Shifra Horn lives in Jerusalem and this is her fourth novel. She has won several literary prizes and is also the author of the international bestsellers *The Fairest Among Women*, *Four Mothers* and *Tamara Walks On Water*.

Also by Shifra Horn

Four Mothers
The Fairest Among Women
Tamara Walks On Water

Ode to Joy

Shifra Horn

PIATKUS

Copyright © 2005 by Shifra Horn
English translation by Anthony Berris

First published in Great Britain in 2005 by
Piatkus Books Ltd.
5 Windmill Street, London W1T 2JA
email: info@piatkus.co.uk

The moral right of the author has been asserted

A catalogue record for this book is available from the British Library

ISBN 0 7499 3635 5

Set in Times by
Action Publishing Technology Ltd, Gloucester

Printed in Great Britain by
Bookmarque, Croydon, Surrey

Acknowledgements

My thanks to Dr Nurit Stadler of the Department of Sociology and Anthropology at the Hebrew University of Jerusalem, who allowed me entry through the front door to 'The Sacred and the Profane in the Concept of Work: The Case of the Ultra-Orthodox Community in Israel', her doctoral dissertation written under the supervision of the late Prof. Reuven Kahane.

Thanks to psychologists Dr David Kahan and Daphna Winter for their advice.

To Eli Shai for his guidance on Lilith.

And to my Hebrew editors, Nili Mirsky, Dr Ilana Hammerman and Tirza Biron-Fried, for their patience and love.

For my loved ones Gili and Peter

Affliction shall not rise up the second time
Nahum, 1:9

O Freunde, niche diese Töne!
Sondern lasst uns angenehmere anstimmen
Und freundenvollere!

Oh friends, no more of these sad tones!
Let us rather raise our voices together
In more pleasant and joyful tones!

Friedrich von Schiller/ Ludwig van Beethoven
The opening lines of 'The Ode to Joy', *Symphony*
No. 9 in D minor

In The Beginning

(Genesis 1, 1)

And life has returned to normal.

What kind of life and what kind of normal?

Despite the ludicrous cliché, I'd like to apply it to my life, but since the upheaval I went through on that Sunday morning, the 20th of January, 2002, my life hasn't been the same and the new one dictated to me has never returned to normal.

'A miracle', that's how strangers defined that moment for me, that second in my life when everything fell apart. But even the people close to me tried to sidestep the horror and refused to call a spade a spade, as if even a mention of the word was life-threatening. They used a strange variety of names as a substitute. Nechama, my psychologist friend, called up her professional lexicon and the highly charged term 'the trauma'; 'the accident' was sufficient for my mother, Louisa, my research colleague, used the words 'the disaster', Prof. Har-Noy, head of our anthropology and sociology department, talked to me about 'your illness', and for some reason or other my husband, Nachum, toyed with 'the episode', while I myself still suffer the anguish of 'that day'.

Ever since 'that day' a rift has split my sense of time. The old one went skyward in a pillar of smoke and its beats weakened until they disappeared altogether, and its place was taken by a new time, mocking the principles of order and organisation and upsetting the familiar division of years and months, day and night, hours and minutes. And this new division of time jeers at me and counts itself in units unmeasurable by any instrument. Since 'that day' long years have shrunk into fleeting moments and what took place in one

1

second never leaves me and in my memory seems like an eternity.

A thousand years earlier, on the Saturday before 'that day', my sleep was interrupted by my wake-up call. I leant over Nachum's sleeping body and my hand feeling for the alarm clock knocked over the glass of water that Nachum religiously puts on his bedside table every night, and the water drizzled down and was absorbed by the pages of the weekend supplement thrown down at the bedside. I grasped the clock and silenced its ringing, and with my skin cringing at the cold I hurried to get up, picked up the newspaper that was heavy, swollen with water, its pages sticking together, and hung it to dry over the still cold ribs of the radiator. Sounds of shuddering and hawking came from it, telling me that the hot water was on its way, making its long stubborn climb from the sweltering bowels of the boiler in the basement, through the hidden pipes buried deep in the walls up to the third floor and our apartment, pushing cold water and air bubbles ahead of it on its long journey. The heating pipes that crawled under the bedroom floor trembled and groaned with the sound of gentle gurgling, like a warm assurance that they would dry out the newspaper before Nachum awoke. I switched on the light in the bathroom and a weak beam of light trickled onto the bedroom floor, lightening black shadows in the darkness of my closet and arranging my clothes for me. I picked out a pair of jeans and the checked flannel shirt that Nachum hates, and then stuck my head under the bed and my hands mixed the darkness, scrabbling for my walking boots. I fought tooth and nail for a long time with the tangle of hooks and laces, and then tiptoed into the kitchen to boil a pot of coffee and gulped it down too quickly; the dark liquid burning its way down my throat into my stomach. When I heard Louisa honking I put the hot cup down on the draining board and hurried into the bedroom, and with lips burned by boiling coffee I planted a loud kiss on Nachum's forehead. He grumbled something about having his day of rest disturbed and turned over, suddenly remembering something, and his head appeared from beneath the heap of blankets: 'Don't forget to turn off the light in the hall when you leave,' he mumbled. I hurried to Yoavi's room; he was sleeping just like my father, his eyelids half open with the whites of his eyes showing, I put my nose next to his sleep-reddened cheek and inhaled his sweet baby fragrance, and left the house. As I did I remembered

2

that I'd forgotten to switch off the hall light, went back inside, switched it off, and took the stairs out two at a time. A cold wind hit me outside and I could see the dark sky above the tops of the cypresses that inclined their heads to me and whispered among themselves as if gossiping about me with the rustle of their branches.

The lovely Louisa quickly got out of the car and her bangles rang out a welcoming tune for me; she tottered towards me in her high-heeled shoes, opened her arms and hugged me and I lowered my eyes to her shoes: 'That's how you're going to visit a Bedouin encampment and climb hills?' In a spoilt voice she replied that she wanted to feel beautiful even when she was out on a field trip, and anyway, who knows who she might meet. I sat down next to her, grateful that she'd persuaded me to go with her, because, as she'd told me on the phone, 'You've got to get away from your religious Jews and their dead for a while.'

Like two feckless young girls embarking on the adventure of their lives we giggled and listened to the army radio station, joining the singers at the top of our lungs. The grey, lowering, threatening sky stole away behind us and was swallowed by the mountains, and small cracks appeared in it until the bright blue firmament was spread out above us, and a wintry, slightly bashful sun warmed my arm resting on the car windowsill, and I said, 'It's so good to get out of Jerusalem, that town's been depressing me lately.' And the further away we drove, Jerusalem receded behind us, the stone buildings vanished, the mysterious alleyways and the graveyards and the ghosts of the dead were erased.

Louisa's car slid along the ribbons of asphalt that were partly covered with alluvium from the recent floods, and before our eyes soft, round hills undulated like young breasts covered in the greenish down from the winter rain, and the narrow furrows made by flocks ploughing their paths with hard, sharp hooves over thousands of years. I thought what a pity it was that Yoavi wasn't with me, he surely would have been delighted by the sheep speckling the hills in white dots, and I began humming his favourite song, 'What do the trees do? Grow,' and when I got to the line, 'And what do the sheep make? Dust,' Louisa asked, 'What's that you're singing?' and I repeated the words and she laughed.

Then suddenly the soft landscape became more jagged. Sharp-edged cliffs soared above us and rocky craters opened their arid, serrated jaws. And the Dead Sea was before us, oily, breathing heavily, and the smell of its breath was the smell of the brimstone that had been rained down on the cities of sin. And vapour rose from the earth like steam from a furnace and sparse grey vegetation barely clung to the cursed earth covering the destroyed cities, and Lot's Wife looked on from above, fossilised and rigid. I thought about the curse visited on this place, 'Because their sin is very grievous', and Abraham's words echoed in my ears, 'Wilt thou also destroy the righteous with the wicked?' I told Louisa that God was right when He turned Lot's wife into a pillar of salt. It's sometimes better to become fossilised than to see the worst.

And the cliffs soared even higher like a noisy crescendo reaching its climax. From high above they lowered an angry stare on the tiny car as it wended its way between them along winding roads, threatening to come down on it with stones and rocks and bury it under them. There was a sudden silence as the radio, as if affected by the desolation all around, faded until it disappeared completely, and Louisa grumbled, offended, 'The radio always dies on me right here,' and she scanned the stations with her bangles jangling, and station after station was caught in her net, filling the car with strident static, and I watched her fighting the elusive notes and wanted to tell her that I envied her but didn't. I envy this lightness of yours, your perpetual smile, that you look so happy, beautiful and elegant even when we're out on a field trip. I suspected that Louisa had asked me to accompany her on this trip out of pity, and poison simmered inside me as I compared the subject of her dissertation to mine. I had no excuse to drive far like her, because while she goes to the wide-open spaces of the Negev in her high-heeled shoes, I wander haunted Jerusalem burial sites like Sanhedria, the Mount of Olives and Givat Shaul in my modest clothes, and my shoes sink into the mud and the piles of dung left standing in the alleyways of Jerusalem's ultra-Orthodox neighbourhoods. As if feeding on carrion I visit the morgues, lie in wait for funerals and perfume myself with the weeping of the bereaved relatives. I bury my life in houses of mourning, find shelter with weeping women in crowded, stifling rooms and try to persuade yeshiva students, who don't dare return my look, to speak to me. I'm tempted to blame Nachum somewhat for my choice of this depressing subject of burial and mourning customs in Jerusalem, because if it hadn't been for him I certainly could have found an exotic subject and travelled the world, wandering among distant and mysterious tribes, and my anthropological studies would have been published in the professional literature and human-interest stories. But to myself I admit that if my father hadn't decided to be buried on the Mount of Olives, I would never have come upon this subject.

I had readied myself for his death for so many years. I imagined where I'd be standing, wondered whether I'd look into the grave when they buried him, asked myself which flowers I'd bring him, and whether I'd cry, and which sunglasses I'd wear, and which blouse I'd wear for the ritual rending, and I learnt verses from the Bible that I'd recite in his memory over the grave, for that book was so well-loved by both of us. But nothing prepared me for what really happened. Before the funeral procession set out, a black-garbed man holding a razor blade came up to me, slit the collar of my blouse and asked me to widen the tear with my fingers, and I did as asked and knew that the rent, that was supposed to symbolise the rent in my inner world, would never heal. Then I was told by the *Hevra Kadisha* burial society people that because of the 'Joshua Ben Nun proscription' I, the daughter of the deceased, was forbidden to join the funeral procession as it began, and that I had to wait behind. I asked for an explanation but they only said vaguely that it was 'the custom of Jerusalem'.

As soon as my father's body, enshrouded in a shabby prayer shawl, was unloaded from the hearse and carried onto a narrow stretcher, the *Hevra Kadisha* people swooped down on him with their flashing eyes and unkempt beards. And I, in my blouse with its torn collar, followed behind them. But they were already far away from me, carrying him in a manic stretcher race, far up the hill that was covered in new tombstones and crumbling ones, and I, short of breath, raced behind them, begging them to slow down, to stop, to wait for me and the other mourners, but they were unfaltering, running, running, and I could see their backs rising and falling, and could hear their feet pounding on the rocks in unison, crunch-crunch-crunch. And my father's body was shaken, bouncing up and down, as if they were intentionally jerking it, and then a withered arm almost fell through the shroud, and I, breathing heavily, begged them, 'Jews, respect the dead, where are you hurrying to?' but they took no notice.

Far behind me my mother and Nachum heading the group of

mourners plodded ahead, all walking slowly, as if spitefully, as if they were taking a Sabbath afternoon stroll.

The *Hevra Kadisha* people conducted the ceremony and finally, when everything was over, one of them placed a small stone on the mound and I heard him say in the plural 'We beg your forgiveness, perhaps we did not do everything in your honour.' I wanted to scream, asking forgiveness isn't enough. That's not the way to treat my father. But they were already busy telling the mourners to stand in two rows, and my mother and I walked between the rows, and they murmured, 'God will console you together with the other mourners of Zion and Jerusalem'; and I actually thought of the children's dance 'We've got a billy-goat', and how we used to dance, couple after couple, prancing between the two rows of children who sang, 'We've got a billy-goat and the billy-goat's got a beard.' I conquered my smile and etched the rows of people on my memory, taking notice of who was present and who was absent, and Louisa's doe-like eyes followed me. She left the row and came over to hold me in her arms, and I patted her shoulder, as if it was me consoling her, and said: 'I'm all right, I'm all right, don't worry.'

Upon leaving the cemetery, near the water fountain, one of those clad in black who had been running with the stretcher came over to me, and with kind eyes, pure as a child's eyes that had never seen any evil in this world, smiled at me when he said that I should wash my hands three times and not dry them. I asked him about the meaning of this custom, and he replied, as if amused: 'To banish the evil spirits.' I told him that I didn't believe in that kind of rubbish, but nevertheless I washed my hands three times, piously, and with wet hands I signalled to Nachum and my mother, who were waiting for me near the gate, that I'd be along a bit later. I was tempted to wipe my hands on my blouse, and only then was shocked to discover that for some reason in honour of the funeral I had worn my elegant black silk blouse and not the tattered T-shirt I wear at night, and had planned to throw out in any event. And again the man clad in black smiled his pure, almost childish smile at me, and said: 'May you know no more sorrow.' I told him I wanted to ask one more question and he said: 'With pleasure,' and I asked why they had to run so fast with the stretcher, and he replied: 'The custom of Jerusalem.' I asked him the meaning of the custom, and he mumbled and blushed and lowered his eyes, looking down at his shoes that were covered in mud, and whispered: 'Because of an odious drop.' I asked him for an explanation, and he told me that a man spills odious drops during the course of his life, and if the children of the dead come to the grave to mourn their father, those children of the odious drops will also wish to come. Millions and millions of them will encircle the dead and demand their share in the inheritance, and will thus endanger his status in the next world. I told him I didn't understand, and he explained to me, 'Those are the sons who have no body.' I asked him for his name and he replied, 'Yosef Warshavsky, pleased to meet you,' despite the fact that I had not yet introduced myself.

When we went to the cemetery on the thirtieth day after my father's death, I asked for him and was given the telephone number of the *Hevra Kadisha* in Jerusalem. During our conversation I reminded him of our meeting at the water fountain at the cemetery exit, and he hesitated for a moment and then said, 'Yes, I do actually remember you,' and I suspected him of lying because of his gentle temperament; after all, he saw so many bereaved people every day. I introduced myself and told him I was interested in burial and mourning rituals in Jerusalem, and asked him whether I could speak to him on the subject at length, for a study I was involved in at the university, and he replied, 'Of course, of course, but first I have to speak to the boss,' and I was surprised that he used such a word. I dictated my telephone number and he promised to make enquiries and get back to me. He phoned me the next day and solemnly announced that I was invited to come over and speak with them. He also promised that they would notify me of the dates and times of funerals so I could attend them, and would even give me a special pass to enter the purification rooms of the dead. 'And I thought you were a closed and secret society,' I said to Warshavsky, who was my first professional contact with them. 'It's a question of public relations,' he replied, 'the *Hevra Kadisha* has a bad image in the secular world. They call us ravens and claim that we get rich off the dead.'

That same week I went over to Prof. Har-Noy and announced that I had found a subject for my doctoral dissertation, and repeated what they had taught us at the department, that the way nations deal with their dead provides a key for understanding the basic values of their culture. The professor grimaced slightly and wondered aloud whether a timid and sensitive girl like me could cope with such a highly charged subject; he assumed that the death of my father was probably related to this choice of mine, and suggested that it might be better if I waited a while until the crisis of mourning passed and then I would be able to choose, level-headedly and with due consideration, a new subject. But I was adamant.

Suddenly Louisa interrupted my thoughts and jumbled them up. 'Did you know,' she said to me, 'that according to the Bedouin legend, Hagar, Ishmael's mother, circumcised herself, and since that time it's become a practice among the Bedouin tribes?'

'And what does the Koran say about it?' I asked

'In the Koran itself there's no mention of female circumcision. Only the call of Mohammed the prophet, who was born circumcised, to only circumcise men. There's an indirect mention of female circumcision in the unwritten law, in a *hadith* that's attributed to Mohammed, which contends that "circumcision is mandatory for men, and an addition for women". Believe it or not,' she added, her eyes fixed on the road, 'all cultures that disfigure the core of a woman's femininity believe that ultimately they are protecting women from themselves,' and added that removing the core of a woman's sexual desire should keep her from having forbidden sexual relations, particularly if her husband has many wives or goes off on long journeys. 'In some tribal societies extramarital relations can end up with the wife's murder to preserve the family honour.' Then she told me about Dr Isaac Baker-Brown, president of the London Medical Society in the 1850s, who, at the end of the nineteenth century, recommended clitoridectomy as a remedy for hysteria or melancholia in women.

And I watched her beautiful face and her ivory-white hands, and in my mind's eye read the long articles written about her and her study, and could see her standing on the platform at international anthropological conferences, and could hear her voice speaking in a soft sensual French accent, and her bangles accompanying her lecture with a soft and captivating peal.

And once again I thought about my own study, and knew that eternal fame would not await me.

We reached Beersheba too soon and parked next to a low building, its plaster peeling, surrounded by sparse grey desert vegetation, with a dusty sign that read 'General Health Maintenance Organisation'. We rang the bell and a weary-eyed guard opened the door for us and asked us in a heavy Russian accent, 'What you want? It's closed today. Sabbath. Where do you want to go?' Louisa flashed him her dazzling smile, shook out her luxuriant curls and clinked her bangles especially for him. I saw the stern look on his face soften. He checked our handbags perfunctorily and directed us to the second floor, where Louisa drummed with her fingers on the door on which a small sign, written in uneven handwriting read: Dr Khalil Abu-Yusuf. Between the gynaecological table's stirrups Dr Abu-Yusuf's back came into view, a dark bald head turned in our direction, and black confused eyes focused on us. A deep scar that had been carelessly stitched and had healed in dark lumps cut across his cheek, and it seemed as if he noticed my look and covered the scar with the palm of his hand and got up. Louisa gingerly waltzed past the table, came closer to him, stretched out her hand and said: 'Louisa Amir, I spoke with you earlier, and meet Yael Maggid, a colleague of mine at the department,' and her bangles clinked merrily. He got up from his seat, the doctor's chair, pulled over another chair, gestured to me to take it, and then asked, 'Coffee?' We politely refused, and he stood next to us, as if ashamed, and Louisa asked, 'And what about you? Where will you sit?' He hesitated for a moment, then pushed the metal stirrups aside and carefully lowered his behind, and I remembered that since I'd had Yoavi I hadn't seen my doctor. Dr Abu-Yusuf looked down at the floor tiles and remained silent, and we remained silent too, until Louisa finally said: 'Do you remember our last phone conversation?' He hastened to interrupt her and said, even before he was asked, that he had seen his last case of circumcision some two years ago, when a young woman came to him to give birth to her first child.

'And since then you haven't seen any patients who have undergone circumcision?'

The doctor lowered his eyes and his fingers began playing with the table's leather straps, and replied that the custom was still practised in some tribes, mainly those that originated from the Nile region, but today female circumcision among the Bedouins was less severe and almost undetectable, limited to straightening the height of the meeting place of the labia minora. Louisa asked him to show her a picture of female genitalia that had been circumcised, since she had heard that he had such a photograph in his possession, but he apologised self-consciously, rubbing his fingers, and said that he couldn't remember where he had put it. But Louisa wouldn't give up and urged him on, 'But we've come all this way to see the picture.' He shrugged helplessly, and I was glad that Louisa, who was used to having her way immediately, was faced with rejection. She fixed him with a stare and asked, 'At least tell me which tribe the woman comes from,' and unwillingly he said, 'Abu Madian,' and Louisa raised her eyes and asked him to draw her a map, and he said that as far as he remembered the tribe had gone northwards, but it might well be that some families had been left behind, and asked what kind of car we had come in because only a jeep could make it to the encampment. Then he took out a medical record decorated with sketches of wombs, ovaries and Fallopian tubes, drew a map on the other side and told us that if we reached the encampment we should look for Umm Mohammed who would undoubtedly cooperate.

The car, used to travelling over asphalt roads, moaned and groaned, and skidded over the rocks along a track steamrolled in the desert, and a reddish desert dust landed on the windscreen, adorning it with lacy patterns. Two tents loomed from a distance in a small ravine, and I said to Louisa that from there we would have to go on foot, and I pointed to a twisted path on the map that the doctor had drawn for us between the wombs and ovaries. Barefooted children clad in rags suddenly appeared from the ravine and ran towards us, yellowish dust clouds following at their heels. We asked them whether this was the Abu Madian tribe and they nodded and led us to one of the tents. Pebbles creaked and crunched under our feet in the *wadi* that had long since dried up, and Louisa, her bangles ringing like wind chimes, clumsy in her high heels, stumbled behind me and yelled '*Merde!*' and took off her shoes, and slowly staggered on in her bare feet, complaining and cursing every time she stepped on a thorn or a sharp stone. I gloated. Her everyday stride, the self-assured, light, elegant step that made men turn their heads, was now a dragging crawl, and the soles of her white well-cared-for feet were covered in dust.

In the large tent, exactly as the doctor had promised, Umm Mohammed sat on a red cushion sucking in smoke from the mouthpiece of a narghileh, her brown face resembling an ancient parchment grooved with deep wrinkles that reminded me of a photograph of an old Indian woman in one of my textbooks. Her jaws and cheeks were deeply sunken into her shrivelled toothless mouth, and her chin, from which a few long white hairs sprouted, protruded, narrow and pointed. She dropped the mouthpiece of the narghileh and called out, '*Tfadalu*, *tfadalu*,' and led us to a seating corner padded with camel hair carpets, and coaxed us to relax on the large colourful cushions that delineated the tent's corners.

I relaxed on one of the cushions and Louisa sat at my side. With gloomy eyes she surveyed the injured soles of her feet, and in a stammering Arabic-Jewish, from her father's house, began to chitchat. Umm Mohammed replied with '*Hamdulillah*' and added in Hebrew, 'Everything's good,' and again Louisa engaged in small talk and the old woman responded with a smile, and again I admired the patient and professional way in which Louisa undertook her fieldwork. Later, after a long silence, Louisa asked a question and the old woman leant over towards her and tilted her ear the way the hearing-impaired do, and later she giggled and said in Hebrew, 'Don't understand.' Louisa repeated her question in a loud voice.

All at once the old woman shed her smiling countenance, her face became sharp and rigid, and she waved her arms and with a loud shout sent away the two young girls who had been peeking behind the curtain, covering their mouths with their hands and shaking with laughter. Then she retreated into the depths of the wizened shell of her skin, her naked jaws moving as if they were constantly chewing. '*Taher el-banat*,' she whispered, purification of girls, 'Now they don't do it. Once they did. Once they did it to all Bedouin women,' she continued, as Louisa hastened to translate for me in a whisper.

'How did they do it to them?' Louisa asked, her eyes glued to the carpet so as not to embarrass the old woman.

'Like this,' the old woman said, and without any pretence of shame she raised her dress to her hips, revealing a pair of dark legs, shrivelled like prunes, and spread her knees, exposing a sagging, almost hairless pudenda, and passed an imaginary knife between her legs. 'Like this,' she repeated and added, 'You need a razor blade,' and with her sinewy palm suddenly took hold of one of Louisa's thin ankles, elbowed me and had me take hold of her other ankle, and with one hand holding Louisa's ankle, she described with body movements and guttural cries that sounded like weeping, how two women took hold of the feet of a girl, and how they forcibly opened

11

her legs and cut. 'It's nothing,' she assured us in her broken Hebrew, 'Nothing, a little piece of flesh.'

'And now, today, do they still do it today?'

'Whoever doesn't want to, no.'

'But are there tribes which you know that do it?' Louisa continued to ask her in Hebrew, without pronouncing the explicit word.

'Yes,' said the old woman, glad that she could speak of another tribe, and listed the names of the tribes, and added that the custom prevailed among those who had come to the Negev from Egypt.

'Umm Mohammed,' Louisa said coquettishly, clinking and jangling her bangles intentionally. 'Why do you need to do it?'

'You have to purify to get married,' the old woman said and glued her greedy eyes onto the bangles, and I thought about Louisa's Yoram, Nachum's partner at the clinic, who's the handsomest and sweetest guy in town, and remembered how that night, when I introduced them, he looked at her totally mesmerised, and during dinner wanted to count her bangles one by one, and he jangled them with a great deal of noise, and when he reached thirty he pretended he was mixed up and wanted to begin again. I then heard her rolling laughter, saw her body bending to his and her arms covered in goose pimples and knew that they would get married even before they knew it themselves.

Umm Mohammed banished my memories and called in the girls she had earlier sent from the tent, and they returned and offered us two glasses of sweet tea on a copper tray, and Louisa looked at them curiously and whispered to me that she was dying to speak to them, but the old witch would surely not let them express themselves.

Our eyes, which had become used to the dimness in the tent, were somewhat blinded when we went outside into the light. The orange ball of the sun was already swinging in the west on a cradle of reddish clouds whose fringes were intertwined with golden thread, and Louisa said that we needed to hurry because she didn't want to drive in the dark. We walked towards the car and a sudden wind began to blow, and as if repelling invaders it propelled us from behind and made us trip on prickly sheaves of uprooted and thorny burnet bushes. Like rough sandpaper, burning sand swept into our faces, plugging our ears, piling up in our sinuses, even penetrating our windpipes. Dishevelled and dusty we reached the car and Louisa plonked herself down heavily on the seat and stroked the soles of her feet and said that her shoes had been ruined and her feet had been ruined, and she patted her hair in the mirror and hissed, 'Ugh, look what I look like,' and added that this trip had been totally pointless and she had gained nothing. A milky film covered the windscreen and made the world outside opaque. Louisa trickled some water on the windscreen until the dust turned into mud, and then switched on the wipers and they squeaked and moved and made furrows, and two clear semicircles restored the landscape to it natural colours.

We drove silently until we reached the main road. A short time later Louisa was in a good mood again and she returned to her favourite subject and told me that there were three methods of female circumcision, and the Bedouins in Israel use the easiest one, probably as a result of the process of refinement they were undergoing, living in the modern-day culture to which they are exposed in Israel. This method, she explained, was analogous to male circumcision, and involved only the removal of the skin covering, called the clitoris foreskin, and then she continued to describe the other methods – the Sunni one, in which the entire clitoris is excised, and the Pharaonic method, which was the most demanding, which is performed on young girls. By this method the clitoris and the labia minora are excised in their entirety, and sometimes two thirds of the labia majora as well. After the excision, the genital labia are sewn together and a small sliver of wood is inserted between the labia, to allow the passing of urine and menstrual blood.

I cringed inside. 'Louisa, enough, enough, I'm getting weak at the knees from your description,' I begged her, and felt that my guts were somersaulting inside me, and I wanted to tell her to stop the car at the side of the road for a minute so I could get out and take a breath of fresh air, but I was afraid she'd tell everyone at the department about my momentary weakness, so I swallowed my saliva and changed the subject to her forthcoming wedding, and she was only too happy to give me a full description of the wedding gown that the owner of that Tel Aviv boutique would sew for her, and Yoram's suit.

We reached Jerusalem too soon. The city welcomed us with dark, low, forbidding clouds that cast dark shadows on the gloomy stone buildings. Louisa stopped at my house, raised her head to the darkening skies, and like a primordial prophet of fury announced:

'Tomorrow there's going to be an horrendous storm, the end of the world.' I was suddenly engulfed in fear, as if the prophecy was directed at me. In the stairwell the aromas of the Sabbath *hamin* wafted oily and aggressive, and I thought about the brown eggs and the meat that melted in your mouth and the soft beans, and my rumbling stomach reminded me that except for the couple of stale sandwiches we had devoured at a filling station on the way back, I had had nothing to eat all day.

There were no smells of cooking in the house. Nachum pecked my cheek and I could hear the rebuke in his voice when he told me that Yoavi had missed me and had waited for me all evening, and later fell asleep exhausted. I hurried to his room and he was sleeping on his stomach, his behind raised. I removed the stuffed animals and dolls that were piled in his bed, kissed his golden cheeks with their peachy down, inhaling his sweet scent. I returned to the living room and to Nachum, who was engrossed in the world news programme, and he asked, duty-bound, 'How did things go?' and I described the sandstorm and told him, in the spoilt tone of voice I had borrowed from Louisa, that I was so hungry and dirty. I devoured cold roast beef and potatoes in the kitchen straight from the pot, leftovers from Friday night, went into the bathroom and filled the tub. Like a happy hippopotamus I lay in the warm water, examining my big toes and gazing at the ceiling covered with stains of blackish mould, and thought about how I could convince Nachum that we finally had to refurbish this nest of ours.

At night Nachum turned his back to me and said that Yoavi had sapped him of all his strength and that he had to sleep because he was going to have a hard day at the clinic tomorrow. After he fell asleep I got out of bed and went into my study and called Nechama. I told her about the day I had spent with Louisa, and about the gynaecologist and Umm Mohammed, and she asked me to describe to her how female circumcision is performed. I whispered to her that I couldn't, and Nechama giggled and said, 'Don't be so genteel,' and reminded me how after Yoavi's *brith* she had to come over to diaper him because I couldn't bear to look at his wound.

Above us on the fourth floor the neighbours were moving furniture. Their dining room table legs were screeching heavily on our ceiling as they dragged it into the corner of the living room. The thin legs of the little coffee table squeaked when it was pulled along on two legs, and I heard the bang when they opened their couch that turns into a double bed at night. 'We sleep in the living room so that each child has his own room,' Levana, our neighbour, explained to me, embarrassed, when one night, while I was trying to concentrate on my work, these noises cracked though my cranium, and I went up to the fourth floor and banged on their door with my fists. Now the couch was groaning above me, squeaking and squeaking, and Levana's voice was begging, 'Moremoremore.' When the noise from above stopped I stealthily returned to our bed, and listened for a long time to Nachum's rhythmic breathing. I lay close to his back, and he woke up and reached back and hugged my thigh that was against his. I licked his ear lobe and murmured, 'What do you say we have another child?' and he turned over on his stomach, his member well protected in the depths of the mattress, and said nasally into the pillow, 'Now? Are you crazy? It's late, we'll talk about it tomorrow.' But I didn't give in and said sweetly, 'Maybe a little girl? A sister for Yoavi? I've always wanted a little girl.' But he didn't answer. I felt his muscles relaxing and his chest rising and falling in a slow rhythm, and I whispered, 'Nachum?' but he didn't respond. I waited a few minutes, and then turned over and fell asleep.

That Day

First thing that Sunday morning, the 20th of January 2002, before the sky had turned pink, Louisa's premonition came true. Lightning flashed and thunder rolled and like a thousand drums warning of impending danger the fat raindrops drummed on the windowpanes followed by hail bombarding the city with its smooth, frozen stones. Frightened by the noise, Yoavi leapt into our bed and his feet were freezing. I chafed them between my palms and suddenly remembered the washing I'd hung out on Friday. I jumped out of bed and ran to the utility balcony from where I could see the sparrows huddling together in a line on our bedroom windowsill, their breasts puffed up and their feathers bristling in the biting cold, like eminent English gentlemen in grey suits waiting patiently in a long queue. I leant over the rail, stretched out my arms to the washing lines strung outside and from them plucked Yoavi's damp clothes that ballooned in the wind and looked like fat little cherubs whose wings were bound with coloured plastic clothes-pegs. Unmoving, the sparrows calmly observed my panicky movements, and I wondered why they'd left their warm home inside the bedroom shutter housing from where I could hear, morning and night, their soft twittering and the chirping of the fledglings. I wanted to show them to Yoavi but by the time I got back inside with the heavy, freezing laundry, they escaped my consciousness as I tiredly mulled over the long week awaiting me.

I hung the damp clothes over the radiator and knocked it with my knuckles as if coaxing it to warm up and start heating the apartment. It responded like a feeble old man with a burst of throat-clearing and hawking. I dressed quickly, woke Nachum, and dressed Yoavi in warm clothing and we held the morning ceremony, a ritual he had recently invented. Like a pious Hasid, each morning he insisted on the order of putting on his shoes and in the evening the order of taking them off. 'So as not to upset the shoes,' the right shoe was put on first and then the left one, and in the evening the left shoe was first to come off and then the right one, and this ceremony of reversing the order had to be strictly observed so that no shoe would suffer discrimination.

I made breakfast and Nachum joined us and with his face buried in the newspaper told me not to burn his toast. Yoavi drank his hot chocolate and drew a brown moustache above his upper lip, and I licked it off and he laughed, 'It tickles!' After breakfast we all went downstairs. The bench, used by the three old Russian women whose smile on light-drenched mornings would sparkle at me with a glint of gold, stood damp and lonely. During they day they sat in the sun and shared their food with the sparrows that clustered around them, and when the shadows fell over the bench they would smack their lips as if kissing noisily, and the suspicious, flea-ridden alley cats would pad towards them, wait at a distance and follow them with narrowed eyes until they threw them a salami end or a pickled herring head. Then they'd spring, pin their prey with their incisors, and scurry away to nibble their spoils in hiding. I called them 'the babushkas' and wondered where they came from and to where they disappeared. From the green garbage dumpster that lay on its belly at the side of the pathway leading to the parking lot came a stench of rotting vegetables. Two cawing ravens fought in the rain over a bloated garbage bag, and with the violence of hungry birds they pulled it from side to side until it burst and its contents spilled out onto the path.

In the parking lot Nachum hurriedly pecked our cheeks, asked me to drive carefully because the roads were hazardous today and sailed off on his way in his huge car. Despite the short distance to Yoavi's kindergarten, I belted him in and he happily sang, 'What do the trees do?' I put on a thoughtful face and answered, 'Grow?' and he laughed and continued, 'And what do the houses do?' and I thought and said, 'Stand.' And then we were passing the concrete wall, that tall barrier of fear they'd built in the middle of the neighbourhood that pierces the landscape and intrudes between our homes, the ones whose sandbagged windows face Beit Jallah, and their houses from where the shooting comes and from whose door-ways the suicide bombers leave on their deadly missions. In their gay colours the concrete blocks decorated with landscapes painted by Russian immigrant artists recreate the blocked view as if trying to put the danger lurking on the other side out of our minds, even momentarily. As always, I was stopped at the pedestrian crossing by the junior traffic wardens, opposite the painting of the tree whose top, which was real, soared above the wall as a continuation of the painting. And by the time Yoavi came to the line, 'And what do I do? No-o-o-thing,' we'd reached the kindergarten. I bent down and he kissed my lips, and before he was swallowed up behind the gate I saw Nikolai, the Russian security guard, pat him on the rump as if hurrying him along.

Then my trusty old Mini refused to budge. As if she knew what was waiting for her, she stood wrapped up in the frozen, dozing silence of a Jerusalem winter morning, and obstinately dug her rubber hooves into the frost-rimed asphalt like an obdurate mule. I tried talking to her with soft, flattering words but she, like a terminally ill patient, only coughed and choked. Again and again I did my best to win her over in that habit I had acquired over the years in the belief that this car, which had been with me throughout most of my adult life, was part of me, flesh of my flesh, for on the road we were a single entity and my movements were part of hers. Every groan, cough, squeak or croak was familiar and predictable, and when I importuned her aloud, my Yoavi would giggle and add sentences and blessings of his own, calling her by her nickname, 'Minimush', a blend of 'Mini' and 'Imush', his pet name for me. For years I believed that only my car and I had this kind of special relationship, until yesterday, when Louisa's car had huffed and puffed up the steep inclines on the way back to Jerusalem, I heard her pleading with it in French, her mother tongue, and just like me she called it by an assortment of nicknames.

But that morning Minimush behaved completely unpredictably. Again and again I tried to start her, to breathe life into her, but with the capriciousness of an old car whose strength has failed she was impervious to all my efforts. I wiped off the beads of hoar frost that had collected on the windscreen and which blurred the outside world, and then fooled her. I slipped the gearshift into second, released the handbrake and rolled down the slope. Reluctantly, the engine farted once and once more and then enveloped us in a whitish fog. I hissed entreaties through clenched lips: 'Nu,

18

please, move already', until she finally answered my prayers.

I felt the engine's tremors running through my body.

We moved slowly down the slope of my street at the edge of the Gilo neighbourhood, she emitting the dissatisfied roars of a frozen, sleepy engine, while the wipers squeaked and juddered, the noise reminding me yet again that I needed to replace them. With no consideration for her ripe old age, I spurred Minimush on until we slid into the wide funnel that drew us into the main road and we passed the white stone monstrosities, the fortified palaces of the nouveaux riches that lay self-assuredly on the land of the Arab village of Beit Zafafa, all dolled up and flamboyant like architectural nightmares.

I twisted and turned until I was opposite the village and the traffic lights that blocked the traffic with a red light. I waited for the green, and the moment it began flashing, from behind me I heard the drumming hooves of the rubber, iron and glass knights, and was overtaken by a mad, noisy tumult mingled with the roar of engines, honking horns and the screech of brakes. Several cars, whose drivers were determined to get there before me, encircled me in the eternal battle of the road. As the red light dawned again, I found myself blocked by the broad behind of the 32A bus whose buttocks were adorned with a 'The Nation Is with the Golan' sticker. The outlines of people packed into a solid block peeped at me through the rear window whose transparency was blurred by a misty film of condensation from the breath of the passengers packed like sardines on this wintry morning. As the car trembled under me in neutral, I scanned the radio stations until I found the Voice of Music and the sounds of Beethoven's Ninth flowed over me in stereo. Distant, mysterious notes, a little violent, echoed from the speakers and crowded with me in my tiny space. I gave myself up to the notes that engulfed me, and I remembered that someone had once said of it that it was the most sublime sound ever heard by human ears.

I gazed at the rear window of the bus in front of me and followed a tiny hand that suddenly appeared and drew lines and dots on the condensation that partly obscured it. The movements of the drawing hand blended unknowingly into the harmony of the notes that sounded inside the sealed space of my car, and was it just my imagination or was the anonymous artist hearing the magnificent work at this very moment too? As the bus began to

19

move and I was left with no choice but to crawl along after it, the drawing was rubbed out with short, slanting, hasty movements and from the clear and illuminated patch that now shone through the filthy window like a gap opened up in the clouds, the clear silhouette of a small head peeped. Energetic, busy hands further cleared the condensation from the inside and a button nose was pressed to the glass, squashed against it like yellow dough, leaving thin breath in its wake. The sweet face of a little girl could be clearly seen through the window, her chin resting on the back of the seat and her earnest eyes gazing at me with interest.

I smiled at the head that had been revealed and waved, the child hesitated for a moment, and then raised one hand and then lowered it, and raised it again; she opened her fingers and then clenched them into a fist the way children wave, and then with both hands as she bobbed up and down. I was very happy with this children's game that had come my way, and waved back and once again she opened and clenched her fingers. Now the dark outline next to her, whose back was to me, suddenly straightened up and the head of a woman wearing a hat turned round and appeared at the side of the little girl's head, and suspicious eyes pierced both windows, mine and hers, until they met mine. My cheerful upraised hand froze in shyness and joined its sister holding the wheel. The larger head moved back from the window and with it was gathered the small, blonde one that was swallowed up behind the seat backrest, with the child's ponytail bouncing gaily behind her head. The lights changed and the bus blew its grey exhaust fumes at me and moved slowly towards its stop at the Patt intersection, stopped below the junction and blocked my lane with its broad backside. Again the little head turned to peep at me and again the mother grasped her and sat her down and again the tiny stubborn hands gripped the seat backrest and the small body climbed up until it was standing on the seat, like a tumbler toy, and curious eyes surveyed me with their gaze.

'Peekaboo!' I called when she again peeked at me and I bent down until I was under the dashboard, hidden from her. 'Peekaboo! Peekaboo!' I popped up but my call failed to reach her, shattering on the thick glass separating us, mingling with the supplications of the soloists preaching peace and love on my radio. 'Peekaboo! Peekaboo!' and I thought I could see a smile on her face and again I disappeared from her view as I bent under the wheel before popping up again.

'Peekaboo! Peekaboo!' and my call was answered by a dull drum roll followed by a blinding flash of lightning and all hell was let loose, and my car was rocked from side to side, 'And the people saw the sounds and the lightning and the mountain smoking'. With difficulty I straightened up and the steering wheel hit the back of my neck and the sweet little head that had peeped out in front of me disappeared, the daylight turned into darkness and my windscreen was filled with fine closely woven cobwebs like a wondrous, enchanted stained-glass work of art. I touched the delicate web and it crumbled at my touch and showered me with a waterfall of shining diamonds that covered my lap and knees. A strong wind hit me through the shattered windscreen, bringing with it a strange smell and a choking mass of smoke was trapped in my lungs. In the terrible silence that suddenly fell after the noise, I heard the 'Ode to Joy' enthusiastically sung by the choir on my car radio, oblivious of what had just happened.

Then came the screams. Inhuman screams like those of animals trapped in a fire.

I tried to get out but couldn't get the door to open. It was an eternity until an unseen hand opened my car door and the notes of the 'Ode to Joy' burst out and joyfully mingled with the moans, shouts and choked weeping. Searing tongues of flame greedily licked the blackening skeleton of the bus whose roof was agape as if frozen in a scream, sending greedy fingers towards my Minimush. A hand grasped my arm and pulled me out into the rain. Where the bus had been standing, a pillar of smoke and flame rose skyward over the low roofs of the houses that shimmered in the heat haze as if in a chimerical, nightmarish dance.

Like a limp rag doll with no will of its own I was passed from hand to hand, and Beethoven's timpanis still thundered dully, boom, boom, boom, and my body was being shaken with the notes. My skin was being stripped and stretched over a drumhead, my hollow body was a sounding board and kettledrum sticks were pounding my back together with the clubs of Alex and his gang of thugs from *A Clockwork Orange*.

'Are you OK? Are you OK?' Dozens of pairs of strange eyes glared at me, and anonymous hands felt my body and rummaged in my clothing and shook the diamond splinters off me. I wanted them to stop, to leave me alone, but I couldn't find my voice.

Then they sat me on the sidewalk and pushed my head down

between my knees. 'Breathe, breathe,' I was ordered and I wondered why they were all speaking to me in duplicate, why they had to repeat every sentence. Look I'm breathing, breathing, and I raised my head and asked the faces looking down at me where the little girl was who was sitting in the back of the bus. I've got to find her and take her back to her mother. But nobody answered. Tottering like a drunkard, I went looking for her and tripped over a shiny, bloated, black plastic bag. There were more bags crowded on the road, side by side in a straight, orderly row like harvested sheaves in a field with the raindrops sliding off them.

I lost control of my body and my dignity. My bowels contracted in a painful spasm as their contents spurted into my panties in a thin, warm stream and made their way down my buttocks, thighs and calves. The stink rose from me as I was laid on a stretcher and I looked upward at sky that had fallen on us. Black rain clouds sailed above me, swallowed up by the pillar of smoke and mingling with it.

I was loaded into an ambulance that forged its way forward with strident siren blasts until it came to a halt. My stretcher was unloaded and they ran with it, making a path between people milling around and rolling gurneys and I was laid on a bed in the middle of a nightmare of blood and cries. Once again hands fiddled with me and again I was told, in duplicate, 'Breathe, breathe,' and I, in my soiled clothes, asked about the little girl and asked to see her, but they silently cut off my pants and shirt and removed my underclothes and I thought about my mother who had said you should always go out wearing clean underwear because who knows what might happen in the street. I remembered that strangely enough I had put on my best panties, the sexy black silk ones with lace flowers blooming on them. Louisa had brought them from Paris, 'And Nachum will go mad for them,' she had whispered as she handed me the small, beautifully wrapped package. Then I tried to remember what I'd been wearing today, but the pile of rags lying on the floor didn't tell me a thing, and an authoritative voice tore me from my thoughts and ordered me to lie down and wait. Despite my benumbed senses I knew I wouldn't be able to get up, filthy and naked as I was, move past the curtain and look for the child. I buried my face in the pillow and refused to look at the fresh-faced national service volunteer who silently cleaned my body with a damp cloth and patiently and gently removed the remnants of shame from it, and asked me to sit up. And I sat on the edge of the narrow bed ashamed of my nakedness before the clothed girl, and I felt pity for my white breasts that flopped onto my chest drooping and ruined like two emptied milk bags, and for the ugly scar that wended its way from my navel, splitting my belly and disappearing into the dark gateway of my vulva, dividing my stomach into two fleshy segments. And the young girl, as though sensing my shame, wrapped a pink soft gown around me, asked me to slip my arms into the jaws of the sleeves gaping in front of me, and knotted the strings at my nape. She sweetly asked me to, 'Lie down and wait patiently for the doctor.'

A far-too-young intern arrived and in a thick Russian accent asked me if everything was all right, and I, dull-witted, repeated all right, all right, and knew that everything wasn't all right and from this moment on nothing would be all right. On my upper arm he inflated the cuff like a black mourner's band and the column of mercury shot up proud and shining inside the glass tube. I looked at the small pimples covering the intern's cheeks and his forehead furrowed in concentration as he leant over me without looking at me, and without asking my permission lifted my gown up to my neck and put his stethoscope to my chest. My pendulous breasts recoiled and he smiled at me and said, 'Cold,' and rubbed it between his palms to warm it and again placed it on my chest, moving my breast and listening to my heart with apprehensive expectation, as though wanting to hear the secrets I'd hidden from him there. 'Now sit up,' he ordered and I sat up and he, as if seeking to shatter my already broken body, tapped my limbs with a little rubber-headed hammer. I watched his hands scuttling over me, seeking hidden signs that weren't there, and I was afraid of disappointing him so I told him that everything hurt and my body was exuding a stench, but he patted my bare shoulder masterfully, straightened the gown over my body just like I straighten the bib on Yoavi's chest, told me I was fine and, before he left to find employment with others whose need was greater than mine, asked me to give the social worker, who would be right there, the phone number of the person closest to me, and drew the curtain with a loud rattle, imprisoning me in the maw of the yellow sheets. My best friend Nechama's number had been erased from my memory and in its place Nachum's number at the clinic popped up.

It was an eternity until Nachum got to the emergency room with a bulging Hamashbir Letzarchan shopping bag and with a concerned expression asked, 'Are you all right?' I told him to wait on the other side of the curtain and as I put on the clean clothes he had brought, which bore the lavender scent of laundry softener, my very bones were riven by a terrible pain and a foul stench assailed my nostrils.

As I felt for the slippers he'd brought, the young girl who'd cleaned me up popped her head in and ordered me, 'Don't leave. You have to wait for the doctor, he'll be right here with your discharge form.' The words 'discharge form' were ground between her teeth as if her mouth was full of gravel. And I got scared and realised that I was imprisoned in a closed institution, a jail, and I had to have a discharge form otherwise I would be shackled in here forever, inside the yellow sheets, on the narrow bed and I'd be given a number and striped pyjamas and passers-by would be able to look at me and read the small notice they'd hang over my bed: *Here Lies a Survivor*.

It took the doctor another eternity to come back and he again asked me: 'Are you all right?' and I was quick to reply that everything was fine and as a memento he gave me the hospitalisation file and on the discharge form he had written in amazingly legible handwriting, 'Mild shock. Discharged in good condition. Recommend check-up next week.' I recalled that diagnosis a few days later when I read about a diagnosis of shock patients in the paper, and the doctor they interviewed described them as patients whose body is unharmed but whose arms are folded securely against their chest and their knuckles are white with straining. I tried to remember if they'd found me like that, with my arms folded, but despite my efforts I couldn't remember those moments.

Nachum took me outside to the parking lot and bundled me into his Volvo that now surrounded us with its steel and glass fortifications. I sat silently at his side and the terrible stink that came from me settled between us, separating and dividing. On the back seat sat the plastic shopping bag into which I had thrown the remnants of my previous life, a small bag of tranquillisers and three Hypnodorm tablets, 'the Rolls-Royce of sleeping pills', of which the doctor told me I was allowed one pill at night.

We made our way in silence up the hill and the hospital vanished behind a curve in the road and was swallowed up by the hills that surrounded it. The day faded into gloom like a smoking cigarette butt and pale yellow lights were already spilling from the windows of buildings. From deep in the Arab village of Ein Karem the ringing of a bell was suddenly heard, another joined it and another and another and more bells were being tolled by the faithful, clappers striking the bronze sides, and a resolute and nervous pealing shook the mountain air and the pale, fading light. I told Nachum that they were probably ringing for the dead, but he reminded me that it was Sunday and the church bells always ring on Sunday, and then he asked, 'Where's your car, and where were you exactly when it all happened?' I leant back against the headrest, closed my eyes and asked him to leave me alone and not ask me anything until we got home.

I opened my eyes when the car came to a halt outside the house and Nachum quickly got out, opened the door for me and held out his hand in a courtly gesture. I ignored him, but then the giddiness hit me again and I was forced to lean on him, and with his arm round my waist and mine round his neck, he led me step by step up the staircase. And when my legs buckled and I stumbled at the door, he lifted me up and carried me from the door to the bed and laid me down like a fragile object. When he covered me with the quilt that felt as heavy as if it was woven of leaden thread, I recalled how on our wedding night, despite my entreaties, he had refused to carry me over the threshold when we got home, saying he didn't like that romantic nonsense that was alright for saccharine-sweet American movies, and patted my behind, hurrying me into the bedroom just like you gee-up a stubborn mule into the stable. There's poetic justice in this world, I thought, as he hurried to the kitchen to make me a cup of camomile tea; here I am carried in my husband's arms, five years after I asked him to.

In the back of the bus I saw a little blonde girl who played peek-aboo with me, I wanted to tell him when he came back carrying a steaming cup of tea, but I didn't. As he carefully brought the cup to my lips and I sipped slowly, I asked him to call Rami. 'Call him now, tell him I need him tomorrow,' and Nachum whispered, 'You don't remember, Rami can't come any more.' 'I don't care,' I insisted, 'tell him I need him. He'll come for me.' Nachum nodded and said, 'I'll call him right away,' and he left the room and I heard him speaking on the phone. When he came back he told me that Rami wasn't home and immediately changed the subject and

25

told me that three-year-old David Wasserstein, a patient of his, who's a bit older than our Yoavi, and his mother had been killed in the bombing. And I remembered my son and asked anxiously, 'Where's Yoavi?' and Nachum calmed me, 'He's with Levana upstairs, he's playing with her Yossi.' He patiently fed me the murky liquid that tasted like medicine, and sat at my side on our bed and squashed my sweaty hand in his strong one and I gazed at the bedroom floor on which lay curled-up dolls and soft furry animals in a gay, colourful pile.

'You know something,' I said to him in a kind of epiphany, 'the "Ode to Joy" from Beethoven's Ninth was used as an anthem by numerous European political groups. The Nazis, the fascists, the communists – they all used it. Every one of them found in it what they were looking for.' And I had no idea why I was saying this and where I'd heard it, until Nachum asked me why on earth I was talking about music right now, and I recalled that the Voice of Music announcer had said it, but I couldn't remember if he'd said it before or after that moment. I told Nachum that the Ninth was playing in my head and wouldn't go away. 'I'm hearing it all the time, the shouts of the choir, the trumpets, the violins, and most of all those annoying kettledrums,' and I added that now I was like Alex from *A Clockwork Orange*, every time I hear Beethoven's Ninth I'll feel nauseous and that will be my conditioning for that piece of music. He didn't even ask why and talked and talked, happy to display his broad education and erudition, and reminded me that Leonard Bernstein had played it on the eve of the fall of the Berlin Wall, and again squeezed my hand in his as if afraid I'd run away from him.

Afterwards I asked Nachum for another Hypnodorm and he asked if I was sure, and I said yes and, drowsy from the tranquillisers, with my hand still in his, I turned my face to the wall. The black beady eyes of Teddy Bear, which Yoavi had dragged with him when he climbed into bed with us early that morning, about a hundred years ago, transfixed me. With my free hand I grasped the bear by his one ear and threw him onto the floor where he landed with a soft rustle on a heap of woolly toys stuffed with straw and bits of sponge, and I thought that perhaps Nachum was right and Yoavi didn't need this zoo and to prepare him for life we should buy him trucks, rifles and pistols like other boys of his age.

I tried to fall back into the black abyss that opened up to swallow me, but Nachum wouldn't let me sink back and talked briskly about the horror and said that they'd called him from the Abu Kabir pathology unit and asked him to send them the dental X-rays of the boy who'd been killed in the bombing. 'David Wasserstein, a patient of mine. They had no other way of identifying him, his face had been totally mutilated. And just imagine,' he added happily, as if he wasn't talking about a dead child, 'I found his file on my desk right in front of me and I've got no idea why it was there because he was only due for a check-up in another two weeks.'

'They say he was a gifted child,' he eulogised him, and in his voice I heard a hint of rebuke and knew that now he was thinking about Yoavi and comparing him with the dead child. 'He taught himself to read and write at three years of age, while our Yoavi is still playing with soft toys and dolls,' he just couldn't resist the comparison.

The tears suddenly burst out and a bitter taste rose in my throat and I smelt the reek of burning bubbling up from every cell in my body. I wanted my father by my side. He would surely caress and soothe and tell me, 'Everything's fine now, Yaeli, nothing bad will happen to you while Daddy's here. I won't let anyone take you away from me.' Then he would undoubtedly go to the kitchen cupboard, pull out the arak that he kept out of Hobson's choice as a substitute for ouzo, draw the cork with his teeth, take a mouthful of the fiery liquid, roll it from cheek to cheek, warming it, and then purse his lips as if in a kiss and spray it over my bare chest and stomach, ask me to turn over and then do the same to my back. Then he'd wrap me in a thick towel, rub and massage my aching limbs with the liquid he'd warmed in his mouth, cover me with a blanket and say, 'And now to sleep, and in the morning my little girl will wake up with no fever and no pain.' Before I fell asleep I'd listen to the sounds of the house and the voices coming from the living room, which was also my parents' bedroom, and I'd know they were both using my illness as an excuse for sipping arak. I would wake up in the morning smelling like the fragrance that rose from the jar of fish-shaped liquorice sweets that was kept in a cool dark place in Shlomo's grocery store in the Bulgarians' alley. And when I asked for a sweet, Shlomo would carefully twist the tin lid of the clear glass jar that was full of shiny, black fish-shaped sweets, catch one for me and quickly screw the lid back on. And once he told me that

27

this smell of liquorice evaporates very quickly and if he didn't hurry to replace the lid, the sweets wouldn't have the same taste because our sense of taste without the sense of smell was worthless. With blackened tongue and lips I'd suck the head of the fish, and by the time I reached its tail the sweet was completely transparent. At that moment, just before it disappeared in my saliva, I'd bring it close to my eyes and through its translucency look at the sun that now turned grey.

Nachum released my hand from his painful grip and told me he was going into the living room to watch the news and despite my asking him to keep the volume down, I heard the sounds through the comatose sleep that hit me. The dramatic metallic voices of newsreaders invaded my bed. I covered my head with the quilt and stuck my thumbs into my ears, but they, more insistent and stronger than me, were fired into the room like bursts from an automatic weapon. Fragments of words, sentences and key terms that in the past few days had been chewed over and over on screen and refused to cohere into a whole picture, again fell upon me like motes of ash that scorched my body and invaded my sleep: At . . . intersection . . . a bomb outrage . . . the rescue services . . . so far the names of . . . I suddenly heard a boom . . . She was only sixteen . . . I suddenly heard a boom . . . I saw . . . I saw . . . I suddenly heard a boom . . .

Again I thought about Rami. I thought about what he would say about what had happened and wondered what he was doing right now. I wanted to call him, maybe I could still persuade him to come back to me, and what Nachum might say didn't matter. Over the voices of the newsreaders I heard the front door open and Yoavi's clear voice asking, 'Where's Imush?' and Nachum saying, 'Shhh, Ima's asleep.' I remembered how Rami had welcomed us home in the spotless apartment when I returned from the hospital with my scarred belly and a baby, red-faced with anger, clutched in my arms, weeping coming from deep within me. With all the excitement of a new father Rami had washed his hands and soaped between the fingers, spread a clean towel over his shoulder and taken the baby from me. With his big hand supporting the head, he took him carefully to his chest, rocked him gently making warm, soft sounds, and played with him for a while before giving him to Nachum. Nachum had held him with both his hands stretched forward and hadn't held him close to his chest and hadn't wanted to sniff his baby smell, and then he'd put him back into Rami's arms and announced that he had to rush off because he had a patient waiting. Rami lowered his eyes to the floor as though ashamed of meeting mine. Then he'd asked me to get into bed and wouldn't let me get up; he moved around the apartment silently, hung out the washing and folded the clean laundry, arranged the cupboards, made okra, rice and a salad for lunch, made me drink some malt beer because it's good for the milk, and when the baby awoke crying, he'd gone into the bedroom and lifted him from the crib, placed him in my arms and gently closed the door after himself. A short time later he'd come back, taken the baby, swiftly changed his diaper and stayed with us far after his hours were up, until my mother arrived with a great deal of noise. Together they bathed Yoavi and I heard her ask him to hold the baby because her hands were shaking with excitement, and his assured voice saying, 'Don't worry, missus, my five brothers I look after.'

When he left me in the early evening, and my mother plumped a pillow under my head, she found a package wrapped in purple paper and in it a bright blue woollen baby suit, and she'd hissed, 'Arab taste,' and repacked the suit in the crumpled paper and put it on the dresser.

I swallowed another pill from the bag the doctor had given me and sleep fell upon me and trapped me in its soft arms, drawing me down into the abyss, to the place the dead go to, never to return.

And there was evening and there was morning, a second day

(Genesis 1, 8)

I woke up in the morning into a terrible racket of a fracas, squawking and beating of wings. Hammers were pounding my temples, a bitter bolus of dried tears blocked my throat and that awful smell which had been with me since yesterday morning rose from the sheets. I heard rustling from the living room. 'Rami, is that you?' I called weakly, and Yoavi trudged towards me in his furry slippers adorned with cats' heads. I was afraid that he'd see the terror in my eyes so I closed them tightly, shielding him from the scenes, and Rami arose before me as if his face had been etched upon the darkness behind my eyelids, although it had been many months since I'd seen him.

Monday was our day. Like on every other Monday morning I'd awaken with some anxiety mingled with a sweet expectation. I'd lie there with eyes closed, waiting for the light knock of his knuckles on the armoured door. I'd never managed to persuade him to use the bell. I told him that the noise of the washing machine, the television set chirping its children's programs, Yoavi's chatter and the morning street sounds blocked out the sound of his drumming fingers. But he insisted and I taught my ears to hear his knocking. Despite my lying in wait for him, ear to the door, I'd never hear his light footsteps coming up the stairs. Rami walked around the house like a cat stepping lithely on its pads, and again and again I'd shake in fear as he appeared out of nowhere. Every Monday, at eight o'clock on the dot, he arrived. Even when snow had fallen on the city and covered it in a freezing woolly carpet, he didn't give up our day and walked all the way, bundled up in an old army greatcoat, crossing the valley that separated his city from my

30

neighbourhood before the wall was put up. He'd greet me with a smile, ask how we were, kiss Yoavi on the cheek, and as part of a lasting ritual I'd ask him to join us for breakfast and he'd refuse, urging me to leave for the university lest I be late, and, like a host waiting impatiently for the departure of bothersome guests, he'd say goodbye to us at the door. When I got back in the afternoon, the baby in a sling and laden with shopping bags, the ruins of the hurricane we'd left behind had been completely erased. Each object was in its place, the china gleamed, the dishes we'd left in the sink had been swallowed up into their cupboards, the old newspapers piled in the corner had been thrown out, and the smell of cleaning wafted on the air. Rami would meet me at the door, rebuke me with, 'A woman mustn't carry heavy thing,' arrange the purchases 'like soldiers' in the cupboards and fridge, remarking that when he got married he'd do the shopping for his wife, so that she wouldn't have to lug baskets like me.

'Shhhh . . . Imush sleeping.' The little one tore me from my memories of Rami. He walked around the bed, dragging Teddy Bear and Tutti, a tattered, filthy scrap of diaper he liked to rub under his nose and sniff like a little drug addict. 'Imush sleeping, don't wake her up,' he sang to himself, probably repeating what Nachum had told him, and I shook myself, again amazed by this son of mine, 'the Angel Gabriel' I called him in my heart of hearts, for there was no other child like him in the world, who knew how to put my needs before his own, that's what I'd tell Nechama and she'd lift up her nose.

With closed eyes I pulled the quilt over my head and with the hand of a woman abandoned groped for Nachum's body.

'Daddy's at work and Imush is taking Yoavi to kindergarten today,' he chirped, reminding me of my obligations.

I switched on the reading lamp and crooked my finger at him and he jumped into the bed with Tutti and Teddy Bear, lay on my belly, stretched out on it and my stomach, empty since yesterday morning, cramped with a slight pain. The small body smelling of sleep curled up in my arms under the quilt and hugged me with its tiny arms, giving my aching body some relief. I sniffed his hair still damp with the sweat of the night, kissed his plump nape with its little wrinkle and with my tongue wiped off the stains of red jelly decorating his cheeks.

'Imush is only Yoavi's,' he mumbled.

31

'Only Yoavi's,' I answered, obedient as an echo, 'Imush is only Yoavi's.'

My promise was swallowed by the sound of squawking, beating of wings and the scratching of talons, and Yoavi pointed to the window-shutter box and said confidently, 'There's a lot of birds in there.' The sparrows had never squawked so loudly before, so something was probably bothering them; and I remembered how they'd crowded together on the windowsill yesterday morning, two thousand years ago. I got out of bed and with sleep-numbed fingers pulled on the shutter cord. A grey morning dimness crawled from outside the window and stole into the room, threatening to over-power the artificial lighting with its gloominess. I was answered with a commotion of beating wings and sharp squawking, and Yoavi shouted that I was hurting the birds and grabbed my hand and asked me to let down the shutter, 'Because that's the birds' house.' When I did as he asked he sang a line from our song, 'And what do the birds do? Fly, fly, fly, until they're tired.' I mustered all my strength and put on my tattered old mauve robe, the one my mother bought me for Yoavi's birth. The robe, whose wool was well worn, was dappled with threadbare patches like chickenpox. Despite Nachum's pleadings, I refused to throw it away, for the memories were stuck to its front in stubborn greyish stains – a memory of breast milk that had dripped and dried on it, the vestiges of whose smell still stuck to its threads despite the frequent washings, and the smells and stains had gathered one on top of the other inside the warmth of the wool, refusing to let go and remind-ing me of the period I wanted to forget. Protected by his familiar, honey scent, I piggybacked Yoavi to his room, but when we held the morning shoe ritual, I suddenly forgot the right order and began deliberating between the left and right shoes. Yoavi sensed my confusion and hugged me and called me silly Imush.

Like stardust on the table sticky with dark plum jam shone crumbs of breakfast cereal and toast with a Milky Way snaking through them. The morning paper lay spotted with blobs of butter and jam and its bleeding headline screaming HORROR AT THE PATT JUNCTION, and the subhead announcing twenty-two dead, most of them children, in the suicide bombing of a bus. And although the little girl was a stranger to me, her death was all mine and I had to know her name and age, discover her parents, and find out where she lived. I scoured the paper's pages that rustled and sighed and whimpered at my touch as I searched it for some sign of her; the names of the victims and their ages flickered blackly in small letters like fly tracks. Meticulously, I read the names and ages and didn't find the little girl among them. Then I checked the photographs of the dead whose names had been released, and they looked at me, neatly arranged in three straight ranks, solemn, brushed and combed, and on the orders of nameless and invisible photographers they showed their teeth in a broad smile, in the momentary action arousing compassion for people striving to look their best and being photographed so they wouldn't be forgotten. I read the names and ages again, and studied the photographs.

My sweet little girl wasn't there!

My sweet little tot had also escaped the list of the injured, and the moment I realised this I was flooded with a tremendous wave of relief, tears of release blinded me, blurred the names and were absorbed by the paper. Now I knew she was safely at home and living her life, and I wondered at this miracle that had happened to both of us, and I wanted to see her again. I went to the sink and with my back to Yoavi turned on the tap, and a waterfall of nearly boiling water flooded angrily into it. I noisily washed the dishes and the bus floated before my eyes in the water, long and swaying, and the lovely face of a little girl smiled at me, and an annoying ringing was suddenly heard and Yoavi woke me up and said, 'Imush, telephone.' By the time I got to my study and wiped my hands on my robe, the answering machine's red light was gaily winking at me and Nechama's concerned message reverberated through the room. In her authoritative voice she had decided for me that I mustn't leave the house and announced that she would be coming this morning by taxi with her Yoeli to take Yoavi to the kindergarten, and added that she would also pick him up from there and it would be better if Yoavi slept over with them tonight until I had gotten over the trauma I had experienced. As if paralysed I stood by the machine from which her voice emanated, distorted and metallic, and by the time I picked up the receiver I was informed by a prolonged monotonic tone that Nechama had completed her speech, and my fingers, racing over the keys and dialling her number, couldn't catch her.

I suddenly heard the rattle of a key in the lock and I got up and ran to the door, calling happily, 'Rami?' and a curly head appeared in the doorway and Nechama, resolute and efficient as ever, stuck her head inside, still holding the key I had given her for emergencies. She studied me with interest, as if this was the first time she'd ever seen me, slammed the door behind her and leant against it heavily, panting with the effort of climbing the stairs.

'Rami? How could it be Rami? You know he can't get here.' With the authority that came with her long years of loneliness, she chivvied me to get back to bed, 'Because in cases like this you've got to rest.' And as her Yoeli and my Yoavi rolled around on the rug with the woolly toys, she made me some verbena tea 'that calms the nerves' and stroked my head with great compassion. And I asked her, 'Can you smell it? Can you smell it?' and she answered with a question, 'What am I supposed to be smelling?' I whispered, 'The smell that's been coming from me since yesterday morning.' She brought her forehead to mine until her eyes became a single Cyclopean eye, screwed up her nose, made noises like a police sniffer dog and complained in an affected tone, 'Ugh, what a stink, run and brush your teeth.' 'Nechama,' I told her, 'I'm serious, I'm carrying the smell of burning, of burnt flesh,' but she dismissed my complaint with a derisory gesture and said it was all in my mind and it would pass, and gave her special whistle to the children, the bugle call from Tchaikovsky's *1812 Overture*. They came running to her and she caught them in her arms and lifted them up, one after the other, and they clung to her neck and clasped their legs around her waist. As we said goodbye I watched her heavy buttocks rising and falling, like the backside of a strong mule, with two children hanging down from both sides, holding her thick hips with their ankles and fighting above her head with their hands entangled. 'And don't you dare go out today,' she passed my sentence as she went down the stairs, 'anyway, you don't have a car,' and she ordered me to disconnect the phone, 'Because you don't need any consoling calls today,' I heard her saying after she disappeared from sight.

I listened to the sounds from the street and when I heard the taxi door closing I hurried to the bathroom and banished from the bath a family of yellow plastic ducks that had put down stakes there since last night, when Nachum had showered Yoavi. Foaming, almost boiling water filled the bath, and steam covered the mirror with condensation. I undressed, stuck my foot into the water that scalded my toes, and I yelled and jumped up and down and quickly opened the cold tap, tested the water again, and slowly immersed

34

first my behind and then the rest of my body. The water trapped me in its hot embrace. I took Yoavi's soap, which was shaped like a green turtle, rubbed it onto the rough loofah until it foamed, and scrubbed my skin as if trying to shed it together with the remains of the tragedy and the smell. I even soaped my forefinger and slid it into my vagina and anus and scoured them from within.

Then I gave myself up to the hair-washing ritual and I shampooed my hair and washed it three times, re-enacting the 'head-cleaning ritual' of my youth which then was an efficient way of cleansing the memory cells and disposing of hard thoughts, and which proved to be particularly efficient in erasing the memory of boys who dumped me. I copied this ritual from the musical *South Pacific* that I saw with my first love, an excited boy with an acne-scarred face who held my one hand with his sweaty one and with the other felt his way over my chest that had just started to develop and I concentrated on brushing his hand away and the actions of the heroine who was washing her hair energetically to wash that man out of her hair. I applied the method next day after seeing my first love in the yard, passionately kissing a girl more developed than me, and I bunked off school in the middle of the day and stood for a long time under a strong spray of water in the shower and washed my tears and washed and washed, digging my nails into my scalp and tearing him from my memory and exploring my soul until the blood flowed and the hot water ran out.

That night, as I wept bitter tears into my pillow, my father came into my bedroom and sat down at the end of the bed. Although he was very thin, one side of the mattress sagged under his weight, and I rolled over to him and he asked me, half jokingly, half seriously, if I had washed my hair thoroughly and whether it had helped, and when I told him, choking on my tears, that it hadn't, he suggested that I go back to the bathroom and wash it again and again until I had washed that boy right out of my head. Then he took my hand and told me that I was so beautiful, and it wouldn't be long before those boys would be standing in line, 'And they'll come to you from all over the country, until your mother will have to drive them away with her witches' broomstick.' And I laughed and laughed until fatigue fell upon me and I gave myself up to sleep, and when I woke up in the morning I found my father lying beside me on the edge of the bed with my hand in his.

I lay in the hot water for a long time and I thought that now my

35

flesh was slowly cooking and would rapidly soften like the meat they put in the Sabbath *hamin*, and bit by bit it would peel off my body and disappear down the plug-hole, and when Nachum came he'd find a bleached skeleton instead of me. Cleansed and red I got out of the bath and towelled myself, but the smell of burning still exuded from every pore and mingled with the fragrance of the soap and the perfume I sprinkled liberally behind my ears and at the base of my neck.

At the bathroom mirror, on whose two panels there were tears of condensation, I stood naked and combed my hair and examined my face that was covered with orange freckles even though I'm not a redhead. My father had once told me that the freckles reminded him of a girl who had not come back from 'there', and I was freckled just like her, and one day, he said, I'd find me a man who'd love my freckles and would even count them one by one, in an expression of love. But Nachum had never admired my freckles.

I gazed at my body that only yesterday had seemed to me to be debased and desolate and now I could see a slim waist, rounded hips and breasts that were as full and upturned as always. I recalled a compliment Nachum had given me so many years ago, before we were married, that the curves of my body reminded him of the Venus de Milo, and on our honeymoon, as we wandered moon-struck through the Louvre, he took me to meet her. I stood to her left, hiding my hands behind my back and my hips pushed forward and head held high, and he photographed us, side by side; one with her breasts exposed, her arms truncated and her body shining white, cold and hard, and the other in a short summer dress, with a soft, warm, suntanned body. At the souvenir shop he bought me a white marble miniature of the goddess. When we got back to Israel and he had the film developed, he claimed that the photograph didn't do justice to my beauty and he stopped calling me his Venus and no longer praised the curves of my body.

Naked, washed clean and perfumed I sat on the end of the bed and considered my steps for the next hour. Nechama's words of warning still echoed in my ears, and the unmade bed, its warm sheets rumpled, tempted me to lie down in its softness again, promising to protect me from the dangers lurking outside. I mulled over Nechama's commanding words: Don't you dare; rest, don't move, and her masterful and protective tone grated on my ears and

I thought how she always takes me under her wing when I'm in a state of weakness. I recalled what she had once told me when we were talking about hysteria, that rest and prevention of stimuli had been perceived at the end of the nineteenth century and the beginning of the twentieth as the perfect therapy for hysteria in women. Then I recalled studies I'd read on shock victims, and I thought that maybe there was some truth in the claim that the victim should be taken back to the heart of the horror as a tried and true method of saving him from his anxieties. The jeans and check shirt I'd worn for Saturday's trip with Louisa were still thrown over the back of the chair, and without a second thought I quickly put them on, still full of desert dust, and called the nearby taxi rank.

The driver waiting for me outside had his arm dangling from the window and I saw the cigarette between his fingers and the smoke curling upward and the long ash, which had not yet succumbed to the force of gravity, clinging to the end and refusing to let go. I got into the back seat, and he flicked the column of ash off and said, perhaps to me, perhaps to himself, that he'd started smoking again after having stopped for six months, and how could you not smoke with the situation as it is, everything going down the tubes.

I lied and told him that smoking didn't bother me and asked him to drive along the Gilo road towards the Patt junction and stop at the bus stop there. He shrugged and asked, 'And then where to?' and I said, 'Then back home.' He flicked his cigarette butt out of the window, looked at me curiously through his rear-view mirror and wanted to ask me something but I looked away and concentrated on the little plastic football hanging from the mirror on a transparent thread. The ball bobbled about during the drive, its black and yellow panels, the colours of the Betar Jerusalem football club, flickering before me like a poisonous insect.

Far too quickly we reached the last stop of the bus that had gone up in flames. There, on an elongated rectangle of charred, blacker than black asphalt, I asked him to stop. The bus's skeleton had been towed away. I made my way through the rubberneckers gathered there. A holy site had been set up there overnight. Bunches of flowers shrivelled from the cold and bound with black ribbons now upholstered the bus stop's benches and several dolls and teddy bears rested peacefully among them like vacationers resting in a long-withered field of flowers. An Israeli flag covered an advertisement for baby formula on the bus stop wall and tattered notices on soft, damp cardboard declared that the Arabs should be deported. Fresh death notices had been hurriedly pasted to the bus stop's supports and dozens of memorial candles for the victims had been arranged to form the Hebrew word *Chai*, living, and tiny flames guttered in the protective glasses. Two soldiers patrolled around the bus stop and a few faded, silent passengers waited patiently for the next bus and crowded side by side outside the shelter as if trying to draw some consolation and security from each other. Above their heads the sun hid its shamed face behind a veil of black clouds that clustered around it, roiling, as if threatening a fresh downpour that would erase the memory of death and in its mercy wash away the dust of the dead that had gathered in the cracks in the roadway.

'May the names of those accursed murderers be blotted out forever,' grumbled the taxi driver on my return, 'Virgins they promise them in paradise. They should be thrown out. Every last one of them. Only then we'll be able to live in peace.' He lit another cigarette and waited for my reaction and I burrowed deep into the seat and told him I'd been there yesterday, that I'd been driving behind the bus when it blew up.

'Anyone sitting at the back of the bus,' he said, 'was killed instantly, and if you weren't hurt by shrapnel then it was a miracle,' he added, looking at me with interest through the mirror over his head as if scanning my face for signs of the miracle that had happened to me. I didn't tell him about the little girl in the rear window who'd played with me, I kept her for myself. I felt that he wanted to go on talking but my expression in his mirror didn't encourage him to go on.

'Where to now?' he asked as if he'd forgotten what I'd told him only a few minutes earlier.

'Home,' I answered brusquely.

The taxi climbed the mountainside along the wide road and the football flickered before me like a dangerous hornet until we pulled up in the parking lot by the house next to mountains of garbage that had overflowed from the green dumpster. 'How much?' I asked, and he waved a dismissive hand, 'There's no need.' And I repeated, 'How much do I owe you?' and with fat fingers he zeroed the meter, turned to me and said, 'There's no need to pay, missus, it's only a short trip.' I asked his name and he told me and

I immediately forgot it, and thanked him. Through the mirror a pair of cloudy green eyes fixed me with a look we sometimes reserve for those slow on the uptake, and he said, 'We should meet only on joyous occasions, missus.'

I hurried to be swallowed up in the stairwell. Short of breath, I climbed the stairs and as if being pursued I opened the door and fully dressed covered myself with the quilt on the bed that still held the warmth of my body. The rattle of the key in the door was heard followed by the routine sounds of Nachum coming home: The door closing, his keys being thrown into the copper bowl standing on the low bookcase in the hallway, the slap of his briefcase on the dining table. Nachum had come home early today. His face peeped at me from the bedroom door and I pulled the quilt up to my chin so he wouldn't suspect I was lying in bed fully dressed. He asked, 'Why didn't you answer the phone, I called you several times to let you know I'd be home early,' and I said I'd disconnected the phone because I wanted to sleep. Again the noises from the window shutter box were heard, and he listened and asked what's that noise from the window, and I told him it was birds, and he said but the sparrows have never made such a racket, and I remembered the sparrows that yesterday had crowded together on the windowsill like refugees in the biting cold and I said that there were probably other birds in there, and he said we've got to get rid of them and finally get that crack in the box blocked up. Then he turned his back on me and quickly undressed. Tiny, tight-fitting, leopard-spotted underpants, which I'd never seen before, gracefully hugged his manhood that protruded in an impressive bulge. He sat down heavily on the bed, bent to take off his socks and new underpants and threw the lot into the laundry basket. Naked and barefoot he padded into the bathroom and I could hear the water needling onto him in the shower. He came out wearing a grey sweat suit and enveloped in a cloud of sweet-smelling fragrance, his reddened feet encased in his squashed check slippers and rebuke in his voice: 'Why didn't you clean the bath, your hair blocks the pipes, the plumber makes more out of our bath than I do at my clinic.' Only then he asked where Yoavi was and I told him that he'd be staying over at Nechama's. He sat down next to me and looked at me and asked how my day had been. I kept him out and lied by saying I'd been sleeping, and he said, that's the best thing for you and asked what is there to eat? I told him I hadn't the strength for cooking and I'm not hungry and there's the roast from Shabbat in the fridge, and he said he'd heard on the radio that there might be snow in Jerusalem tonight and there was nothing in the house, and I said lovely, it'll be Yoavi's first snow, and there are eggs in the fridge.

When I heard the clatter of plates I hurriedly undressed and put on my flannel nightgown and took a tranquilliser. I gave myself up to the sweet feeling of slackness that spread through my body, and the mattress beneath me swallowed me up and I slept dreamlessly. I awoke to despairing words, stronger than me, falling on me and I floated up to wakefulness and asked Nachum to turn up the volume on the TV newsreader's voice and he shouted back, 'I thought you wanted to sleep,' and I insisted, 'Turn it up a bit,' and I heard the standard formula: Today the funerals were held of . . . She was a young girl who loved life . . . He was to celebrate his marriage . . . He left a pregnant wife and three children . . . A foreign worker who arrived from Romania only a week ago . . . a boy killed with his mother. And I didn't hear anything about a three year-old girl who had been brought to her final resting place. Then the newsreader announced that right after this service broadcast we'll bring you the weather forecast, and I could already hear the meteorologist saying, 'Tomorrow will be a . . . ' and I knew that there would be a tomorrow, because the weather forecast had said so.

Then there was silence and Nachum fell onto the bed and shook the mattress and pressed himself against my body and with his fingers, which had suddenly come back to life, pinched my nipples and slid into my depths that had dried and hurt me. I lay on my back with my eyes closed and saw the little girl whose name I didn't know with her nose pressed against the window and her breath surrounding her face like the halo of a saint in a Christian icon.

'Peekaboo,' I whispered, half asleep.

'Are you crazy?' Nachum said, recoiling from me, 'I'm trying to seduce you and you're playing peekaboo?' and he turned his back on me, hurt.

'Did Yoavi have something to eat?' I asked his retreating back, and he mumbled, 'Yoavi's at Nechama's, have you forgotten?'

'Did you read him a story?' And I asked him to call Rami now and try to persuade him to come tomorrow because the house was in such a mess. But Nachum didn't reply, and I, whose sleep had been disturbed, snuggled up to his warm body and tried to gain some consolation from it. But his body was rigid and his back hostile. I got up, went to my study and stood at the window. In the light of the streetlamp I could see the first snowflakes dancing in the air. I watched them for a long time, but it was a light fall that melted as it touched the ground. I felt my body chilling, needles pierced my flesh and my heavy limbs were paralysed. I was frightened of going back to the warmth of the bed lest I lose control of my sleep and those scenes would come back in a nightmare. I tried to rid myself of the bad thoughts, but they came back again and again like black birds of prey, screaming and pecking at the bodies of the dead.

And there was evening and there was morning a third day

(Genesis 1, 13)

My eyes were open when the sounds of screeching and banging came from the window shutter box, in perfect synchronisation with the buzzing racket from the alarm clock at Nachum's side. I leant over his body and silenced the clock, and Nachum, refusing to open his eyes, turned over. I woke him with a light shake and asked him to take Yoavi to kindergarten because I hadn't slept a wink all night. He jumped out of bed in a panic, ran to Yoavi's room, came back and said reproachfully, 'Have you forgotten that he slept over at Nechama's last night?' And I remembered and hid myself under the quilt that still held the warmth of his body and asked, 'Is it snowing?' Nachum said that the noise could drive you mad and there was something the matter there, and he took the shutter cord and raised the shutter one click at a time, and one beam at a time the morning light came through and stole onto the floor, and squares of light fell onto the quilt, and the darkness of the room was mingled with the softness of dawn. The awful screeching drowned out the whistle of the wind outside, beating on the windowpane, begging to come in, and Nachum cursed those damned birds that wouldn't let him sleep.

He left the room and returned carrying an aluminium ladder spotted with bird droppings, leant it under the window with a bang, climbed up and loosened the screws holding the cover of the shutter box in place, and angrily exposed the thick plastic roller. Straw and assorted rubbish lined the box, and bits of cotton wool, egg fragments, scraps of plastic bags, dry leaves, feathers and fluff, and other stinking matter dripped onto the rug. Nachum hit the bottom of the box with the screwdriver's handle and was answered with a whistling screech, and a bolt of black lightning fled the scene, hitting the closed window again and again, which shook and rang in pain. A forked tail, pointed pinions, a beak gaping in a scream and sharp, crooked talons shot from wall to wall; as if blind the bird crashed into the ceiling light, knocked a book off the sideboard and smashed into Venus de Milo. My armless goddess shook and swayed, and a shattering sound was heard as she fell from the height of her place of residence. As the bird was hissing above my head I shouted to Nachum, 'Open it, open it, open the window,' and he struggled with the handle until a cold wind was suddenly blowing over me, and the beat of wings could be heard above me, and the screeching gradually diminished.

In the blessed silence that fell I heard Nachum's angry voice saying, 'The bastard nearly gouged my eyes out.' And I asked, 'Where are the sparrows?' and he replied, 'There aren't any. She drove them away.' I asked who 'she' was and he hurried into the study, came back with *The Birds of Israel* and asked me to find the bird, because it had flown around so quickly and it had been hard to follow, and I said I remembered a sharply forked tail, something like a swallow's, and he leafed through the book and leafed again and then announced, 'Unbelievable. It's a swift. It took over the shutter box.' Then he opened the window again and shook out the rug outside, and the wind tried to snatch it from his hands and he fought the billowing rug that threatened to fly away. Afterwards he swept up the straw and dirt that covered the floor, and said he'd called a joiner to close up the box so that no birds could nest in it. 'And the sparrows?' I asked, 'What'll happen to the sparrows?' Nachum shrugged: 'How many times do I have to tell you that birds just bring dirt and lice?' I told him I was dead tired because I hadn't slept all night, and curled up into the warmth of the quilt. The morning's sounds – the banging of the frying pan in the kitchen, the hum of an electric toothbrush, the flow of water in the shower and the voices of the morning's TV interviewees – all imbued me with a sense of false tranquillity and I fell asleep in the morning light.

I awoke to the sudden peal of the telephone next to me, 'Those ultra-Orthodox of yours and their funerals can wait,' and as if from a dream I heard the rumbling voice of Prof. Har-Noy, 'The main thing is for you to recuperate from this illness and become your-self again.' I lifted the receiver and thanked him, wanted to

terminate the call, but he shouted, 'Wait a minute, there's somebody here who wants to talk to you,' and a caressing French accent
sang in my ears and Louisa's voice breathing gently called me *ma
chérie* and a sweetness filled me, and I heard her gold bracelets
accompanying her hand movements with their gay jangle, and she
said, 'Rest, sweetie, there's no rush,' and she asked if I wanted her
to visit me and whether I needed anything from the grocery. I
quickly replied that there was no need, and in any case I'd be back
at work tomorrow, and thanked her for her kind words, and she
asked, 'Are you OK?' and I replied confidently, 'I'm fine,' and
wound up with 'See you tomorrow.'

I got out of bed unsteadily. Repellent smells followed me as I
emerged from the depths of the quilt, enveloping me in an aura of
stench. I felt for my slippers and stood on a cold, hard object.
From the darkness of one of them I pulled out a small marble
figurine. My goddess, who had found a hiding place in the warmth
of the artificial fur of one of my slippers, had lost her head.

I fled to the bathroom. The odours had got there before me. The
mirror reflected a crumpled face. Hair tangled wildly around my
head like a Gorgon's, swollen eyelids, lashes stuck together with a
yellowish secretion, one cheek furrowed with pillow crease marks.
I lay in the hot, almost scalding water for a long time, immersing
myself and dispelling the odours in the water and the foam of
fragrant soap. My fingers and toes showed granny wrinkles when
I rose from the bath, purified. I put on my faded mauve robe, plea-
surably inhaled the smell of Yoavi's laundered vomit, and suddenly
felt weak and my legs trembled and I remembered that I had had
nothing to eat for two days. I hurried to the kitchen and, with
hands shaking with hunger, opened the fridge. There were two
lonely eggs shining whitely, a half-full bottle of Coca-Cola, and a
sagging bag of milk whose sell-by date had come and gone. I
turned my back on the fridge and its door closed, shaking free two
worn magnets in the shape of dinosaurs; I put them back on the
door, but they refused to stick and fell to the floor again. Impatiently I threw them into the garbage pail on whose bottom I
discerned eggshells and a half-burnt slice of toast. I retrieved the
toast, stuck my teeth into it and my mouth filled with scorched
crumbs, and I thought, that's probably how you feel when you
chew coal. Then I looked for the Fruit House magnet and found it
hiding among Yoavi's drawings that were stuck to the fridge with

alphabet magnets, next to 'things to do' memos, emergency phone numbers, prescriptions, and the phone numbers of plumbers and pizzerias. I dialled the number of the Fruit House, above which was a picture of a bunch of purple grapes. I told Zvika the manager that I was sick and would he do me a favour and deliver an order, which I dictated. He replied in his trust-evoking basso, 'No problem, you'll have it by noon,' and he told me about Moshe Dvir, the dairy products deliveryman, 'You must know him, the guy that delivers eggs and cheese and such. His son was on his way to school on that bus and got killed, and Rosa, too, the new immigrant who teaches violin at the community centre, she was there, and now she's in hospital seriously injured.' A wave of nausea flooded over me, but he went on, 'Go figure, today it's them and tomorrow it's us.' I didn't tell him that I'd been there too, I just asked him to get a move on it because my house was empty, and he said, 'Sure, sure, I'll send Hamid right away and you have a nice day now.'

I went back into the kitchen and to the fridge, took out the pair of eggs, cracked them on the rim of the frying pan and poured their viscous contents onto the turbid pool of oil in it. Pleasant crackling and bubbling noises came from the pan, and the frying eggs stared at me, yellow and shining, floating in a cloud of white that hardened and browned at its edges. I wolfed them down straight from the pan, poking and wounding their eyes with a fork and finishing off with the remains of a day-old roll whose crust was stale. When the kettle whistled I poured the boiling water into a cup, added a teaspoonful of coffee and hurriedly sipped the dark solution, burning my tongue in the process. Afterwards I sat in the bedroom for a long time listening to the birds that had come back to the window shutter box, until I got myself together and went into my study. I switched on the computer and put up the last interview I'd had with Yosef Warshavsky, my liaison with the *Hevra Kadisha*. I stared at it and couldn't understand what I'd written just before 'that day'. Once again remorse stole into my heart: the research subject I'd chosen, Burial and Mourning Customs in the Jerusalem Ultra-Orthodox Community, wouldn't contribute a thing to science, and even if I didn't complete it, it wouldn't be missed in the world as we know it. Despairingly, I counted the months and weeks and days and hours I'd spent in the kingdom of the dead, and discovered that I'd met twenty corpses face-to-face, taken part

45

in twenty-nine funerals, visited eleven homes in mourning and had nine meetings with Yosef Warshavsky and three with his superiors.

I thought about how and when I'd inform Prof. Har-Noy that I was giving up my research, and decided I'd enlist 'that day' as an excuse and explain that I was no longer capable of facing the grief of others. In a theatrical gesture of despair I'd once seen in a movie about an author deserted by inspiration, I put my head on the keyboard; my nose pressed on one of the keys, and an interminable monotonic ticking came from within the computer. When I raised my head, hundreds of tiny aitches were winking at me. Guiding the mouse, I clicked on 'Close' and the screen winked 'Save?' I seriously considered the offer and decided to accept it, and all those aitches were saved in a file called January 22. I switched off the computer, went back into the bedroom and fell heavily onto the bed. Pipes hidden in the walls murmured softly as if talking to one another and the open-shuttered window cast dancing orange maculae of noontime sun onto me. I closed my eyes to them, but they danced, nimble and brilliant, behind my closed lids. I covered my head with the quilt and gazed open-eyed into the blessed darkness. When I plumped the pillow under my head my fingers encountered something hard and round. I pushed back the quilt and cold marble eyes stared at me. Not a single curl on the severed head of my goddess had been disturbed. I got up, threw Venus's head into the wastebasket and added its armless marble torso. Then I buried my nose and eyes in the pillow and wept tearlessly.

I awoke in the afternoon to the sound of the door opening. Nechama was standing in the doorway looking at me, and my Yoavi came joyously to me, his legs clasped around her waist and a new doll in his hand. 'Shhhhh, Ima's not feeling well,' came Nechama's hoarse voice.

Nechama, my good friend and saviour from all my tribulations. Each day I thank my lucky stars for bringing us together that first time in the gynaecologist's waiting room. My tummy wasn't yet showing, but hers protruded from under a thick covering of fat. When she heard me mention when I was due to the religious woman sitting next to me and who was interrogating me about my bowel movements during my pregnancy, she broke into the conversation, saying, 'What a coincidence, I'm due in the second week of October too.' I replied that you couldn't tell she was pregnant and blushed right away, because I didn't know whether she'd taken my remark as a compliment or an insult, and I shut up in embarrassment. The religious woman used my silence as a loophole and again interrogated me unabashed, asking if I had observed, before becoming pregnant, the purity of the family. Amused, I listened to her, and before I had a chance to reply she said that bathing in the ritual bath guaranteed beautiful, healthy children, and Nechama gave me a wink. When I came out after the examination and Nechama went in, I waited for her. She stormed out after a few minutes, didn't even see me, impatiently rummaged in her purse, pulled out a pack of cigarettes and a transparent plastic lighter, stuck a cigarette into her mouth, lit it, drew the smoke thankfully into her lungs, and her features softened somewhat. Then she saw me, answered my hesitant smile with a smile of her own, and asked if I was waiting for a taxi. I didn't want to admit that I'd been waiting for her and said that I'd parked my car not far away, and she asked where I lived and I told her Gilo, and she announced, 'I'm in Patt, you can drop me on your way home.' As we walked to the car I wondered about asking her to put out her cigarette, and maybe mention incidentally that smoking is harmful to the health, but she had already squeezed herself into the car and was telling me, 'I'm Nechama and I can't understand why you were listening to that nudnik. She bothers every new face she meets.' I told her I thought that the woman was a bit dim, and that my name was Yael. We drove in silence and her cigarette smoke filled the car, and although it was a rainy winter's day I opened my window and stuck my head out. When the burning ember began to scorch the filter she again rummaged in panic in her purse and took out another cigarette and lit it from the dying stub that she threw out of the window on my side and greedily sucked in the smoke. We quickly reached her neighbourhood: nondescript apartment blocks that had been put up hurriedly to block the expansion of the Arab village of Beit Zafafa. With no identity the buildings stood side by side, as if giving away their occupants and candidly declaring that in these boxes lived faceless people with no dreams. They had been roughly patched up over the years, balconies had been added and balconies had been closed in, windows torn out, and parts of the walls had been coated with cheap cut stone that threatened to peel off.

I drove along the neighbourhood's main street and asked where she wanted to be dropped, and she said, 'It's all right, wherever.'

I insisted on taking her right to the door, and she smiled and said, 'I usually walk home from the clinic, so in any case you've saved me a walk,' and she stayed in the car for a few more minutes, sucked on her cigarette end and told me she was a clinical psychologist specialising in pre-schoolers. My eyes were focused on the blackish down above her upper lip, her nicotine-yellowed teeth and her greyish skin devoid of make-up, and she asked me, 'And you, what do you do?'

'Imush not feeling well ... shhh ... ' I heard Yoavi loudly repeating Nechama's caution. I jumped out of bed and Yoavi slid from Nechama's waist and leapt into my arms. 'Imush well, Imush well,' he exulted.

'Coffee?' Nechama asked, her head popping round the kitchen wall. 'Thanks,' I replied and heard the fridge door opening and she called to me and her voice sounded as if it were coming from an empty water cistern, 'Do you know there's nothing in your fridge? Not even milk for coffee. I'll run to the grocery and get you a few things.' I remembered the provisions that hadn't yet been delivered and I told her that I'd phoned a big order to the grocery, and then there was a knock at the door and Hamid, Zvika's deliveryman, stood panting in the doorway, his shirt stinking of sweat and his black curls sticking to his forehead. With a self-effacing smile he put down the loaded carton on the counter, and I wanted to yell at him for taking so long, but Nechama diverted me and began dancing attendance on him and asked him where he lived. 'Abu Tor,' he murmured through lips clenched in bitterness, as if he was being forced to answer a police interrogator's question. Nechama mustered one of her rare smiles: 'So you've got a an Israeli ID card?' and he nodded and she enquired sweetly, 'So what's it like there in your neighbourhood?' and he stared at her suspiciously as if he couldn't comprehend what this woman wanted of him, shrugged, and answered, 'Fine,' and she stuck a bill into his hand, far more than I usually tipped, and said amiably, '*Shukran.*' I knew she was doing it only because he was an Arab. Hamid didn't look at her and said, 'Have a good day,' even though it was almost night, and fled, leaving a fine wake of sweaty male body odour behind him. When the door closed I asked her if she'd kiss a Jewish deliveryman's ass the way she'd kissed Hamid's. The pulsing blue vein in her neck told me that she was enlisting all her

48

strength not to rise to my bait. Her eyes measured me with a compassionate look and focused on my stained robe. In a sour voice she again asked, 'Coffee?' and I said, 'I don't want any.' She sent me back to bed, as if I were suffering from an incurable disease. Yoavi followed me with Tutti and Teddy Bear and sat down next to me. Nechama took control of the kitchen. I heard her opening drawers and slamming doors, making free with my cupboards. And again her voice asking, 'D'you want a cup of coffee?' I didn't reply and she said, 'Whether you like it or not I'm going to pamper you, and I'll even warm the milk for your coffee.' I heard the clang of pans and the hiss of milk boiling over, a smell of burning filled the house and I shouted from the bedroom that the milk was boiling over, but she had already come in, a cup of coffee in one hand and a cigarette in the other. She sat down heavily on the bed next to me, prised off her shoes with her big toes and dropped them on the floor and, after placing the cup on my bedside table, spread herself out on the bed, on Nachum's side. I heard the springs protesting under her weight.

'What have you got there in the window-shutter box?' she asked as squeaks and screeches came from it.

'A family of swifts has moved in with us.'

'What are you going to do? You can't live with that racket.'

I said that Nachum was going to get a joiner to seal up the box cover, and Nechama said it was impossible because they're particularly stubborn birds, and maybe we should try and smoke them out and, if that didn't work, put down poison. 'Kill them? Are you out of your mind?' I replied, shocked, and Yoavi, who was playing with his dolls at our feet, said hotly that you mustn't kill birds. I didn't want to continue with this subject lest we shift from driving out birds to expelling Arabs, and said reprovingly, as if she were to blame for my condition, 'I didn't sleep a wink all night.'

'Of course you didn't.' Nechama put one arm behind her head and sucked on her cigarette. 'Watch out with your ash,' I told her, 'you know how Nachum hates you smoking here.' But she ignored me. 'What are you thinking of? That this trauma will go away without therapy? And apart from that, I didn't get any sleep either because of the shooting and noises from your neighbourhood.'

'Shooting?' I asked.

'Yes, shooting, they were firing at your neighbourhood from Beit Jallah again. And then there were helicopters and tanks, the

49

whole *gescheft*. If you didn't hear, then you slept like a log.'

'I didn't sleep either,' piped Yoavi, confirming what she'd said. 'There was shooting all night.'

'I can't fall asleep at night,' I complained. 'But in the morning, after Nachum goes to work, I manage to get some sleep.'

Smoke penetrated my lungs and I coughed, and again Nechama ignored it and said that this insomnia was just a symptom, and if I didn't treat the root cause of the problem, I'd probably lose control over my life. Then she announced, 'We've got to talk,' and sent Yoavi to his room, because she wanted to have a quiet talk with Ima. And he, obedient and eager to please, clasped his Tutti and went to his room. Nechama stroked my hair gently and asked in her professional tone, 'Have you thought about how to deal with this trauma?'

'There was a little girl there, about Yoavi's age. She had blonde hair in a ponytail. She was sitting in the back seat of the bus, and I don't know what happened to her,' I said, finally managing to tell her the awful story.

Nechama was silent for a moment, looked away, and asked again. 'What do you intend to do now?'

I said that I had to know what had happened to the little girl. Apart from that I was functioning normally and I'd be back at the university tomorrow. I didn't tell her that yesterday, just one day after the bombing, I'd gone back to the site and that I was considering stopping my research.

'Even the strongest person can't suffer a shock like that and get right back into routine,' Nechama declared solemnly. 'This trauma will come back to you in all kinds of ways. If you don't want to talk to a professional, then you should put down what you're going through on paper. Writing can help. You need to know how to dispose of that filth, otherwise it may harm Yoavi and your married life.' And I said that if she heard or read about what had happened to the little girl, of about Yoavi's age, who had been sitting at the back of the bus, she should tell me, even if the news was bad.

Nechama got up to hug me and her heavy breasts squeezed against me. Then she went out and called Yoavi. I heard a small smacking sound as she kissed his forehead, and knew that as always she was ruffling his curls, and I listened as she told him that Ima hadn't been feeling so well lately, and that he should be

50

a good boy, and I heard him reply joyfully, 'Then we'll have a baby?' and she asked in surprise, 'How come a baby?' and he answered confidently, 'Because Shlomi from the kindergarten's Ima didn't feel well and in the end a baby came out.' Nechama's laugh rolled to me through the open door, she whispered something, and I could hear the disappointment in his voice: 'So there's no baby?'

I got up from the bed and Yoavi came running, hugged me and put his ear to my belly as if seeking to make sure that there was no baby. I stroked his head, and a pair of long legs and a pair of short ones walked heavily to the front door. Nechama stopped on the landing for a moment and asked me to think about what she'd said, and that I shouldn't hesitate to call her, even in the middle of the night, and she hugged me warmly, squashing Yoavi who was standing between us, and announced that it was awfully cold and her old bones forecast that it would snow tonight, and Yoavi chirped, 'Good, snow,' despite his never having seen snow in his short life, and Nechama, almost cautioning, repeated, 'Think about what I told you.' She walked heavily down the stairs, whistling to herself, and I stood there, my finger hovering in readiness over the light switch lest she be left in darkness.

'We're sisters,' Nechama had told me at the beginning of our acquaintance and we both had sworn that our relationship would be based on trust, mutual support and keeping promises made, and we would have our babies on the same day and raise them together. I recalled how she had broken that promise and given birth three days before me. I sat at her side holding her hand for ten hours in the labour ward, wiping away the beads of sweat from her face until the final labour pains began, and followed her to the delivery room. My path was blocked by a bouncer in the shape of an elderly sister in white orthopaedic shoes spattered with small drops of blood. Amazed, she inspected my belly. 'In your condition? You want to see all this? How long before you're due?' and wouldn't let me in. I waited in the corridor with Nechama's mother who, in honour of the occasion, was wearing a pink Chanel suit with matching shoes, and I thought how could anybody ever find in this slim, elegant woman, whose blonde hair was gathered in a conservative bun, any relation whatsoever to Nechama. She, too, despised smoking, she told me, and all the time we sat there, waiting for news, she delicately interrogated me as to whether I knew who the father was, and if he was willing to pay child maintenance, and complained about Nechama who wasn't willing to marry him, but to have his child she was more than ready. I lied that Nechama didn't confide in me about everything, because I couldn't tell her that this grandchild, who was at that moment making its way into the world, had come from a test tube costing a few hundred shekels and that her daughter would never know the identity of the donor father. For my part, I almost asked her if Nechama was adopted, because there was not even a hint of a resemblance between them, but I bit my tongue and kept quiet.

By the time the sister came out carrying a red-faced and angry-looking baby, I was exhausted, and I looked at the buttons of the tiny fists that had escaped the diaper and were waving around in disquiet, as if seeking to hit out at all the world and its wife. We looked at its tiny monkey face and its hair-covered ears that stuck out like the handles of a jug, and we made the appropriate cooing noises that women usually make on seeing a minutes-old baby. When he was taken back we laughed and hugged and I told her that another uncompromising fighter for justice, just like his mother, had just come into our cruel world. And her mother looked at me confusedly and asked, 'What? What?' and I realised that Nechama had even avoided talking to her about her political activity. Then I went to the stern-faced bouncer and said that now everything was over, perhaps she'd give me permission to go into the new mother's room. She smiled and turned sideways to let us in. Completely engrossed on the bathed infant they'd placed on her still protruding belly, Nechama was crooning, 'Yoel, Yoeli, Yoelili, Yoelchuk, Yoelileh, Yo-Yo.' I kissed her forehead and said I'd never seen such a beautiful baby, and her mother asked eagerly, 'Is he like his father?' and Nechama, despite her exhaustion, winked at me and we both burst out laughing.

Three days later I went to bring her and Yoeli home. She was waiting in the corridor wearing her tent dress, her belly still in evidence and Yoeli cradled in her arms, his hairy ears hidden under a white bonnet, and he was wearing the blue suit I'd bought him. With her lips slightly clenched and the impatient look of a heavy smoker suffering withdrawal symptoms, she held Yoeli out to me and, as her fingers were scrabbling in her purse for her first cigarette in three days, right there, in the corridor, in front of everyone, my waters broke and warm amniotic fluid dribbled down my legs and into my shoes. I was taken straight to the labour ward and she and her Yoeli went home by taxi.

I heard the ring of keys thrown into the copper bowl and the slap of his heavy briefcase on the dining table, and was torn away from my memories, and Nachum was standing in the bedroom doorway like an unwanted guest. Crossly, he asked, 'Why are all the lights on?' and sniffed the airless room and said, 'Nechama's been here. How many times have I got to ask you to tell her not to smoke in our apartment?' Only then did he ask what there was to eat, and I told him there was probably some of the Shabbat roast left, and he said he'd already finished it, and I remembered Hamid and said that I'd done some shopping and he'd probably find something in the fridge. Nachum went into the kitchen from where he yelled, 'What have you spilt on the cooker? It's completely black!' I didn't tell him that Nechama had heated milk for coffee, and I heard the hiss of an aerosol followed by the sound of scrubbing, and Nachum shouted, 'Where's Yoavi?' and I replied, 'Playing in his room.' He came back to me with a sleepy Yoavi in his arms, and said in reproof, 'Guess who I've found asleep on the rug in his room, among all his toys and dolls?' and he gave me that look men give their wives when they suspect them of neglecting their children. Yoavi yawned and stretched and said he was hungry, and Nachum asked me drily if I wanted him to fix me something as well, and I said there was no need.

Smells of toast, fresh salad and scrambled eggs came from the kitchen. My hunger was aroused and I wanted to ask Nachum to make some for me too, but I'd already told him I wasn't hungry. When they finished eating and I heard the sounds of Yoavi being showered and put to bed, I sneaked into the kitchen and took the frying pan from the sink. With a fork I scraped off the remains of egg, and in my enthusiasm tore the Teflon coating and, afraid of Nachum's anger, I hurriedly washed and dried the dishes and returned them to their places, and so he wouldn't detect my crimes, I pushed the frying pan deep into the cupboard and thought that at the first opportunity I'd buy an identical one.

'Imush, kiss,' Yoavi called from his room. My hands still wet, I hurried to him and he hugged my neck, almost choking me, and said he had a secret to tell me, and I asked what secret and he whispered in my ear, 'I love you best in the whole world.' Tears almost choked me and I whispered back, 'And I've got a secret to tell you,' and his body tensed and I told him, 'And I love you best in the whole world.'

I sat by his side for a long time, his hand in mine, until his grip slackened and he fell asleep.

That evening, while Nachum was watching television, I tried putting what had happened down on paper. But the language of my forefathers, my ancient language, which for so many years had been trippingly on my tongue, wouldn't agree to come to my aid. I begged and pleaded with it to find me the words and it, as if exhausted by the horror, closed its vocabulary to me, stood to one side, distant, looking on and not intervening. 'Even with a tremendous effort, we would be unable to describe the catastrophe in words,' so my father had once told me when I grilled him about what had happened to him over there in the camps. Determined to discover what he was concealing from me, I once rummaged among his things and found, in the drawer of his bedside table, under the padding of an old newspaper, a yellowing photograph. A lovely little girl of about three wearing a sailor suit smiled at me, her head adorned with a big ribbon that shadowed her features, her face freckled like mine, and her blonde hair cascading in Shirley Temple ringlets. I knew that this girl, who had been hiding from me in the darkness of that drawer all these years, was a competitor for my father's attention. I knew that he thought about her, looked at her at night, and without knowing why, I felt that she was as important to him as I was. I couldn't restrain myself and showed him the photo and asked who she was, and he didn't answer. I goaded him, making fun of the huge ribbon in her hair, and he snatched the photograph from me and warned me never to dare go through his things. When I cried he immediately gathered me into his arms, and stroked my head, soothing me, 'Sha, sha, sha, my little one,' and promised that nobody would ever take me away from him. I asked, 'Who would want to take me away?' and he buried his nose in my hair, inhaled me deep inside him, and said that my hair smelt good. To this day I can feel his heavy breaths tickling my scalp.

Another time, when I asked about the place it was forbidden to talk about, he told me that you didn't always have to say everything. You could sometimes find what you needed to know in silences, in the spaces between the words. These spaces, he said, are part of the language of silence that is stronger and more important than any other. Those days I wandered between two languages: my mother's and my father's. His was the language of silence, concealment and pain, while hers was the tongue of cackles, bleats of laughter, and the consoling sounds of pampering.

They started moving furniture on the floor above us, and soon Levana would start moaning 'Moremoremoremore', and I longed to collapse into the depths of language, the language of my father. To be constantly silent, not to talk, not to write, and perhaps that way the horror enshrouded in a thin mist would vanish. But I was bound by Nechama's dictum and reread the little I had written. Hollow words that voided the experience of its potency, like the empty, jaded and terribly predictable report given by the TV newscasters. But still I was trying, and with a blunt needle was laying patch on patch and erasing what I wanted to forget, but the awful descriptions just wouldn't come. 'Fire, fire, fire, fire, fire, fire,' I suddenly typed and a whole page of flames was written on the screen, threatening to overflow onto the next page.

'Are you coming to bed?' Nachum asked from the bedroom, tearing me away from my thoughts, and I replied, 'In a minute,' and told the computer 'Shut down' and declined its offer to save the document and switched off. A shiver of cold gripped me and I thought that again they'd switched off the central heating too early, and made a mental note that I had to speak to the head of the house committee about the heating and the neglected garden. I went into the bathroom, filled the bath with hot water and ignored Nachum's complaining voice asking me to stop that noise already. My skin burning, I towelled my body and put on a fresh nightgown. I lay down next to Nachum and he pleaded with me to stop tossing and turning because he couldn't get to sleep and he had a hard day tomorrow, and apart from that he was dead tired and because of the episode that had happened to me he was also functioning as a mother, because I was neglecting the child and the house. Hurt, I asked him if he'd prefer me to sleep in my study, and he said do what you want, and I took a pillow and a quilt and went into the study and lay down on the checked couch, which had been my bed in my parents' home.

Now I knew that Sunday's nightmares and ghosts would steal in to me in the darkness of the night, crawl like disgusting maggots over my skin, gnaw at my flesh and leave my whitening skeleton in the vague darkness of my life. I fled my thoughts and went into the still-steamy bathroom, wiped the mirror weeping condensation with the sleeve of my nightgown, looked into my eyes and saw a tiny furrow of anger that had been ploughed between the brows, and I was concerned that it might put down roots there and spread to my entire forehead. I took the bag of pills and fished out the 'Rolls-Royce' of sleeping pills and swallowed it without water. When I went back to the study I could see snowflakes in the window, dense and thick this time, floating down like ballet dancers in tulle tutus under the strong spot of the streetlight. Sleep was already besieging my eyes and I could feel its veil capturing my body, damming my mouth, and I fought against it. I forced my drooping eyelids open and looked out of the window to see how the white blanket of illusions was forming and covering the tops of the cypresses, wrapping the garden in its softness and making illusory white flowers grow on the honeysuckle that had long since withered and died, and I thought about Yoavi who in the morning would be able to see his first snow, and I was glad that the snow was covering the blood and stifling the pain and ugliness. I went back to the couch and laid my head on the pillow, and before the drug vanquished my body I thought again about what Nechama had said and admitted that she was right, I'd been through a severe trauma. Ever since that little girl had vanished in smoke and flame before my eyes, my life had been radically changed and would probably never be the same again. I promised myself to speak to her in the morning, right after I'd taken Yoavi to the kindergarten, and I sank into the black oblivion that makes us forget all the promises and vows and oaths and prohibitions.

And there was evening and there was morning, a fourth day

(Genesis 1, 19)

A blanket full of lead weighed down on me, contracting my chest and squeezing my lungs. Iron fingernails scraped plaster from the walls sounding like shrieks of pain, and someone next to me gasped, with heavy, frightened, rapid breaths. My body was paralysed, and only my hands pulled the blanket over my head, protecting it. But the whistling breath lay beside me in the darkness, curling up in the hollows of my body and I discovered that it was mine, erupting from my lungs. I got out of bed with the blanket wrapped round my body, and ran toward the sliver of pale light gleaming beneath the bedroom door. The bedside lamp was switched on next to Nachum. He was sitting up in bed, his back supported by the pillow, and scowling in annoyance he listened to the shrieking clatter. I said, 'What are we going to do about it?' and the words that came out of my mouth tasted like ashes, and Nachum jumped out of bed, and with eyes almost closed went to the bathroom and re-emerging, armed with a squeegee, pounded against the window shutter box, and a chorus of birds defied him with agitated, ear-splitting shrieks, and Nachum swore that he'd take care of the problem before the day was out. I lifted the blanket on his side and curled up beneath it in the warm hollow left by his body and fell asleep.

I awoke to a soft murmuring sound: Yoavi was sitting on the rug at the foot of the bed chatting quietly with his stuffed animals, and once again I wondered at the consideration shown by this three-year-old. He looked up at me, smiled sweetly, revealing the dimples in his cheeks, and announced calmly that it was snowing outside, as if snow was a matter of routine for him. I crooked my finger and he leapt onto my stomach with his Tutti in tow and whispered in my ear as if revealing a secret, that Daddy had left, and he'd already had breakfast, and that he must put his boots on because Daddy said there's snow outside and it's wet. I kissed his dimples, the ones on his cheeks and the ones above his bottom, and he gurgled with pleasure. We went to his room and I dressed him, and I was just about to observe the ritual of 'which shoe goes on first', but he said that when it's snowing he had to wear boots. I searched the closet and found the red boots I'd bought him at the beginning of the season, with the picture of Winnie the Pooh hugging a pot of honey, and as soon as he saw them he squealed with joy, the ritual completely forgotten. Only later, wearing the boots, he shuffled behind me to the kitchen and said, 'Imush, we forgot.' And I asked, 'What did we forget?' And the corners of his mouth trembled as if he was about to start sobbing as he said reproachfully, 'Which shoe we put on first.' I answered impatiently that I thought we only did that with shoes. Disappointed with my answer, he turned and walked out, and although I knew that it was bothering him, I didn't offer to adapt the ritual to boots.

At the front door, above the radiator shelf, which was still hot, lay the property tax envelope and next to our typed address was Nachum's scrawl; he liked to recycle official documents and used envelopes. Sharp, angular letters joined into words, rising and falling like black goats on a hill, and informed me:

'I'll be at a *shiva* house during lunch break. If you feel all right and want to join me, an interesting anthropological experience is in store for you. The Wassersteins, 28 Admor MiLubavitch Street, in Rechess Shu'afat. Yoavi's had breakfast. Go by taxi. Kisses, Nachum'.

Yoavi was wearing a thick coat with a woollen scarf wrapped round his neck, and I clutched his hand as we walked down the stairs. Streaks of snow dotted the world, bringing frozen flowers into blossom on the bushes and covering the garden in white mounds and slushy puddles. There was a puddle on the pavement with oil stains floating on it, glistening and multicoloured like a rainbow, and Yoavi skipped into it in his red boots, mixing the colours, which quivered and shuddered and the puddle became turbid, and I suddenly saw his sweet face reflected from it twisted and distorted and I pulled him out in alarm. We trod muddy snow that hardened and creaked under our feet, and collected small lumps of glistening snow from white patches that gathered on the windscreens of parked cars, and Yoavi squeezed the snow in his hands and licked it and said, 'It's cold, very cold. Like ice cream with no taste.' I explained that snow formed from tiny flakes shaped like stars, and no two are alike, just like the children at the kindergarten and the people on the street. And Yoavi gave the matter some serious thought and confirmed the finding, saying that in his kindergarten there were Ethiopian children and Russian children and even one Arab boy, and no one looked like anyone else. I promised that if there was still some snow in the afternoon, we would take a small lump and put it on a piece of black paper and look at the flakes through a magnifying glass and see interesting shapes of stars.

We arrived very late at the kindergarten. Nikolai the security guard was no longer waiting for terrorists at the gate. Because of the cold, he'd been allowed to sit inside on a child's orange plastic chair, and he warmed his huge hands on a steaming cup of tea.

Once again Shoshana the kindergarten teacher treated me to one of those reprimanding looks she reserves for idle mothers like me who bring their children to kindergarten late, not taking the morning assembly into account. I fled her admonishing looks and went back home. I looked at Nachum's note and knew immediately I had to go. I sprayed my body with perfume and put on my 'field outfit', the clothes I wear when visiting ultra-Orthodox-neighbourhoods – a long skirt and a heavy sweater that obscures the contours of the body, and I called the Gilo taxi rank. To the controller's irate question, 'Where to?' I answered, 'Rechess Shu'afat,' and he replied in an irritated staccato, 'Half an hour. It's snowing. The roads are icy. No taxis available. Wait outside.' I tried to tell him that if it was snowing I wouldn't be able to wait outside, but he'd already hung up.

I sat in the kitchen sipping my coffee, which had gone cold, and my fingers dug unheedingly into the bread, extracting soft chunks out of it and kneading them into small balls, which I lined up in front of me like soldiers on parade. My father detested this habit of spoiling bread, and I thought that in that he was like Nachum, who hated waste of any kind. He always complained that a loaf of bread that had been left to me resembled a mountain that had a tunnel dug through it, and was impossible to slice. It occurred to me that they were alike only in this, my father and Nachum. In everything else they were entirely different. Nechama once told me that women whose relationships with their fathers were normal tend to marry men who remind them of their fathers, and I wondered to myself why I had chosen him, Nachum, this anal man, as Nechama liked to call him. I liked to think that my love for Nachum had blinded my senses, that I fell in love with him at first sight, that being in bed with him was wonderful. But I had married him and that was that. He was simply there when I wanted to get married. And my mother, who after she was widowed started dabbling in the spiritual and believed in reincarnation, the signs of the zodiac and numerology, told me that it was my karma, and that in a previous life I must have tormented Nachum, made his life miserable, and now it was his turn to pay me back.

Twenty-five minutes later I went downstairs. I thought I'd wait for the taxi on the discoloured wooden bench where the old Russian ladies always sat, but it was wet and covered in dry leaves and a tiny snowman was slowly melting, its carrot nose lying next to it. I stood by the bench beneath the olive tree that cast its shadow over it, and thought that the tree should be protected with wire netting, because during the last olive picking season its branches had been shaken too much and had finally broken.

When heavy rain started beating down again I escaped into the dimness of the stairwell and stepped on decaying split fruit with little tubercular nodes, which had scattered on the path leading up to the building, the fallen fruit of a tall tree whose thorny branches were bare. It used to be a lemon tree, but neglect and dryness had turned it into a bitter-orange tree. When they wanted to uproot it Levana protested, and said of it affectionately, as if it were a sentient being and an old acquaintance, 'What do you want from this poor thing? I make great marmalade from it, and if you want I'll bring you some.' And she hurried into the kitchen and returned with a small bowl of pale viscous jam, peppered with shredded peels. I tasted the bitter sweetness from a teaspoon and told her that the marmalade was excellent and she walked over to the white lacquered sideboard, on which stood ancient volumes of the *Children's Encyclopaedia* and dusty dolls in national dress, removed a jar filled to the brim and presented it to me like a victory trophy. I remembered that the jar sat untouched in our pantry, and we had never tasted it. I decided that the house committee must do something about these trees and the hedge of fragrant honeysuckle that had withered during the summer, and I remembered something I'd once heard: 'Planting a garden is believing in tomorrow.' If our garden withered so long ago, then one might assume that none of the twenty residents in the building believed in tomorrow.

Twenty minutes passed before I heard the impatient honking of the taxi driver from my hiding place in the stairwell.

Rain beat loudly on the taxi's roof and its long windscreen wipers darted across the windscreen with a jarring, squeaking sound. The driver rolled down the window and I saw a large paunch rubbing against the steering wheel, and a bald head turned toward me: 'Where to?' I plopped down heavily in the back seat and gave the driver the address, and asked him to go down Gilo toward Patt junction and go on from there to Jaffa Gate. He said that way was much longer and suggested the dual carriageway, Derech Begin, as an alternative, but I insisted and he shrugged and said, 'Makes no difference to me, you'll pay more.' Near the accursed bus stop, piles of disintegrating flowers piled up around it, he slowed down, rolled the window down and shouted to the lone man who stood there, 'Death to the Arabs.' Then he rolled up the window and as if to himself he said, 'May their name and memory be obliterated,' and immediately declared to the interior of the taxi: 'The day before yesterday I took three of the wounded to the hospital in my taxi, and it took hours to wash all the blood off the seats, and you wouldn't know it but I changed the upholstery only last year.' I remained silent. His eyes peered at me in the mirror: 'You look like a Lefty to me. Don't you care about what happened here?' I asked what a Lefty was supposed to look like and what made him think I was a Lefty, and he said, 'Never mind, love.' And he shut up. My body tensed and I sat on the edge of the seat, and very close to his ear I suddenly confessed, surprised at myself that I was telling him of all people, that I'd been there, that I'd been driving behind the bus, and the bus had come to a halt at the bus stop and blocked me off. I also described the little girl who'd played peekaboo with me, and I added that I hadn't found her listed among the dead in the newspaper. And he said softly, 'Thank God,' and again peeked at me in the mirror. I added defiantly that I was on my way to the *shiva* house of one of my husband's patients who had been killed in the bombing, and he asked, 'Whose? What's his name? I remember all their names.' I answered, 'David Wasserstein, a little boy he was treating.' And

61

he proudly contributed his part: 'The paper said his mother was killed with him.'

We were on the slope of the Cinematheque road heading toward Ben Hinnom Valley, the valley of heinous and ruthless atrocity, now spotted with snow like a malignant skin disease, like blanching leprosy. And the valley sought to draw me into it, with petrified arms it tempted me to join the celebration of bereavement, and I thought about Ahaz and Menasheh the Judean kings who had sacrificed their sons to Moloch who dwelt in the valley, his exploding belly hanging down and covering his genitals, insatiable and demanding moremoremore. I asked the driver to drive faster, and the monstrous inferno followed us with its gaping maw. I smelled the stench of its heavy, choking breath and its ravening jaws snapped shut behind us in disappointment, with a sound of nipping teeth chattering futilely. I thought about the little girl whose name I didn't know, about this city that eateth up its inhabitants, about its sons whom we were unable to save from being slaughtered at the knife and death by fire, and about my Yoavi who did not know any other reality. My brain was ablaze. I searched for tricks to rescue him from the bloodthirsty god, and from the suicide bomber who had been designated to us and had already started his murderous training and was meticulously preparing for the blood ceremony in which his spilled blood would mingle with Jewish blood. And now, after giving his flesh a good wash, serenely straps on his explosive belt, ties the black band of the *shaheeds* around his forehead and ponders on the afterlife promised to him by his dispatchers and the preparations being made for him there in Paradise. About the virgins waiting for him, trembling with desire, their legs spread only for him, the hero. And my ears heard clearly and candidly the terrible curse put on my Yoavi even before he was born, at a Women in Black demonstration, in which I had participated for the first time in my life. The face of that woman in the red coat, contorted with hate, appeared before me once again, and the dreadful things she said came back and reverberated in my ears: 'Your son will die in a terrorist attack just like mine did.'

Now we were climbing the road that ran beside the walls of ancient Jerusalem just before Jaffa Gate, the walls that bore the scars of war and the scabs of siege and the scorch marks of conflagration, and we turned eastward towards Damascus Gate. Citadels, minarets, bell towers and gold and silver domes rose up behind it, touching the sky.

Leaving the walls behind we twisted upward with the busy road towards Shu'afat, passing Jewish neighbourhoods that had been built on disputed land. At the French Hill junction I scrunched down into my seat as child peddlers in tattered clothing damp from the rain surrounded the taxi as it stopped for a red light, offering their wares: brooms, coloured dusters, plastic clothes pegs, dustpans and floor cloths. They flocked around us, beating on the windows with frost-chapped fists. I automatically checked the button to make sure the door was locked. I avoided the doggy eyes of a small boy who voicelessly pleaded with me through the closed window, and when I averted my eyes I met, in the opposite window, the squashed face of another boy, whose runny nose left a thin smear of mucus on the glass. In a flash the driver opened his door and screamed at them, '*Rukh min hon*!' and waved his arms, and they fled like a flock of startled chickens.

The red light, that had stayed that way forever, turned green, and before we had a chance to move off it turned back to red, and again the children surrounded us as if they hadn't been driven away just a moment earlier, and the driver shouted at them again as if he'd never done it before. From the depths of the soft seat in the heated taxi I thought about the absurdity of that traffic light, that showed green for just a few seconds before changing back to red for minutes on end, and how, so arbitrarily, it dictated that long queues of cars peopled with irritable drivers and troubled women, wait at the entrance to and exit from the Arab neighbourhood.

It was only when we finally got going that I felt compassion for those children. Instead of going to school they were risking their lives going down to the roads to earn a living and evading closely guarded checkpoints imposed by the closure and encirclement and curfew, and I thought that our fear of them had made us impervious to their hardship. I decided that on the way home I'd ask the driver to stop and I'd buy a few things from them.

As it stopped raining we reached the recently built neighbourhood that already showed signs of neglect. Saplings that had been planted at the edge of the sidewalks had withered, weeds dominated the soil, and small piles of garbage and building debris could be seen on the empty plots between the buildings. Strollers, children's bikes and plastic toy cars crowded in the yards and entrances to the apartment buildings, and men's white vests, small fringed prayer shawls of all sizes, baby clothes, cotton diapers and long-sleeved, high-collared dresses fluttered on the clothes lines, sure signs of a neighbourhood turned Orthodox.

I asked the driver to stop outside a tiny store over which a huge sign announced 'Eliahu – Fish'. I went inside to enquire about the address. The neighbourhood fishmonger dried his chapped hands on his black apron, silver-flecked with fish scales, and asked in a singsong voice, 'And what might madam want?' I looked into the concrete pool against the wall. The gaping pink and grey mouths of carps circling in the knowledge of certain death shouted voicelessly. Again he enquired, 'And what might madam want?' and I didn't want to disappoint him by just making an enquiry, and replied, 'A fish.' 'Big, small?' he asked, and I said small. His net was already pursuing the fish, and one by one he pulled them out and presented them, flopping about and suffocating, and asked, 'Like this?' and I said, 'Smaller,' and apologised, 'I've got a small family.' He finally caught one. 'This is the smallest. It will just about make two portions of *gefillte* fish, but if madam insists,' and I answered confidently, 'It will be enough. I've got a small family.' And then it was in the air, flopping softly onto a sheet of newspaper spread out on the counter. With a magician's dexterity the newspaper was wrapped around it and from the tail of my fish hung a headline from the religious daily, *Hamodia*, which informed its readers about some *kashrut* inspectors who had been caught in some act of impropriety or other. Diapered in news the fish was placed in my arms, its tail lightly slapping against my chest and its gaping mouth gasping for air. I didn't know what I'd do with it. The fishmonger came to my rescue and said that if I wanted it really fresh, then 'The minute you get home you put it into the bath with cold water.' I said I'd only be getting home in an hour's time, so he courteously suggested keeping the fish in his little pool. He quickly stripped it of its newspaper shroud and like a released spring the fish leapt onto the entrails-and scale-covered counter, and the man grabbed it by its flapping tail and dropped it into the small aquarium whose sides were covered with greenish algae, keeping it for me until I got back.

I returned to the taxi and the driver asked, 'So where's the street?' and I remembered that I'd forgotten to ask, so I went back into the shop and the fishmonger was already on his way to net my fish and I said, 'I forgot to ask you the way to Admor MiLubav-itch Street.' He pointed with his bloodstained cleaver and without looking at me explained that I had to get to the 'Moriah' taxi rank and from there left to the 'Yir'at Dalim' synagogue and I'd find it right there on the corner.

Lots of dilapidated baby strollers crowded the lobby and the doors of battered mailboxes swung on the peeling wall. We were greeted by cooking odours that wafted on the mixed aromas of washing powder and the faint stench of diapers soaked with urine and faeces. The stairwell wall bore the obituary announcement: 'The Lord is a God of Vengeance. Woe unto us that calamity has befallen us. How were the pure and innocent souls cut down by wrongdoers. My pious wife and pure son, Batsheva and David Wasserstein, may the Lord avenge their blood.' I went up to the fourth floor, and breathlessly entered through the open door, on which an identical obituary notice had been fixed. As I went inside I was hit by the sour smell of people who strictly observe the precept of not bathing or changing their clothes throughout the seven days of mourning. The scenes that were so familiar from other houses of mourning were here, too: the cloth-covered mirror, 'so that evil spirits will not don the images seen in the mirror', or perhaps 'lest the mourners adorn themselves before it and digress from their mourning'. Squat memorial candles burned on a low table, and a Torah scroll in a splendid velvet cover was standing, in the custom of strictly observant Jews, in a small cabinet with glass doors, for 'a mourner who calls a prayer quorum to his house must also bring a Torah scroll'. Dozens of black felt hats covered with wet plastic supermarket bags, gathered in a secret conclave, were lying on the dining table in the corner of the living room and their owners, bearded young men in white shirts and black yarmulkes, stood in the middle of the room, swaying back and forth in prayer. Fumes of mothballs and mildew rose from the heavy coats piled on the radiator to dry.

Nachum wasn't to be seen in the mass of murmuring, swaying men. I stood in the doorway self consciously, studying the people in the room and the toes of my shoes, until a woman whose eyes were red and puffy with weeping extricated me, took my hand and led me into a side room. Stale, stifling air welcomed me into the room whose windows were closed. I could hardly breathe. Women in dark dresses, their artificial hair beautifully groomed or covered with fine hats, were crowded onto two beds standing facing each other in the small, bare-walled room. Others were sitting on a mattress placed on the floor, their backs to the wall and their legs outstretched. They looked at me inquisitively.

'This is Batsheva's room,' wept an older woman, her rough hands trapping mine, and I nodded and mumbled, 'May you know no further sorrow,' and she introduced herself as Bilha, Davidl's grandmother and Batsheva's mother, inspected my clothes and hair and asked, 'And who are you?' I stammered my name and she asserted, 'You're probably one of Avshalom's friends,' and asked if I knew him from the army. 'Avshalom?' I repeated, and she said, 'Avshalom my son-in-law. Davidl's father.' I told her that my husband is Dr Maggid, David's dentist, and immediately cursed myself for using the present tense. She hesitated a moment, trying to place me among the friends, and her eyes lit up as she said, 'Dr Nachum Maggid is an excellent dentist, and Davidl's got a lot of problems because he sleeps with a bottle of milk in bed, and the sugar in the milk is ruining his teeth.'

As if suddenly remembering she burst into weak sobs, and a young, white-faced woman got up from the floor and with a face devoid of expression quickly pushed me aside, embraced Bilha with protective arms and led her to the mattress, sat her down, put a cushion behind her and rocked her in her arms like a baby and whispered, 'Cry, Ima, cry, it's best to cry as much as you can right now. Afterwards you won't have the strength.'

I escaped the bedroom. As if afraid of awakening sleepers I cautiously walked down the dark passageway to the lighted living room. The crowd of men had finished praying and I found Nachum there, camouflaged like a chameleon in his wrinkled black trousers and white shirt with the eternal sweat stains under the arms. I recalled the nickname I'd once given him, 'Zelig'. That's what I called him for a long time after we went to see Woody Allen's *Zelig*, and to the surprised looks I explained that Nachum, just like Allen's hero, would always manage to blend into any group of people, Chinese, blacks or Hottentots, and I didn't miss out the animals and claimed that if he hid in an African swamp, I wouldn't manage to find him in a flock of pink flamingos or a herd of mud-covered hippopotami.

'Come on, I'll introduce you to David's father,' he whispered and pulled me to the other end of the room, where I saw him for the first time, sitting on a mattress folded in two. His eyes flashed at me, deep blue, and a silver-framed photograph was pressed to the blond beard that fell to his chest.

'Yael, this is Avshalom,' Nachum said loudly, and whispered to me: 'His father.'

I bent down and saw the rent that had been cut in his shirt, and his honey-coloured side-locks hiding behind his ears. I whispered my condolences and automatically extended my hand, but he didn't take it and just laid the photograph upside down on his knees, buried his face in his hands and groaned through their spread fingers. As if mesmerised I looked at his hands and was suddenly envious of the woman whose man he had been. I had never seen hands like them. They were powerful and gentle, strong and vulnerable, and in my eyes they were the epitome of the beauty of all men. Involuntary thoughts suddenly arose in me, and I saw his hands running over my body and I blushed, and immediately banished the terrible scene and tried to imagine them touching the sacred and the profane, holding his son and stroking his head, tearing a piece off the Sabbath *challah*, leafing through a book and smoothing his beard. I have no idea how long I stood there, looking at those magnificent hands covering his face. Silence suddenly fell on the room and into the stifling air stole some hesitant conversation, rumours circulated, promises were made, lies were told, and the coming of the Messiah was reported, as was the consolation of grief and that each terrorist outrage brought us closer to redemption.

I went down the stairs with Nachum with great difficulty. At the entrance, by the mailboxes, three men in air force uniform and the force's peaked caps stood whispering, looking somewhat embarrassed. They gave us a weary glance and ran up the stairs.

The taxi, which I'd totally forgotten, stood waiting for me right next to Nachum's car and its windows were completely misted up. I knocked on the window, but the driver had his seat back in the reclining position and was sleeping the sleep of the just. I opened the door and shook him by the shoulder and told him I didn't need him, and asked him how much I owed him. He stared at me through narrowed eyes, grumbled something as I paid him and sped off. I got into Nachum's car and he told me off for not sending the taxi away and having to pay for the wait. I sank into the seat and thought about Avshalom, and wondered what happened to a man whose belief was steadfast and had been so severely punished through no fault of his own.

By the time we reached the junction where the Arab children and their wares were waiting, the last vestiges of the green light were flickering and Nachum put his foot down, ran the yellow light and mumbled as if to himself that you had to be careful there, because they'd already fired at a Jewish car. I turned my head and saw the neglected children blurring into the distance until they became small black dots, with the brooms they held standing up behind them like bruised and faded peacock tails.

My eyes filled with tears as I recalled Yehuda Amichai's poem, and thought that God didn't really take pity on kindergarten children, and even less on schoolchildren and adults He no longer took pity at all. I turned my face to the window so Nachum wouldn't see my tears and wiped them away with my sleeve, and when I blew my nose he said I'd probably caught a cold and I should take care not to give it to Yoavi. Then he added, somewhat irrelevantly but with a touch of admiration in his voice, that they say that Avshalom, Davidl's father, is a computer whiz. In his free time he teaches yeshiva students and ultra-Orthodox women to use computers and the Internet. And I asked in amazement, 'An ultra-Orthodox man? Computers?' and Nachum said he was surprised at me: 'You come and go in their homes, you're the one who's supposed to know that society inside out,' he said, and added that we with our prejudices about the ultra-Orthodox see them all as parasites, but 'there are some who make a contribution to society,' he announced proudly, as if he'd adopted Avshalom as a relative.

And I couldn't stop thinking about the amazing hands of that stranger I'd met today.

In the evening Nechama brought Yoavi home and said she was in a hurry and didn't stay. Nachum bathed Yoavi and put him to bed, and I went in to kiss him goodnight, turned off the light, and the moon and stars I'd stuck onto the ceiling before he was born glowed phosphorescently. The child stuck his Tutti to his nose, inhaled its smell and asked me not to go, and with his free hand grasped three of my fingers. I sat next to him until he dropped off, and remembered that I'd forgotten to pick up my carp at 'Eliahu – Fish' and that I'd surely saved it from death and now it was swimming at leisure until it died at a ripe old age.

Then I went into our room and found Nachum sprawled on the bed speaking on the phone in a low voice. When he saw me he said a quick goodbye and hastily replaced the receiver. I asked who it was, and his greenish expression avoided me as he answered, 'Some patient who wants an appointment tomorrow.'

I went into my study and again tried to reconstruct, on Nechama's advice, the events of the past few days. For a long time I stared at the screen that flickered patiently at me, but my thoughts wandered. I decided to try and concentrate on my thesis and opened up the 'Lilith' file that dealt with the winged, long-tressed demon, consort of Sammael the Devil, who flew in dark rooms and collected the seed ejaculated by those who sleep alone. In secret she became pregnant from the ejaculated seed and filled the world with her offspring, demons all, and their number is greater than that of all the world's human inhabitants. 'No man in the world can evade Lilith's visits,' confessed Warshavsky, my *Hevra Kadisha* liaison, 'so that's why they must observe the custom forbidding children to follow in their father's footsteps.' I told him that I was more concerned about the long-haired two-legged Liliths that lay in wait for men outside the home, in broad daylight. Warshavsky laughed and added that a tale from Ben Sira related that this Lilith, robber of sperm and husbands, was Adam's first wife, and because they were both created in God's image at the same time, she had not accepted authority and demanded equality from her husband. I told him that among my feminist friends Lilith was considered to have been the first feminist, because she had demanded total equality, even during sexual intercourse, for she, too, wanted to be on top, and Warshavsky blushed and said that as Lilith had been punished in Adam's time, she bore a grudge against his descendants and killed babies in their cradles. I abandoned the computer in panic and ran to Yoavi's room and listened to him breathing softly for a long time. On the fourth floor the furniture was shifted, and I heard the bang of the double sofa being opened. In an effort to divert my attention from my neighbours I went back to the computer and found myself typing automatically, 'Avshalom, Avshalom, Avshalom'. An entire screen of Avshaloms flickered at me, and when I reached the next page I put in my name and Yoavi's, and I could see my fingers typing of their own volition, 'Yael, Avshalom and Yoav Wasserstein' and 'This Is the Happy Home of Avshalom, Yael, and Yoavi'. I got frightened and quickly erased the lot, and just to make sure I switched off the screen and the computer and destroyed the file with the incriminating evidence. Assailed by pangs of conscience I joined Nachum who was lying spreadeagled on his back, wrapped myself up in the bit of quilt he'd left me and with my eyes I felt the room's shadows: the wall closet, whose brown, wood-grain Formica had peeled away from the edges here and there, the small nightstand at my side of the bed, that was always piled with books and journals and which now cast a large shadow on the wall, and the white camel-hair rug I'd bought in a Bedouin village in Sinai, and that was now grey in the darkness.

Later I heard shooting. With closed eyes I could see the rounds as they were shown on television – glowing arcs flying over my neighbourhood's houses like the fiery tails of so many comets. Then lights came on in the neighbour's house across the road and infiltrated the room through the slits in the shutter. Dogs woke up and barked angrily, the voices of newsreaders came from radio loudspeakers, the demanding and monotonous wailing of a baby came from one of the apartments, and this mélange of sounds was joined by my husband's snout, that emitted soft snores.

I wanted to shout 'Quiet, enough already, shut up!' but didn't. I swallowed half a tranquilliser. When I got back into bed I was beset by anxiety. I suddenly feared for the fate of my mind, and thought that pills like that, that give us tranquillity, must surely kill a lot of brain cells, and wondered if they also weakened nerves, that were fragile in any case. Who knows, maybe I was already addicted to the drug. My limbs fought against sleep and I tossed and turned. I wanted to rush to the kitchen and make a cup of strong coffee that would weaken the drug's effect, but Avshalom's hands suddenly appeared from the sea like the masts of a sinking ship and I gripped them, and the ship sank and sank and I was dragged into the depths with it, and my legs trembled with the slight tremor that heralds sleep, and I slowly sank into a slumber that rocked me like a baby, and its tongue lapped at my feet like wavelets.

And there was evening and there was morning, a fifth day

(Genesis 1, 23)

At three am I awoke to the wavering nocturnal call to prayer of the muezzin from Beit Zafafa, which echoed sweetly in the darkness. The voice rose and fell, now entreating, now in rebuke. I waited for him to finish his prayer, but another muezzin suddenly answered him like a distant echo, and the two were joined by a third, then a fourth, and the echoes of their dull trilling reverberated in the heavens, competing one with the other as if in a holy relay race to the attentive ear of Allah the Omniscient. And those metallic notes, amplified by high-powered loudspeakers, mingled with the frightened beating of my heart. I sat up in bed, switched on the reading light and I wanted to wake Nachum and ask him why the muezzins from Beit Zafafa, Beit Jallah and Bethlehem didn't synchronise their watches so their calls to prayer could be heard in unison. But Nachum was lying on his left side, his light snores still bubbling from his mouth as from broken plumbing. His so-familiar features had changed so that he seemed like a stranger.

I lay down again beside him, and compassionately embraced the father of my son and kissed his chest, on which a few curls sprouted. He mumbled something and turned over, presenting his backside to me, and I pressed myself to him, squashing his buttocks to my belly, but he kicked out at me in his sleep and a sharp pain pierced my left leg. Hurt, I moved away and damp with sweat left the bed and went into Yoavi's room. In the doorway I tripped over the house he'd built from his Lego blocks and trod on one that spitefully stabbed itself into my heel. I moved the furry animals, brushed away the curls that fell onto his face, stroked his cheeks and sniffed his body. A smell of damp puppy came from

71

him and from under his half-closed eyelids I could see the rapid eye movement of a dream. I covered him with his quilt and sat down next to him, trying to soothe my body with the help of his regular breathing. I sat there for a long time, listening to his sleepy mumbling until my throat tightened and I went into the kitchen, got myself a glass of water from the tap and sat down on the living room couch, listening to the angry cats fighting and the sounds of passing cars. Of their own volition my fingers dialled Nechama's number.

A sleepy voice answered, 'Who's there, what's wrong?'

'Nechama, it's me.'

'Do you want to come over? I'll put the kettle on for coffee,' she announced, fully awake now, as if she were used to answering my calls at four am.

'No, forget it. I'll be OK,' I said, suddenly regretting the weakness that had overtaken me.

'Are you sure?' she asked with a yawn.

'Yes, of course, I'm sorry I woke you,' I murmured.

I could see Nechama sitting up in bed, switching on the light and bringing the alarm clock to her face to check the time.

'What's wrong?'

'Every little sound wakes me up. Those muezzins in the morning,' I grumbled.

'What muezzins?'

'From Beit Zafafa, and maybe from Beit Jallah and Bethlehem too,' I said, and suddenly realised that this had been the first time I'd heard the muezzins' call since I'd moved to Gilo.

'Maybe you should go out of town for a night or two? You've got to get away from this depressing atmosphere of Jerusalem.'

'Where can I go?'

'How about your mother? You haven't been to see her for long time. So *yalla*, go tomorrow. She deserves to spoil you a bit. I'll pick up Yoavi from the kindergarten and he can sleep over here.'

As the pink light filtered through the slats of the shutter I went into the bathroom, and through the window I could see the moon turning on its bed of soft morning clouds, the edges of which were embroidered with the first gleams of dawn light. Two hours later I waited for Nachum in the kitchen with a splitting headache. Nachum looked in surprise at the festive purple suit I was wearing on just an ordinary weekday, and asked how I'd slept, and didn't wait for a reply and opened the fridge and asked where the milk was, and I told him I was taking a day off and going to my mother's. It seemed that he hadn't listened to a word I'd said, and with his head stuck inside the fridge and his hands feeling around he joyfully informed me, as if seizing an opportunity, that I'd been grinding my teeth all night. Then he sat down heavily at the table with an empty milk bag in his hand, and said resignedly, 'There's no milk so don't forget to buy some today,' and asked me to open my mouth so he could see what was happening in there, and he said I was suffering from bruxism, nocturnal grinding of the teeth, and if I carried on I'd end up with broken teeth and fillings, and I'd have headaches and jaw pains. He understood that I was over-wrought, he said as if consoling me, and added that this was apparently my way of dealing with the episode I'd experienced, and if it recurred during the next few nights, he'd fit me a night mouth guard that would solve the problem. I could see him fitting me with a metal muzzle like a ferocious dog and sealing my mouth with it and tightening the screws on both sides of my jaw, and I wanted to say something but couldn't open my mouth and move my tongue, and a choked, hoarse barking came from my chest and my mouth was filled with a rusty taste. Before he left the apartment with Yoavi he said he'd try and get home in the afternoon with the joiner, and they'd get rid of those birds and seal the hole in the window shutter box, and a goodbye kiss burst on my cheek, too close to my ear.

The tiny blue car I'd been given by the insurance company until my own was repaired awaited me in the parking lot. It bore a big diagonal banner, something like the broad silk sash on a beauty queen's chest, announcing that this vehicle is a replacement car and the property of the Citadel Insurance Company, the best and most dependable firm in Israel. A wintry sun shone in the cloudless sky, melting the glassy crust on a little puddle, and slowly thawing the blooms of frost that had flowered on the sidewalk during the night and which crunched beneath my feet.

Once again I saw cars stuck in the morning jam. I zigzagged between them, avoiding the buses that crawled along the death lanes, their backsides emitting clouds of whitish smoke, and they stopped at their stops, taking on passengers while others alighted, as if everything that had happened was already forgotten and was etched only on my nightmares.

Despite the replacement car never having taken me to my mother's house, it seemed that I didn't have to drive it at all: it led me there confidently, like a horse that knows the way to the stable. It devoured the miles, its tyres emitting cruising sounds, cheekily overtaking far bigger cars and trucks. We reached the coastal plain in very good time, and along the Ayalon Freeway the city's tower blocks gleamed in the silvery greyness, and huge tempting billboards flickered with promises that would not always be kept. The traffic swirled around me at dizzying speed, cars cut in left and right, and I turned left and drove towards Jaffa. Grey strips of a sullen sea peeped between the buildings, and turbid waves heavy with silt rose and threatened to flood the promenade. At the entrance to the city the moonfaced clock whose hands had stopped moving many years ago smiled at me from the heights of its tower, and from there I twisted and turned through the alleyways of the Flea Market. On one of the corners, over the alcove shop that had been boarded up with rough rotting planks, there was still the sign with its peeling paint, 'Vicki – Knitting Wool and Needles', my father's wool shop that had been named after my mother.

With a screech of new brakes I pulled up outside the house. An unfamiliar car was blocking my father's 1977 Ford, which had not been driven since the day he died, forcing me to mount the kerb. My tiny car groaned and climbed it with a great effort, and I heard its underbody scraping the asphalt with a noise that made me shudder. A sudden gust of wind came in from the sea through the narrow alley and hit my back as if trying to drive me away, weeping in its path dust and dry leaves and old memories, and blowing up plastic bags like coloured balloons and carrying with it newspapers whose headlines bled, their news old before it left the presses. In an impatient squall the wind turned the pages and puffed events into conflict and mixed up the flow of days and disasters. For a moment it swirled around me as if loath to part, then suddenly vanished down the street, its face to the sun and carrying with it, up and up, the memory of the dead and the echoes of lamentation and weeping.

I stood outside my home. A single Arab family had once lived there in comfort, but since the War of Independence Jews had lived there in more cramped quarters. Up to the time I moved to Jerusalem I had never lived anywhere else. Its walls, with their fading pink paint, were covered with scabs that revealed its exposed flesh of bricks and iron ribs that had oxidised and rusted. Windows veiled with latticework and rickety balconies whose balustrades were swollen with salt and dampness hung above me. I quickly crossed a plot of stubborn couch grass that crawled towards the stairwell, whose floor tiles, decorated with a carpet design, were finely cracked.

I went up to the second floor and rang the bell, which merrily sounded the rising and falling chimes of Big Ben. There was an oppressive silence that lasted for an eternity, and then I heard bursts of laughter and my mother's voice shouting towards the door, 'Go away. I'm busy. Come back tomorrow.'

Like a refugee I stood on the threshold of the locked door of the house that was once my home. Now I stubbornly wanted to go back to it, to discover in it something that had not been completed, to follow the memories, to try and understand.

'Ima, it's me, Yael. Open up.'

Again silence, and then rustling. Her soft slippers slid over the floor inside. She opened the door a crack and welcomed me in the doorway with an embarrassed expression and flushed cheeks.

A breath of fetid, mildewed air hit me, and the sad mess of a helpless woman was revealed in the background. Behind her, above the couch whose flowers had faded although it was always covered with a check wool blanket, peeped 'Father's Map', which proudly proclaimed the borders of the expanded Kingdom of Israel, borders that had become blurred under the plastic covering whose transparency was now opaque with age, tiny drops of whitewash and fly droppings. That map, whose four corners were affixed to the wall with four steel nails, had never been taken down, and when Zalman the Painter came every three years to whitewash the house before the Passover festival, my father would lay down the condition that the map would not be taken from the wall, and instruct Zalman to paint carefully around it, standing over him and making sure he didn't touch it. Today I believe that he feared removing it from the wall for even a moment lest its temporary displacement put paid to his territorial aspirations.

I couldn't rid myself of that map either: it was spread before me from my room that opened onto the living room, peeped at me from the kitchen and the balcony, and if a stranger found himself on our doorstep he would see it right in front of him. In our neighbours' houses and in the homes of my friends, its place of honour in the living room was reserved for embroidered tapestries of aristocratic girls in splendid crinolines, or hunting scenes from distant lands, and cheap reproductions of the great masters.

Every Friday, before the Sabbath candles were lit, Father would take his wooden ruler that was worn with use, and lovingly pass it over the borders of the Promised Land. 'You must always begin in the north on the map,' he would announce as if to himself, stretching on tiptoe, and the ruler would caress and merge with Turkey's southern border. 'And now we move southward,' and the ruler would glide over the Red Sea and the great Sinai Desert, and move upwards to the fertile Nile delta, flank it on the left and come to a stop in the Mediterranean to the west of Port Said. From there he would move in a flash over the Mediterranean border and cross eastwards, sail over the Jordan River, climb northwards, join up with the banks of the Euphrates and from there overlook Damascus. And Father would conclude his journey and say that with borders as extensive as those, no one would destroy us. Then with much pomp and circumstance he would take a heavy tumbler from the sideboard and his bottle of arak, 'To strengthen the heart and soul,' pour the clear liquid, knock it back, slam the tumbler down onto the table and ask, 'Why do we bang the glass onto the table?' and without waiting for a reply he would answer his own question, 'Because when you drink arak all the senses should enjoy it: the mouth that tastes, the nose that smells, the eye that sees, so why should the ear be denied?'

Father had a custom of taking pleasure in 'the promised borders' in the presence of guests to our house, and every time a new friend visited me he would ask her with excessive politeness to stand in the living room, and with his ruler he would sketch the borders of our land, as they should be.

'Yaeli, why didn't you tell me you were coming?' my mother scolded me.

'You say you like surprises, so here I am. Maybe you'll let me in?'

She reluctantly moved aside and I sidled in through the narrow opening she'd left me. The living room seemed more neglected than usual. Piles of yellowing newspapers whose corners had curled from the sea's dampness were waiting at the door. The colourful macramé curtains, which she had crocheted over many years from bits of leftover wool that Father brought her from the shop, were grey and heavy with dust. Clothes discarded carelessly made love on the floor and couches in an orgy of rags. Orange peel and leftover food were piled on the table next to disintegrating round lace doilies, and I knew that if I moved them I'd find a deposit of dust balls under them. The entire mess was looked upon sadly by the sentimentally valuable potted yucca my father had lovingly tended for two decades, and now it stood there drooping in misery, its pointed leaves withered and its thin stem writhing in the agony of death.

'I can't really blame you for being so untidy,' I recalled what Nachum had once told me patronisingly, 'it's enough just to look at the state of your mother's house.'

'Vicki, who is it?' came a male voice from the bedroom that once had been mine.

I blushed. My mother was making out with men, and my nights were dry of love and saturated with fear.

'Why don't you come back later?' my mother begged in a whisper, 'Go visit your friends and come back in an hour. I'll have lunch waiting for you.' I didn't understand how she could have forgotten that I no longer had any friends here.

'I'm going back to Jerusalem, and if you want to know what's wrong, phone me.'

Her expression became serious. 'Has something happened to Yoavi? To Nachum?'

'They're both fine.'

'Have you been fired from the university?' she asked, a small cloud of concern covering her face.

'Is that the only thing you care about?' I whispered angrily. 'I wanted to talk to you, but if it's not convenient for milady, we can do it by phone.' And I slammed the door behind me.

'Yaeli, what's wrong, wait,' she ordered in a choked voice from behind the closed door and opened it wide and ran after me down the stairs, her open robe revealing a pair of proudly upturned breasts. 'Wait, I'll tell him to go. Give me a moment.' Ashamed by seeing her nakedness, I raised my eyes to her face. An intrusive sunbeam that forced its way through the layers of black clouds suddenly shone on her face, and like a powerful spotlight cruelly revealed the deep lines that had been hidden under a heavy layer of face powder, the age blotches that spotted her temples with patches of brown, the eyes clouded with old age, and the folds of wrinkled skin that trembled beneath her chin.

'Wait,' she tried again, 'I'll tell him to leave.' And her face clouded as if she'd suddenly remembered something. 'But I've got nothing in the house.'

'I don't want anything. I didn't come here to eat.'

'Wait,' she said, ignoring my reply, 'I've got some chicken and coleslaw in the fridge. Wait, if you don't want to eat, I'll wrap it up, take it for Yoavi.'

Ashamed of my mother, I hurried to get away from there. I drove to the seafront and the sea hiccuped dirty foam at me, and again that children's song, 'What do the trees do' played incessantly in my ears: 'And what does the sea do? Seee-a. What does the sun do? Day.' I thought of Yoavi, who would certainly have been happy to see the sea even if it was rough, and of my father, who would sail me on its waves in the summer in an inner tube, and buy me prickly pears chilled with ice.

I parked outside Margaret's restaurant, got out of the car and sat down on the terrace under the green wings of faded canvas that flapped at each other; but the owner of the neighbouring garage waved, trying at attract my attention, and told me that Margaret was ill and the restaurant was closed.

I walked beside the wall that protects the old buildings from the vagaries of the sea, and thought how dare she screw around like that, when only eighteen months earlier my father had died in her arms.

'Your mother is a woman who gives herself to the delusions of love, she'll feel flawed without a man at her side,' Nechama told me when my father fell ill, and forecast that my mother would find a new love in double-quick time. And I yelled at her then, fool that I was, 'How can you say things like that about my mother, she told me that if he dies, she'll go with him.'

And the waves, resolute and stubborn iron rams, tried to breach the fortified wall and broke against it in spent anger, spraying me with tiny splinters of salt and crumbling my thoughts. Sudden, hard rain fell, and sky and sea and land merged into a single grey and melancholy mass, and the sea vomited seaweed and dead fish and broken seashells, and my wet hair whipped about my face as I ran to the car and sat down on the narrow seat and rested my head on the wheel and I wanted to weep for Davidl, and the little girl who had disappeared, and Yoavi, and my life and my mother and my dead father.

I pitied my father who my mother was now betraying, as if she'd waited patiently for him to leave her life so that she could screw around with other men. How could she do that to the man who had loved her so much? I wept for my father and knew that I had begun mourning him while he was still living, many years before his death. There was something fragile and fleeting in him, as if he were wavering between death and life. And despite his learning how to laugh, I'd hear in his voice the ghosts of his family who had died and from whom he had not parted. His life here in this world had been the life of a displaced person, a brief and temporary stop leading him to the greatest moment of all, in which he would again meet his dead, so he had once told me in a moment of intimacy, and afterwards he had changed his mind and asked me to forget what he'd said.

On the way home I again fed myself on my anger at my mother.

By the time I reached Jerusalem the windows of the stone buildings were gleaming in orange hues, and long shadows were cast from the streetlights that had not yet come on. I crossed the Valley of the Cross and joined a long line of cars on their way home. In Gazelle Valley the whitening skeletons of deciduous trees were casting their harsh bony shadows one on top of the other and concealing behind their branches families of gazelles that I'd never seen. Suddenly I was overtaken on both sides by a police car and an ambulance, their sirens blaring a plea and their warning lights flashing red and blue. I slipped into the gap opened up by the cars making way for them and sped after them. I lost them at the Patt junction and the two halos, one blue, one red, raced one after the other, cruised along side by side, until they blended into a single, glowing purple aura. And the lights flashed through the reddening traffic lights and climbed up and up the mountainside towards my neighbourhood until they disappeared and the sound of the sirens was no more. I drove up the steep incline towards my neighbourhood, which had been built in the spate of construction that came in the wake of the reunification of Jerusalem. I saw its buildings from afar and thought about the architects who had carried out some unsuccessful architectural experiments in it: romanticism had stuck its sticky fingers into the hard rock and in it had hewn flamboyant arches and had torn round balconies out of it and had filled the building stones with all kinds of symbols and historical references, and miserable imitations that had been inspired by the surrounding Arab neighbourhoods. We hadn't learnt a thing from our Arab neighbours, I thought as my car neared the fences. They build their houses on the slopes of the hills so as not to disfigure the skyline, while ours rise like arrogant, ostentatious lighthouses on the summits. My anger had ebbed as I entered Gilo, and by the time I reached our street I'd sketched out in my mind the conversation I'd shortly be having with Nechama.

'You'll never believe what I'm going to tell you,' I said to her a short time later on the phone, 'my mother's having an affair, and she was so busy screwing that she had no time to talk to me.' A warm laugh rolled down the line to me. 'What did I tell you?' she said, unable to restrain herself, 'Don't you think that's a lot better than killing yourself? And don't deny that you're jealous,' she added emphatically.

From the bedroom I heard the key turn in the lock and the sound of the door opening, and I hurriedly ended the call, saying that Nachum had come home and we'd talk later. And as I replaced the receiver I remembered that I'd forgotten to ask about Yoavi and say goodnight to him and wish him pleasant dreams.

Nachum glanced at my purple suit and asked in his inimitable way, 'How was your day?' I didn't bother to mention that I'd told him that morning that I was going to Jaffa to see my mother, but only asked, 'Where's the joiner?' Nachum slapped his forehead and mumbled, 'How could I have forgotten,' and asked about Yoavi. I said that Yoavi was sleeping over at Nechama's, and he said it wasn't good for the child to sleep there night after night, and he picked up his keys from the copper bowl and went out. I called Nechama to tell her that Nachum was on the way to collect Yoavi, and she said that the kids had already had supper and showered and Yoavi was in his pyjamas, and in the background I heard the doorbell ringing, and Nechama whispered, 'It's probably Nachum,' and replaced the receiver. A few minutes later they were home. I put Yoavi to bed and went to the bookshelf to look for a bedtime story. When I turned round his eyes were already half closed. I kissed his cheek and whispered in his ear that I loved him most in the whole world, and he mumbled and put Tutti to his nose. In the living room Nachum was already sprawled out in his armchair, he blew his nose loudly and asked with some trepidation what there was to eat. I replied that I'd just got home and hadn't managed to prepare anything, but there was probably some of the Shabbat roast left in the fridge, and Nachum complained that he'd told me yesterday that the roast had long since been eaten, and his gloomy eyes fixed me in rebuke as if to say, you've been lying around at home doing nothing for a week now, and for a week I've had nothing to eat. I offered to make him an omelette and salad, and he said, 'If I'd wanted an omelette and salad I would have made it myself.' I recalled how my father used to come home dead tired from 'Vicki – Knitting Wool and Needles', and lift my mother into the air, and as if he hadn't seen her for days on end he'd kiss her passionately on the lips, and then hurry to the kitchen, fill the kettle and make her a cup of tea, steep tiny greenish mint leaf fish in it, and then ask her what she'd like him to make her for supper.

From the day they'd met on the beach, he a Holocaust survivor from Greece and she a long-legged, full-figured native Israeli, they had loved one another until my father's dying breath, so my mother told anyone interested in listening. He had died in her arms, 'Just like that, he died on me,' as if she'd forgotten that two years earlier he had gradually waned until she begged me to get him out of the house.

In the first year of mourning I was afraid that she would make good the threat she had uttered on the day I married Nachum. Mother had never believed that Nachum was the man of my life. A few hours before they led me under the wedding canopy she had shooed everybody out of the room, closed the door after them and asked, 'Are you sure you love him?' I replied angrily that if I didn't love him I wouldn't be standing there in a wedding dress, but doubt was already gnawing at me when she asked, 'But what do you love in him?' I thought a while and said, 'His industriousness, his perseverance, that he's so organised, and calm, and educated.' And Mother shrugged, insulted, and shouted, 'But that's not enough! What about the butterflies in the stomach, and the excitement, and the weak knees, and the sleepless nights?' and I replied just as Nachum had when I'd asked him where the butterflies in the stomach had gone, that all those things appeared in romantic novels and saccharine-sweet films and not in real life. Nachum and I, I'd stressed then, based our relationship on friend-

81

ship and mutual trust and feelings of warmth and affection. Then Mother shouted loudly, 'And what will happen if, God forbid, he drops dead? Will you feel that your life is over?' and she didn't wait for a reply and added emphatically, that if, God forbid, anything happened to Father she'd kill herself, because life without him wouldn't be worth living.

Two hours later I was standing at Nachum's side under the wedding canopy at the ceremony that was held on the beach. The hazy air frizzled the women's hair, and I felt as if I were breathing droplets of water and that my lungs were as heavy as a drowning man's and I was about to suffocate and die. My eye make-up ran down my cheeks in black drips and I wiped away the perspiration with my white glove that became covered in yellow, pink and black stains, like an artist's palette. Then the rabbi broke into 'The voice of joy and gladness', and my heart was filled with confusion and fear. I didn't love Nachum the way my mother loved my father. In my heart of hearts I admitted that I'd chosen Nachum because he was a responsible guy, and thrifty, and well off, because I wanted security, and a house and order. And when Nachum smashed the glass in commemoration of the destruction of the Temple and we were now man and wife, I suddenly became frightened. I wanted to shout, I hardly know this man at my side, and how could two people so different commit themselves, because of a scrap of paper and a piece of metal, to live together for life, sleep in the same bed and eat the same food from one pan.

The smell of frying onions came from the kitchen. Nachum would shortly pour the egg into the spitting frying pan and make himself a scrambled egg with onions. I recalled how I'd first met him at the students' dental clinic: He was a dentistry student wearing a white coat that obscured the paunch that had just begun to show, and I was a student with toothache. He politely asked me to sit in the chair, inclined it backwards, examined my teeth with his magnifying mirror and tapped lightly on the painful tooth. I shuddered, either from the pain or the fragrance of his aftershave. Afterwards he stood tense and attentive at the side of the dentist who treated me, and when I groaned with pain he held my hand and said in the plural, as if he, too, was poking around my teeth, 'We're almost done, patience, we're almost done.' When I got out of the chair and he removed the bib from my neck, I thought I'd fallen in love with him. I went back a week later to have the filling polished, but another intern took care of me. I enquired about Nachum and went back to the clinic on his day. When he bent over me I looked into his eyes that were looking into my mouth, and complimented him on his hands that were so gentle and deft that I wasn't feeling any pain, and he smiled and his hand rested on my chest as if by chance. When I got out of the chair he took off the bib and asked for my phone number.

Sounds of eating came from the kitchen and I was angry with Nachum for not bothering to ask if I was hungry as well. And again I thought about Mother – how she'd always loved dramas and tragic scenes, just like in the Egyptian films they showed on TV on Fridays, and how she'd announced over Father's gravestone on the thirtieth day after his death that she'd soon be joining him. Like a Greek widow she insisted on wearing black for a whole year, and shut herself up in the house and didn't stop talking about him, as if at any moment he would be coming in to hold their daily ritual, kiss her on the lips and tell her loudly and ceremoniously that he loved her. I tried adopting this custom with Nachum, but he refused to cooperate with this cloying romanticism, because real life, he told me, was completely different.

'Who was he?' I asked Mother, when she called later that evening and apologised profusely.

'Yoskeh.'

'Which Yoskeh?'

'You know, Yoskeh Ben-Nun, the one who used to be our neighbour.'

And I suddenly remembered. The two families had lived in adjoining apartments. Ours and theirs. Yoskeh, his wife Sarah, and their daughter Tzillah. Before the war, Mother told me, the house had belonged to an Arab family, and when they had fled, the building was declared abandoned property and was converted into numerous apartments. Yoskeh, who as a member of the 'Egged' bus cooperative had friends in high places, was given the huge lounge and the servants' room with its adjoining kitchen, while we made do with the bathroom with its fine marble bath, and two tiny rooms – running rooms, my mother called them and constantly sighed that her house was like railway carriages, and if you wanted

83

to get into the back room, my room, you had to first go into the front room, that was the living room, the hall, the dining room and my parents' bedroom; the floral couch was opened up into a bed at night. My room overlooked one of the market alleyways, and at night I'd listen to the fall of the metal shutters as they were slammed down, the screeching locks and then the silence of the alleyway that was sometimes broken by the staggering footfalls of drunks. Until Yoskeh built himself a small outhouse in the common yard with a shower and toilet, he and his family used our bathroom, and Mother cooked in their kitchen until Father fitted up a cooking corner on the balcony.

'Our neighbour Yoskeh's got a heart as big as a house,' my mother once told me and added in awe that he was a member of 'Egged', and that 'Egged' members got to travel for free on the bus, as did their wives and children. One day, Yoskeh, whose neck and huge hands were sunburnt and whose voice was cracked, rough and warm, disappeared together with his wife Sarah and their daughter Tzillah, who was my age and my best friend. Two brawny porters hastily emptied their house of boxes and furniture and loaded them onto a truck. Then the three of them crowded into a shiny black taxi and the driver sped after the truck that was loaded with the bundles of their life and enveloped them in its exhaust smoke. And I heard one of the neighbours saying that the Ben-Nun family had left the neighbourhood because Sarah had caught Yoskeh in an act of betrayal. In those days, when there were spies everywhere, I thought he'd betrayed Israel. That night my father opened a new bottle of arak, drank straight from the bottle and in the morning he told me, breathing anise fumes over me, that now Yoskeh had left he could buy the other apartment and enlarge ours.

For a long time I quizzed my parents about why they'd left without saying goodbye, and never got an answer. 'People move all the time,' my mother would say, and when I persisted she added hurriedly, 'I've got something on the stove.' And my father would clench his teeth and grumble under his thick moustache in long sentences in Ladino, and I suspected he was cursing.

My father couldn't raise the money to buy the Ben-Nun's apartment, and a new family of immigrants from Iraq that had come from a transit camp settled in next door. The Ben-Nun name had never been mentioned again, until this very moment. As I was still pretending to be angry, I stifled my curiosity and didn't ask my mother for further details about Yoskeh and how they'd found one another, although I knew she was dying to tell me.

'Is it all right if I come to Jerusalem tomorrow?' my mother asked, playing her last bargaining chip.

'Do whatever you like,' I replied, and informed Nachum right away that my mother was planning to visit us on the coming weekend, and asked him to try not to comment on her untidiness and cooking.

That night I worked late. I wanted to exhaust my body so that sleep would come to me light and ephemeral. I fought the keyboard, tapping and hitting it until the letters on screen flickered and flew before my eyes. Afterwards I stole carefully into the bedroom, took a quilt and pillow and covered myself up on the couch in my study. For a long time I watched the colourful tropical fish sailing peacefully between the corals and water lilies of the screen saver, and couldn't fall asleep. Again the smell of burning rose in my nostrils, and I saw my little girl smiling at me without fear, and I was afraid that the moment I closed my eyes the scenes of that horror would come back. Again there was the sound of firing from the direction of Beit Jallah, and I knew that the helicopters would shortly be in the air searching for the shooters, and the tanks would fire their shells, and the dogs of Gilo would bark bitterly, and the dogs of Beit Jallah would reply with broken howling, and babies would cry, and TV sets would be switched on in the middle of the night and they would report on the incident. I listened to the sounds for a long time until the first muezzin sounded his call. I waited tensely to hear what the Beit Jallah muezzin had to say, but his voice was hoarse, apparently from terror of the cannons.

When the cacophony finally died down I tried to fall asleep with my eyes open, like my father who slept with half-closed eyes, so that you really could see 'the whites of his eyes', and he once told me that he slept that way to catch the Angel of Death before he managed to take him by surprise. But then the bodiless head of the little girl appeared and hovered before my eyes like a silver helium balloon, with its string like an umbilical cord. And the child smiled at me and called, 'Peekaboo,' and her features suddenly blurred, dissolved and changed, until I found myself looking at Yoavi's face. And my son waved his chubby hands through the rear window of the bus, and clenched and opened his fingers and said, 'Peekaboo, peekaboo,' and then he was hidden from sight. When I raised my face to the sky I saw his silvered face hanging over me, and the string tying the balloon's mouthpiece was swinging above my head. I jumped to catch it and failed. And Yoavi rose and rose until he became a distant silver dot that covered the moon with its shadow as in an eclipse. I shook myself out of the horror until I awoke.

I went into the bathroom and took a Hypnodorm and with petrified limbs lay down on the narrow couch and tossed and turned until a pale light filtered through the slats of the shutter. I listened to my heart ticking like a time bomb, and to the noise of the garbage men throwing the bins around, and the beep-beep of a car alarm as it was disabled by an early-riser driver. The wail of a distant siren made me shudder suddenly with a familiar fear and I waited for another wail, and when it didn't come I heaved a sigh of relief, because one siren in our city means nothing much, but one wail after another is bad news.

And there was evening and there was morning, the sixth day

(Genesis 1, 31)

'Ima doesn't sleep at night,' I heard Yoavi summarising my condition in the morning as I wrapped my aching body in the warmth of the quilt. Nachum slammed the wardrobe door, and as he straightened his tie informed his reflection in the mirror that he'd got up in the night to pee, and when he hadn't found me in bed he'd looked in Yoavi's room and the study, and seen me asleep there curled up like a foetus with my head almost touching my knees, and in a position like that it was hardly surprising that my body was aching and my neck stiff. 'Why the tie? Where are you going today?' I whispered, and Yoavi tried to get some order into my strange sleeping habits and announced with the confidence of the very young: 'You don't sleep in the morning, you should only sleep at night. In the morning the birds make a noise and you've got to get up.' And Nachum said, 'I've got an important meeting today,' and fluttered a kiss onto my cheek, and Yoavi repeated insistently: 'You don't sleep in the morning, you should only sleep at night.' I promised to tell him, when we got home from the kindergarten, the story of the daytime butterfly and the night-time moth, and I felt for his lips with mine in our regular morning ritual, and a kiss sticky with jam was pressed onto my mouth. After they left I reinforced my grip on the bed, listening to the morning sounds coming through the shutter slats with raucous gaiety, and looking at the dust motes yellowed by the sun, I fell into sleep.

Weak and shaking and with a bad taste in my mouth, I awoke to the screeching of the birds voluntarily imprisoned in the window-shutter box.

I decided that I had to visit Avshalom again.

I ignored the replacement car that was standing in its parking space and walked towards the stop on that accursed bus route. I hurriedly climbed the three high steps that led me inside and stood by the driver for a few moments wondering where to sit. I slowly made my way down the narrow aisle, inspecting the faces of the people sitting on the plastic seats on both sides of the bus. Two Ethiopian women wrapped in white embroidered garments were talking quietly and the younger one, who looked like a child, was playing with the chocolate baby that smiled happily at me from her lap. A boy whose long hair had sprouted spikes stiff with gel and his girlfriend whose hair was purple and cropped and who had a gold stud in her nose were sitting close together and their fists were clenched as if they were in a dizzying descent on a roller-coaster. An elderly religious man was hunched over a book and mumbling prayers and oaths, and a schoolgirl in her uniform and a dark-skinned soldier, whose rifle stood between his knees, sat in the last-but-one row. I grasped the metal bar over their heads and waited until we passed the ill-fated stop: nobody was waiting and nobody wanted to get off. The night's rain had washed away the placards into the gutter and kneaded the obituary notices into pulp. The bus accelerated past the stop, remote from the disaster, and as if on an unheard command all the heads turned to the windows on the right side of the bus and the eyes looked at the grey wreaths that had long since withered and disintegrated on the purple bench that was now left behind. The old religious man suddenly gave voice to his prayers and the soldier announced loudly that he was on his way to Ramallah to stick it to all those motherfuckers, his mouth impressive with its stories of heroism while his fingers played with his unit insignia that revealed his desk job. 'On the morning it happened,' the schoolgirl said, 'all the birds vanished from the sky because the birds are the first to know.' And our song played in my head, 'And what about the birds? They fly, fly, fly until they sing a lullaby.' And between the lines the girl said that she'd woken up late that morning and missed the bus because the driver hadn't seen her, and he always waited when he saw her. And if she'd got onto that bus she wouldn't be talking to him now. I moved past them, sat down on the back seat and pushed my back-side into the middle seat facing the aisle, exactly where my little girl had been sitting. I turned my head and looked out of the rear window. A bored driver was waiting behind us at the junction and concentrating on the toothpick he was using. I tried to catch his eye but he didn't see me.

I turned my head to the front of the bus and watched the passengers getting on, sharpening my senses and looking for telltale signs. In the interpretations that had been written it had been explained that they readied themselves for death by purifying their body, and so they wouldn't appear suspicious they shaved their beards and removed all their valuables. After all, anybody about to leave this world would not be wearing an expensive watch or a gold chain.

The soldier and the old man got off at the city centre and a young man got on, bent under a heavy backpack. His protruding, lifeless eyes, over which arched thick, connected eyebrows, scanned the half-empty bus.

Of all the empty seats he chose the one next to the schoolgirl, sat down next to her and rested his backpack in the aisle at his side. The girl shrank away and stuck her face to the window. I looked at his back. Prickly bristles were stuck to the collar of his festive white shirt, as if he'd just come out of the hairdresser's. His black hair was slicked down with oil and his nervous fingers, which were playing with the cord of his backpack, revealed his malicious intent. I considered my options. Should I tell the driver of my suspicions? I rejected this possibility immediately: he would blow himself up on the spot. Then I thought I should free myself of responsibility and get off at the next stop. In paralysing fear, my eyes not leaving his back and my body ready to either jump at him or through the window, I cursed the red lights and the heavy Friday traffic that was crawling along when everybody was in a hurry. Just before we reached the stop the boy leant sideways, his fingers opened his pack and rummaged around inside. I knew that this was it, it was going to happen right now. I got up heavily and my cry was choked back in my throat. The smell of hardboiled egg and pickled cucumber wafted in the air, as the young man pulled a thick sandwich from the depths of his backpack. I sat down again. Anybody going to his death wouldn't be suffering such pangs of hunger.

Torrential rain hit me as I got off the bus opposite 'Eliahu – Fish', and I thought about my fish that I'd saved from death. A tall man stood under the awning, his black beard whipping about his face, his coattails flapping around him and his free hand struggling with an umbrella that had succumbed to the wind. The pregnant women and the prams had vanished from the street, and only a few yeshiva students were running in the rain in black hats covered with plastic bags. I walked among them with my gaily flowered umbrella, and climbed the hill to Avshalom's house.

As if announcing the end of the seven days of mourning, the obituary notices for Davidl and Batsheva had been torn down from the walls of the neighbouring houses, and new ones, announcing new dead, had been stuck up in their place. A few little girls in brightly coloured dresses were playing ball in the lobby, throwing it from hand to hand and against the wall in a precise game of catch whose rules I didn't know, calling to each other by name and shouting commands in Yiddish. As soon as they saw me Chaya'leh and Sarah'leh and Rivka'leh stopped playing and asked, in Hebrew and in unison: 'To the Wasserstein *shiva*?' I nodded and they announced: 'Fourth floor. Left door.'

The door was ajar. Avshalom, who was sitting on a mattress facing the door, saw me. I felt that he was happy to see me. I nodded a greeting and walked towards the women's room, but he gestured me to come over to him. I stood facing him with my head bent towards him. With lowered eyes, lest his eyes meet mine, Heaven forbid, he whispered: 'Dr Maggid told me that you were there in your car when it happened.'

I nodded in reply.

'You were there?' he repeated hopefully. I realised that he hadn't seen my nod.

'Yes,' I whispered.

'Maybe you saw them before it happened?' he asked and handed me the photograph. I saw a happy family, father, mother and son, dressed to the nines, upside down. I turned the photograph over and it suddenly became heavy and I almost dropped it; the eyes of the little girl were looking at me from the silver frame. She was smiling at me with a tiny, hesitant smile, golden curls peeping from beneath a big yarmulke. I felt I was going to pass out. A chair was pulled towards me from somewhere and I fell onto it, my heart pounding in my throat. I lowered my head and gazed at the sweet face that had been destroyed in fire and smoke.

'It's her,' I wept, and immediately corrected myself, 'it's him. I saw him just a second before it happened. He was sitting on the

90

back seat. I thought he was a girl.' A glass of cold water was pushed into my hand and I sipped it absently. Avshalom reached for the photograph and kissed it. 'We let his hair grow. We were going to take him to Meiron in the summer. To the *halakeh* ceremony of the first haircut.' He was silent as I wept, choked and sniffled. Somebody handed me a tissue. I blew my nose loudly, wiped away my tears and apologised, 'It was all so sudden.' We were silent for a long time and I looked at him looking at them. Then he stole a glance at me and asked, 'How was he, Davidl?'

'He was playing with me,' I replied with difficulty, in a voice turned hoarse, 'he played "Peekaboo" with me. It's a game I sometimes play with my own son.'

Avshalom raised his eyes to me, two deep blue pools, and then lowered them and asked, 'Davidl? How did he look? Did he look happy?'

I tried to hearten the bereaved father: 'He looked like a happy child.'

'And Batsheva, how was Batsheva? Was she playing with him as well?'

'I didn't manage to see her,' I stammered, 'but she turned round once, to see who he was playing with.'

We both wept. He on the floor and I seated on the chair, and a young man took the glass of water from me and offered me a box of tissues. I took a few and poured my soul into them, my grief, and thought about the little girl who was a little boy. And Avshalom whispered words of consolation to me, as if my dead were lying before me, and asked me to go to the women's room and tell his mother-in-law what I'd told him. But I wanted to stay with him and weep with him, and laboriously I got to my feet and went into their bedroom. A wave of choked weeping and groans greeted me, and I knew that the news had reached there before me. Bilha got up, put her arms round me, stuck my face into the wide cleft between her breasts and asked me to tell everything from the beginning. What did they look like? What was Davidl doing? How did he smile? How did he wave? And did you know that he was a gifted child? He already knew all the letters of the alphabet and to count up to ten. I felt relieved when I heard her speaking of him in the past tense. I sat at her side on the mattress and told the women in the room the story that came back to me every night in my bed. I described the tiny hand that had scribbled lines and dots in the condensation on the window ('He probably drew letters,' the women sighed), and how the little hand had cleared the condensation ('An inquisitive child. He wanted to see everything and know everything.') I described the blonde head I had seen and that I'd thought he was a little girl ('Sweet and beautiful like a girl,' the sighs answered me, 'he had golden curls, ringlets, ringlets'), the button nose pressed against the window, the two hands waving happily at me, his jumping on the seat, and how he had popped up several times as we played 'Peekaboo'.

Bilha's chest rose and fell heavily, she groaned and then let out a wail. I found myself holding her, and she rested her head on my shoulder and I stroked the hair of her wig and tried to soothe her, and was surprised to discover how easy it was for me to embrace and console a strange woman. It hadn't been so simple with my mother. When my mother wept over my father's open grave, I was unable to support her. I asked Nachum to go to her, because I didn't have the strength. Nachum had clumsily tried to clasp her shoulder, but she pushed him away and stood upright by the grave, proud and inconsolable. She mourned her dead as if she were alone in the world, as if he had been hers alone, and not mine. And I, as much as I tried, couldn't squeeze out a single tear. And before they covered him with soil it was as if I could hear him whispering to her, 'My lovely one, I love you.'

Now the tears flowed from me, for my father as well. Bilha was in my arms and the women around us murmured over and over, 'The Almighty will comfort you.' I asked to see Davidl's room. 'He's locked it,' Bilha apologised, and I understood that Avshalom had closed the windows, drawn the blinds and locked the door, because he wanted to preserve Davidl's smell as it had been on his last morning. 'He goes in by himself when he wants to feel the child. Perhaps he'll let you,' she said and went to him, and returned with a key clasped in her fist. She struggled a little with the lock and the door groaned and opened and we entered the Holy of Holies. The light was switched on in my honour and the door closed behind us so that Davidl's smell wouldn't escape. The warm and pleasant fragrance of laundry softener mingled with sour milk and the honey scent of a baby that had not yet become a child, that same familiar smell that wafted onto me from Yoavi's room after a night's sleep.

Davidl's room was big and crowded with furniture. An old,

white-painted wooden chest of drawers, a single chair and a new single bed, still covered with transparent plastic sheeting through which I could see the red mattress with its dancing bears. I remembered that we had to buy Yoavi a new bed. 'Yoavi doesn't need a cot anymore, it's time you treated him like a big boy,' Nachum had been preaching at me for the past six months, and had even offered more than once to take time off and go with me to the furniture shop to buy the child a new bed. Half hidden by the wall cupboard was an unmade cradle overlooked by a picture of a righteous Jew with a white beard and kindly eyes, upon which a mobile of dancing bees hanging from the ceiling cast its shadow. A few books and a red ball lay in a small straw basket. I was hit by pangs of conscience because of the abundance of soft toys, dolls and other playthings that filled our house to overflowing. Bilha awakened me from my reverie, opened the door a little, shoved me out, followed me and locked the door. The men in the living room were on their feet, their backs to me as they swayed in prayer. Taller than the others by a head stood Avshalom; with his broad shoulders and solid stance he seemed out of place. I was sorry that I couldn't say goodbye to him before I left. I wanted so much to go back and see him, talk to him, look at his wonderful hands, and I didn't know how.

I walked back to the bus stop by the fish shop, waited for the bus and looked at my reflection in the dusty window. Eliahu suddenly came bursting out of his shop and the fish scales on his apron glinted in the sun that had emerged from behind the clouds, and he said, panting slightly, as if imitating the fish swimming in his pool, that I'd forgotten the fish I'd bought, and he apologised and said that he'd sold it to another customer who insisted on having a particularly small fish, but he had a new one for me, from a shipment that had arrived just today for the Sabbath. 'It doesn't matter,' I said, and thought that in spite of everything I hadn't managed to save it. But he insisted that I come inside: 'You've already paid me and you have to be given something in return, I don't want to be guilty of a transgression.' Once again he dipped his net into the turbid water of the pool and repeated the ceremony of bringing fish up in the net until we found the smallest, especially wild and strong, that rebelled and leapt and evaded Eliahu's hands that were trying to wrap it up in newspaper, until it finally yielded and the loops of a swaying plastic bag containing the mummy of a panting, jumping fish, were hung over my arm. On the bus that made its way back I sat right behind the driver with the fish expiring on my knee.

A soft and silvery landscape of distant olive trees burst in through the windows, and I saw Avshalom, I recalled the baby smell that had filled the locked room, and over and over I heard what Bilha had told me: 'Yours was the last face that poor child saw.' And although I had not conceived him, and it had not been my blood that flowed when he was born, Davidl was mine too, I had a part in him, even though for only a few minutes. And now he was dead. Once more I was filled with terror as I remembered how that woman in red had cursed me, a curse that in the end had harmed another child, Davidl. And I asked myself whether the curse was edging towards me, whether it was now my Yoavi's turn.

A long line of children was standing on both sides of the bus's route, and my Yoavi's thin, lovely body stood out among them. They stood patiently in the biting cold, in the rain, neither crying nor complaining, and the Angel of Death passed among them, dressed as an Arab terrorist whose face was masked and his body swollen with explosives. With fingers of dynamite he pointed at the children, choosing his victims. Now he became a Nazi thug in his splendid uniform amusing himself with the selection, and pointed with his riding crop at a delightful, freckled little girl with a huge ribbon in her hair, the little girl that my father had hidden in a drawer.

I begged his forgiveness. Once I had accused him of concealing the horror, but now I understood that with his silence he had succeeded in finding the strength to forget in order to survive, to go on living and save me, my mother and the whole world from his nightmares. A person's memory is a strange thing, I thought when I saw from afar the wall in my neighbourhood, sometimes he'll remember something insignificant, and sometimes he'll try and forget something of value, bury it deep in a locked drawer of secrets. During those few minutes on the bus I suddenly felt a great closeness to my father. Both of us were survivors, he from there and I from here. I rolled the word 'survivors' around my tongue and thought that our language had done a great injustice to those who had come back from there. They were called 'survivors' here and all of them were put in the same basket: the survivors and the heroes and the fighters. With a single word they had been turned into helpless people who sat in the camps waiting for rescue. One Holocaust Remembrance Day my father had come home late at night, as he usually did on that day. When he and Mother had opened the couch to go to sleep, I heard him tell her that the term 'the ashamed' should replace 'the survivors'. He had been so ashamed at the *aktions* and selections, ashamed when they had taken his family and he hadn't been able to protect them; he was ashamed every day anew when he ate the rotted meat soup, ashamed before those who had died at his side in their bunks, ashamed when he met the Red Army soldiers who liberated him from the camp, ashamed before my mother when he was unable to laugh, and was ashamed afresh each day for having survived. At that moment on the bus, as I recalled his words, I decided that I would try, like him, to erase the scenes and banish the smells and sounds. I wouldn't talk about them and I'd refuse to reconstruct them in my memory. Only that way would I perhaps rid myself of them.

I got off the bus quickly at my stop, leaving the fish that was still flopping around weakly on the seat, to its fate. The doors closed, the bus coughed and drove off. There was a sudden squeal of brakes, the doors hissed open, and the bus stopped by my side. I was convinced that someone had found a bomb and I ran with all my might, but then one of the passengers got off and ran after me shouting, 'Lady! Lady! You forgot your fish!' and he caught up with me with my bag and its fish in his hand. I thanked him and took the bag. The fish lay inside cold and heavy and lifeless. I didn't know what I'd do with the corpse when I got home, and deliberated on whether I should throw it into the nearby dumpster. The bag described a high arc in the air, missed the opening and fell onto the pavement with a loud slap. I changed my mind. Maybe it was still alive. I walked faster and hurried home. I filled the bath and tried to peel off the fish's newspaper overcoat, but the pages stuck to its scales. I put the half-dead fish and the newspaper into the water. The fish sank to the bottom and lay on its side, revealing a whitish belly. Bubbles rose from it and burst on the surface. The resurrection of the dead took place before my very eyes. A few weak wags of its tail helped it shed the newspaper, it bobbed to the surface like a cork and immediately swam back into the depths of the bath, its body twisting like a corkscrew, as if it had lost its equilibrium.

*

'There are moths that fly at night and butterflies that fly in the daytime,' I told Yoavi when Nechama brought him home in the afternoon after the Sabbath Eve ceremony at the kindergarten. Yoavi waited until she left and immediately jumped onto my bed in his shoes, because at Nechama's he wasn't allowed to get onto the bed wearing shoes, so he had once told me with the astonishment of someone who has seen natural order undermined.

'Moths are brown and grey and dark, just like the colours of the night,' I went on, 'and butterflies are coloured in every possible colour and they're beautiful and dazzling and they're like flying flowers. In the daytime, when the sun's shining in the sky, the moths go to sleep, but the butterflies fly around merrily and happily from flower to flower, drink the sweet nectar from the flowers and eat the pollen. And the moths only wake up when darkness falls on the world.'

'But at night all the flowers go to sleep,' Yoavi said, 'so what do the moths eat?'

'Clever boy,' I said, hugging him to me and telling him that moths eat paper, clothes and woollen sweaters, and they also chew on tree bark. But sometimes they also find a flower in the forest that doesn't want to go to sleep either.

He listened open-mouthed, and then summed up the story: 'Once upon a time Imush was a butterfly, now she's a moth,' and immediately asked with a worried frown, how it had happened. I told him that I had a lot of work, 'And at night, when the house is quiet, and Abba and Yoavi are asleep, Ima can work in peace.' But he wasn't satisfied: 'If Yoavi is quiet all day, can Imush work in the daytime and sleep at night?' I choked at the thought of the heavy burden I'd unnecessarily put on his little shoulders, and quickly steadied my voice and told him that I'd got used to a moth's life of darkness, and promised that one day I'd be a butterfly again, just like Yoavi.

'But Imush is beautiful like a butterfly,' he shouted, hugging me and burying himself in my lap. Then he remembered something important, detached himself from me, ran to his room and shut himself in. He came out a long time later, offered me a colourful scribble and explained that he'd drawn a moth with colours. I caught him up in my arms and inhaled his smell, trying to banish the fears and smoke with the sweetness of his fragrance.

Again we heard the sound of shooting and the burp of automatic fire, and Yoavi escaped my arms and said indifferently, 'Oof, they're shooting again,' and I told him I had a surprise for him in the bathroom. 'Sur-prise', he repeated after me, his eyes sparkling as he dipped his hands into the water. 'A fish?' and I confirmed, 'A fish.' Disappointedly he said that this fish wasn't as pretty as the goldfish in the kindergarten aquarium, and besides, it swam funny, like a spinning top. And he went to his room.

Nachum came home with a shy and brawny young man. 'Meet Yuval the joiner,' he introduced us, and added offhandedly that he'd just heard on the radio that three houses in Gilo had been hit and two women had been lightly wounded, and that the police were telling the residents of Gilo to stay indoors. Then he led Yuval into the bedroom, closed the door after them and asked me not to come in, because Yuval was going to get rid of the birds and seal the window-shutter box.

Afterwards he went into the bathroom to wash his hands and came out almost running: 'What the hell's that in the bathtub?' I remembered the poor fish and said, 'Can't you see it's a fish?' and he asked in a mixture of fear and hope, 'And what do you intend doing with it?' I told him I didn't know, and he decided for me, 'It's a carp. Maybe you'll make *gefillte* fish for me? You know how I love fish.' I replied that I would never kill that fish, and he declared that I was crazy and why waste money on a carp if I wasn't going to cook it. Then he grumbled that he couldn't take a bath because it was occupied by the fish, and I said, 'So take a shower,' and he looked at me as if to say that since the 'episode' there was something wrong with my head. Then he opened the fridge and announced that there was nothing in the house: 'Your mother will be here soon,' he scolded me, 'and it's Friday and they'll be closing the grocery soon.' I went out and hurried to the Fruit House, hugging the stone walls surrounding the buildings, protecting myself against a stray bullet. I didn't bother prodding the tomatoes and testing the lettuce, and carelessly threw groceries and vegetables into the cart. I came out with two heavy carrier bags on my arms. Again I hugged the walls like a frightened alley cat. I crossed the street quickly and heaved a sigh of relief when I reached the entrance to our building. On the stairway I met Yuval the joiner on his way out, his thick hair adorned with a pointed black feather, like a victorious Indian warrior, and grey dust and bits of straw stuck to his blue overall. He greeted me and moved aside to let me pass, but I stood where I was: 'Just a minute, what did you find in the box?' and he gave a big smile: 'You wouldn't believe it, lady. Lots of birds' nests. A whole settlement. They'd really dirtied it in there, and two or three black birds almost flew into your house. But they won't be back. I've closed up the box real good.'

Once inside I put the bags down on the kitchen counter and went into the bedroom. I helped Nachum sweep up the piles of dirt, and told him that I'd got used to the sound of the birds and now I'd probably miss them.

In the evening I heard my mother's laugh coming from the stair-well. The laugh preceded her, infiltrating the apartment, sliding its thick body under the door. Pink-cheeked, my mother hurried to appear in its wake in a new red wool dress that hugged her figure and proudly showed off her wide hips and breasts, and on her arm a shopping basket of plaited plastic twine, filled to the brim with goodies. Yoskeh climbed the stairs heavily after her, carrying before him a new paunch he had nurtured over all the years he had been out of our life, on one shoulder a wide-strapped bag, his two hands grasping the handles of a big pot from which came the aroma of chicken soup, and under his sweaty arms my mother's quilt and pillow. He put the lot down in the doorway, as if afraid to come inside, kissed my mother carefully on the forehead, and left.

Then I remembered I'd seen him, that Yoskeh. He had come to our house when we were sitting *shiva* for my father, he'd sat and kept quiet amid a crowd of noisy men, and I, immersed in and focused on my bereavement, hadn't paid him any attention.

My mother had already taken over the kitchen, put her shopping basket on the counter, and I could see the deep mark its handles had left on her arm. Then she took possession of Nachum's apron, the black one with plastic breasts I'd brought him on my last trip to London, tied it round her waist, ran to the mirror, looked at her reflection, laughed aloud and told me and Nachum that hers were more beautiful than the ones on the apron. I could see the dark blush crawling over Nachum's face and reaching his forehead and ears. Then she went into Yoavi's room, awakened him from his afternoon nap and took him into her arms. He hugged her with closed eyes, rested his head in the hollow of her neck and crushed the plastic breasts with his body. Her head bent to him and her lips kissed the top of his head and murmured, 'My lovely boy, how

I've missed you.' And with Yoavi clasped to her like a baby monkey she went into the kitchen, and together they took food-stuffs from her basket and clanged pots and frying pans, and talked and talked, and soon the smells of the dishes I loved filled the air. I sprawled on a kitchen chair and Yoavi sat on the counter, his legs dangling, and he told my mother his own, improved version of the story of the butterflies and moths, while Nachum walked around treading on eggshells, careful not to blurt out anything untoward.

Then my mother went to take a bath and closed the door after her and came out dry and wrapped in a towel. 'You forgot the carp in the bath. It's too late to make fish balls of it now.' I told her to take a shower instead. 'And what will you do with the fish? Should I make some fish balls for Shabbat?' Reproachfully I asked her, 'Have you forgotten I don't eat fish? And she yelled back, 'So what about Nachum and Yoavi? Don't they deserve to have a nice piece of *gefillte* fish?'

We sat down to eat. Nachum recited the blessing over the wine and in the background the TV screen flickered silently, reviewing the week's events. Once again I saw the bus going up in flames and the stench of scorched flesh filled my nostrils, and my mother said that something was burning in the kitchen, and I thought that it was the smell coming from me and that they didn't dare tell me.

She came back carrying a big tray loaded with slices of roast veal and little potatoes in olive oil strewn with tiny rosemary leaves. I looked at the bleeding lumps lying among the potatoes and thought how alive the roast looked, trembling and wounded. I announced that I didn't feel like meat this evening, and immediately remembered that I hadn't eaten meat all week, and that maybe I'd try vegetarianism, because millions of people all over the world avoid eating meat. As they all stuck their forks into the pink and rubbery meat, I was suddenly nauseous and left the table on the pretext of a headache. From inside I heard Nachum telling my mother that ever since 'that episode' Yael hadn't touched meat, and Yoavi's piping voice asking, 'What's a 'pisode?' Nachum didn't reply and Yoavi repeated his question until he was almost shouting, 'What's a 'pisode? What's a 'pisode?' and Nachum relented and said, 'Ima had a little accident, a teeny one, and she hasn't been feeling very well.' Then I heard Yoavi's mollified voice asking for some more meat, and my mother's encouraging tones, 'Eat lots of meat and you'll be a brave soldier and protect Ima.'

Yoavi's reedy voice objected saying, 'Don't want to be a soldier,' and Nachum said something I didn't catch.

It was a long time until Nachum lay down beside me, fragrant and naked. He reached over and tried to hold me, but I eluded him. I failed to understand why, on this particular night with my mother staying with us, he wanted to make love. I wanted to ask him where he'd been all those other nights, but I didn't. I whispered that I just couldn't make love with my mother, who is a light sleeper, on a mattress in Yoavi's room and listening to every sound. He grumbled something in disappointment, turned his face to the wall and complained that I was turning him off each time anew, and that I shouldn't dare blame him for evading me later. And as if he hadn't been at the height of sexual excitement only a moment earlier, he easily slipped into a deep sleep. I lay on my back in the dark and stroked myself and thought about Avshalom, and my body refused to relax and calm down. I stole into the bathroom, swallowed the last Hypnodorm tablet I found in the hospital bag, took a couple of swigs from the wine bottle that had been returned to the fridge, and sank into a dreamless sleep.

I slept right through Saturday, awakening intermittently, and my family tiptoed around me and whispered behind my back as if plotting against me. From in a dream I heard my mother telling Nachum that after all the girl had been in a major incident, and we should try and understand her behaviour, and now she was probably scared of her own shadow. I covered my head with the quilt and thought about my trip to Japan right after my release from the army. On the southern island of Kyushu I'd met people living at the foot of an active volcano that spewed rocks and lava and ash from its maw. And the city itself, its houses, trees, sidewalks and cars, were all covered in a thick layer of ash. Summer and winter the inhabitants walked around under their umbrellas to protect themselves from the ash, and the children wore hard hats. Perhaps our situation was better than theirs. I sank into a deep sleep again and dreamt that everybody was walking around the streets of Jerusalem wearing white steel helmets, and Japanese paper parasols decorated with pink cherry blossom protected us from the bomb shrapnel.

I woke up towards evening when Nachum shook me and said that my mother was leaving and wanted to say goodbye. She burst into the room, hugged me through the quilt around my body, and said that now we were equal, because I'd evened the score: 'You've been asleep all day and didn't have time for your mother,' she claimed, and added in a whisper that Yoavi had wet his bed and something should be done about it.

When the doorbell rang my mother fled into the arms of Yoskeh, who was waiting in the doorway, afraid to come inside despite my entreaties. He looked at her with the expression of a whipped dog looking for love in the wrong place, and she said, 'So, get the stuff already, what are you waiting for?' Again he stuck the quilt and pillow under his arm, hung her bag over his shoulder, took the empty soup pot by one handle, and she put her arm through his overloaded one and they left together. I heard her laugh echoing from the stairwell, and my anger at her raised its ugly head once more. I wanted to believe what Nechama had said about my mother living correctly, that she wasn't betraying my father's memory. And my father, who loved her madly, was probably looking at her from above with a satisfied smile. After all, he hadn't wanted her to be buried by his side or that she immolate herself on a funeral pyre like an Indian widow.

From the street I heard the car doors slam shut and my mother's voice calling to me and Yoavi. We went out onto the balcony and she thrust her upper torso through the car window and waved her handkerchief dramatically. I picked up Yoavi to wave goodbye to Grandma, and he carried on waving to her with both hands even after Yoskeh's car had disappeared round the bend. Something in the babyish way he waved her goodbye reminded me of what I wanted to forget. And again Davidl's bodiless head rose before me, and his two hands waving to me, and his eyes in his pale face looking at me reproachfully.

It was only when I went back to bed and wrapped myself in the quilt that I remembered that I hadn't told my mother anything about Avshalom and Davidl and Batsheva.

And the clouds? They fly, they fly

I awoke to soft, pale, pink light filtering through the shutter slats and drawing broken lines and circles on the bed. 'I slept for almost five hours last night,' I said, making Nachum part of my joyous awakening, and he, still drugged with sleep, hugged me gently and said, 'I knew sooner or later you'd get over this madness,' and immediately started preaching that it was high time that we started functioning as a family, because since 'that episode' of mine nothing was right in this house. I ignored the lecture and went into Yoavi, who this morning had not jumped onto us in bed as he did every day. He greeted me drowsily, and said he'd tried to be a moth and hadn't slept all night. An acrid smell came from his woolly pyjamas. I lifted him out of bed and my hands felt damp. Yoavi buried his face in my stomach and confessed that the pipi had just trickled out, and that I shouldn't tell Abba. I promised him that it would be our secret. I gave him a fireman's lift to the bathroom, where the fish was still fighting for its life, washed his body in lukewarm water and my heart lurched at the sight of his protruding shoulder blades and round baby's bottom. I bit my lip lest I be tempted to bite his bottom. And Yoavi laughed and said and the water was tickling his willie and he had some more pipi. I told him he could pee in the shower, and he gave me a conspiratorial look and screwed up his face and made a great effort to force out another few drops for me, and I washed him again and wrapped him in a thick towel. I hefted him onto my shoulder like a sack and announced that I had a little boy for sale, and he responded with a happy laugh.

When he sat down at the table he asked me if I'd be a butterfly today.

On the way to the university we passed through the city centre, because Nachum had to collect a package at the main post office. Empty streets yawned silently, traffic lights flashed in vain, and the few cars sped along the street as if fleeing for their life. A few people with haunted looks, keeping to themselves, passed through the empty streets as if escaping a suicide attack that hadn't yet happened.

We parked outside the post office right next to three Russian musicians, two violinists and a contrabassist, whose heavy, suited bodies were seated on folding canvas stools too small to accommodate their large backsides. Gold-toothed smiles that flashed through the white stubble of their faces shone at the passers-by who hurried past. I was filled with compassion at the sight of the contrabassist's wrinkled suit and flaming eyes surrounded by deep wrinkles, and asked Nachum to give them something on his way into the post office. He groused that he didn't have any change and vanished inside. I got out of the car after him. The mildewed smell of jackets too long in storage arose from the musicians. I rummaged in my purse and took out a twenty-shekel note and put it into the contrabass case whose empty purple velvet maw was open in thanks. The three thanked me with a vociferous 'Spasiba' and the violins burst into a rasping melody and the contrabass bim-bammed along with them. I had no idea what they were playing until a skeleton-thin man wearing a pained expression and an outdated heavy jeans jacket that was far too big for him appeared at their side. He gave me a grey look with one arm across his chest and the other beating time in exaggerated gestures. From deep inside his concave belly his basso profundo boom-boomed away. He sang a complex and unfamiliar arrangement of 'Jerusalem of Gold' in my honour.

I stood there, the only listener to a pavement concert, the pavement gleaming with thousands of dark circles: blobs of blackened chewing gum, cigarette butts and sunflower seed hulls bearing testimony to the fact that there was once life in this city, and a small audience began gathering around them and I suddenly felt afraid that a gathering like this was an invitation to a suicide bomber. I disengaged myself from the musicians and singer, and went back to sit in the car. When Nachum returned he said he had some good news for me and, in the morning, after we dropped Yoavi at the kindergarten, he would drive me to the garage because my car was ready. I thought about my old, beloved and perfidious Minimush, and could see the fine glass web that had been woven on her windscreen. I felt as if fingers of flame were reaching out at me. I didn't want to see her again, let alone drive her. I blamed her for everything that had happened to me, as if she had intentionally led me into that death trap. Had she not taken her time and started as usual that morning, and not wasted my time with failed attempts at starting, I probably would have avoided the horror. Only later, sitting in my room at the university, I suddenly realised that if it hadn't been for Minimush taking her time, I would never have known about Avshalom and the most beautiful hands in the world.

My car had led me to him deviously, like a magic pumpkin.

At the approach to Mount Scopus the windows of the Hyatt Hotel followed us – polished, shining, bored and chilly eyes. Against the backdrop of the deep blue, almost sapphire sky, like the door-frames of Arab houses painted blue to ward off the evil eye, the wind scattered and regathered the clouds. 'And the clouds? They fly, they fly', protean, creating downy palaces and flying towers, leaping from window to window, their reflection in the window-panes like on a huge screen.

We got to the university and I made my way past students walking along the never-ending corridors, bumping into one another, preoccupied, like worker ants, with no identity, making their way rapidly in the depths of the earth, jostling one another and feeling each other's antennae until they reach their objective. A feeling of depression flooded me, as it always did when I walked those corridors that resembled a mythological labyrinth at whose end the ravening monster awaits us all.

I was welcomed by shouts of joy in the department secretaries' office. Noga hurried to make mint tea and confessed in a whisper that it had been boring without me. I silently thanked her for not asking any questions. I sat down heavily at my desk, jaded and exhausted, and Noga handed me a cup of tea and a slice of chocolate cake from her daughter Maya's birthday party yesterday and, as if she'd suddenly remembered, asked about Yoavi and gave me a consoling look. Then she said she'd watered my plants in my absence, left the room on tiptoe, and I heard her in the corridor, announcing that I was back. I examined my two miserable begonia plants that I had stubbornly insisted on growing under the cold hum of the fluorescent lighting. Despite Noga's tending, my plants had died standing, withered and crumbled while still tied to the bamboo cane, like Christ on the cross. The overwatered soil had sprouted crushed cigarette butts adorned with red hoops, Louisa's lip-prints.

Prof. Har-Noy stuck the end of his red nose into the room, shaking his shock of damp white curls like a dog coming out of the water, and I knew that once again he'd walked to Mount Scopus from his Rehavia home, and as always he hadn't taken his umbrella. With a kindly expression he showed me his teeth, asked how I was, and without waiting for a reply thundered that I shouldn't overdo it on my first day back after 'your illness', and it would be best if I just gave an hour of exercises in the writing course. 'Nothing will happen if your students wait awhile, because I've found you a sub,' he said, and like an announcer at a boxing match he trumpeted the name of the winner: 'Louisa.'

A shudder ran through me. I hadn't yet died and she was already rushing to take my place? And why hadn't anybody bothered to inform me? And why was he talking to me about an illness when I hadn't been ill at all, when I just couldn't fall asleep at night.

The rumour of my return spread through the faculty's corridors and knocked on every door, and as if in a procession I was passed by lecturers, tutors, secretaries and even two of my favourite students. They all put on a happy face, waved through the open door, lied barefacedly that I looked wonderful – 'Like you're back from a holiday' – and declared, like conspirators who had made sure their stories were consistent, 'We're so glad you're back with us.'

Like I had somewhere else to go back to.

Louisa arrived at midday and gave me a bear hug that somewhat thawed the hostility towards her that I'd accumulated, called me '*ma chérie*', sat down on my desk and began telling me how hard it had been with my students: they hadn't understood her and she hadn't understood them. Following this experience, she said, she'd decided that only research was for her, not teaching. I wanted to ask her why she'd used my plant pots as an ashtray, but I didn't.

She came back in the afternoon and peeped in and asked if I was going home. I told her that Minimush was in the garage and she offered me a lift. On the way home she chattered happily about her wonderful Yoram, the preparations for the wedding and the amazing caterers they'd found on the recommendation of friends. I listened and silently hated her. I showed the contents of my bag to the blue-uniformed Nikolai who was standing at ease at the gate, and although he saw me almost every day, he asked me to open my bag. Once again thick, foreign fingers rummaged through the intimateness of my life. And my bag, swollen with cares, vomited up a cellular phone, a frayed tampon, an electronic appointments diary, out of date prescriptions, a packet of headache pills, a dried up dummy, an old parking ticket, balled tissues, a topless lipstick, a letter I'd forgotten to post and a few sticky sweets. And as Nikolai probed I thought about our bags that divulged our secrets and of Nechama who quoted Freud as saying that a woman's handbag symbolises the female genitalia.

My Yoavi was in the yard, hanging from the tall fence, and like a little monkey stuck his hand through the bars and shouted, 'Imush, I'm here.' He was wearing an unfamiliar pair of red trousers, and he waved a bunch of big sheets of paper in my face. I exclaimed over his drawings, all of which bore the rounded handwriting of Shoshana the teacher: 'From Yoavi to Ima, a butterfly'. I asked whose trousers they were, but Shoshana surprised me from the rear, addressing me loudly and authoritatively as 'Dr Maggid!' and although I hadn't completed my thesis, and it was doubtful if I ever would, Shoshana always insisted on this salutation. She asked to speak to me, and right there, in the yard, in front of everybody, she informed me reprovingly and with a gloomy expression that Yoavi was wetting himself again, and that something was evidently troubling him. Back hunched with insult I took Yoavi's warm hand and we went inside. A strong smell of urine and oranges and stale bread and rubber boots welcomed me. I felt dizzy and held onto the smooth wall, the bottom half of which shone with pink oil paint. Yoavi pulled me after him and together we made our way between small orange plastic chairs arranged in a half-circle for morning assembly, and passed the doctor's corner and the dolls' corner and the cookery corner: Yoavi wanted to show me the nature corner. He stood on tiptoe and from a low shelf took down a jam jar with cloudy water, and cyclamen, anemones and narcissi with blackened stems, then replaced it carefully and ceremoniously proffered me a few shrivelled bulbs, snail shells empty of their dwellers, and a bird's nest with no eggs. Above all these a placard with crooked letters: 'Our Country's Winter Flowers'.

On the way out I took a transparent plastic bag containing a pair of wet trousers and underpants from Yoavi's hook, and hurried him outside. I wanted to run away from there, from the stifling smells and from Shoshana. But she was lying in wait in the yard and called after my retreating back not to forget to wash the trousers and bring them back tomorrow, because they're Rotem's. On the way to the car I asked Yoavi whether Rotem was a boy or a girl, and he said, a girl, of course she's a girl. Louisa opened the door for us and was happy to see him and said he was a big boy and a real hunk, and when he grew up she'd want to marry him. And Yoavi slanted his eyes at me and told her gently, so she wouldn't be offended, that he was only Ima's, and when he grew up he was going to marry me. And Louisa laughed and told me in English, so we've got us another Oedipus.

When we pulled up at our house I asked her if she wanted to come up for coffee and hoped she'd refuse, but she said, 'Sure, why not.' At the door I announced, 'Straight into the bath,' and Yoavi said, 'But there's a fish there,' so I told him, 'Then into the shower.' Louisa crowded into the tiny bathroom with us and burst out laughing when she saw the fish swimming around in confused circles and asked, 'What's this doing here?' and I replied, 'It's a long story,' and she sat on the edge of the bath as I peeled the red trousers off Yoavi and in disgust threw them into the laundry basket. I turned the warm water onto my son and he grabbed his penis and complained, 'Hot!' and Louisa said in English that if she had a boy she wouldn't have him circumcised, because circumcision was actually maiming and she couldn't understand how such a primitive custom had survived until the third millennium. When we went back into Yoavi's room I was dragged into a discussion with her, as if she'd already had a baby, and I asked her if she didn't care that throughout his life her son would be the odd man out, and she shrugged and replied in English that if maiming made the child feel like everybody else, then it was a return to the ancient tribal custom of branding and tattooing the body so that everyone would look alike, and she added that uncircumcised men give their wives greater pleasure and enjoy sex more, and was

107

about to go into detail on the whys and wherefores, when I said, 'Louisa, you're way off your subject. You're supposed to be dealing with female circumcision.' And Yoavi complained, 'Now you're speaking English because you're telling secrets.'

After she'd left I was all Yoavi's. We played with the dolls' house and his soft toys and watched cartoons until Nachum came in like a wet blanket and announced that he'd had a hard day and what was there to eat.

Nechama called in the evening and said she'd heard from Shoshana that Yoavi was wetting the bed again, and that something had to be done about it right away, because bedwetting in children who had already stopped was a sign of emotional distress, and she was not to be pacified until she had accused me bluntly: 'You've projected your anxieties onto him and now he's freeing himself from them by wetting his bed.' I remembered that I hadn't yet washed Rotem's red trousers and impatiently replied, No more, I'd had enough of the whole world snooping into Yoavi's peeing, and she said, 'Who's "the whole world"? Who else has talked to you about it?' but she immediately softened her tone: 'But you know I only want what's best for you.' I replied that I sometimes felt that everybody was poking around in my life and I was just a bystander, looking on and not taking part, and she said I was a little oversensitive after the trauma I'd experienced and I should remember that she is my best friend and always willing to help. I said, 'See you tomorrow,' and ended the call with a feeling of distress. I was angry with her for interfering in my life and I felt a sudden need to blame her for everything, even that curse on Yoavi when he was still a foetus in my belly. But right away I blamed myself: ever since I first met her in the gynaecologist's waiting room I'd opened the door wide and asked her into my life.

I recalled our second meeting, how we'd sat in my car and she lit a cigarette and told me about her activities in the 'Women in Black' movement, and the left-wing women's group she had founded. Nechama exhaled and said gravely that we had to act, and asked me to join a 'Women in Black' demonstration that Friday at noon in Paris Square. She warned me that I had to be strong, that passers-by usually got at them and sometimes argued, and there were some who cursed and threw rotten vegetables. Completely overwhelmed by this charismatic woman who sought my friendship, I declared that I was ready to do anything for peace, and

108

when we parted I knew with certainty that we would meet again outside the doctor's waiting room, and maybe even become close friends.

We met again in the waiting room two weeks later, and she said sourly that the doctor had forbidden her to smoke but she didn't give a damn, and she'd show him what a lovely strong boy she'd have. As I drove her home she made me privy to an intimate secret and told me that she'd become pregnant on the thirteenth of January precisely, and I was surprised and said, 'But that's my date too, Tuesday, the thirteenth of January.' I didn't go into detail about how I was so sure, and I didn't tell her about Nachum who was doing thirty days reserve' service and came home on a surprise one-day leave on the thirteenth of January. 'So we're both on the same day?' Nechama said softly, and when I nodded enthusiastically she solemnly hugged me as a significant other in destiny. And I almost suffocated from the smell of the nicotine in her hair, and her voice grew hoarse when she whispered in my ear that from now on we were bonded, and although she didn't believe in fate, it was clear to her that our meeting hadn't been by mere chance.

And in the fourth month of my pregnancy I joined her at the 'Women in Black' demonstration.

Afterwards the night, with its dark tongue, licked the heaven and the earth, and all their host gleamed and glinted from the windows as if hanging by a hair, and when I went into the bedroom Nachum turned off the light, turned his back and mumbled goodnight. I lay in bed and began thinking about Avshalom's hands and couldn't fall asleep. I slipped into the bathroom, checked the hospital medication bag, found it empty, and remembered that I'd already used all the pills. I went into my study. The computer welcomed me with a monotonic hum and the screen flickered at me with sea hues. As if mesmerised I followed the colourful tropical fish sailing along serenely and silently as if keeping a secret in the screen saver's aquarium. I touched the keyboard and they vanished and the screen glinted at me in tones of silver, awaiting my commands. I didn't know what command to give it, and I got up and stood at the window and looked towards Beit Jallah immersed in the blackout. A pair of soft car headlights flickered in the dark and vanished behind a darkened building, flickered again and vanished again. Absently I tore off pieces from the broad strip of masking tape that the previous tenants had stuck on the window frame during the Gulf War. I'd never managed to get it all off. When I moved in here with Nachum I'd cleaned the apartment thoroughly and had wanted to remove the memento of that war from the windows, but Nachum said that it wasn't worth the effort, that in any case Saddam Hussein would lose it again and we'd have to reseal the room.

The telephone suddenly rang and my mother was on the line. She hurriedly said that she hadn't been able to fall asleep because she'd suddenly remembered that she'd forgotten to ask me if we'd replaced our gas masks and whether Yoavi had a hood mask. The papers were full of stories about the new war in Iraq, she apologised, and enlisted to her aid all her necromancy and sorcerers, the Tarot cards and astrological charts.

'But why are you calling in the middle of the night?' I asked, not wanting to admit that I'd been thinking about the selfsame thing at the very moment, lest she start lecturing me on telepathy and a mother's gut feelings. But she simply said that if she hadn't called now, she probably would have forgotten to speak to me in the morning.

Now I really couldn't sleep. I decided to tidy the house and I tidied it with a previously unknown zeal. I loaded the washing machine, dried the laundry on the radiators, folded the dry clothes, ironed Nachum's shirts, checked store cupboard and fridge, made a shopping list for the morning, made a pot of vegetable soup, fried schnitzels, peeled potatoes for chips and prepared a cream sauce for spaghetti. Then I decided to bake some bread as well. I took pleasure in the thought of Yoavi and Nachum awakening to the aroma of baking in the morning. I couldn't find any yeast, but still I persevered, kneaded the dough into a coil, and I opened and reopened the oven, sniffing the smell emanating from it in curls of vapour. Just before morning I took out a flat confection, incredibly heavy and hard, that brought to mind the bread my father had hoarded for years, and which my mother and I had wanted to get rid of.

My father had a weakness, a weakness for bread. 'You mustn't throw bread away, bread is the staff of life,' he repeatedly said. He'd collect the leftovers in a white enamel box, and when they had dried he would grind them up in the mincer and put the crumbs into plastic bags. The bags would accumulate in the kitchen cupboards until the breadcrumbs sprouted multicoloured layers of fungus, and my mother would surreptitiously throw them out. Father would cram the green-coated leftover bread that was unsuitable for breadcrumbs into bags, go down to the beach and there distribute his staff of life. The gulls would see him from afar, and like flashes of white lightning, in a screaming, noisy flock, flap around him heavily, and their voices hoarse with greed could be heard from far away. More and more gulls would hear the sound and gather around him, landing heavily on the sand and trudging towards him on their red stilt legs. With necks outstretched and beaks agape they hurried to hobble to him, and he would shake his bags with great devotion, crumbling the bread with his fingers and throwing the crumbs onto the beach, into the water and into the air as well. When the gulls were sated and stood aside, their beaks pecking at the roots of their feathers, waves of sparrows and bulbuls and starlings would gather, and grey doves that fanned their tails in his honour, and receive the offering from his hands with chirruping and squawking.

After his death my mother discovered in the depths of his wardrobe and the space between the bedroom ceiling and the roof loaves of bread that had become fossilised over the years, their crusts as thick and tough as steel. Weeping, we collected the loaves, whose weight had increased with the passing years, loaded them into my car and drove to the beach. With a great effort we carried the heavy bags to the place where he used to stand, and waited a long time for the gulls to come. But they didn't. We spread the bread where the waves kissed the shore, but the loaves sank into the soft sand and refused to budge. I rolled up my trousers, picked up a few loaves and strode into the sea, but the water was loath to accept my offering and threw it back onto the shore. Again and again we tried, my mother and I, to throw the loaves far out into the waves, and again and again the sea vomited them up. We left the beach as the day darkened, and lots of hard loaves of bread that the gulls refused to eat and the sea failed to permeate, cunningly stole up behind our retreating backs.

My fish. I tore up the inside of the *challah* left over from Friday and crumbled it into the water in the bath. My fish lay on the bottom, grey and exhausted, refusing to rise to the surface and gather up the bread with its lips.

What does the Sun make? Day

On Monday morning I fully intended to get my life back on track.

That morning Nachum found me in the kitchen, gazing at the sun's rays that came to me through the shutter's slats and cast a flickering sunglow on the floor in an undecipherable picture. His bare feet moved towards me, trampling the lucidity of the light and scrambling the picture.

'Tell me. Are you crazy? What have you been doing in the kitchen?'

I suddenly saw the mess I'd left behind. 'I was only trying to bake bread for us, for the morning.'

Nachum shifted his weight from one foot to the other. 'Are you sure you're all right?' and not waiting for a reply, added hesitantly, 'We're going to pick up your car from the garage this morning.'

I automatically acquiesced, and like a fully functioning wife asked, 'Coffee? Toast?' and Nachum nodded and opened the front door and picked up the newspaper, sat at the table and said as if to himself that two days had passed without any terrorist attacks, and the ministers now had time for rubbish. I didn't ask what rubbish the government was dealing with, because since that day I had refused to find out what the papers were writing about.

Yoavi welcomed me with wet pyjamas and an apologetic smile, 'It leaked out again.' I consoled him and said, 'Don't worry, it sometimes happens. Maybe we should talk to Nechama about it and she can tell us what to do,' but Yoavi was alarmed, 'No, not Nechama, she'll tell Yoeli and he'll tell everybody at kindergarten.'

We acted like partners in crime: Yoavi quickly took off his wet clothes and I tore the sheet from the bed and shoved the lot into the washing machine, and Nachum told me to hurry, and I thought that perhaps Rami might come today because Monday was our day.

I first met Rami in Nechama's stairwell: I was heavily climbing the stairs, one hand on the banister, the other on my hip, my huge belly before me, exhausted from its fight with gravity. He greeted me warmly, as if it was he I'd come to visit. His honey eyes laughed to me, and with an apologetic smile, with a broad, knightly gesture, as if spreading a red carpet before me, he quickly put a tattered floorcloth beneath my shoes so I wouldn't dirty the steps he'd just washed. When I asked Nechama who that nice young man was who was washing their steps, she didn't know. I arranged my next visit for the same day, and that time, too, he spread the floorcloth at my feet and smiled sweetly at me. I asked his name and he said, 'They call me Rami,' and without me asking he volunteered that he was from Beit Jallah, and was taking evening classes at Al-Quds University and he cleaned houses during the day to save money for his marriage to Julia, the girl to whom he had been betrothed when he was little.

On my next visit to Nechama I suggested that he come and work for me. He asked, 'Monday, eight in the morning OK?' and I replied, 'Yes, it's OK.' Two days later he was there. I was at home at the time, a few days before I was due, trying to concentrate on the paper I was supposed to submit, and my doughy fingers tapped the computer keys with difficulty. Rami walked around me with amazingly light steps, as if afraid to disturb me at my work.

It was because of Rami that I had my first row with Nechama. We were sitting in a café, and I told her in passing that I'd asked Rami to come and work for me. She silently took a long drag on her cigarette and blew the smoke right into my face. I thought she'd done it on purpose, and I couldn't restrain myself and told her, 'You can poison yourself and your baby if you like, but why do you insist on poisoning us as well?' She angrily stubbed out her cigarette in the plate still filled with droopy lettuce, and I heard the dying hiss of the ember suffocating in a pool of vinaigrette. Her dark eyes pierced me, and I focused on the down on her upper lip that seemed stiffer and blacker than usual.

'Who do you think you are?' she flashed in a searing voice, spraying me with flecks of spittle, and told me that employing an Arab home help perpetuated colonialist enslavement, and raising her voice, said, 'How dare you employ an Arab in a lady–servant relationship?' I was so angry that my belly ached and I feared that the sac holding the amniotic fluid would break, and I retorted that her own building committee employed Rami to wash the stairwell, and I couldn't see the difference, and then I ran out of breath and told her that I'd had it with her hypocritical preaching, and added bravely that she shouldn't dare to smoke again in my car.

'So I'll walk,' she shot back, 'don't do me any favours.'

Even after we'd calmed down a bit and walked together to my car, I couldn't but shout at her that at least I was offering him a job with a fair wage, and I wasn't sitting on the fence dressed in black and yelling hollow slogans condemning the occupation. A silence fell and in silence we reached her house. Before she got out of the car I said that we didn't always have to agree with one another, and Nechama opened her arms in a conciliatory gesture and hugged me, and our bellies met as if in a kiss, and I told her that now our babies were talking in a language we'd never understand, and they were probably laughing at those crazy mothers of theirs. And Nechama smiled and offered me her little finger and wrapped it around mine and asked hesitantly, 'Friends?' and I answered, 'Forever.'

'Imush, you're dreaming,' Yoavi said, smiling. I hurriedly put the powder into the washing machine, and as I pressed the start button I decided to call Nechama and ask her to send me her cleaning lady because I was losing control over the mess in the house.

Arabic graffiti and brightly coloured Palestinian flags adorned the walls of the houses in the Arab village of Beit Zafafa, and every passing child with a schoolbag on his shoulder seemed to me to be a suicide bomber. I shuddered, and Nachum told me to calm down. We twisted through the village's narrow alleyways to where the road widened and like a black funnel poured us into the garage area of Talpiot. The sharp smell of engine oil lay on the air, spiced by charcoal smoke and the smell of meat roasting on *shawarma* skewers. Nausea choked me and I could feel my stomach turning over. I put my head between my knees, the way my father had taught me when I complained that I was going to be sick on the tortuous drive from Jaffa to Jerusalem. I breathed deeply to counteract the nausea, but the morning coffee and toast and jam made their way into my gullet.

I yelled to Nachum to pull over. Outside a small greengrocery I opened the car door and threw my guts up. I wiped my face and hair with the handkerchief Nachum handed me through the open door. Blind to my distress he scolded me from the depths of his seat, far from the stench of my own depths, 'You probably ate something that was off.' The nausea rose again and in a high arc I vomited my bile and groaned, and a woman with a coloured kerchief round her head came out of the shop and asked in Arabic-accented Hebrew, 'Lady, what's wrong?' and sat me down on a straw-covered stool she dragged outside, vanished into the dimness of the shop and reappeared with a glass of cold water into which she had squeezed a lemon. She patiently helped me drink the sour water, wiped my face with a damp cloth, and said, 'Poor thing, you pregnant?' My face contorted, I spat out the bitter saliva that had accumulated in my mouth, and the woman suggested that I come into her house over the shop and rest. But Nachum had already gotten out of the car and supporting my back he sat me down in the passenger seat and thanked the woman who had pushed her head through the window and was looking at me in concern.

'Are you all right?' he asked, and I at his side, voided and aching, and the sour smell of insides coming from me as I replied, 'Yes, yes. It was probably something I ate last night.' 'Maybe you're pregnant?' he said, trying to make a joke of it, and I dug my nails into the flesh of my hands and asked him to drive on because I had to get to a meeting, and I didn't tell him what I wanted to shout aloud – how can I be pregnant when we don't fuck?

We drove between mountains of tyres and engine entrails, through alleys blackened by used engine oil, until we stopped outside a garage with a sign over it announcing, 'Benny's Body Shop'.

And then I saw her.

Clean and polished my treacherous car stood waiting for me. Her bonnet glowed with new paint, the lashes of her wipers blinked up and down shyly, and her round frog eyes were open wide in wonderment, as if scrutinising me with interest.

I checked her from every angle. In one fell swoop all the signs of her long road life that had been etched on her body had been wiped away, together with my fingerprints.

She was no longer my car.

'The car's fine now,' the garage owner announced to Nachum, and carried on talking to him as if I wasn't there: 'The chassis wasn't damaged, we changed the wheels and hubcaps and polished and waxed it,' and wiped his greasy hands on a piece of newspaper. I closely watched his hands that were covered with black oil and grease. Almost absently he crumpled the pages that bore the horrors almost certainly read about by the mechanics during their morning break, between the coffee and the cake. A wrinkled ball was deftly tossed into the cylindrical rusty can at my side. I glanced sideways into it. The balled newspaper that had swallowed up the nightmare rested on the innards of chopped up cars and plastic bottles and oily-sided cans.

And, as if the car wasn't mine, carried on his man talk with Nachum: 'You've no idea what she looked like when she was brought in. Almost a write-off. And what can I say, your wife was dead lucky. I don't understand how she came out of that mess alive.'

I bit my tongue as I pulled over a white plastic chair with a filthy split back that rocked as befitting a chair in a garage, and sat down in silent acceptance. The words passed over me loudly – carburettor, battery, head gasket, tyres, starter. I managed to understand that the bonnet had been replaced because the old one had been peppered with shrapnel as had the engine itself, several long nails had been pulled out of the passenger door and some had even penetrated the upholstery. He couldn't understand how the lady had come out unscathed.

I had been close to death, so the owner said, and it hadn't wanted me. It had sent Davidl to me to save my life.

I reconstructed the last few seconds before the horror. How I had bent under the wheel in the game I had invented for the little girl and me, and that's where my head had been when the bus blew up.

Nachum went over to my car, raised the bonnet, started the engine, listened to its sound, and like a learned expert announced that it was as good as new, switched off the engine and slammed the bonnet shut. Solemnly, he handed me the keys: 'Are you OK? Can you drive?' and I just about managed to get up from the chair: 'I'm fine.' 'OK, 'bye,' Nachum said, 'see you this evening. I'll be late because I've got a patient who can only come after eight, and it's a complicated procedure. Don't wait for me for supper.' I heard him whistling gaily to himself as he got into his car and adjusted the driving mirror downwards, inspected his face, squeezed a zit above his chin that I hadn't seen, patted down his hair over his forehead, and sailed off on his way.

I remained alone with her. I wanted to run away and forget her, but I couldn't get out of there because the garage owner, who had finally acknowledged my existence, looked at me inquisitively, the way you look at a rare animal, and again declared that it had been a divine miracle and that God loved me.

'Don't you want to take her out and see how she is?' he asked, and left me no room for indecision: with greasy hands, with absurd ceremoniousness, he opened the car door for me. I sat down heavily on Minimush's driver's seat and she cruelly stabbed me in the behind. I got up in a panic and scrambled out.

'What's wrong?' the owner asked anxiously, and I said that something had stuck into me. Eager for battle he went to the car, his black snail-horn fingers extended, feeling and probing, and with a triumphant cry he offered me on the salver of his hand a square splinter of glass, as perfect as a crystal, and said it was a piece of the shattered windscreen and suggested that I keep it as a memento of the miracle that had happened to me. 'Make a piece of jewellery out of it,' and of their own volition his fingers wandered to his neck, felt around under his shirt and pulled out a yellowish bullet with a hole in it, threaded onto a gold chain. He kissed the bullet, was momentarily embarrassed, and carefully replaced it under his shirt. I knew he was dying for me to ask about the bullet, but I didn't say a word, and he ended our conversation in some disappointment, 'Well, goodbye, and don't worry, your car's in great shape.'

I unclenched my fist and looked at my battle memento, and then closed my hand around it again. I had been stabbed, and yet I felt protected from any misfortune. 'Affliction shall not rise up the second time,' I recalled my father quoting the prophet Nachum. It had already happened to me. A bus had blown up in my face and it wouldn't happen again.

I got into Minimush and started the engine. She gave herself easily to my touch and took to the road, her new tyres drumming ostentatiously on the surface. I urged her on and tried to become as one with her again, to talk to her and blend into her movements as in the past. But my car was a stranger, it ignored me and didn't accede to my requests.

Its outer skin had been preserved, but its soul had left it with the bus that had exploded.

And the stench. The stench I thought I'd got rid of cunningly came in through the air vents and crawled round my ankles, clasped them in its sickening transparent arms and climbed up me until it reached my nostrils. I closed the vents and turned off the heating, but as if mocking my efforts the smell continued to flow over me from some invisible source until it finally kicked me out of the car. I closed the windows and doors, imprisoning the reek inside like a dangerous animal.

I flagged down the first taxi that came along and asked the driver to take me to the university.

In my office I grabbed the telephone and called Nachum's clinic and told Hagit his hygienist, who answered my call in a piping voice full of self-importance, that I needed Nachum urgently and I didn't care if he was in the middle of complicated gum surgery. I told him I was fine, but the car stank and I couldn't drive it and I'd left it on Hebron Road, and that he should come right away.

Nachum sighed and said I was just being hysterical, and resignedly declared that he would pass up his lunch and pick me up, and we'd drive to my car together. When he disconnected I waited for a couple of seconds. It was not without reason that I suspected something when I heard the click of the receiver being replaced, and I knew that Hagit had again listened to my conversation with him, and she'd certainly heard him call me 'hysterical'.

A dense stench trapped inside the car and trying to escape assailed me as I opened the door. But Nachum declared that it was the smell of fresh paint and new brakes, and nothing was smelling and that I'd disturbed him for nothing. I insisted that we swap cars, and he grumbled, 'You'll scratch it. You're not used to driving a big car,' and I said, 'Then I'll use taxis all day,' and he was alarmed, 'But that'll cost the earth.' He eased himself into my small car, adjusted the seat and the mirrors, and with hands unused to a manual gearshift he stuttered away. I sat down on the leather seat of his splendid boat and hurriedly drove away.

I went back to Talpiot and parked outside a recently opened car showroom. Coloured banners fluttering around the building promised inexpensive, safe and economical Korean cars. I went inside, dizzied by the abundance of models and colours. And as if buying a new car was an everyday occurrence for me, I pointed at a blue car and said, 'That one.' I called my bank and asked them to release funds from my provident and study funds, and didn't care when the manager himself said that they hadn't yet matured and I would incur penalties.

I wanted to have the new car right there and then, and was disappointed when the smooth-talking salesman in an orange jacket told me winningly that I'd have to wait between a week and a fortnight, and asked my name and repeated it over and over: 'Yael, if you want the car right away, or tomorrow to be more precise, you can have this red one. I've got to honest with you, Yael, it's got some miles on the clock, because we've used it for test drives. Yes, Yael, you're right, it's got a few scratches, but they'll come off easily with waxing.'

I hesitated for a moment because I was thinking of Nachum who had never liked red cars and scorned the people who drove them and called them all kinds of rude names. But the salesman quickly stepped in with a promise of compensation, a new stereo system, and was already leading me to the office to sign the papers for the red car.

Excited by the first significant purchase I'd made in my life, I didn't go back to work but went to visit them in Nachum's car.

I enquired in which bloc and plot the Wassersteins were, and drove slowly through the marble labyrinth of the dead until I reached the place. There were two mounds of earth there, side by side, one large and the other small. Small stones had been placed on them, memorial candles planted in the soil were burning, and small wooden markers announced simply that here lay Batsheva Wasserstein, née Cohen, and David Wasserstein, may the Lord avenge their blood.

I stood looking at the fresh graves for a long time. Then I found myself asking Batsheva's permission. Permission to love her husband.

In the distance I heard the gravel crunch under the hurrying feet of the stretcher bearers, and the subdued voices of the people following the deceased. I was suddenly engulfed in a tumult, and tens of thousands of offspring of 'the odious drop', seminal fluid, the children of Lilith, transparent and bodiless, were pulling at the hem of my clothes, making me remember the study I'd abandoned and rebuking me harshly for my laziness. I shook my clothes and pulled my hand away from their tacky clasp. These children are dangerous, Warshavsky had told me. They flock to the funerals of their fathers to claim their part of the inheritance. In their grief they may take pieces from the body of the deceased, and sometimes they attack his legitimate children. I gave him my anthropological opinion that the attempts to keep them away probably stemmed from the fear that these children, that have no substance, will tell the legitimate children stories best kept secret, describe the father's deeds and count all the 'odious drops' he had ejaculated in the course of his life. Warshavsky blushed and said that my theory was interesting, but that in any case they had to be exorcised, either by shaking the stretcher or by reciting psalms and circling the grave.

I wanted to flee from there, far from the children of Lilith, from the *Hevra Kadisha* people, the tears, the graves and the mourners. And suddenly I decided that I never again wanted to see a funeral, and I'd never again sit in a house of bereavement I didn't know.

Before I left I placed two small stones on the mounds of Batsheva and Davidl, and made my way out of the world of the dead, from the ghosts and the demons and the children of Lilith.

At the cemetery gate I washed my hands three times and didn't dry them, and explained the custom to a young woman who had come out and was standing weeping at my side by the tap. She told me through her tears, 'But you don't look religious.' I didn't reply and hurried away.

Then suddenly I saw him walking straight towards me. Dragging his feet, his shoes scuffing the gravel, his head slightly bent and his eyes to the ground.

And as if we'd arranged to meet exactly at that place and time, I hurried to him. I walked towards him heavily and the gravel crunching beneath my feet echoed the sound of the gravel crunching under his. My heart pounded wildly as I came up to him, barring his retreat route.

He raised his eyes and his look flickered over me and away, and he immediately lowered his gaze. I knew he hadn't recognised me.

'Avshalom?' I said, and he again raised his eyes and again I was washed by blue sea waves, and I could see the wheels in his brain turning, trying to place me in time and place.

'Yael,' I said, making it easier for him, 'Yael Maggid.'

'Mrs Maggid?'

I nodded and he asked, 'What are you doing here?'

Stammering, I said I was an anthropologist researching burial customs in Jerusalem and so I was here, and he said he was on his way to visit them.

In my stupidity I mumbled, 'May you know no further sorrow,' and immediately remembered that he no longer had a family. He nodded politely, as if I'd wished him long life or some similar blessing, and walked away.

I wanted to run after his retreating back. To explain to tell him I'd fallen in love with him. Apologise that it hadn't happened to me for many years. Describe my love for him as a kind of nagging thought that wouldn't go away. But I didn't say a thing.

Trembling all over I walked back to the car and thought of what my mother would have said about this meeting. She certainly would have claimed that nothing happens by accident. Everything's decided in heaven. Even the death of Batsheva and Davidl had to happen so that I would meet him.

As I started the car I told myself that I'd met him purely by chance. There had been no intervention of fate. His loved ones had died and he was visiting their graves. I tried to slow the beating of my heart that was galloping crazily. But my body betrayed me. I had no control over my heart, I thought, it was just a muscle. The cardiac muscle. It decides when to gallop and when to be calm.

On the way home I stopped in Beit Zafafa, in the parking lot in front of Faradus, the grocery store owned by the brothers Naim and Abdallah, that was also open on Saturdays and the Jewish holidays. From behind the cash register I was warmly welcomed by the younger brother, Naim, who quickly came out from behind the counter and informed me with a shy smile that they'd just received a fresh shipment of Shamouti oranges, the ones I always bought from him, and he also had hot *pittas* fresh from the oven, and hummous, and cooked fava beans. We walked together through the spacious shop that was empty of customers.

I shrank at the sight of the piles of withered lettuce, wizened carrots, unwanted bananas that had blackened, and felt sorry for the brothers Naim and Abdallah and for the fruit and vegetables that were rotting and fermenting in their boxes. I went over to a pile of avocados and took one whose skin was hard, but the fruit split at my touch and spread a smooth, dark and revolting paste over my hand. I wiped it on my jeans so that Naim wouldn't see, and was guided to a pile of red, overripe tomatoes. I carefully felt a few – they were all too soft, and Naim said quietly that they were good for cooking. I stuffed a few into the plastic bag he handed me, and thought that I'd make spaghetti sauce from them. I chose a few more items and Naim went back behind the counter and apologised for the quality of the produce, and said that since the bus 'that blew up right here outside', it had been a week since he'd had any customers from Gilo.

Before I unloaded my shopping onto the counter I hurried to the bathroom. The crumbs of the *challah* I'd spread in the bath clouded the water. My fish lay panting on the white bottom. I took out the plug and opened the tap with fresh water for him. It seemed that the fish had revived a bit and was getting back to himself when his head broke the surface and he avidly gulped the air. I sat on the edge of the bath for a long time wondering what I was going to do with him. My hands pursued him in the water, but he, despite his weakness, evaded my grasp, slipping between my fingers. I took out the plug again, drained the bath until he was lying on the desolate bottom, stunned and damp and flopping about. I grasped his tail with revulsion, threw him into the mop bucket and filled it with water. I went downstairs with the bucket and my fish in it to Nachum's car and drove to the university campus at Givat Ram. The elderly guard at the gate rummaged in my purse and glanced into the bucket and wanted to know what I meant to do with the fish. I barefacedly lied that it was for research purposes in the School of Biology, and the guard said, 'You'd do better to take it home and make some *gefillte* fish.' I thought about throwing it into the fountain by the administration building, but it was dry and a few dusty coins thrown in by students and visitors lay on the bottom. I went on with my search until I found a small pool covered with water lilies by the side entrance to the botanical garden. I poured my fish into it and he said goodbye with a couple of flips of his tail. I knew I'd saved his life.

In the evening Nachum came home and solemnly announced that he'd driven my car all day and it was in great shape, didn't smell and didn't stink. 'I can't touch that car,' I told him that night, 'as far as I'm concerned you can get rid of it, I'll never drive it again.' And Nachum looked at me compassionately and suggested that I consult Nechama or any other psychologist, 'Because that smell's inside your head, I can't smell it, Hagit couldn't smell it, nobody could smell it.' I wanted to ask him why Hagit was sticking her nose into my car, and I raised my head from the pillow, leant back on the headboard, and said, 'I've got to talk to you.' His body tensed and his face became grave, and he lifted himself up too, and sat beside me, his breath shortened in excited expectation.

'I bought a new car,' I announced drily without looking at him, and quickly added that I'd opened my provident fund and I'd be getting the keys tomorrow.

His voice rose in a sharp scream: 'You bought a new car? Are you crazy? Without talking to me?' and immediately tried to control his voice and asked calmly, 'What kind of car did you get?' I told him I didn't remember what make, but it was a Korean car.

'How could you buy a car and not know what make it is?' he panted, albeit he again tried to control himself and added, 'Anyway, it's your money, you can do whatever you want with it, and you didn't have to use the lame excuse of the smell to buy a new car.' I wanted to ask him what I hadn't asked earlier, what exactly was Hagit doing in my car, and suddenly realised that I didn't really care, and I turned my back on him and said I wanted to go to sleep.

Sleep that night was light and brief, and this time I blamed it on the excitement of getting my new red car.

Me? I ask

My mother called in the morning and over the line sang, 'Happy Birthday to You', reminding me that it was my birthday, and 'Thirty-five today,' she had to grandly add my age. And I thought of my father, who once told me that thirty-five is the age we should leave this world; because thirty-five years is more or less the life span of our teeth, and once the teeth go it's time to return your soul to The Creator, just like sheep that die at five or six, once their teeth have become worn from chewing and ruminating. From the end of the bed Nachum asked, 'What did your mother want?' 'Nothing, just asking how I am,' I replied, and wondered whether he'd remember my birthday.

He drove me to the car showroom and completely ignored me during the journey. Excited, I went inside and with great ceremony was handed the keys and the promised radio. The heady fragrance of a new car banished any thoughts of the smell of burning, and the thought popped into my mind that somebody really should invent a spray with the smell of a new car, one that you could squirt into an old car and give its owner the illusion of freshness and renewal. I put the small fragment of Minimush's windscreen that I'd kept as a memento on the dashboard, switched on the wipers and together with them erased the vague guilt feeling evoked by my betrayal of my old car. I wondered about what nickname Yoavi would invent for the new vehicle when he saw it for the first time, and what I'd tell him when he asked about Minimush.

Loud laughter wafted towards me in the department's corridor.

Louisa was sitting at my desk surrounded by a small drove of visiting tutors from Tel Aviv University. Her great legs, encased in alluring black net stockings, were crossed provocatively, and she was laughing loudly at a joke someone had told as her bangles accompanied the laughter. As if it wasn't my office as well, I self-consciously stood in the doorway and she called, 'Come in, come in, you've got to hear this one,' and asked a young tutor whose sweet face was like a child's to retell the circumcision joke. He repeated it, blushingly, and again they all burst into roars of laughter, and I cleared my throat and made a supreme effort but didn't even manage a chuckle, and so as not to insult him I smiled and said, 'Very funny.' Now I realised that since that day I hadn't laughed once. Maybe I'd forgotten how? Just like my father, when he had reached that place, and had seen his family being led to the crematorium, his laugh had fled from him and vanished. Like machinery in everyday use – when it isn't oiled, it gets rusty and its cogs become eroded and finally it's thrown onto the scrap heap.

After he came to Israel he had forced himself to laugh now and again, but despite his efforts all he'd managed to get out were the muffled sounds of stifled weeping. And my mother, who possibly loved him because of this, tried to teach him how to laugh. When she first met him on the Tel Aviv beach, so she told me, he was all skin and bones, his lips twisted sideways and his smile worn and bitter, revealing more than it wanted to obscure. He smiled so as not to weep, she said.

Back then she was a young girl, laughing and carefree with sun-gold curls, brown skin and a freckled face. Every Saturday she'd sit by the lifeguard's tower with boys and girls her age, standing out like a traffic sign in the red swimsuit she'd knitted for herself. Around midday when the sun was at its zenith, the tower cast a shadow over the gang and they'd lie next to each other, a boy's head on a girl's stomach, and tell stories and joke, and their stomachs shook with laughter and the heads on them bounced and bounced.

Week after week he'd sit there, looking at the happy band, his body roasting in the sun. Until she saw him and said to her friends, 'Look at that poor survivor, he's so alone,' and she invited him to join them, just like that. Awkward and embarrassed, red from the sun and his shame, he got up and she made room for him on her towel, and he, his arms folded on his chest, sat on the edge as if afraid of defiling it with his touch. She told him not to be shy and asked to see the blue number tattooed on his arm, and asked him questions about that place, and he answered evasively in polished school Hebrew, and made them all laugh, including her. The following Saturday he was waiting for them on the beach as usual, and again she asked him to join them, and thus week after week, until he became a member of the crowd and he'd get there early and keep the shadiest place under the lifeguard's tower.

My mother, who hadn't realised that she'd begun falling in love with him, had stubbornly tried teaching him to laugh, and asked him to go to a movie at the Mograbi Cinema. She had laughed aloud and he stared sadly at Charlie Chaplin and his pity went out to the pathetic *nebbech* in tramp's clothing. But she didn't give up and started clowning and wearing weird clothes and hats and making funny faces. And he'd stare at the girl making a laughing stock of herself while not arousing a laugh from him. When nothing came of her efforts, she'd tickle his armpits and feet, which were particularly sensitive, and he responded to her efforts with deep sighs. Once again she patiently explained how you lift up the corners of your mouth, and show your teeth and breathe in and out while vibrating the soft palate and uvula, and she opened her mouth wide and showed him her uvula, and he wanted to please her and let out a loud bleat. As a last resort she sat facing him one day and laughed loud and long for no reason, trying to infect him with her laugh. And so it became a habit, and she fell in love with this man who was in love with her, and she'd laugh and laugh until a web of deep wrinkles was etched at the corner of her eyes, and he'd look at her lovingly and call her 'comedienne', but wasn't infected by her laughter.

'While he was there with another six million,' her father, my grandfather, who died before I was born, had told her, 'we here were eating our fill and going swimming in the sea and to the cinema. He is a true hero,' she said, repeating his words for me, because heroism is the ability to withstand such suffering day after day and year after year, to lose everything and to go on wanting to live.

As if in thrall my mother was drawn to his suffering and sought to bring him salvation. She begged him to tell her, seeking to peep into the dark abyss that gaped in his soul, and when he refused she kissed him on the lips, entreating and assuring him that she would be strong, and even if she saw the depths she would not be over-come with giddiness and be drawn into them. But he, trapped in his solitude, constantly on his guard and suspicious, persisted in his refusal. Haunted by guilt that she had not been there with him, my mother wanted to know everything that had happened, she read books, listened daily to the search for lost relatives programme on the radio, and followed people in the street who had numbers tattooed on their arms. The more she investigated, the less she understood. When I was older she taught me to ask him questions and listen to him, and then she'd ask me what he'd said and related, and then compare her knowledge with mine. He would inject his anguish into me without words, like poison flowing from an IV bag drop by drop right into an open vein. His fear flowed through me, gnawed at my flesh and sucked the marrow from my bones, I was afraid that my own fate would be similar to that of the little girl with the huge ribbon in her hair, whose photograph I'd found in his drawer. I thought about her often and tried to compare my face with hers and my likes and dislikes to hers. Did she, like me, like tomato salad, did she like to skip rope and go to the beach, how many girlfriends did she have, and did my father rub her back with arak when she wasn't well.

Together with him I'd listen to the search for lost relatives programme on the radio and then watch him go into the yard for a smoke, that's what he told me, and he'd stand by the high fence that surrounded the house, his shoulders shaking with stifled sobbing. I didn't tell him that at the Holocaust Remembrance assembly at school, I, his daughter, had been chosen to deliver the annual address. I had proudly declaimed what my mother had dictated about my father, that he was a Holocaust survivor, loudly recited the number tattooed on his arm, and added that when he had come out of there he had looked like a skeleton, and when you looked at him today it was hard to believe that he was the same man.

On that special day Father would flee the house and come home late at night, and in the morning his breath would be redolent with the fumes of anise. Once, during an argument between them, I heard him tell Mother that those Ashkenazi Jews had taken every-thing from them, and now they were even robbing us of the Holocaust.

When he found a job as chief mechanic at a textile factory in

Bnei Brak and was given, for key money, a small apartment in Jaffa whose Arab tenants had fled in the war, they decided to get married. But he had a condition: they would not have children. He didn't want children, my mother told me years later. She lived with him like that for almost twenty years, and went through three abortions to please him; only when she thought her time had passed and she stopped taking precautions, she carried me in her belly for five months and didn't tell him, until he remarked that she was putting on weight.

Louisa looked at me with some concern and told the tutors who had been telling a string of jokes about circumcision and foreskins, '*Yalla*, enough, move it, we've got to work a bit.' They left the room leaving echoes of their laughter behind, and she slid off my desk, pulled up a chair, sat down, and asked me to sit beside her, stroked my cheek and said, '*Ma chérie*, what's to become of you? You know that since the disaster you were in I haven't heard you laugh.' And I said, 'But what can I do, I don't feel like laughing.' 'It will probably come back,' she said, 'just give it time.'

My father's laugh came back on the day I was born. Mother liked to describe how my fifty-something-year-old father had looked at the squalling bundle cradled in her arms, and on his lips a tiny smile had dawned, a minuscule smile, that spread all at once and took hold of all the wrinkles on his face, and suddenly his laugh came back. She said that his eyes had laughed, too, and she was infected by his laugh as she sat in her bed with me in her arms, and she laughed so hard that her whole body rocked, trembling and languishing from the difficult confinement. The nurse who came running took me from her in fright, fearful lest the poor baby be dropped onto the floor. Since that day laughter had dwelt in our home. They both laughed at the simplest of things, stifled giggles could be heard late at night from their bedroom, and laughter accompanied me next morning as they looked into each other's eyes and laughed for no reason at all; when my father came home from work and she fell into his arms, they would sniff each other's necks and laugh aloud.'

Just as his laugh had come back, it disappeared again. Immediately after my wedding my father began quarrelling with me over trifles, and Mother would stand at the side and plead with me with a look, leave him be. But I wasn't willing to give up. I didn't see the signs and didn't forgive him for getting old, and thought we were having one of those routine quarrels between a daughter and a father who refused to accept her growing up.

This wasn't how I wanted to say goodbye to him. 'Murderer, murderer!' a stranger screamed at me, his face grey, sunken and contorted with hate. 'Murderer, help!' came the words muffled by the thin blanket that covered a thin and twisted body. Yellowing teeth, revealed to the last molar, smiled at me slyly from a glass of water on the cabinet, and I wanted to ask why they'd taken his teeth from him, and what they were giving him to eat that he no longer needed them. Like a prosecutor in a murder trial he pointed a sharp, rigid finger at me: 'Murderer!' I stroked the accusing finger and the thin arm, whose tattooed number had faded to tiny dots imprinted between the folds of shrivelled skin, and whispered, 'Abba, it's me, Yael, I've come to see you.' But he fixed me with his hollowed eyes whose whites were filmed: 'Go away.' I pulled over a plastic chair, sat down beside him, told him that Yoavi had sent him kisses, and from my purse took out a finger painting in purple and red, with Shoshana the kindergarten teacher's rounded handwriting wishing: 'To Yoavi's Grandpa, a speedy recovery, from Yoavi.' His eyes refused to see, and he whispered as if pleading for his life: 'Go. Go now.'

Shamed by the glances of the other visitors who were also standing there awkward and helpless at their loved one's bedside, I drew the orange coloured curtain and thought that this skinny, withered body was no longer my father. Now the body suddenly got out of bed, the IV needle was pulled out of his arm and blood spurted onto the sleeve of his striped pyjamas. I ran from the room to the nurses' station, grabbed one of them by the arm and in tears uprooted her from her seat and screamed into her astonished face: 'He mustn't wear stripes!' 'What stripes?' she enquired in a thick Russian accent, and I wanted to tell her how, for his birthday, I'd bought him pyjamas, and how he'd looked at the heavy, striped material with eyes drawn into slits, and how he hadn't expressed happiness or hugged me. Next day I found the pyjamas in the big garbage bin in the yard. 'He can't wear stripes,' my mother said, trying to soften the blow, 'it reminds him of there.' But now I just dragged the nurse to his room, our feet tripping over an overturned

IV stand that blocked the doorway like a police barrier, and we saw my father in his wet striped pyjamas on his knees by the bed and bawling like a baby. We lifted him up, fragile and weightless, and she lectured him sternly, 'Mr Shemesh, not nice. Your daughter comes and you do this?' and he looked at me with hatred and hissed, 'Go away.' We took off his pyjama jacket with its bloodstained sleeve, and I could see his deeply sunken chest as if his lungs were in a permanent state of exhalation, and the thin ribs stretched beneath the transparent skin with sparse white hair stubbornly clinging to it. They brought him a clean jacket and I pleaded, 'Maybe you've got one without stripes?' but the nurse replied impatiently, 'No. Everybody here wears stripes.'

Exhausted and vanquished in the final battle of his life, my father lay on his back and only his pale lips mumbled angrily, 'Go away.' The nurse looked at him interestedly, searching for signs that might reveal the reason for this hatred. I avoided her eyes. I smiled bravely and looked for somewhere to hang Yoavi's painting for Grandpa, but couldn't find an appropriate place on the wall with its yellow, sick oil paint. I rolled it up, shoved it into my bag and went out into the corridor.

I was watched by ancient heads from the doorways, like a flock of bald eagles waiting patiently for carrion, their eyes empty, their look hollow, their toothless jaws incessantly chewing their tongues and the inside of their cheeks, and their sinewy feet shuffling in slippers in the measured gait of bowed people with no place to go. Feeble in mind and body, they lay on indulgent mattresses covered with rubber sheets, protection against the betrayals of their bodies, and waited, open-eyed, for their time to come.

'Do you know what they do with babies' foreskins in Israel?' Louisa asked, shaking me out of my gloomy memories and trying to make me laugh, and I replied, 'Louisa, I'm not in the mood for jokes today.' She suggested that we play hooky and go to the Malcha mall, because there was nothing like shopping to raise the spirits, and I said that I'd already bought myself a new car that morning. She raised her eyebrows in amazement and said, 'You're kidding! So why aren't you happy?' and I replied that I'd probably feel a lot better tomorrow. 'And we'll have a laugh like we used to?' Louisa begged and I said sure, and recalled how my father's laugh had come back a few days before he passed away. My mother informed me on the phone that he'd suddenly sat up in bed, looked at her and started to laugh. I drove to the hospital like a madwoman, but my father was already lying on his back with his eyes half opened, the way he always slept, so that the Angel of Death wouldn't surprise him. I could see the whites of his eyes, but he couldn't see me by then, and didn't laugh, and didn't cry, and didn't call me 'Murderer'. His chest rose and fell like a bellows, as if after a hard run, his urine collection bag was filled with orange-coloured fluid and nobody had come to change it, and the IV stand stood uselessly in the corner with bent head. Anton, the Filipino who relieved my mother at night, stood at my side and crossed himself. I ran out and burst into the doctors' room and shouted to his doctor, asking what was happening to him, to my father, to Mr Shemesh. He shrugged helplessly and raised his eyes to the fluorescent strip lighting humming on the ceiling, as if trying to hint that now everything was in God's hands. 'But why hasn't he got an IV, why hasn't anybody changed his bag?' and the doctor said, 'Please calm yourself, madam, it will only be another few hours.' 'What will?' I asked, but the doctor had already turned his back to me.

We stayed there all night until my mother asked me to go because Yoavi was probably missing me, and I drove to Jerusalem. When I reached home Nachum was waiting at the door, the telephone in his hand and his look saying it all. When I got back there, they told me he'd died in my mother's arms.

On the way to the hospital I knew that my mother had done it to me again. Even at the moment of his death she hadn't wanted me with him. I only plagued her in life. They should never have had me.

She hadn't let them take her away, they told me at the hospital, she said he'd wake up soon, and her arms encircled him tightly and her nails dug into his cooling flesh, until the doctor came and gave her a sedative injection and loosened her fingers from his body.

Tears suddenly flowed from my eyes and Louisa hugged me and said, 'Yaeli, come on, stop it now, how about some ice cream?' and she pulled me up from the chair and propelled me all the way to the cafeteria, her bangles jangling gaily. We sat facing the arid vista of the Judean Hills spread before us, and I felt miserable and exhausted like an old woman when Louisa enthusiastically told me about the arrangements she'd made for the hall and the flowers, that would be red and white, and how grateful she was that I'd introduced her and Yoram. I giggled bitterly and heard myself saying, 'Louisa, who knows, maybe one day you'll blame me for it,' and she bristled, 'Stop it, Yaeli, what's wrong with you, snap out of it,' and suggested that the four of us go to a movie together in the evening. I told her that Nachum would be home late.

When we got back to the office I tried to immerse myself in the lesson I had to give, but couldn't concentrate, and Louisa came in with a bunch of colourful anemones and kissed my cheek and said, '*Mazal Tov, ma chérie*, may you have a long and happy life, and don't think for one minute that I'd forgotten.' Grateful for the gesture I asked when her birthday was and she said, 'What, you've forgotten already?' She'd had her twenty-eighth birthday about two months earlier, she reminded me, and I thought of my father, whose life had begun at Louisa's age, or so I believed, for there hadn't been a single photo of him as a baby or little boy at home, and when I was little I thought that there were people who were born grown up. He had been twenty-eight when he had been photographed at the military hospital after his liberation from the camp, his eyes sunken and his cheeks fallen as if he was sucking them into his mouth. His skinniness was obscured by a jacket far too big for him, and his stick-like legs in short pants looked like pestles in a mortar inside the impressive leather boots he'd taken from a dead German soldier.

In the afternoon I went to Shoshana's kindergarten, I opened the red door, and the new-car smell met the children, and Yoeli jumped in, yelling happily, 'A new car, a new car.' Yoavi stood by the door, his big honey eyes staring at me in frightened surprise. I explained that this was my new car and his face darkened: 'Where's Minimush?' 'Minimush was so very old that I had to replace her,' I said. He immediately asked, 'And she wasn't hurt?' I tried to placate him and said that Minimush was just a car, an old car that had to be replaced by a new one, but he wouldn't let up: 'But where is she now?' I mollified him, saying that the people who'd buy her would take good care of her and love her just like we had. 'But when you're old I won't change you,' Yoavi reassured me and finally agreed to get in. 'We'll miss her, won't we?' he said, and immediately, as if the whole thing had been forgotten, started jumping on the new seats with Yoeli, and the plastic covering reminded me of Davidl's new bed and Avshalom and his wonderful hands. And Yoavi's head was already stuck out of the window announcing to the kindergarten children standing inside the fence, 'My Ima's got a new red car!' and one of them who was hanging on the fence and whose face was smeared with chocolate spread, retorted, 'So what? My Abba's car is bigger.' We drove home, Yoeli imitating a car engine and his hands spinning an imaginary steering wheel, and Yoavi deep in thought at his side. I thought that Yoavi had never played with cars and never asked to sit in the driving seat. I asked him what he wanted to call the new car and he looked at me through the rear view mirror and said, 'First we've got to get to know her and then we'll see.'

When we got home I poured them both a glass of chocolate milk and made sandwiches, and then I said I was tired, and on my thirty-fifth birthday I shut myself up in the bedroom in mourning, the same mourning that had been continuing since my childhood, when I grieved for my father many years before he died. I had never forgotten that in his heart of hearts he constantly looked forward to being reunited with his murdered family.

Later that afternoon I drove the children to Nechama's and she greeted me with a bear hug and asked me to keep some time free for her in the evening, 'So we can celebrate your birthday together,' and she opened the fridge door to reveal a sumptuous chocolate cake she'd bought for the occasion. I promised I'd do my best to get back early, and from my new car called the number I'd found in the health maintenance organisation's directory, and made an appointment to see a 'homoeopath specialising in bedwetting problems'.

Beneath the cold hum of the fluorescent light the specialist asked me since when had I suffered from nocturnal bedwetting, and I squirmed a little and said, 'It's my three year-old son.' He stared at me accusingly and asked, 'When did you get divorced?' I stammered that I was still married, and was immediately shocked by my use of the word 'still', lest a prophecy that would come true had wormed its way into my words.

'I can't treat a bedwetting child by remote control,' the specialist stated, and demanded that I come to the next appointment with the child and the father, because we had to talk about the child's emotional state at home and the kindergarten. Then he said that in

133

contrast to psychotherapy, homoeopathy helps children who won't necessarily cooperate with a psychologist. I kept quiet when he asked if something had happened at home, if something in the child's environment had changed and, encouraged by my silence, he promised to prepare a homoeopathic medicine that would balance the child's subconscious, treat the root cause of the problem and return him to optimal functioning. I thanked him and paid his exorbitant fee without batting an eyelid. As a parting shot he declaimed about the symbolism according to which water is analogous to emotion, and the release of water through urination is like an emotional release.

I knew I wouldn't go back to him. After all, Nachum, who believed solely in conventional medicine, would never agree to therapy with anybody he viewed as a charlatan and a humbug. On the way to Nechama's I considered whether I should ask her for help, but the whole business of bedwetting was immediately forgotten when she opened the door with a big smile, blocked it with her behind and said she wasn't going to let me out until we'd celebrated properly, and led me to the table on which the cake stood proudly with a single candle stuck into it. Yoeli and Yoavi were standing by the table, and with tiny, eager fingers were picking at the chocolate icing.

Afterwards Nechama laid on the table two drawings the boys had done, each bearing the legend 'Mazal Tov', and Yoeli had even signed his name in mirror writing and crooked letters, and they all sang 'Happy Birthday' hugely out of tune, and we all had cake that was a little too rich. I didn't tell her about my visit to the homoeopath.

When I got home with Yoavi, Nachum welcomed me with a triumphant smile, as if to say, you thought I'd forgotten, eh? On the table stood a huge bouquet of white gladioli, their thick stems stuck into the awful cut glass vase that had been bequeathed to Nachum by his late mother.

In bed that night he handed me a small box and a thin gold bracelet glinted at me from its purple velvet cushion. 'Nice, isn't it?' he said, 'I ran all over town to find you a present.' I wanted to ask him why he'd bought me a piece of jewellery, because I didn't wear jewellery, and whether Hagit had helped him choose it, but I held back. He clasped the bracelet around my wrist and said, '*Mazal Tov* my sweet.'

I wanted to weep but couldn't.

In the morning Yoavi jumped into our bed and his pyjamas were dry and warm, and he asked me to take him to the bathroom. He proudly showed me his semi-erect penis, and announced: 'Now it's hard and it's nice, and after I've done a pipi it'll be soft.'

When I went to pick him up from the kindergarten in the afternoon, I met Shoshana and she looked at me with overweening friendliness and loudly addressed me as 'Dr Maggid', so that the other mothers waiting at the gate should know that she had children in her kindergarten whose parents were doctors. I asked her how Yoavi was and she said just fine, and when I saw him running towards me in the trousers he'd worn in the morning, I was relieved and thought that perhaps the problem had resolved itself.

In the evening we hosted the monthly residents' meeting. I got home breathless from the university and quickly tidied the living room, then put Yoavi to bed and he insisted on us singing 'What do the trees do?' and only when we got to the last line, 'What do I do? No-o-thing! I just ask,' he consented to close his eyes.

In the doorway, ten minutes late, stood our chairman Micha Barnea, and one after another came his flock of chickens, so Nachum called his yes-women deputies. Micha sank heavily into Nachum's TV chair, adjusted the backrest, drummed on the arms with his thick fingers that were covered with a tangle of curly red hair, studied those present with half-closed eyes, smiled at one woman and scowled at another and announced, 'So let's begin.'

I half listened to the balance sheets he read quickly and to his claims of a rise in the price of central heating fuel this winter. Then came the main item on the agenda: The Situation. It was unanimously decided to impose a special levy on the residents, a security levy, for renovating the front door and the intercom, because in such troubled times we had to prevent the entry of undesirables, and that at the same time, if there was a little money over, the mailboxes would also be refurbished. I interjected and put the question that had been bothering me all the time, 'And what about the honeysuckle?' and Micha asked, 'What honeysuckle?' and I replied, 'The fragrant honeysuckle. The hedge at the entrance that died a long time ago.' And the chickens cackled as if on command, and Micha glared at me and said, 'Fragrant honeysuckle? That's all you're thinking about when we're trying to raise the level of security in the building?' and he rejected my question and announced that he would not bring the matter up for discussion. I didn't give up. I raised my voice and said that we had to do something about the garden before the spring because it was in a terrible state. But Micha had already adjourned the meeting and I heard myself screaming at him, insulted, 'Why aren't you willing to discuss my request?' and he fired a barb at me from his eyes and then fixed them on Nachum as if demanding that he control his wife, and my husband may-he-live-and-be-healthy shrugged as if telling him in sign language, I gave up hope long ago, and I shouted, and couldn't believe that the shouts were coming from me, that the garden was no less important than security and that anyone who doesn't plant a garden is not thinking about tomorrow. And Micha raised his hand and said in a conciliatory tone, the way you speak to a fractious child, 'Mrs Maggid's right, but because of The Situation there are priorities,' and emphasised the last word proudly and added that if Mrs Maggid wanted a garden, then she should enlist a few women volunteers, and threw a glance over the room and his flock of chickens cowered in their chairs. 'Buy some plants,' he suggested, and added innocently, 'how much can a few plants cost? Bring me the receipt and I'll find a few shekels to cover the cost.' When he said goodbye he patted my shoulder in a gesture of appeasement and Nachum said, 'Hold on a minute, Micha.' And Micha blocked the doorway with his thick body and I heard them whispering and I could have sworn that Nachum told him, Look, since that episode she had she's been a bit unbalanced.

So why? Because

'Now we're going to play like big boys,' Nachum announced as from behind his back he pulled out a round package wrapped in crinkly orange paper with a blue butterfly stuck on it, handed it to Yoavi and said, 'It's a present for you.' Yoavi eagerly tore off the wrapping paper, revealing a red plastic ball, and immediately came over to me, stuck it into my hands and started playing with his dolls. Nachum didn't give up, he grabbed him under the arms and plucked him out of the heap of toys surrounding him in a soft, coloured circle, lifted him up until they were face to face, and said slowly: 'Yoavi, enough with the dolls, now we're going to play like big boys, and Abba's going to teach you to play football.' Yoavi's legs flailed the air and Nachum relented and stood him on the floor, took the ball from me, placed it in front of his right foot and kicked it gently towards Yoavi. The child became frightened and covered his eyes with his hands, ran to me and buried his head between my legs. Tight-lipped, Nachum went over to him again, tore him away from me, turned him around and hissed, 'Then we'll play catch.' He told him to hold out his hands and threw the ball to him from a short distance, but Yoavi's hands opened and the ball fell to the floor and bounced softly.

Still Nachum didn't give up: 'Now watch how Abba plays catch with Ima,' and threw the ball to me. I caught it and threw it back to him, but it hit the sideboard and his mother's cut glass vase with the white gladioli that were already yellowing, rocked slightly as it considered falling to the floor. Nachum ran to it, steadied it and said angrily, 'Your mother throws a ball like a girl,' and Yoavi turned his back to us and said, 'I don't like balls,' and went to his room. 'Your son can't even catch a ball,' Nachum shouted bitterly. When he was disappointed in him he called him 'your son', and only infrequently, when he wanted to boast about him, called him 'my son'.

As he was about to leave for the clinic, he stopped at the door as if remembering something: 'Don't you think it's time he had his hair cut? With all those curls he looks like a girl.' The door had just clicked shut when Yoavi's head peeped out of his room, his eyes wide: 'Has Abba gone?' he asked, and when I nodded he came to me, hugged me and whispered into the hollow of my neck, 'Is Abba angry with Yoavi?' and I planted my lips on the top of his head so that he wouldn't see my eyes and know I wasn't telling the truth: 'Angry? Of course not! Abba loves Yoavi very much.'

But I knew that he knew I was lying.

When Nachum came home late that night and announced that he was 'dead tired', I let him fall asleep alone and stole into Yoavi's room, stroked his head perspiring on the pillow, followed his rapid eye movements as they danced in a dream beneath his almost transparent eyelids, brushed the damp curls from his forehead and gathered them in my hand; I tried picturing him with long hair gathered into a bouncing ponytail, just like Davidl's, and I thought of Davidl's father, Avshalom. I longed to see him and his beautiful hands again, talk to him about what had happened, tell him about Yoavi, and inform him that since that terrible day that had bound us together, my life was not the same anymore.

On Friday evening we entertained friends for some gloomy staring at the TV set and filling bellies with peanuts and other such non-nourishing delicacies. Yoavi, who had woken up, burst into the living room, Teddy Bear in his arms and Tutti over his mouth, and complained that he couldn't sleep.

'Oh, how long his hair is,' Louisa enthused, 'he's as sweet as a little girl.'

I glanced at Nachum and saw the horrified expression on his face. 'Yael thinks it's nice,' he said and looked around for support and understanding. 'She'll grow his hair and in the end she'll take him to Meiron for that religious ceremony of the *halakeh*, the first haircut.'

I jumped at the chance: 'You know what, you've given me an idea. That's what I'll do with him! I believe it'll be a powerful experience that will stay with him for the rest of his life.'

There was an embarrassed silence. Louisa jangled her bracelets, shook her curls and displayed her erudition: 'The word *halakeh* is colloquial Arabic, and it means haircut or shaving,' she stated.

Nachum gave one of his bitter smiles and I heard him say to Yoram in a stage whisper, 'I really can't understand her lately. I think that since that episode of the bus she's been a bit unbalanced.' I blushed as sympathetic looks were directed at me, asked who wanted more coffee, and blinded by tears ran into the kitchen with Nechama at my heels. 'Don't let that anal creature do this to you,' she demanded. 'Be strong, don't break down.' And I answered, 'I'm not crying because of him,' and she asked, 'If it's not because of him, then why?' And I blew my nose and said that since that day I couldn't stop thinking about Davidl and his father. 'Why his father?' she asked, astonished.

I finally made my confession to her. I couldn't believe that it was me uttering the words: 'I think I've fallen in love with him.' Nechama burst out laughing and pulled me to her, and in the way you pacify a crying child she tut-tutted and said, 'Enough, enough, *sha, sha*, love, don't cry, it's only a little romantic heartache, a tiny twinge you've decided to cherish. It'll pass.'

After they'd all gone I told Nachum I was tired and that we should leave the washing up until Saturday morning, but he disagreed and stood at the sink in his ridiculous apron with the plastic breasts. I piled more and more dishes onto the draining board and whispered, afraid of waking Yoavi, 'Yes, that's what I'll do. I'll take him to Meiron,' and he murmured something like, 'You're out of your mind,' and 'We'll see.' When he finished the dishes he put a plastic bag round his right hand, and with an expression of disgust on his face collected the damp remnants of food from the stainless steel sink tidy and threw them into the garbage can.

That night he turned his back and didn't speak to me. I didn't know what he was angry about – that I'd let him wash the dishes or Yoavi's long hair. Or maybe both.

After he'd fallen asleep I slipped into Yoavi's room and gave myself up to the nocturnal ritual. In the light of the bedside lamp I sat beside him and ran my fingers through his long hair. Tiny white, shiny and elusive eggs were stubbornly stuck to his hair, hidden and then revealed among his curls, and I declared an all out war on them and thought why did we deserve this. Weren't all the

139

plagues the Jewish people had suffered enough, blood and flames and pillars of smoke? Terrorists, suicide bombers, bombings, economic crises, businesses collapsing, recessions, budget cutbacks, the Sea of Galilee's water level, the shrinking Dead Sea, the plague of road accidents and the plague of killing the firstborn, and on top of all that, now we had a plague of head lice too.

I planned vengeance, because nobody, not even the tiniest of creatures, was going to suck my son's blood. As pearls of sweat covered Yoavi's forehead, I joyfully plunged my fingers into the tangle of his curls and began making mincemeat of them. In the weak light of the bedside lamp I made paths in his hair, opened roads and lay in ambush at the roadside. With the joy of victory and lust for revenge I caught a louse, plucked it from its hiding place, placed it between the nails of my thumb and middle finger and squashed its grey body. I placed the cadaver on a piece of white paper and watched its tiny legs flailing beneath its crushed body. Again my nails were extended, searching for another victim, and Yoavi reminded me of his existence and suddenly fluttered his silken eyelashes, opened his eyes for a second and asked, 'Imush, what are you doing?' and put his hands up as if to brush away an annoying mosquito, and then he lay down, his head filled with undeciphered dreams and hidden lice, and slipped back into the tranquil sleep of babies.

I went back to bed and Nachum and rehearsed the scathing remarks I'd direct at Shoshana the kindergarten teacher in the morning. It was unthinkable that the kindergarten was once again suffering a head lice epidemic, something must be done, announce a group hair-washing campaign, and send home any infected children.

In the morning I ignored her fawning good morning and took her to task saying that Yoavi had caught head lice from one of the children, and demanded that all the necessary steps be taken. She looked at me, shocked, and said that I, too, wouldn't be best pleased if she decided to send Yoavi home because of head lice eggs, and that it wasn't educational and children could develop a trauma. Then other mothers joined the discussion and a small circle closed around us and I could see Shoshana winning them over and them shrugging helplessly. And then Nechama came along with Yoeli, put her heavy hand on my shoulder and whispered, 'Come on, Yaeli, really, head lice aren't our biggest tragedy.' I shook her off and hissed, 'Don't you dare interfere, in any case you couldn't care less if your Yoeli's head is infested with lice and that my Yoavi probably got them from him.' She paled and her hand fell from my shoulder. 'Yael, you're losing it, get a grip.' I left hastily, angrily slamming the iron gate behind me, and I saw Nikolai, the Russian guard, awakening from a doze.

In the afternoon, when I collected Yoavi, I lowered my eyes in the face of Shoshana's angry look as she returned my greeting through clenched lips. Yoavi met me with a long face and on the way home told me that Shoshana was angry with me and Yoeli was angry with him and that the kids had said I was crazy. I turned my head and looked at my son fettered in his car seat and told him, 'Of course you've got a crazy mother. Your mother's crazy about you.' And Yoavi gave me a sad smile and reached out and lifted himself up a little and embraced my neck from the back.

And at night, I again stole into his room to complete the mission. And as my fingers moved towards Yoavi's head as if of their own volition I again saw Lousy Yaeli being sent home with a note from the school nurse safety-pinned to her blouse. And I saw my father, too, and the pallor spreading over his face, and I heard his shouting, into which a note of despair had stolen, that here in the Land of Israel there should be no children with lice and least of all his daughter. And that night in the bathroom with four hands, hers and his, shearing my hair. The scissors clicked mockingly above me and long tresses of honey-blonde hair slid onto the sheet and piled up on the floor. A lethal mixture of equal quantities of kerosene and vinegar was poured over my head and the stinking solution burnt my scalp that was furrowed with fingernail scratches.

My father sat beside me on my bed all night. I wept into the pillow and he silently held my hand. Then he unfolded his handkerchief and dried my tears and consoled me saying that he promised that my hair would grow again very quickly and be even more beautiful than the hair that had been shorn. I went to school with my head covered with a colourful bandanna, and they called me 'Lousy' and 'Turniphead' and 'Baldy'.

My father's promise didn't come true. Just like his promise that I'd find myself a man who'd love my freckles and count them one by one.

In the morning I went to the local pharmacy. As I approached the counter an elderly pharmacist hurried over to serve me and I whispered that I wanted a powerful preparation for treating head lice. And he asked, 'What? What?' and I repeated my request and he shouted, 'Ah, head lice.' He searched the shelves and came back with an orange-coloured bottle bearing a gruesome close-up of the disgusting creature and told me, in German-accented Hebrew, 'Only this solution does the job thoroughly. The shampoos you buy at the supermarket only tickle the lice.' A woman standing behind me, her head covered in a coif, suddenly stuck her oar in and said that she too recommended it, and she had, thank God, a lot of children and grandchildren and in her experience only this solution works 'and kills them, and afterwards, because of the smell, they don't come anywhere near the hair.' I ignored her, angry that she'd eavesdropped on our conversation, and turned to leave, but she grabbed my sleeve and added, 'I wish those lice on our enemies, they multiply like the Arabs and should all be killed.' I didn't want to get into a discussion with her, I just turned my back and left. I stood on the corner until I saw her come out, and went back inside and the elderly pharmacist welcomed me warmly and enquired, 'And what have we forgotten?' and I replied with equanimity, as if asking for a carton of milk at the neighbourhood grocery, 'Hypnodorm,' and he asked, 'What, what did you say?' and I hesitantly repeated, 'Hypnodorm?' and he, his eyes narrowing behind the lenses of his glasses, replied, 'Madam, that's only on prescription. It's so strong that we keep it in the safe with all the drugs that can kill you,' and he pointed at a metal door set into the wall.

I left with the orange-coloured bottle with its picture of the monster burning my hand.

I called Nechama in the afternoon and suggested that Yoeli come over to our place after kindergarten, have supper with us and sleep over. Nechama couldn't restrain herself: 'Aren't you afraid of my son's head lice?' I picked them up at the kindergarten. At home they played on the rug and head touched head, and I thought that their lice, that were probably related, were chatting, exchanging confidences and copulating in an orgy with a cast of thousands. I felt a terrible itching on my scalp, and thought that their thread-like legs were running all over me as well. I quickly ran the fine-toothed comb through my hair and screamed in horror at the sight of a grey louse caught in the comb's teeth, its legs flailing helplessly. I quickly drowned it in the sink under a stream of hot water.

In the evening I prepared them a royal banquet. When they'd finished I announced, 'To the bath,' and goose-stepped with them to the bathroom. I emptied a whole bottle of bubble bath into the streaming water and an acrid smell of green filled the closed room. Like desert islands their heads stood out in the sea of bubbles, and they laughed and said and they were bathing in cream and they tried tasting it and screwed up their faces and spat it out. For a long time I heard them laughing and then Yoavi's spoilt childish voice, 'Imush, the water's cold.' I ran in and Yoeli said, 'We're going to melt in the water soon.' I told them to shut their eyes tight, and they screwed up their eyes so hard that it furrowed their foreheads and around their lashes. I lathered their heads with the solution and its reek pervaded the air and Yoavi said, 'Oof, it stinks,' and then he screamed, 'Imush, it burns, it's burning my head!' And Yoeli suffered in silence. I waited five minutes, as the instructions said, and first rinsed Yoavi's head, and I was gratified to see that his slicked hair covered his neck and fell almost to his protruding shoulder blades. Then I rinsed Yoeli's cropped head, and shampooed both their heads with regular shampoo and combed their hair, and between the comb's teeth I could see lice cadavers and dead eggs. I changed the bedclothes in the children's room and our bedroom and shoved them into the washing machine and set it to 'Boil'. Exhausted, the children fell into bed and this time I didn't hear the happy chatter that usually came from there.

Once they'd fallen asleep I went into the bathroom, washed away the last of the foam and washed my own hair with the solution, and rewashed it, ridding myself of every last vestige of the bloodsuckers.

'Abba did it,' said the mite proudly when he greeted me at the kindergarten that day. 'He said I'm a boy, not a girl, and boys don't have long hair.' And as though Yoavi had shed his natural baby sweetness all at once, I could now see the delicate features of a little boy. Beneath the mercilessly cropped hair a pair of huge eyes gazed at me, a curved forehead that had been concealed under the curls, and it was as if the features he would have in his adulthood were now revealed. With small, calculated gulps of air and saliva I choked back the anger that roiled inside me, and could feel it fermenting in my stomach.

I kissed the child's shorn pate, and tiny blond bristles tickled my lips.

That evening Nachum and I didn't exchange a word. That night we quarrelled in low voices behind the closed door. 'How could you do that to me, and behind my back too! Why did his hair bother you? In any case he'll grow it when he's a teenager.'

'What do you want from me?' said Nachum, on the defensive, 'Yoavi was complaining that the kids at kindergarten were bullying him and calling him a girl. I didn't want him to suffer. And apart from that, he's far too delicate, and you add insult to injury by buying him dolls like a girl, and soft toys too. What do you want? To raise a limp-wristed queer?'

I wrapped myself in my robe and grumbled angrily that all those soft toys were compensation for the real animal that Yoavi wanted, a pet, a dog or cat, that Nachum wouldn't permit us to have in the house, claiming that 'They're dirty.'

'Yoavi, before Abba cut your hair, did they call you a girl at kindergarten?' I asked the child next morning.

'It's not true,' the toddler replied, insulted. 'I'm a boy.'

'But the children at kindergarten, what do they call you?' I asked, changing the wording of my question.

'They call me Yoavi.'

And She Conceived and Bore

(Genesis 4, 1)

'And she conceived and bore' – that was how women miraculously conceived and bore children in ancient times of the Bible: Eve the Mother of all Life, our Four Matriarchs, the wives of the Prophets and Judges, the wives and concubines of the Kings. The biblical scribe nimbly skips over the nine months of pregnancy, passes over descriptions of copulation, morning sickness, swollen ankles, mood swings, the rounding belly, the pressure of a weak bladder, the anxiety, the fears, and the death of the husband's desire. Faithful to his method, he also conceals from his readers descriptions of delivery, labour pains, blood, the great tearing, and the scream of the baby.

For the result is what counts: 'And she conceived and bore'.

'If a woman had written our Book of Books,' I told Nechama in the gynaecologist's waiting room, 'she would have definitely found more words other than "and she conceived and bore".'

Yoavi was conceived on January the thirteenth. On that day Nachum came home for a single night's leave from a lengthy stint of reserve service. I started undressing him at the entrance to the house, paving the hallway with his uniform and my clothes. Naked and laughing he skipped behind me into the bedroom, and his trousers and underpants, which had dropped down to the uppers of his chunky army boots, bound his ankles in fabric hobbles and hindered his progress. I pushed him to the bed and he lost his balance, fell heavily onto it and his head banged against the head-board. He lay on his back, his angular legs sticking out, his member erect and sturdy. I fumbled with his laces, untying them impatiently. I removed his dusty boots and pulled off the grey woollen socks, which had hardened with sweat and dirt, from his feet. I pulled his trousers off over his ankles, and in underpants he wrestled with me as if begging for his life. He hadn't bathed in a week and he surely stank. But I bent him to my will. Naked, I sat on him and his fingers dug fiercely into my buttocks until I screamed and he loosened his grip, and I felt him dissolve inside me leaving behind a small puddle that moistened my pubic hair, and he quickly rolled me off him and apologised: 'I wanted you so much that it happened too fast.' Then he rushed into the shower and spent a long time washing off my smell and his, and by the time he returned to me, bathed and perfumed with his member erect and asking for more, I remembered with alarm that I had forgotten to insert the diaphragm, and I ran into the shower and tried to douche the semen out of me with a powerful stream of water.

And she bore. I lay in the labour ward for two days with inducing solutions dripping into my vein. Students and doctors and nurses and all and sundry came and went and pushed their fists into me, and hands wrapped in gloves raped me one after another, and heads consulted over my belly and counted my 'dilation' on their fingers. I wanted to flee, to get off the narrow bed, leave everything and crawl into a cave, where, protected under the cover of darkness and silence, I wanted to give birth to my child. But cold shackles fettered my ankles, the needle of a drip pierced my flesh and dripped poison into my body, and the straps around my stomach were attached to a monitor, emitting sounds of galloping horses. Exhausted and humiliated, hurting and helpless, I felt like an assaulted woman. And then came the mad race to the operating theatre, the hasty shave, the epidural, my feet and hands tied, the screen erected between me and my belly. I heard them talking, I heard the surgeon's instructions and Vivaldi's *Four Seasons* playing in the background, and when 'Spring' came they slashed my stomach from top to bottom, exposed my womb, cracked it open and pulled out the baby. I lay on the bloodstained sheets, hazy from the drugs, and beyond the screen I heard the cries of the baby who had declined to come out. Before I had a chance to recover from the sharp transition between pain and the joy that was expected of me, they showed me the little bundle that was responsible for my suffering, still smeared with my blood and baby wax.

A stranger's gaze opened up at me, steel-grey eyes inspected me, and tiny red and wrinkled hands, like a chick's feet, twitched about in every direction. And I screamed uncontrollably, so Nachum makes a point of repeatedly reminding me, and which torments me each and every day when I encounter Yoavi's sweet face in the morning: 'Take it away from me, I don't want it, I don't want him.'

Everyone present said: 'Congratulations Mummy, you have a boy,' and I cried because I thought my son's fate was sealed and he would die in a terrorist attack or a war. And then, in the middle of all the pandemonium around me, Nachum, whom I'd forgotten, suddenly leant over me and whispered: 'Another soldier for the State of Israel.' I wanted to leap up from the bed with all the tubes and cables attached to me, and with the incision that had not yet been stitched with needle and thread, and stick my fingernails into the face of my son's father and tell him that I hated him, but I didn't have the strength.

The next morning he came to see me bearing a huge bouquet of wilted and pathetic-looking yellow roses, leaned over the transparent cot beside me, and inspected the baby who lay there like an Egyptian mummy, only his serious red face sticking out of its shrouds. The petals fluttered onto the floor and into the cot. Beyond its transparent sides peered sad and pensive eyes like those of an old man. In those moments I believed that the sensory mechanism of newborn babies is more developed than ours. Even this baby, who had been born by mistake, knew that he was unwanted and would never be loved and surely sensed my fears – for he was condemned to die in a terrorist attack.

Nachum tore me away from my thoughts and asked what we should call him, and I said that the flowers he'd brought me had known better days. He practically ran out of the room and I thought he wouldn't come back, but a large plastic bottle of Coca-Cola with its top cut off appeared at the door with him, and he filled it with water, shoved the pathetic bouquet into it, placed it on the cabinet next to me, and said that he hadn't slept all night, that he'd been thinking about the name we'd give the boy, and suddenly blurted out: 'Yoav.'

Yoav, Yoavi, Yo-Yo, I rolled the name around in my head, and forgot about Yoav, the captain of David's host, and only remembered Yoav the hunk from high school who was a year ahead of me and never noticed me. I nodded weakly in agreement.

A whole year passed before I taught myself to take pleasure in his sweet smell, laugh to him and be amazed at his sensitivity. I once apprehensively asked Nechama whether he remembered those bad days of my rejection and fear and whether he would hate me and seek revenge when he grew up.

'Children have a remarkable ability to combine the good and the bad they have experienced in their short lives, and they're blessed with a natural ability to rectify bad experiences,' she soothed me.

But I wasn't soothed. To this day. Because I wanted a girl anyway.

Eight days later, my body battered and exhausted, I stood at the circumcision ceremony, leaning on Nechama, and before averting my eyes from what was taking place I saw Louisa standing very close to the *mohel* and her head almost touched the baby's exposed body. I knew that she wouldn't miss a single stage of the process. With the sobbing of the tormented baby filling the air, the *mohel* announced the name. 'Yoav, Yoav, Yoav,' everyone murmured like an echo, and the *mohel* said ceremoniously: 'This little one will be great, like Yoav the captain of David's host.' His words brought back to me what I had forgotten. Perhaps Nachum was right, I thought, when he said that immediately after the birth I had been afflicted with a kind of temporary madness. That is the only excuse I have to justify the fact that I agreed to the name.

The first night after the circumcision, when the baby screamed in pain in his cot, I read the Second Book of Samuel and the first chapters of the First Book of Kings. The image of Yoav, the blood-thirsty warrior who had thrice betrayed King David's trust, appeared before me with alarming clarity, and David's curse rang harsh and scathing: 'And let there not fail from the house of Yoav one that hath an issue, or that is a leper, or that leaneth on a staff, or that falleth on the sword, or that lacketh bread.' And David's wrath was not assuaged until he commanded his son Solomon, 'And thou shalt bring his hoar head down to the grave,' and the blood he spilled shall return 'upon the head of Yoav, and upon the head of his seed forever'.

I told Nachum that it was unthinkable that my son should be named after a Biblical murderer, and that we had to change his name.

'Of the two of us, you're the Biblical scholar, no? You should have thought about it before.' I heard the contempt in his voice, and said what he wanted to hear: 'I went through a difficult delivery. I was unbalanced.' But he argued that it was too late, that it was impossible to change the name, and if Yoav wanted to change it, he could do so when he was eighteen. Then he added that he hoped his son wouldn't follow my Leftist tendencies, and warned me not to dare take him to any Peace Now rallies, and especially not to 'those lunatic lesbians, those Women in Black of yours', he spat out spitefully.

During my university days I believed that the two peoples, theirs and ours, must repress the harsh memories of the past, forget the fallen, the hatred, the destruction and the lust for revenge. Forgetting, I thought, was a basic condition for settling the Jewish–Arab conflict for, if we didn't forget, the seeds of evil would pass from father to son and from mother to daughter for all generations.

In my first year I had already marched bearing a red and black banner in a Peace Now demonstration outside the Prime Minister's office. A solid chain of police officers protected us from the rabble that cursed and threatened to break through and wreak their vengeance upon us. Later, when I met Nechama, I went with her to a Daughters of Peace rally whose slogans were: feminism, peace, coexistence and incorporating Palestinian women into the discourse, only women would be able to put a stop to the sacrifice of their sons to Moloch. It all sounded to me like the right path towards resolving the conflict. In our audience, young Palestinian women sat in a separate group, well dressed, educated and proud. As if in a fantasy, I only saw the aura and did not delve any deeper, did not bother to decipher the facial expressions, to internalise subtle intonations, or decode the foreign body language. We were living in euphoria in anticipation of peace and did not hear them when they told us that their situation in the Occupied Territories was not good, there were no political horizons, and there wasn't really peace, and we didn't understand when they explained that it was almost impossible to speak of the hardship, the pain, the despair, the injustice. At every meeting they would stand up and attack Israel and the settlements and we in turn would stand up and attack Israel and the settlements, and afterwards I'd go home with a sense of relief that today I had struck a blow for truth, and would go to bed feeling that we had a partner for peace. Later, when the al-Aqsa *intifada* began and our group broke up with a whimper, I remembered how we Jewish women had spoken with them, softly, apologetically, trying to appease them and salve our consciences, and they looked at us with strong resolve. And how I tried in vain to establish an intimate language with them, a language of women, and talked to them about my pregnancy and my longing for a girl. If I had a boy, I said, I would never let him fight your sons. But they fixed me with suspicious looks as if marking me, marking all of us.

Only once, on that ill-fated Friday, when I was four months into my pregnancy, I gave in to Nechama's pressures and joined a group of about ten women dressed in sombre mourning clothes. Together we stood in Paris Square facing the King's Hotel, behind the fountain that had long since dried up and had been converted into a flowerbed. Black, determined, and mute, I carried a banner cut out of black cardboard in the shape of a hand calling to Stop the Occupation, I thought of my father and his map, and I tried to shut out the cursing and swearing that labelled our group 'Lesbian Enemies of Israel. Arab-Fucking Prostitutes', as if the very act of our standing there brought out of the men everything they had against women. And we, silent and proud, stood there and bravely looked our abusers straight in the eye.

My eyes followed a young woman who stood a short distance from our group, her face like that of a statue sculpted from white marble, blue and slightly slanting eyes, her fair hair cropped short. I liked her face and the way she was dressed – a long red coat of soft wool that hugged her slim figure attractively. I'd seen an identical coat in the window of the Summit Boutique but hadn't dared go into the shop because of the price.

The woman stood a short distance away to the side, watching us with great interest, but did not join the revilers. I was sure that she identified with us and was waiting for us to invite her to join us. I smiled at her and she responded with a shy smile. It seemed as if she wordlessly understood me: she approached us, and like a witness in a police identity parade she walked past us, inspecting us with a penetrating gaze. Up close I saw heavily made up eyes, furrows of bitterness that stretched from the corners of her nose down to her chin, and a slightly opened mouth, like an unrealised scream. She lingered in front of me for a long time, and unashamedly stared into my eyes. I lowered my eyes and thought of starting up a conversation with her, but she turned away from me and moved on to Nechama who was standing next to me, and continued walking slowly to the end of the row of demonstrators. Then she slowly retraced her steps until she stood before me once again, and her eyes, like blue barbs, pierced me and refused to let go. I smiled at her in embarrassment, but this time she didn't return my smile. Suddenly her face contorted and she hastily rummaged in her bag, took out an orange and threw it at me. The firm orange struck my stomach hard, and as if in a nightmare I saw her face, twisted with hatred, and a single eye twitching in front of me. She drew closer, raising her hand as if to gouge out my eye with her angular fingers, and whispered in a husky voice: 'Your son will die in a terrorist attack like my son.'

I was horrified. I didn't understand how she could see the baby in my womb, for my stomach was still flat and protected by a heavy coat. I threw down the black cardboard hand and fled, Nechama panting at my heels calling me to stop. She caught up with me in Ramban Street, near my car, and wrapped her arm round me, and I sank into her embrace and sobbed, 'She said my son would die in a terrorist attack like her son.' And Nechama soothed me: 'I was standing right next to you and I heard no such thing. You're just imagining it.' I was angry that she didn't believe me and screamed in the middle of the street, the passers-by looking at me in astonishment: 'But that is exactly, exactly what she said to me!' And Nechama persistently: '*Nu*, and let's say she did curse you. How can an enlightened woman like you believe in curses? And anyway, the woman is insane.' Now she told me that the woman in the red coat came almost every Friday afternoon in search of a victim among the demonstrators and cursed her. I knew she was lying and insisted: 'But how did she know I was pregnant? And that I was going to have a boy?' Nechama shrugged and I said I'd had enough for one day, and drove home burning with horror. As I climbed the stairs I felt the foetus in my stomach kicking for the first time.

Since then death had lain in wait for us like a fuzzy spider patiently and dutifully weaving its web, threading translucent drops of morning dew like a pearl necklace, and a perpetual black cloud hovered over my head, roaring and humming. The evil thoughts assaulted me like green carrion flies. Think positive, I told myself, only positive. Negative thoughts have a way of being self-fulfilling. Afterwards for some reason I wanted to believe that an effective method of preventing the worst was actually to think about it.

I never went back to stand in the square.

But Nachum, who liked to count my sins, would repeatedly remind me of my transgression, even though I made a point of giving a wide berth to that square, even when the Women in Black weren't there.

By Night on My Bed I Sought Him Whom My Soul Loveth

(The Song of Songs 2, 3)

'I'm in love with him.'

Brandishing a sharp knife Nechama carved the bloody steak on her plate and then licked the bloodstained blade intently.

'You're sure you love him,' possibly asking, possibly making a statement.

'I think so.'

She looked at me, and a spark of pity was kindled in her eyes. She chewed and chewed for a long time, and when she finally swallowed the chunk in her mouth she picked up the cigarette that was burning slowly in the ashtray and inhaled smoke deep into her lungs, and blew it onto me, and then lowered her head again to the steak in front of her.

'I can't understand you,' she said in her smoky voice. 'You put all kinds of crazy ideas into your head, and refuse to let go.'

I was silent.

'"I'm in love with him,"' she mimicked me mockingly, 'How do you know? How many times have you even seen him? When did you ever get a chance to talk to him properly?'

After she'd chewed at length and swallowed another chunk of meat, she softened her tone a little: 'You know that this love of yours is hopeless. It's completely fallacious. Nothing but a spoilt woman's daydream. And what worries me most of all ...' I waited tensely to hear what she had to say, but she was concentrating on her fingers that were burrowing in a pile of toothpicks. She selected a toothpick with great care, slowly stripped it of its thin paper and idly picked her teeth. 'And most worrying ...' I reminded her, and she shook herself and removed the toothpick from her mouth and looked at me in genuine concern. 'What worries me most is that you really and truly believe what you're saying. That you were meant for one another because of a coincidence. So what if you saw his son on the bus. He didn't herald anything about love. And don't talk to me about karma and destiny. That suits your mother, not you. You know I don't believe in that nonsense,' she concluded and sat comfortably in her chair, waiting to hear what I had to say. I looked at her: 'Nechama, it's much simpler than you think. I've fallen in love with him. That's all.' She leant towards me: 'So how do you explain that you've fallen in love just like that, one fine day, and with a yeshiva *bocher* no less, whom you barely know.' I tried to justify myself, find excuses, to tell her that it was pointless seeking rational reasons for love.

'You're not convincing me. Perhaps you're convincing yourself,' Nechama said.

I tried again. 'I feel that we have something in common. Perhaps because of his anguish, perhaps that's what draws me to him.'

'Anguish,' Nechama snorted in contempt, emitting plumes of whitish smoke.

And like a fool I continued confessing: 'And also because of his hands, you should see his hands. I fell in love with him when I saw his hands.'

'His hands?' she repeated in disbelief.

'There's something mesmerising about them. Magnetising. I can't explain it. Apart from which he's also an attractive man.'

'That's not enough,' she grumbled.

'When I saw his hands I wanted them to touch me,' I tried to explain, but didn't tell her that I felt envious of his deceased wife whose body those hands had loved. 'The moment I saw them I wanted to sleep with him.'

Nechama chuckled and said that she couldn't see me rolling around the bed with a thickly bearded man, and that when this *dos* removed all the layers of his clothes and I saw his pale and emaciated body, my desire for him would surely dissipate. And then, as if remembering something, she added, 'Actually, you've always been attracted to *haredim*. Even in your doctoral thesis. Who chooses subjects like that these days?'

I bit my lip and remained silent. Encouraged by my silence, she continued talking: 'You're suffering from troublesome thoughts,' she said, diagnosing my condition. 'Your love for him will always be one-sided and unrequited. And perhaps that is precisely why you can't get him out of your head. He's suffered a terrible tragedy and it's doubtful he'll ever recover from it, and above all he's a *haredi* and you're secular. It's a lost cause.'

Afterwards she called the waitress and ordered chocolate mousse, and I grumbled and told her that she was so rational and it was impossible to talk to her about love. And she said, 'I'd rather be rational than deranged.' I didn't want to come out at a disadvantage and said to her, 'So let's conclude and say that Cupid's arrow struck me and I fell in love with an ass,' and she finally smiled at me.

We were served with two spoons and a chocolate mousse whose pinnacle was sprinkled with greenish crushed pistachios. Nechama got in first and submerged her spoon into the brown, porous substance, brought the spoon to her mouth and sighed with pleasure.

Behind me I overheard a conversation between two young girls.

'He just tore my heart out. Tore it out just like that, without a second thought. In the same way that I'm tearing into this.'

And the second one said, 'But he was handsome that shit, handsome like a prince.'

'Handsome but no good. I was crazy about him, wild.'

'But from the start he made scenes.'

'True, but what can I do. As soon as I saw him, so handsome, an arrow pierced my heart. Broke it, I was so mad about him.'

And Nechama, as if continuing the conversation going on behind us, said that people talk about love as they would about war, and added that I should comfort myself with the mousse and that she would be prepared to kill for mousse like this. I carved out a little of the viscous substance for myself, and the brown mound collapsed. 'How can you talk like that about mousse?' I said self-righteously, and she said, 'Enough, stop being so heavy, loosen up a bit, start enjoying life.'

I licked the spoon and my throat dried from the sweetness. 'Why am I even bothering you with love, what do you know?'

Nechama didn't believe in love. In her defence she would cite studies that claimed that it was nothing more than biochemical activity that occurs in the brain, a small molecule that is released and attaches itself to other substances from the adrenal family, and together they create a sensation of elation and euphoria that is nothing but a temporary psychotic state. She also said that the substance remains active in the brain for only four years, after which it evaporates, and proof of that are the statistics reporting that the greatest number of divorces are registered after four years of marriage.

She had no intention of experiencing this fantasy; on the contrary, she avoided it like the plague. She repeatedly claimed to me that true love, great, pure love is that which forms between a parent and child and which is based solely on giving. Giving that is not threatened by desertion. She would then pick up her Yoeli, brandishing him in the air like a victory trophy, kiss him on his mouth and his fat baby cheeks, and announce to the whole world: 'This is my one and only love.'

Afterwards, as if to appease, she admitted that I, unlike her, was actually capable of love, and even characterised me as 'addicted to love.' In my eagerness for a romantic relationship, she said, I tended to form impossible ties that were liable to end in frustration.

The next day I thought about Avshalom and the conversation I'd had with Nechama as I made my way to the university, listening to the army radio station, because since that day I had avoided listening to the Voice of Music lest heaven forbid I again hear Beethoven's *Ode to Joy*. Notes of contemporary music went wild in my car, lively and animated, and the car glided along the wide road that had been paved coercively on the land of the Arab village of Beit Zafafa. A new palace was being built beside the road, and I remembered that about two weeks ago, when I passed through there a few minutes before the terrorist attack, I'd seen iron rods, and yellow mounds of sand and hewn stones, and I thought about those quick builders who build themselves houses in such a short time. Like the unripe fruit of great delusions, the houses of Beit Zafafa were built so close to one another, so inappropriately to the village. Like overly painted young women swinging their hips on the catwalk in a beauty pageant, they competed with one another with huge living rooms, galleries, ornate balconies, windows decorated in Oriental style, observation towers, cornices, walls, and arrow slits. With abandoned and self-indulgent coquettishness the houses crawled down the primeval slopes, bit into them voraciously, uprooted ancient orchards and olive groves and invisibly and completely encircled the village. They battered down its gates, took over the square and reached with their stony, greedy arms towards the houses of the Gilo and Patt neighbourhoods.

I quickly passed the village and reached that damnable bus stop and looked away, in the habit I'd adopted, and then I was passing between the little boxes of the drab housing projects clad in pinkish hewn stone in the Katamon neighbourhood. I left its commercial centre behind, the falafel and *shawarma* stands and their plumes of smoke, the sandwich and vegetable sellers and the filling station buzzing with thirsty cars. At the traffic lights of the junction just before Begin Boulevard, I could hear the wailing of the ambulances, telling us all in their stentorian tones to clear the way. I stuck close to the pavement and counted them. When I got to the seventh the catchy tune suddenly faded out to be replaced by a Hebrew song replete with longing and sadness, that was in turn cut off by the dramatic announcement of a newsreader who declaimed, in the sombre tones used only for events of this kind, about a bombing that had just occurred in Jerusalem's Machaneh Yehuda Market. So far there were four dead, not including the suicide bomber. The number of dead would probably rise as many of the wounded being evacuated at this moment were in critical condition, and in the same breath he dictated the emergency telephone numbers that could be called for further information. I felt bad. I wound down the car windows and inhaled the outside air saturated with exhaust fumes, and with my last remaining strength drove on to the university. I parked in the parking lot, stumbled out of the car and hurried to my office. I put my bag on my desk, the bag that had suddenly become heavy, as if I'd filled it with rocks, and sat next to it fatigued and exhausted.

Grey wintry light poured into the room through the narrow oblong window, and terror stole up behind me. Its cold, merciless fingers clutched my neck. I fought for air. My heart felt endangered and increased its pulsing. Nausea rose in my throat. I fought the strangling hands, tearing off a collar button from my damp blouse. I tried to get up and didn't know where I was going, I wanted to call for help and couldn't find the words, until Louisa came in and saw me, 'as white as a sheet,' and I mumbled in a choked voice, 'My heart, my heart.' I was put onto a stretcher, strapped down lest I fall off and a needle was stuck into my arm

157

and fluids were dripped into my body from a transparent bag, and they ran with me through the maze of corridors with everybody looking at me and they loaded me onto the wailing cardiac intensive care ambulance. I lay inside it, an oxygen mask over my face and Louisa holding my hand, and I told her I was going to die and asked her who would raise Yoavi, what would become of him.

'Everything will be OK, you'll see,' she interrupted and stroked my head.

I was rolled into a room filled with beds and on them people with faces as yellowed as ancient Torah scrolls, and the life draining from their bodies was illuminated by green flickerings and angular graphs on television screens. Flashing instruments, giving off light in a plethora of colours, were in charge of their fragile souls, counting the little time they had left in soft beats, with gay rising and falling beeps, as if they were conducting a symposium in an arcane language.

In the ward I was met by a petite nurse, as flat-chested as a little girl, with soft, compassionate doe eyes, who said softly in an American accent, 'Just one more tiny prick, just one more and that's it.' I knew that she knew I was dying, and she was talking to me so sweetly out of pity, the way you talk to small children. Then a large needle was stuck into my arm and she took a blood sample, a very big sample, and put it into several test tubes. I was bound to the ECG machine, and with great interest the girl inspected the rolls of paper it spewed out. I followed her expressions and how she wrinkled her nose sprinkled with freckles until it showed fine lines, and I asked, 'What? What can you see?' and she quickly evaded my questioning and beat a retreat, as if I were infected with a contagious disease. I studied the blue blotch that had begun to show on my arm, from where she'd drawn the blood. They'd soon be coming to tell me that I had only hours to live.

Through the window Nachum and Louisa were peering at me, they waved and Louisa spoke to me in sign language I couldn't understand, and I couldn't hear her bangles as she blew me kisses.

And I, like a glutton for punishment, fortified myself with my illness and believed that here I'd be able to sleep safely. The instruments responsible for me would watch over me and come to my aid. Serene and consoled I wrapped myself in the sheet, until I found a pair of spectacles with bottle lenses staring at me. A very tall middle-aged doctor was bending over me. For some reason I concentrated on his white, tangled eyebrows that sprouted above his eyes like small wheat sheaves that had been stuck on for a joke, and he broke into my musings and asked, 'May I?' and gestured at the bed. Of course, I told him, and he sat down carefully on the edge of the mattress as if fearful of wrinkling the sheet.

'Good news. We didn't find a thing. You're healthy and can go home.'

I grasped the bed rail. 'But I've got chest pains. And I'm nauseous and choking and sweating.' A flash of derision flickered in his eyes. 'So what happened to me?' I asked, and he whispered, as if fearful that the other patients might hear, 'What happened to us was a teeny panic attack.' He spoke to me in first person plural, like I was a baby, and teeny, he said, not even tiny. And without a word of goodbye or courtesy, as if I weren't a worthy patient, he abandoned me as well. Feeling guilty for having nothing wrong with me, I lay there, frightened of leaving the room and its machines. Through the glass I saw the doctor talking to Louisa and Nachum, and his benevolent eyes suddenly hardened, and sceptical glances were shot at me and pierced the glass and landed next to me, scalding me with their chill. I prayed for a teeny, harmless heart attack, which would justify the brouhaha I'd caused. And behind my back the terror had returned, panting. I was gripped by mortal fear and knew that my worn-out heart would not withstand another bout. It would rebel and expire, and I'd die and prove to them that my complaints had been fully justified. But then the little nurse came in, detached the drip and demanded that I get up. Now her tone was tired and indignant. I wanted to ask for just a little more time, so if I had another attack they'd be able to examine my heart at the height of the pain, they'd see the symptoms, they'd understand that I was in a life-threatening situation.

Nechama suddenly appeared at the window, flushed and panting, and, with the lordliness of a woman conscious of her size that dwarfed all around her, she spoke to the tall doctor, said whatever it was she had to say and then she was at my bedside helping me up. At the reception desk they put my discharge form and a fresh handful of tranquillisers into her hands.

Alone in my pain and misery I lagged behind my well-wishers like a patient at death's door who had been forced from her sickbed too soon. I walked to his car with a long trail of shame in my wake. I was convinced that everybody was pointing at me, at the bogus patient who had the nerve to invent an illness right now, just when the doctors had more patients than they could reasonably deal with, and in the subterranean operating theatres, like industrious dwarfs with bloodstained hands, they were patching up people who had once been whole.

Nechama stayed at home with me, and after Nachum had left she said that the phantom heart attack I'd experienced was what the doctors called an anxiety or panic attack, and she called it PTSD, post traumatic stress disorder, and as she offered me a cup of tea she added with a wink that it was probably accompanied by pangs of conscience and anxiety because of my love for Avshalom, and that these attacks were particularly common in people suffering from unconscious conflicts. If I didn't deal with my problems, I'd go on getting these attacks and then I'd reach a stage of mortal fear of fear itself.

When Nachum came home he said he'd thought about the attack I'd suffered and had come to the conclusion that I had to get back to my research. 'You've got to keep yourself occupied. Busy to the point of falling off your feet and not thinking about the episode any longer.' He believed, so he said, that if I came into contact with people in a state of bereavement, I'd be able to overcome my own individual mourning and fears, 'Because in this city of ours there are people who've gone through experiences far worse than yours.' Then he thought a bit as if in two minds and added, 'Why don't you call the father of that patient of mine, whatsisname, David, the child that was killed on the bus with his mother. He's *Haredi*. You can talk to him about burial customs for terror victims. It sounds to me like a new and interesting aspect of your research.'

Of all the people in the world, he suggested Avshalom? I knew how inappropriate it would be to talk to him about burial customs regarding his loved ones and how appropriate it was for Nachum to suggest such an insensitive solution, and dry-mouthed I asked, 'And what if he doesn't want to meet with me?' and Nachum replied confidently that he believed that Avshalom would consent. 'There's something that binds you both. After all, you were the last person to see his wife and son alive.'

That evening on the phone I told Nechama about the proposal, and she chuckled and said mockingly, 'So Nachum suggested you call him, eh? So go ahead, do what your husband tells you. Maybe this crazy love will pass faster than you thought.'

I backed up. 'Call him? What can I tell him?'

Nechama giggled. 'You've got the perfect excuse. You're an anthropologist, you can surely come up with a subject for research on the *dosim*, and he'll be happy to help.' And as we were about to finish our talk, she added, 'Remember what they say: all's fair in love and war.'

At night, once Nachum was asleep, I went to the freezer and took out the bottle of vodka we kept there for guests and which I used as a substitute for my father's arak, and poured the clear liquid right down my throat. A frozen ringed snake slithered from my mouth to my stomach, bit me in the belly, its venom bubbled into my bloodstream and drugged the terror that had become an integral part of me.

Next morning I knocked at Prof. Har-Noy's office door. He welcomed me beaming: 'And how's our girl this morning?' he roared. 'Fine, thank you,' I replied, and added that I needed to talk to him. His face fell. 'You know I don't like these talks. They're never good news.' He took off his glasses, breathed on the lenses, polished them energetically with the tail of his wrinkled shirt that was always outside his trousers, and said, 'Ah, well, come on in,' and shifted his bulk to let me in and closed the door behind us.

'I've decided to change direction with my research,' I hastily announced, trying to get the news out of the way as quickly as possible.

He took off his glasses again, as if forgetting that he'd just cleaned them, breathed on them, industriously polished the lenses on his shirt-tail, and studied me with his naked eyes in a compassionate and concerned look, as if saying that you have to tread carefully with people who've gone through a violent trauma, because they temporarily lose their sanity. When he frowned I realised he was making an effort to temper his response. He didn't ask which new subject I'd chosen, he just enquired tiredly, 'Why?'

I took a deep breath and told him that since that day I'd found it hard to deal with burial customs and mourning. 'I find myself weeping during the interviews and while I'm writing. The subject's depressing me. I need another one, something new and optimistic.'

The compassion in his eyes voiced something I'd never heard. 'So your entire research and data gathering and the hours you've spent on interviewing people, isn't it a shame to waste all that work and effort?' So I added confidently that nothing would go to waste, that I could teach the subject in a seminar and I believed that I'd have a lot of takers, the subject was very fashionable at the moment. Then I tried arousing his curiosity: 'My new subject is also related to the ultra-Orthodox community.'

Prof. Har-Noy looked at me and his thick brows suddenly arched, tenting his eyes, and a pair of long, perpendicular furrows were ploughed above the bridge of his nose, lending his face a scowl. The acquaintanceship of years told me he wasn't angry, but rather concerned and attentive. I looked deeply into his eyes, which despite his advanced years maintained a playful and youthful sparkle, and said that the subject I was mulling over was 'The Ultra-Orthodox Community in an Era of Change,' and that it could even focus on 'The Computer and its Integration into the Social Fabric of the Ultra-Orthodox Community in Israel.'

He didn't look at me as he said, 'You know I can't approve the change. You'll have to submit a new research proposal. Ten pages at least. We'll have to convene the research committee to approve your new subject. And why have you chosen this of all things?'

I replied enthusiastically, 'Today this conservative society is undergoing a process of change. True, it's slow, but it's still changing. There is a tremendous tension between the community's need to make a living and its spiritual existence, and it seems that there's something in the computer's logic that appeals to people who are used to the logic of the Talmud.'

Then I told him that in my previous research I'd found that in recent years all kinds of manuals dealing with livelihoods and financing had been published, aimed at this community. The books provided advice designed to ensure success in the various fields of making a living without harming the worship of God and study.

The professor remained silent while I was totally carried away: 'In this research I can clarify how, if at all, they face up to the temptations of the Internet and the pornography it offers, with all the chat rooms and forbidden movies and all that. That's why they're having this heated debate on the question of 'The Computer: Pros and Cons.' Their newspapers are full of clashes of ideas, manifestos and all kinds of proscriptions. And all this is evidence of the critical importance they ascribe to this matter.'

Prof. Har-Noy's face brightened and I applied a little more pressure: 'An examination of all these dilemmas, even in a gender framework, will reveal the ways in which the community is dealing with a changing environment. If we take the ultra-Orthodox woman as an example, her role was to stay at home and raise the children. Today, through the computer, she can work from home and continue in her traditional roles.'

The professor hesitated for a moment. 'Are you sure that this is the right time for a study like this, when the high-tech market is at an all-time low?'

I quickly took up the gauntlet, saying, 'Now is precisely the right time. My research will show how they're dealing with the new situation.'

Prof. Har-Noy said the subject sounded interesting, and he asked me to submit a new written proposal, and then asked how I proposed to go about the subject. Although I hadn't yet spoken to Avshalom and obtained his consent, I said that I had an ultra-Orthodox contact who was a computer expert, and in his free time he taught yeshiva students, religious college students and *haredi* women. 'He'll direct me to his students so I can interview them in depth. And apart from that,' I declared, 'I can always do direct observations of the behaviour of yeshiva students during their studies, and of course I'll interview the executives of high-tech firms that employ *haredim*.'

Before I left his office he warned me that he didn't believe that anybody in the academic world outside Israel would be interested in the subject, and that he doubted whether the efforts I'd invest would garner a positive reaction worldwide. 'But if you want to go for it, I'm with you. And don't forget the seminar on mourning customs,' he added, reminding me of my academic obligations.

That afternoon I looked up his number in the telephone directory.

Avshalom immediately recognised my voice and said, 'Shalom, Yael.' I believed I detected a hint of happiness.

'How are you?' I asked the so-hackneyed question that had become habit even when the world around us was falling apart, and I immediately hated myself, and he replied seriously and in the plural, 'Thank God, we're trying to get over it, and how are you all?' 'Much the same,' I replied, and fell silent. He waited patiently on the other end of the line and I could hear the expectation in his breathing. I began by describing my request, wording it cautiously and stammering a little, and he hesitated momentarily and said that he liked the idea, but first he'd have to consult his rabbi, and then he asked for my phone number. I gave him my university office number.

Every day I asked Louisa if there were any messages for me, until after a week had passed I heard his voice on the phone. The rabbi had said that there was a problem of religious privacy, he said, and suggested that during the time we spent together we either kept the door open or asked one of the neighbours to sit with us. Impatiently trying to find shortcuts, I asked, 'So when can we meet?' and after a brief pause, as if he were checking an unseen appointment book, he replied with a question: 'Next Thursday, at five in the afternoon?' Lying, I said, 'Great, I'm free,' and at the end of our conversation I found it hard to replace the receiver. I was scared of Nechama's reaction, because that day and that time were set aside for our sacrosanct weekly meeting that we'd made every effort to maintain despite all kinds of temptations.

I called and told her about the appointment I'd made with Avshalom, and she said, 'I'm happy for you and I'm already preparing you express therapy for a broken heart and grief.'

I could see her lips curling in an ironic smile, and imagined that her smoke rings were around my throat, strangling me.

Like Nimrod the Mighty Hunter

(Genesis 9, 9)

On Thursday of that week I was with him.

Before leaving the house I spent a long time at my wardrobe. At first I put on a white sweater and a long jeans skirt, my camouflage garb for religious funerals, with whose help I successfully blended into the congregation of mourners. A lipstick stain showed pinkly on the sweater's collar and I changed into a black blouse. In the mirror I saw a woman settler. I stripped, and stood for a long time in panties and bra looking at myself in the mirror and with my thumb and forefinger pinched a small layer of fat that had cunningly settled on my belly.

Then I tore from its hanger the long black dress I'd bought about a thousand years earlier for Louisa's upcoming wedding. It slipped over my curves in restrained splendour and its high collar set off my greenish eyes and pale face. I added a string of freshwater pearls I'd never worn, a gift from Louisa after I'd introduced her to Yoram. I smiled at my reflection: a self-assured intelligent woman, good looking with a great figure, returned my smile. Pleased, I left the room. In the mirror in the passageway I was passed by a black-attired Greek widow, sad-faced and hard-eyed, in permanent mourning.

That wasn't how I wanted to look at our first meeting. Actually, black suited me, I thought as I went back inside and again looked into the mirror. Better to stay a widow, I answered myself, it's far more convenient and clean than divorce, and it saves all the revolting fights and quarrels over the children and property, and it also obviates social criticism and tut-tutting. As I pulled off the widow's weeds, I suddenly realised that this was the second time the thought of divorce had passed through my mind. Again I went to the open wardrobe and deep inside, in a remote corner, I found a green pleated skirt I'd bought a week before I'd discovered I was pregnant and never worn. It reminded me of a time I wanted to forget. I didn't know if I'd manage to wiggle into it. I pulled it down forcefully over my head and it stuck a bit over my chest, slid over my ribs and stopped at my waist. With great effort I buttoned it and looked at my green lower torso. The skirt hid my belly and set off the hips. I added a white silk blouse and checked that my bra didn't show through it. I gathered my hair in a band, and pleased with the result I left the room.

I'd never paid so much attention to choosing my clothing.

He left the front door open wide, told me to sit down in an armchair and gave me a cup of tea. I heard the drumming of the children's feet as they ran up and down the stairs and the bouncing of a ball in the entrance hall. I sipped the oversweetened tea and opened the questionnaire I'd prepared with Prof. Har-Noy's help.

His eyes avoiding mine, Avshalom calmly answered question after question, lowering his eyes again and again as if looking for something. I industriously took down things that were of no interest to me at all and for an instant I caught his blue glance. He hurriedly lowered his eyes again and slapped his forehead and said, 'What kind of a host am I, I forgot to offer you another cup of tea.' 'There's really no need,' I said, but he'd already gone into the kitchen and I heard the water running and then the kettle whistling on the gas. Once more two cups were placed on the table, separating us like a steaming fortification. Again he went into the kitchen and came back with a bowlful of cookies with Smiley faces, the kind small children like. I wondered if they had been kept since Davidl's time.

I quickly sipped the boiling tea and burned my palate and tongue. I turned away from Avshalom so he wouldn't flinch at the sight of my pain-twisted face. I saw him glance at me and when I turned my face to him his eyes again avoided mine.

We said goodbye after an hour, and as he took me to the door he asked, 'Same time next Thursday?' I nodded my reply and thought to myself that he evidently needed these meetings no less than I did.

I drove straight to Nechama's to collect Yoavi, told her about the meeting with Avshalom and as I did so I looked at the faint moustache above her upper lip, and again considered, for the thousandth time, whether I should tell her it was time she finally got rid of it. She said she was beginning to like this Avshalom of mine and suggested that I ask him something about his past, because she had the impression that his education was not necessarily religious. 'You always think you know it all,' I accused her, and she shot back, 'That's my gut feeling. Just ask him straight out and you'll see that he wants to talk. I've got a feeling he's more interested in these talks than you think.'

When I got back home with Yoavi, Nachum was already there and welcomed me with a sour look. 'How can you go out and leave such a mess?' He raised his voice and pulled me into the bedroom and pointed at the pile of clothes and hangers I'd thrown onto the floor as I'd rushed to the meeting with Avshalom.

'You're just like your mother. I can't live like this. You've got to be tidier,' he reprimanded me, annoyed.

Then he looked at me, as if seeing me for the first time in his life, and asked, 'Where did you get that green horror you're wearing? At some flea market? In Jaffa? Where your father's wool shop used to be?'

I felt as if something was exploding inside me. I undressed quickly, letting the blouse and skirt slide from my body to the floor, crossed the pool of clothes that had formed at my feet, and left the room, making sure I switched off the light and left Nachum and the mess in darkness.

I went to the next meeting in a new, dark blue woollen dress I'd bought at the Malcha mall. I sipped the strong tea he made and said that for the purposes of my research I had to ask him a few personal questions. I mustered all my strength and as if reading from the page asked in a single breath: 'Where were you born? Do you have any brothers or sisters? Are your parents still alive? What kind of education were you given?' He put out his hand as if seeking to halt the flow of questions, smoothed his beard, and his eyes smiled at me for the first time.

'Are you sure you really want to know?'

I followed his wonderful fingers as they stirred his thick blond beard, and nodded. Avshalom turned serious, sipped his tea and whispered, as if someone outside the open door might hear him:

'Up to about eight years ago my name was Nimrod. I was born in a *Hashomer Hatza'ir* kibbutz, Kibbutz Shikmim in the northern Negev. My parents are still living and I've got two younger brothers.'

'Nimrod?' I repeated in disbelief. I wanted to ask him, 'So what the hell are you doing here?' but I couldn't. He read my thoughts: 'You probably want to know how I ended up here?' and I nodded silently. 'Where do you want me to begin?' he asked, and I whispered, 'With the name, your name, Nimrod.' 'Well,' he said, 'as you know, a religious Jew would never be given that name.'

Although I knew what he meant, I said that as far as I knew Nimrod was a biblical name. Again he smoothed his beard as if just discovering it, and as if in an admission of guilt whispered that at the time the name was fine for someone born in a kibbutz and whose parents had looked for a name of an ancient biblical hero for him as 'he was a mighty hunter before the Lord.' Then he shifted restively on his chair and said, as if declaiming: 'Nimrod was evil and cruel. In any event, that's how he's described in the legends of our Sages. When the sons of Noah crowned him their king, he sought to rebel against the Lord, and so he was named Nimrod, from the Hebrew root "to rebel." He was the one who suggested to the "separatist people," the descendants of Noah, that they build the Tower of Babel, which was also known as "The House of Nimrod," and it was a house of idolatry. Another legend tells that he threw Abraham into a fiery furnace after he smashed his father Terah's idols.'

'And Avshalom?' I asked. 'Why did you choose that particular name? After all, Avshalom, too, wasn't exactly a paragon of virtue, he rebelled against his father, David, and the name isn't accepted in the *haredi* world. As far as I remember,' I added, 'I've never come across a *haredi* man named Avshalom.'

'You're right. The rabbis were not exactly enamoured of the name I'd chosen and they tried to persuade me to choose the name of some righteous man. But there you are, Avshalom was my favourite Biblical hero, and in the end I somehow convinced them. They realised how important it was for me.'

'But in all Israel there was none to be so much praised as Avshalom for his beauty; from the sole of his foot to the crown of his head there was no blemish in him,' I said, quoting the passage I'd learnt by heart after our first meeting. Avshalom was silent,

168

and I was silent with him. We remained quiet for a long time until I broke the silence with the obvious question, 'And how did Nimrod become Avshalom?'

But it was as if Avshalom had detached himself from me and sunk into distant thought, in places where I had no foothold. I repeated the question, but he ignored it, jumped up and went into the kitchen and asked if I wanted another cup of tea, and he didn't wait for a reply and came back carrying two steaming cups. He put them down on the low table between us and sounded exhausted when he said in a suddenly hoarse voice: 'Please, not today. I can't talk about it right now.'

'So when?' I urged him, and he thought for a moment and promised, 'When we meet next week,' and I was happy that we'd have another meeting, and Avshalom would be mine for another hour and perhaps another after that.

When I got home I found Nachum sprawled in his armchair facing the flickering TV set, with the newspaper covering his face like a lampshade. He moved the paper slightly, looked at me, and said, 'You seem happy lately.' I nodded joylessly, and he hid his face behind the paper again and said offhandedly, 'It's good that you're coming out of it, I was worried, really worried that you weren't going to pull through.' Hands whose skin was dry and cracked from frequent washing in antiseptic solution smoothed the pages of the paper with stubby fingers whose nails were pared to the bone. I compared his hands with Avshalom's. And again his voice came from behind the paper, 'How's your research going with Davidl's father, whatsisname ... ' I replied angrily and reprovingly, 'His name's Avshalom, but he used to be called Nimrod.'

Nachum showed absolutely no interest in knowing why the man had changed his name, and I looked at him and suddenly noticed that his paunch had thickened a little. I recalled how he'd first come to my parents' home, wearing a blue jacket and trousers with knife-edged creases, holding a small bouquet for me and a box of chocolates for my mother, or the other way round, and how he'd promised to have me home before midnight, 'Like Cinderella,' he'd added with an annoying giggle that grated on me. At eleven thirty I opened the front door and found my father waiting on the couch, beneath his map. He said that Nachum seemed like a decent, reliable boy, and I was happy that he was pleased, but next morning Mother uttered the famous sentence that this boy of mine was neither fish nor fowl. 'If you marry him you'll have a lack-lustre life,' she declared.

And I thought that I'd never loved Nachum. The first time I saw him I thought he had a nice face just like my father and that I'd surely come to love him the way I loved my father.

But later the nice disappeared and only the face was left.

I turned my back on Nachum and his newspaper and went into Yoavi's room and bent over him and inhaled him into me, and he opened his eyes and held out his chubby arms from his sleep and hugged me and whispered into the hollow of my neck, 'What do the trees do?' and I answered, 'They grow,' and I kissed his cheek and suddenly wondered when that sweet smell would disappear and fields of bristles would sprout on his cheeks, and Yoavi closed his eyes and asked, 'Stay with me a bit,' and I sat beside him for a long time and waited till I heard Nachum's snores, and only then I went to our bed and curled up on the far side and started thinking about Avshalom. I touched my breasts and ran my fingers over the buttons of my nipples, and they responded joyfully and came erect, and I saw Avshalom's mouth over me and his lips feeling for my breasts, and he found a nipple and sucked it gently, and I fought back my groan and felt my fingers in his chest hair, and Nachum stopped his snoring and woke up and reached out from the edge of the bed and touched my belly and asked, 'Are you all right?' 'I'm fine, go back to sleep,' I reassured him in a choked voice, angry with him for intruding on my lovemaking with my beloved, and I covered myself with the quilt and sniffed my fingers, and thought about Nimrod and Avshalom and knew that I loved them both.

'Who was Nimrod?' I asked him at our next meeting, and as if part of a set ritual he asked, 'Would you like some tea?' and without waiting for a reply he went into the kitchen and came back with the two cups, went back again, and I could hear kitchen cupboards being opened and closed, and he came back with a plateful of Smiley cookies, even though he hadn't seen me taste them last time.

'Nimrod was an air force pilot,' he began, speaking in the third person, as if talking about someone who had died a long time ago, 'a combat pilot who fought in the Lebanon War.' In my mind's eye

I removed the thick beard from his face, and he became a pilot in a grey coverall. His voice suddenly sounded different, and a different man sat facing me, a man who told me that Nimrod had believed in what he had done and loved the air force and really loved flying. 'Even in battle the pilot doesn't soil his hands with blood,' he said as if apologising, and I imagined him cruising in the sky, winging happily above the clouds: for neither the sounds of explosions nor the screams of the wounded or the noise of collapsing buildings reach the cockpit.

'What type of plane did you fly?' I asked, my curiosity aroused, and a tiny smile spread on his lips and I was as happy as if the smile had been for me, and he said, 'A Phantom. The Vietnam War workhorse. What difference does it make?' I didn't know what to reply and he said that my question was actually important because the previous generation of pilots, those who had served before him, had the privilege of flying the light and elegant French aircraft. And then the Phantom came along, the cruel, heavy beast from the United States that didn't have even a hint of French chic, and together with the plane our air force had adopted the American fighting spirit.

'So what happened to him, to Nimrod, what was the turning point?' I asked.

His life had changed when they began sending him on interdiction sorties. The command echelon would set up the target, explain exactly which terrorists were hiding there and plot how to reach them on the map. 'We'd reach the target, press the button, feel the aircraft jump as the bombs were released, see the pillars of smoke down below, and then fly home clean and in one piece.' And Avshalom cleared his throat and sipped his tea. 'It was only later that I found out other things.'

'What, for instance?'

'When you drop your bombs on an interdiction mission you intend to hit a military target or a building housing terrorists. But my commanding officers knew, in fact everybody knew, that in those clearly specified targets there were also innocent people. Children.' His voice broke as he described how he'd drop his ordnance and just see the building, not the eyes of his victims.

'And when children are killed you inevitably think about the children you yourself might have in the future.'

Again he asked if I wanted another cup of tea, although I hadn't touched the one in front of me, and rushed into the kitchen and rattled plates, turned the tap on and off, foraged in the fridge and came back empty-handed, and sat down facing me and took up his story where he'd left off. 'And then those reports began appearing in the papers and on the foreign TV channels.

'I'll never forget the day that a newspaper headline, and I don't even remember in which paper, proclaimed: 'The Pilot That Drops the Bomb – How Can You Sleep at Night?' Since then he'd begun torturing himself at night. 'When you announce that you're not sleeping nights, they try and reduce your mission load. But it always rebounds on your buddies who have to do your job. I started taking sleeping pills, half a pill at first, and when I'd wake up at three in the morning I'd take the other half. I'd get to the briefing fuzzy and be given my mission. Before each sortie I'd demand all the information, who was inside the buildings and whether there were any children there. I knew that the terrorists used civilians as a human shield and my superiors weren't always able to answer my questions. At every debriefing I interrogated them about the casualties.' When he'd discovered that he'd killed two children he cracked up and asked not to be slated for interdiction missions and volunteered instead to bomb anti-aircraft batteries. 'A pilot has an advantage over the regular soldier,' he explained, 'in that nobody can force you to execute a mission against your will or the dictates of your conscience.' And once, when they'd sent him to bomb an anti-aircraft position and he'd discovered it was located in a public building, on the roof of a school or a hospital, he'd dropped his bombs in the sea and returned to base with a clear conscience.

His eyes roamed the room and came to rest on the photograph of Davidl on the sideboard. 'In my view there's no difference between a missile fired from a plane at a building housing terrorists, and children playing in a nearby alley are killed, and children killed in a suicide bombing of a bus. Both are innocent victims. The error committed by a pilot is no less grave than that of a suicide bomber who acts out of malicious intent.'

I felt I had to defend him, to remove the ignominy from him: 'The suicide bomber does it with the intention of murdering, and you attacked interdiction targets in self-defence.' But Avshalom looked away and asked me for the thousandth time, 'Another cup of tea?'

172

I shook my head and asked how he'd found his way to religion of all things.

He absently touched his black yarmulke, as if making sure it was still there, protecting his head, and gazed at a distant spot on the wall.

All at once the man sitting opposite me changed into a *haredi*, speaking in their language.

'I felt like a murderer and looked for a way of atoning for my actions. To beg forgiveness. The blood of the innocents I'd killed shouted at me from the ground. In the air force they'd taught us how to fly, drop bombs, execute the mission, but they didn't teach us how to free ourselves of the blood and the stench of death that stuck to our hands.'

And so, after serving for some years as a flying instructor, he'd left the air force and enrolled at the 'Or Sameach' yeshiva in Jerusalem.

'I remember the boys at the yeshiva talking to me about transgressions like calumny, saying the Grace After Meals without due devotion, lustful thoughts and spilling one's seed on the ground. Unlike them I felt like Nimrod from the texts – evil and cruel, his hands dripping with the blood of innocent children. For the first time in my life I fasted on Yom Kippur and went to the synagogue. I was taught how to stand and when to bow and when to beat my breast and declare that I had sinned. Then, in front of everybody, I declared: "I have trespassed, I have been faithless, I have robbed, I have spoken basely," and I added to that long list the word "murdered," and each blow of my fist on my chest cleansed me of my sins a little. In the synagogue they spoke of the calamities and dangers that the New Year brings to the sinner, and I knew that if I did not make a full repentance, I would never be forgiven, because it was then that that the Almighty decided who would live and who would die. Who by the sword and who in war.'

'And Batsheva?' I asked, finally managing to speak her name, 'was she from a religious home?'

'Batsheva was my girlfriend back when we were conscripted into the army and was with me all along. She supported me and understood. To make life easier for us, her parents, who were traditional Jews, became ultra-Orthodox.'

'And your parents?' I dared to ask.

'They ostracised me. They'll never understand how their son the

173

pilot, the pride and joy of the kibbutz, lost his mind and became an unenlightened religious Jew. They didn't come to our wedding or to Davidl's circumcision ceremony on the pretext that they didn't want to sit separately, he with the men and she with the women. Batsheva used to write to them and send them photos of Davidl, but they wouldn't forgive me. Even after the tragedy they still bear a grudge.'

'And your brothers?' I asked.

'They're still living in the kibbutz,' he said, 'and sometimes come to visit. They also came to the funeral and the *shiva*.'

He suddenly buried his face in his hands and whispered, 'It wasn't enough. I failed.'

'How did you fail?' I asked in surprise.

'I failed to save them. I didn't succeed in atoning for my sins. They had to die because of me. Davidl and Batsheva paid for my crimes with their lives.'

And he wept and said that perhaps he hadn't repented fully, that perhaps he had been too preoccupied with the material world, with his work, and too little with study of the Torah. 'It's all because of my pride,' he groaned. 'I didn't want to be supported by the community's institutions, my rabbi told me that my work in computers would interfere with study of the Torah, but I felt that I had to make a living and support my family.'

In my mind's eye I again saw the two heads looking at me, one big and dark and the other small and blond. Davidl and Batsheva gazed at me with an accusing look through the window of the destroyed bus.

I wept with him, because I knew: their death had been necessary in order to create this unexpected conjoining between Avshalom and me.

And my mother's voice came to my aid: 'Nothing is coincidence,' I heard her saying, 'there's a guiding hand. Fate devised a fiendish plot and did everything so you'd meet.' Nechama was wrong, I silently rejoiced. Our meeting was not random. His tragedy would safeguard Yoavi and me.

'Trouble shall not rise up a second time.' The sentence my father loved quoting from the Book of Nachum played in my head, the sentence he used when he embraced me. With oaths and imprecations he would assure me that nobody would take me from him, because trouble that had beset someone once would never beset him again.

My skin itched with excitement. Stimulated and merciless I longed to wind my arms and legs around Avshalom, to sink nails and teeth into him, to bind him to my body with my hair, to link his life to mine. I wouldn't let him go. We had to be together. His Davidl had died so that my Yoavi would live. Through him the curse would be removed.

Agitated, I got up and told him I had to go. He didn't try to stop me.

I didn't know where I found the strength: I went to him and held his feverish head in both my hands. His body trembled close to mine, and I knew that he knew that his dead had united us. But he was suddenly alarmed and broke away from my arms. 'Shall we meet next week?' I asked fearfully, and he, pale and exhausted, nodded silently.

I got into my car with its smell of newness, and my hands, that had earlier held Avshalom's head, burned on the wheel. I thought about my old Minimush, which on that morning had intentionally refused to start so that she could lead me to him.

I drove my new car and my eyes roamed the road, following her, following my old car.

And the Woman Was Very Fair to Look Upon

(The Second Book of Samuel 10, 2)

The ringing of the telephone suddenly assaulted us with extended
talons and unravelled our conversation. His mind wandered and for
long moments he deliberated about answering. But the ringing was
insistent and encircled us and put up a bastion between us, until he
finally and unwillingly said that it was probably an emergency and
he had to take it, and got up and went into the kitchen to take the
call there, and when he returned said he'd been called to a *minyan*
of mourners in Neveh Ya'akov, and apologised and asked me to
wait for him because he'd be right back after the prayers. He left,
softly closing the door that had remained open since I entered his
apartment.

As the sound of his footsteps faded on the stairs, I quickly
looked for the bathroom. Throughout our conversation I'd been
sitting facing him in pain and suffering, my thighs held tightly
together and my buttocks clenched. We'd been talking for a long
time and I was frozen in my chair, not daring to change my position and move the fresh cup of tea he'd brought for me. My
bladder was about to burst but even so I was shy about asking him
where the toilet was.

Although he'd already left I made sure the door was closed.
With great pleasure I emptied my tea-filled bladder, and like a
dextrous and silent wine waiter pouring the elixir onto the wall of
the glass I directed the flow to the sides of the toilet bowl, so that
no sound would be heard. Then I went into the bathroom to wash
my hands, and there, on the rail of the absent shower curtain, hung
a horrifying monument commemorating the dead wife: a white bra
whose cups were as small as those of a young girl, and three pairs

of white cotton panties with no frills. I touched the underwear that had been hung up to dry two thousand years ago, and hardened dust stuck to my fingers. I washed the ashes of the dead from my hands and a pale and faded face looked at me disappointedly from the mirror of the medicine cabinet over the sink. That mirror, that had looked at her face innumerable times, now scanned mine and probably compared my features with hers.

'Mirror, mirror on the wall, who is the fairest ... '

I dried my hands on a pink terrycloth robe that was hanging from a hook behind the door. Embroidered on its pocket was a monogram of three Hebrew letters, *Beth, Shin* and *Vav*. Probably a present from him. I stuck my hand into the pocket and pulled out a balled tissue that I straightened out and sniffed.

Later, when I was telling everything to Nechama, I said that I wanted to know her. I wanted to know who the woman he'd loved was, I explored her smell and searched for traces she'd left behind. So I also opened the cabinet and rummaged around inside it. I found a bottle of liquid paracetamol, baby cream, a yellowing paper bag containing headache pills, a bunch of simple black hairgrips held together with an elastic band, a comb missing some teeth with a few curly hairs caught in it, a pack of sanitary pads and a little bundle of gauze pads for testing the clean days of the menstrual cycle.

'Cosmetics?' asked Nechama, and I said I'd found no traces of her beauty – no face cream, no make-up, no perfume bottles, just a half-used pink lipstick hiding chastely in the corner of the cabinet.

I came out, passed Davidl's locked room and went straight into their bedroom. A four-door wall cupboard finished in light Formica hung from the wall facing the window. Two joined single beds covered with colourful counterpanes. A cheap wicker bedside table stood by each bed.

I lay down on the bed by the window. The mattress shifted under me and the bed moved slightly towards the window. I leant over, lifted the counterpane and saw the two metal wheels attached to its feet: this had been hers – the menstrual bed. Next to the reading lamp on the bedside table was a tattered prayer book and at its side a dark hairband, in whose velvet folds a few light brown hairs had been caught. I opened the drawer: a few black hairgrips, Nivea hand cream, a thin colourful head kerchief, and the September,

New Year issue of *The Family*. The cloth bookmark in the middle had been left at 'Cooking for the Festival with Leah' which contained a recipe for 'Roast Veal in Honey.'

I rolled onto the other bed: the permanent bed, his bed. A wall reading lamp stretched its curved neck towards me, and its transparent pear-shaped head inspected me. Fixed to the wall over the bed-head was a simple board that had been screwed into place. The photograph in its silver frame, a few religious books and a purple velvet phylacteries bag, whose embroidered flowers were topped by a yellow crown, stood on his bedside table. I lay on his bed where Batsheva, on her clean days, had lain by his side. I took off the counterpane, sank my face into his pillow and sniffed it. A faint scent of soap came from it. I was swallowed up into the softness of the mattress, pleasure filled my body, and tranquillity came upon me and caressed my eyelids with its feathery down. I was so tired, tempted to close my eyes and sleep and sleep and sleep, for a thousand years perhaps, until he came searching for me, fought the dragon and the thorny barriers, found my room at the top of the tower and wakened me with a soft kiss on my lips.

With difficulty I shook off sleep and got up from the bed.

I had to know her.

From my seat on his bed I opened one of the cupboard doors. It yawned slowly and a strong smell of mothballs wafted from it. It was her side.

Dresses hung on simple wire hangers, arranged side by side at regular intervals. Long-sleeved, high-collared, and lacking personality they crowded there like hunched, scowling, skinny and chaste women waiting patiently for an important event in their lives. At their feet lay two pairs of dark round-toed, flat-heeled shoes. By the cupboard wall, upright on their splendid high heels stood the privileged festive shoes, their black patent leather sparkling, toes pointed, and their golden butterfly buckles glistening. Behind the next door, that squeaked lightly when it opened, a few ironed blouses were stacked one on top of the other in perfect order. Beneath them there were three wooden drawers. I pulled one open to reveal some plain cotton underwear in all their meekness. The drawer below opened with difficulty, and heaps of rolled up dark stockings were piled in it. In the bottom drawer there was a mess of colourful head kerchiefs, wound into each other as if seeking consolation.

'I had to feel her. Put on her clothes. Wear her shoes,' I later confessed to Nechama.

I took off my blue woollen dress, and in my bra and panties scanned hanger after hanger, feeling the material with my fingers, sniffing the armpits as I tried to detect her scent. I rejected dress after dress until I found the dark green one with white spots shining gaily on it. I put it over my head and squirmed in the darkness, feeling for the neck, the sleeves, the waist. With the dress tight on me I reached behind me, found a row of buttons and trapped them one after the other. My body was imprisoned inside the fabric. The dress gave off foreign smells of perspiration and mothballs, its high collar squeezed my neck and threatened to strangle me for my chutzpah.

Yael in Batsheva's dress, sad and depressed, a thick-waisted dwarf, looked out at me from the mirror on the inside of the cupboard door. I blamed the distorting mirror for reducing my height and widening my body. Again I reached behind me, undid the buttons and tore off the dress. And again I moved hanger after hanger and absently chose a black dress. This one gave itself to me easily and willingly. I looked at my reflection again. The dress obscured my curves, its thick cloth slid over my breasts and completely erased them. It was a threadbare maternity dress.

I deliberated over the shoes and finally chose the patent leather ones. As I picked them up I saw the worn soles and the dry cracks in the polished leather. My feet in thick woollen stockings were far too big for them. I took off the stockings and with much effort pushed my feet into the shoes.

I stood at the open kerchief drawer for a long time. I took out a purplish one, wrapped it round my head and tied the ends at my nape. A woman in a bloodstained bandage looked out at me from the mirror. I ripped the kerchief from my head and selected another, a dark-blue one. I folded it diagonally and spread the resulting triangle over my head and tied the ends behind. Then I rummaged in the drawer and found a white headband, and put it on my head. I pushed the stray strands of hair that had escaped the kerchief underneath, making sure that not even a single hair would show.

A strange woman, with my eyes, gazed blankly at me. My time unravelled and lost its beat, and I was shocked to see Avshalom standing behind the woman in the mirror. He was wide-eyed. His voice shook my back: 'Batsheva?'

I turned to him. Transfixed, he stood in the bedroom doorway, his figure outlined like a portrait in the doorframe and his face as if he'd seen a ghost. He opened and shut his mouth, voiced a clicking sound as if he had detached his tongue from his palate to say something, and then turned his back on me and fled. Batsheva's maternity dress scorched my skin, my heart pounded in my throat, and my stomach roiled with heartburn. I reached behind me, my fingers trembling as I struggled with each button, groping and missing, until I managed to free myself from the dress. Like a dry leaf it shed itself from me and fell around my ankles. I took off the headband and kerchief, hurriedly put on my own dress, returned the clothes to the cupboard and left the room.

He was standing in the kitchen, his back to me, his body bent over the sink and his face to the window. Almost absently he asked, 'Please go.'

A strong wind plucked at the power cables shaking overhead, as black and dangerous as evil serpents. On seeing me it slapped me, flinging dust into my eyes and lashing my face with a thousand tresses of hair. It pursued me to my car, pushing and shoving at my back, driving me away from there.

By the car I fought against it, barely managing to get the door open, and it slammed into it, seeking to rip it from its hinges, whistling and shrieking as if begging to be let in and drive away with me. All the way home it bombarded me with round missiles of ice that beat like iron battering rams against the bodywork and windscreen.

I reached home with great difficulty. Leaving my car to its fate I ran towards the house. Like an angry bull the wind assailed the abandoned car, rocking it back and forth and trying to overturn it. On the stairs, halfway to the apartment, the car called me back with pleading, demanding hoots of its alarm. The wind answered it with its shrieking and frightened neighbours switched on lights and lowered shutters, their eyes sweeping the darkness, looking for the hooting car.

Pursued by the wind, red faced, hair tousled and clothes awry, I went into the apartment.

Complete silence. Nachum was in his armchair, his paper on his lap and the TV flickering dumbly before him. I said hello and wanted to escape to the bedroom, but he lowered his eyes to my feet and asked, 'What's this? Where are those weird shoes from?' Alarmed, I saw that I was still wearing her shoes and told him that I'd stepped in a puddle, filling my shoes, and one of the faculty secretaries who had a spare pair in her car had given them to me until mine dried out. Nachum remarked that my friend had a strange taste in patent leather shoes, and who was she, and I replied that he didn't know her, she'd come from a temping agency and probably wouldn't be with us for long. I put the shoes into a plastic bag and hung it by its loops on the front doorknob, lest I forget them at home.

Next morning while I was dressing Yoavi, the phone rang and Avshalom said quietly, as if nothing had happened, 'You forgot your shoes and stockings here.' I was relieved that he'd called and asked if he'd be at home after I'd finished work. I wanted to apologise, to explain and justify myself, but he replied in a cracked voice that there was no need, he didn't want to understand the whys and wherefores, and let sleeping dogs lie.

We exchanged bags at his door like a couple of secret agents. I asked him when we could meet again, and he replied that he didn't know right now and when he found time he'd let me know. I went down the stairs with a shopping bag bearing the legend 'Rachel Modes – Quality Women's Clothing' and my shoes and stockings inside, heavy on my arm. When I turned round I saw him standing on the landing, one hand holding my bag with Batsheva's shoes inside, the forefinger of his other hand hovering over the light switch, and he waited until the light went out so he could switch it on again for me.

He called again a week later and asked if we could meet again.

'I gave all her things to charity,' he said as I sat down in the armchair. I lowered my eyes. He'd done it for me so I wouldn't again be tempted to touch her things. And as if something had snapped inside him, he got up and rushed into the kitchen and came back with two cups of tea and a plate of Smiley cookies. I knew he'd gone to dry his tears, and when he came back with moist eyes I looked at the toes of my shoes and apologised again for putting on her clothes, but he cut me off with a gesture.

'They buried them in their clothes,' he said. 'They couldn't even ritually cleanse the bodies. They said that in the case of Batsheva and Davidl, who died a violent death, the dead had to buried in their bloodstained clothes, because the blood is the soul. And I don't know what she was wearing that day. Maybe you could see? Do you remember?'

I shook my head and he said that when they'd carried her to the grave on the stretcher, her hand, the one that had remained whole, had peeped out from under the sheet, and he had wanted to hold it and take her, step by step, to her grave, and he hadn't known with whom to walk first, his son or his wife. 'Those innocent souls were murdered for no reason. They unknowingly stretched out their necks for slaughter.' And Avshalom hid his face in his beautiful hands, and I wanted to kiss those suffering hands, to draw the pain from his body into mine. And he, as if feeling the burn of my lips, clenched his fists and folded his arms on his chest and sank into a long silence. And I couldn't restrain myself: 'What about the anger, what about the desire for vengeance?' He stared at me for a few moments and then raised his eyes, to his God, in all probability, but his look was blocked by the ceiling and the ugly worldliness of the colourful lampshade hanging from it.

'In cases like this we say, "May the Lord avenge their blood,"' he finally said.

'And that's all, you don't feel the need to take revenge on the people who sent the murderer?'

'I'm not interested in vengeance. I don't want to have bad feelings like that.'

'But why do you think that God brought this calamity on us?' I dared to ask in the plural.

'I believe that the Almighty, blessed be He, puts us to a difficult test every day.'

'And after what happened, do you still believe in such a test?'

'The Lord giveth and the Lord taketh away, blessed be the name of the Lord. He put me to a test, a terrible test. He didn't choose me by chance. He knows I'm strong and will withstand it.'

'Wouldn't you want to ask the Almighty, blessed be He, for a little quiet after two thousand years of restrictive laws, and persecutions, and exiles, and Holocausts ... '

But Avshalom ignored the question and just stared at the lampshade, and a shadow passed over his face as he suddenly said, 'There was a terrible quiet there. Like in a cemetery.'

'Where?' I asked in surprise.

'The pathology department. I didn't find them at the hospital and they took me there by taxi, to the forensic medicine department. It was so quiet there. People spoke in whispers, as if they were frightened of waking people sleeping. And there were pine trees there and a green yard and flowers in plant pots.' After a brief silence he added, 'They asked me questions in the office, and they wrote the answers down in a printed questionnaire in black letters, like an obituary notice.'

'What did they ask?'

'They wanted their personal details for identification, and I didn't know how to describe them. I didn't know how to describe my loved ones. But they insisted.'

'And what did you tell them?'

'I said that Batsheva is a beautiful woman, that she's got honey-coloured eyes and light brown hair and clear skin, and she's got a deep dimple on her chin, and when she laughs there are fine wrinkles around her eyes, like delicate sunbeams. And her hands, her hands are soft and loving, and her big toes are tiny and chubby like a little girl's.'

'And Davidl? How did you describe Davidl?'

'When they asked me about Davidl I said that he is a perfect copy of his mother, of Batsheva, especially when he smiles. And although the room was full of people they listened to me patiently, and asked for further identifying marks, like birthmarks, scars, teeth, and I didn't know what to tell them. Then I remembered that Batsheva had a scar on her forehead, from when she had chicken-pox, and they said it was impossible to identify that scar and asked for their dentist's name. Your husband's name had been erased from my memory, and all I could tell them was that his clinic is in Emek Refa'im. That's how they found him.' And Avshalom told me how, in spite of everything, he had held onto the hope that they were among the survivors, until they came to him with a grave expression on their faces.

'I asked to see them,' Avshalom wept, 'just one more time. Because how was I to know that it was them? How could I know it was over for them? How could I go on living?

'And what did they tell me?' he asked and didn't wait for an answer, 'They said that if I wanted to remember them as they were, it would be better if I didn't see them. But I insisted, and in the end they agreed to let me see one of Batsheva's hands. One, not both. They stood me by a glass partition, behind which was a stretcher with a small mound covered with an army blanket. I couldn't recognise her body. They lifted the blanket slightly and I saw the hand and the finger with the wedding ring. And with Davidl they just showed me his curls, no more. It was some small consolation to hear that they'd both been killed instantly and didn't suffer at all.'

'And what of your God? Where is He while His chosen people are afflicted like this?'

Avshalom said that God has His own reasons and doesn't have to explain His actions to us, and then he asked if I wanted another cup of tea, and his voice sounded weary. I shook my head, but he still went into the kitchen and came back empty-handed and said, 'The night before that morning I was working in the computer lab until the early hours, and I didn't want Batsheva to be alone in the apartment with Davidl, and they went to spend the night with her sister in Gilo. She left there early in the morning, she had an appointment with her gynaecologist.' He rolled a Smiley cookie in his fingers and added, 'I think she was pregnant. I asked them to check it at the pathology department, but they said that her body was so badly mutilated that it was impossible to examine her.'

The satanic face of the woman in red smiled evilly at me: 'Your son will die in a bombing, your son will die in a bombing,' I heard her keening like a spiteful child. I felt the foetus kicking in my empty belly, and bent forwards twisted in pain. I dug my finger-nails into my palms and stopped the cry that threatened to burst from my throat: I want to be pregnant. By you. I want us to have children. I quickly hunched over the teacup, which was still full, and gulped the boiling liquid. It scorched my mouth and crawled down my gullet, setting my innards on fire. I hiccuped in pain and he looked at me and told me about the last time he'd seen her, the evening before her death, how he'd said goodbye to her and Davidl with a peck on the cheek. 'Living as if somebody was going to die any minute would be unnatural,' he said, as if apologising, and added how badly it hurt that it hadn't been a proper farewell.

I nodded to him and said that our lives were so fragile, and he said that had he known what was going to happen, he would have told her what she so much wanted to hear from him and those words had never passed his lips. I thought to myself that he would probably have said he loved her, and how beautiful she was, and how much he admired her wisdom and generosity, and perhaps he might have asked her if she was happy with him.

The bolus in my throat suddenly dissolved and I was flooded with weeping. I wept for Batsheva and Davidl, for my life with Nachum, for Yoavi who had been cursed before he was born, and for my father who had died and I hadn't managed to weep at his graveside. I wanted him to come to me, touch me, hold me in his arms and wipe away my tears. But he didn't move and watched me weeping. 'And what now?' I asked him. 'How long can I go on crying? It's never-ending.' And he gave me an apologetic smile, as if my weeping was his fault, and told me, 'It's good that you can cry, it will cleanse you,' and I knew that he knew I was weeping not only for his Batsheva and Davidl.

Again that sharp, relentless pain creased my belly, and my bowels wrenched like labour pains on an empty stomach. My groin was damp and I got up and bravely announced that I was going to the WC: 'the WC,' I said, purposely using a reserved euphemism. I quickly took off my panties and saw the dark, damp stain that had come early, pulling a red tongue at me from the material of the panties. I peed quietly, directing the flow to the side of the bowl lest he hear the sound from the living room. Then I lined my panties with handfuls of toilet paper that had been cut into square pieces in order to observe the Sabbath precept. I flushed the toilet and wiped the seat and checked that I hadn't left any incriminating evidence. When I went into the bathroom to wash my hands, I saw that the shower curtain rail was bare, and the pink robe had vanished from the hook.

'We have to go on living, we have to preserve the sense of life. Nothing, not even the cruellest act, must extinguish that feeling,' he told me as I said goodbye.

In the car I thought that Avshalom was the only man in my life, except for my father, of course, with whom I could weep.

This wasn't the way I'd planned it. I didn't mean for what happened to happen. But afterwards I was unable to stop. I went all the way, and afterwards I felt a huge relief, but burning shame as well.

Over and over, like a silent film, I run those moments through my mind. I was sitting facing him in a new grey skirt I'd bought for the meetings with him. My hair was flowing and fragrant because only an hour earlier I'd been to the hairdresser's I hadn't visited since my wedding day, and my face was lightly made up.

We sat facing each other in the living room. The front door was open, because that was what the rabbi required. The voices of the children playing outside gradually faded. The winter dusk filled the room with shadows, darkening Avshalom's face, subduing the senses, obscuring my thoughts. But he didn't get up and switch on the light. The cookies smiled at me from their plate, the two teacups had long since been emptied, and Avshalom buried his face in his hands and wept. Traces of white that I hadn't noticed before streaked his hair.

I don't remember what made him weep then, but there was no shortage of reasons.

Trembling with fear and desire I went to him and with my fingertips touched the beautiful fingers covering his face. I later justified this act to Nechama by telling her that all I'd wanted to do was ease his burden of memories. But I knew that I wanted to make him forget his dead and tell him, Let's stop everything, forget everything, begin at the beginning, a new life.

His warm tears flowed over my hand and he didn't pull his hands away. I was flooded with a deep compassion. I wanted to tell him that there was no random chance here, that Batsheva's and Davidl's lives had been sacrificed to that we could be together. And with his head still buried in his hands I put my arms round him and felt his firm, broad body trembling under my hands. I wanted him to hug me because his embrace would protect us, Yoavi and me, from any misfortune. Because affliction shall not rise up a second time. For only a man who had lost a wife and son would know how to protect us and eradicate that woman's curse.

Quickly, before I could change my mind, I told him everything I wanted to say:

'Take me, take me instead of Batsheva, and I'll give you my Yoavi for a son, and we'll raise him together.'

In a flash he got up, detached himself from my arms, clenched his fists and hid them in his pockets, and his damp eyes were wide in horror: 'You're a married woman!' I heard him shout. 'A married woman!' Then he sat down and I returned to my seat and remained silent, because I'd run out of the words I wanted to say. Like sinners we lowered our eyes to the floor, not daring to look at one another. Then he politely asked me to leave. I picked up my purse and coat and took my time putting it on, perhaps he would change his mind and ask me to stay. But he didn't.

Yet I left the front door open after me, maybe he'd have a change of heart and call me to come back. From the yard I looked up at his window. The closed blind didn't blink and the curtain remained still. All the way home I thought about what I'd said. I reconstructed the movement of his body responding to my embrace, the holding of the damp hands, the cry of 'Married woman!'

I knew it hadn't been the right moment.

Next day he called and asked me to come, he wanted to see me today, if I could find the time, of course. Eagerly, I asked if it was convenient for me to come now, and he said, 'I'm at home today. Whenever you like. Just tell me when?'

All the way there I made promises and vowed vows.

'I'm sorry,' he said at the door and left it wide open. I followed him into the living room. He didn't look at me but at the ugly lampshade hanging from the ceiling, and said, 'I was too over-wrought and hurting yesterday. I couldn't relate to what you proposed. But it's an impossible proposal for me.' Then he said that when a man loses his first wife it is as if the Temple has been destroyed in his time. 'I love her. It's a love that's impossible to erase or replace. You of all people should know that I'm still in mourning. I don't know when I'll be able to stop. If I can at all.'

I swallowed my saliva and didn't say, 'But I want you.' I said instead, 'There's so much love in you. So much giving. And the dead can no longer take it. You gave them their share in this world, and now they're buried, and this love of yours can't reach them.'

'Every day I love them anew, more and more,' he said, his expression blank.

'But they're dead. You mustn't be afraid of life. You said your-self that we have to go on living.'

I asked him to reconsider my proposal. 'It's serious. I thought a great deal before offering myself to you,' and I added that I'd agree to accept the precepts of the Torah, and even go to the ritual bath and cover my head. I confessed that I was considering divorce. 'Even before I met you. I can't go on living with my husband,' I told him. He listened attentively, and I silently thanked him for not asking me to detail why I couldn't go on living with my husband.

At the door, as I was leaving, he suddenly shot at me, 'You've got a child. You have to consider him, too.' And in a parting shot he said, 'Even the altar weeps for the man who divorces his first wife.'

I looked at him and smiled a bitter smile and said that in fact, I too was a widow, a widow buried while still living. I turned my back on him and walked along the dark landing. The light came on and I turned round. Avshalom was standing in the doorway, his finger on the light switch. Then he went back inside and closed the door behind him. As I stood in the parking lot I looked up at the fourth floor and saw the curtain move slightly. I knew he was looking at me as I got into the car.

His look accompanied me all the way home.

Next day he called me at work and said that he had talked to his rabbi, and the rabbi had decided that he was not the right man for my research. He quickly dictated the name and number of one of his colleagues, and politely added that it had been a pleasure talking to me, and said goodbye. And I said, 'Avshalom, we can't say goodbye this way,' but he replied quickly, 'Please. Don't call me again. You're putting me to a severe test.'

I looked at the receiver burning my hand for a long time, until Louisa came with her bangles jangling merrily and she looked at me and said, 'What now, *ma chérie*? You look like you've lost a pound and found a penny,' and I replied, 'Leave me alone, Louisa,' and picked up my purse and drove home.

You Are Hereby Permitted to Any Man

That night I told Nachum: 'I want a divorce.'

I'd practised for this moment for such a long time, learning the four words I was going to say by heart. I'd enjoyed it. I wanted him to pale, plead for his life, make promises, tell me he loved me. And I would harden my heart, tell him everything I hadn't dared to say for all those years, tell him it was too late, and then I'd turn my back on him, and like a Hollywood actress leave the room with grace and my head held high.

Nothing could have prepared me for what actually happened.

Nachum peered at me over the evening paper and didn't seem at all surprised as he replied quietly, 'Fine,' as if it were all his idea and he'd already decided for both of us. I was suddenly frightened and asked, 'Are you sure?' and he replied, 'Yes, I think it will the best thing for all of us.'

Nausea rose in my throat, and my body was trembling as I asked, hurt, 'Don't you love me any more?' and he replied in the past tense, 'I loved you so much.' Although I knew the answer, I repeated the question, 'But now, don't you love me now?' and he said, as if to himself, that I had no idea of how much he'd loved me. 'I loved you madly,' he said, raising his voice. My own voice immediately rose to a sharp scream, 'And now? What about now?' and he remained silent, and I shed ugly, miserable tears, angry with him for not fighting for me, for not begging me to stay. 'What happened to us? When did it end?' I shouted, and he shrugged like a scolded child and avoided my eyes. I didn't give up and shook him by the shoulders and screamed, 'Tell me what happened to us!' and he replied as if consoling me, 'Yaeli, it was over between us

189

a long time ago. Long before Yoavi was born.' I suddenly remembered my son and wept, 'And Yoavi, what will become of Yoavi?' and Nachum replied quietly, 'I will always be his father.'

I suddenly realised that he'd planned this divorce in secret, behind my back, long before I'd thought of it, and bitter bile bubbled inside me and on its way to my throat it burned until it collected in greenish bitterness in my mouth, and venom burst from me: 'His father? And where have you been until now?' Nachum said he was sure that after the divorce he would see the child more often than he did at present, and apart from that there were so many children at Yoavi's kindergarten whose parents were divorced, it had almost become the norm. And I screamed bitterly, 'And that's what salves your conscience, that divorce has become the norm?' And although I knew I'd never loved him the way my mother had loved my father, the tears burst from me, and weeping I asked if there was another woman, and again his eyes avoided mine, and I stated a fact, and my vocal chords almost exploded: 'You've got someone else!' and I suddenly heard him reply quietly, 'Yes.' 'Who is it?' I demanded, and he didn't reply, and I shook him by the shoulders with all my might and asked if I knew her, and he answered me with an offhanded 'Yes,' and I demanded her name and he refused to tell me. By now I was beside myself, and wallowing in my insult and hurt I counted off the names of the prime suspects, and they stood there patiently on this identity parade, in a long straight line, and then I marched them past him one by one, announcing the candidates' names like in a beauty contest, and they walked towards him and he sat there in his armchair like a lord, disqualifying them one by one.

At the head of the parade of whores marched the lovely Louisa. Nachum spluttered, 'Are you crazy? She's engaged, and apart from that Yoram's my best friend.' After Louisa came the wives of our friends, and after them I didn't forget to put Shoshana the kindergarten teacher and Levana our neighbour onto the list of floozies, but he rejected them all with a derisory gesture. I finally enlisted Nechama, too, even though he called her 'the fat one with the moustache'; and so, with Nechama walking slowly at the end of the line, I ran out of candidates. 'No,' he repeated, and in his voice I heard a dim echo rolling between snowy mountain peaks, hitting a high mountain and causing a terrible avalanche that sowed death and destruction in its path, burying people, trees and chalets.

When the storm passed I asked him if he'd decided to play Truth or Dare with me, because the whore's name would come out sooner or later, and it would be better all round if I heard it from him and not from others.

With a great effort he finally blurted it out: 'Hagit.'

I shuddered and asked if it was Hagit his hygienist, and as he nodded I could suddenly see her plunging necklines, her breasts rippling, soft and flaccid, as she bent over the patients' mouths, and the skin of her chest, spotted and wrinkled like crêpe paper. And I saw her dry hair, dyed iridescent blonde, and her face daubed with a thick layer of make-up. With trembling lips I said bitterly that her efforts had paid off, that whore, and she'd finally caught herself a dentist even at the cost of breaking up a family, and I demanded to know how long the affair had been going on. Nachum ignored the question as if it hadn't been asked, and I asked, shouting, whether our friends knew, and he was silent but his look told me 'Yes.' 'Nechama too?' I asked – asserted through my tears, and he admitted that Nechama had come to his clinic one day and interrogated him about the gossip she'd heard, and he had denied the rumour. Again I asked him how long the affair had been going on, and how many times a week they'd met, and how was she in bed, and was her body more beautiful than mine, and he suddenly answered all my questions magnanimously, as if he'd got a load off his chest, probably happy that he'd finally freed himself of the taxing secret and the lies.

Rejoicing in my tears I demanded to hear everything, everything, in all its gory detail, and it peeved me to death that everybody except me had known, and I wailed, 'How could you do something like this to me?' but he suddenly responded with a vigorous attack, and blamed me for his infidelity, and shouted that none of this would have happened if I hadn't neglected him emotionally and sexually. My fingers shot out, fingernails extended, to scratch his ugly face, slaughter him, puncture the vein standing out on his temple that was pulsing madly, and now my nails were in his thinning, greying forelock, tearing out a tuft of hair. Nachum caught my wrists and his face reddened as he screamed, 'Who do you think you are, that only you can do it? D'you think I'm blind? That I didn't know you'd fallen in love with that *dos* of yours? I'm a human being too, I need love too!' Droplets of viscous spittle sprayed from his mouth and seared my face like acid, and I couldn't wipe them off because my hands were imprisoned in his. I bleated, weeping, and shouted that at least I hadn't gone to bed with Avshalom while he was sleeping with that whore Hagit and God knows who else, and everybody knew except me.

Yoavi suddenly woke up and screamed loudly, and Nachum immediately let go of me and pushed me away. I ran to my son, tripping over the pile of toys in the doorway, and then I was at his side, and he was sitting up in his cot and crying with his eyes closed, Tutti pressed to his nose. 'Don't be frightened, it was only a scary film on television, it'll be quiet now,' I assured him, and Yoavi opened his eyes, stared at me confused, the tears soaking into his pyjamas and his body swaying back and forth, back and forth. I was alarmed and called his name, but he didn't respond. I picked him up, his body warm and heavy with sleep, and shook him gently until he woke up and asked me to sit with him, and he grasped my hand, begging me not to go, not to ever leave him.

I heard Nachum leave the house and start his car.

When Yoavi fell asleep I went into the bathroom and saw my face in the mirror, the red, swollen eyes, the dishrag lips and the fine lines of bitterness at both sides of my mouth. I put my arms under the flow of cold water and saw the last vestiges of the white finger marks that Nachum had left imprinted on them. I washed off the spittle he'd sprayed onto my face and thought how pitiful my husband was, that despite the large selection he'd had to choose from, in his laziness he'd taken the most readily available, that whore Hagit who was par for the course. His patsy. Like a bad, greasy dish from a fast food kiosk.

Nachum didn't come home that night, and in the morning, after I'd taken Yoavi to the kindergarten, I drove to Nechama's clinic.

'Nachum's left me! You knew, everybody knew, and nobody bothered to tell me,' I shouted after driving out a father and son who were with her. The father looked at her helplessly, waiting for her to say something, and she told them they should leave now because this was an emergency, and promised to make up the time they'd lost next week. 'In any case you only had five minutes left!' she called after their retreating backs, and immediately turned to me and angrily said that no Greek tragedy justified me driving her patients away. 'When they come back next week,' she promised,

192

'I'll tell them you're mad and suicidal, and that's why I had no choice but to see you.' Then she hissed through clenched lips, 'You just didn't want to know. You shut your eyes. The writing was on the wall. You refused to see it.'

'If you knew, then why didn't you tell me? Your best friend?'

Nechama went on the defensive. 'I heard rumours, I didn't have proof. I couldn't tell you about my suspicions.'

'You could have at least saved me the shame of everybody knowing except me.'

'Is that what's bothering you?' she shouted angrily. I shrugged and she repeated, 'Is that what's bothering you? Not the life of lies you lived with him? You were two lonely, pitiful creatures under the same roof. Can you remember the last time you fucked him? Did it happen at all apart from that time you conceived Yoavi? Thank your lucky stars that he wants to leave, some men don't even know how to separate! And anyway, what difference does it make to you who's leaving whom? You should thank God it's over like this and not with you being committed to an asylum! Because I was afraid for you. Really, I was afraid for your mental health. It's not because of the bus. The bus was just a trigger.'

Then she made me a cup of tea, wiped away my tears, and until her next patient came explained that the infidelity had been inevitable. 'Nachum simply did it before you. If Avshalom had agreed to cooperate, we both know you'd have slept with him a long time ago.'

Although I knew she was right, I couldn't let go of the sense of being the victim. I interrupted her, screaming in insult, 'But he cheated on me, don't you get it? He cheated on me with that Hagit!'

Nechama chuckled. 'And you cheated on him in your mind with Avshalom. Admit it, how many times a day do you fantasise that you're sleeping with him, eh?'

'So you're trying to tell me that you justify what Nachum's done?' I yelled, 'You're justifying his pitiful cheating? What about love? Do you believe he loves that ugly cow?'

'Love,' Nechama exclaimed derisively, 'You're talking to me about love? How many times have I told you that love's a load of hocus-pocus! Love's got nothing to do with it!' and she repeated her hackneyed theory that men's infidelities play an evolutionary role whose purpose is the replacement of a partner that ensures the offspring of the new woman's genetic diversity that constitutes an option of survival for the man's genes.

I took a handful of tissues from the box on her desk, blew my nose loudly and shot at her, 'I really don't understand why you're preaching at me instead of behaving like a good friend and siding with me and telling me that Nachum's a rotten bastard and an adulterer.'

I stormed from the room, and so she'd know I was angry I slammed the door behind me and startled the next patient who was sitting in the waiting room. When I got home I heard her voice rebuking me over the answering machine: 'Stop feeling sorry for yourself and concentrate on Yoavi, you've got to talk to him about the change that's going to take place in his life. If you need help, I'm always here for you.'

That night, drugged with tranquillisers and dozing on the couch in front of the flickering TV screen, I waited for Nachum. At two in the morning I crawled into bed until I was awakened by Yoavi. I looked at the clock and saw it was already 8.30. I hadn't heard the alarm. Concerned, Yoavi looked at me and asked, 'Is Imush a moth or a butterfly today?' and didn't enquire about Nachum. I dragged after him into his room and dressed him, didn't offer him breakfast and took him to the kindergarten. Then I called the university, told them I was sick, lay on the bed and swallowed another pill. I dozed and awoke intermittently and didn't answer the phone even when I heard Nechama's voice screaming in concern: 'Yaeli, pick up. If you don't call back I'm coming over and I'll use my key.' I called her receptionist and asked her to tell Nechama that I was at home asleep, and that she shouldn't dare come over, and disconnected. I woke up in the afternoon with a blinding headache and hurried to collect Yoavi from the kindergarten before Nechama got there.

We didn't go back home. We drove to the German Colony and went into a toy shop and I told Yoavi that I wanted to buy him a toy, 'Whatever you want.' Yoavi kissed me and said, 'Thank you, Imush,' and ran to the pink shelves where the girls' toys were. He deliberated for a long time between the various dolls and cookery sets, and I tried in vain to pull him away to the boys' shelves and tempt him with cars and building toys. He finally asked me to get him down a half-naked baby doll with a blue diaper around its private parts and a bottle clutched in its hand. I looked at this plastic horror with its frozen face, bloated cheeks and wide eyes. When we paid for it the shopkeeper showed us the tiny hole in its mouth, that fitted the bottle's nipple exactly, and the other tiny hole in the lower body from which the water dripped and wetted the diaper.

As we left the shop Yoavi said he was going to call the doll Bobo because he was a boy and not a girl, he kissed its bald head and promised me he'd take good care of him and wouldn't forget to feed him and change his diaper.

Then we drove to the playground in Talpiot. We sat on a bench and had something to eat, and Yoavi played with Bobo and asked me to pour some juice into his bottle and he fed him through the hole in his mouth. The bluish diaper was immediately stained purple, and Yoavi got scared and said that the baby had blood pipi. I told him it was because of the juice, and he asked if his pipi too would be blood-coloured because he'd drunk the juice as well, but he didn't wait for a reply and ran to the swings and asked me to push him. I sat him on the swing and asked him to hold the ropes tightly and pushed his back and he yelled, 'More, Imush, more, Imush.'

The swing squeaked and squeaked and the sound dug another scratch and another into the scab of my old wound, which opened and started bleeding. I saw her, the three year-old girl on the swing in her white Shabbat dress, her eyes rounded and damp with fear, and at the corners of her mouth a smile that had withered. Reluctantly, I recalled that warm Shabbat when my father took me to the playground, lifted me up and sat me on the swing. And I gripped the ropes of Yoavi's swing, my knuckles white with effort, and rough fibre curls scratched my palms and tore the skin. And my father wrapped my hands around the ropes in his fists and told me to hold on tightly, so I wouldn't fall off. And he stood behind me, holding on to the ropes and swinging me up into the sky, and letting me go down, down to the ground, and up again and down again.

Yoavi's voice screaming in terror and laughing with delight intermingled with the sounds of my screams and weeping, because my father had suddenly let go of my hands. He was no longer holding onto the ropes with me, his back was retreating with giant strides until his figure became blurred and disappeared from my sight. I was alone in the world on the high swing between heaven and earth. I called him in a weak voice and then with loud weeping, until he suddenly came back to me, his black box camera in his hands and his voice soothing, '*Sha, sha, sha*, my sweet Yaeli, I was only taking your photograph!' but his abandonment of me had put down its decaying roots deep inside me. Since then the photograph had lain at the bottom of the photograph box, the tin box that in its sweeter days had contained small tablets of bitter chocolate. After Father's death, when the photographs had been properly arranged in an album, I saw that photograph again, and all the ancient musty fears had crawled out at me like hairy worms. And I pushed the swing and pushed it, more and more and more, and Yoavi's laughter turned into tears, and I suddenly heard his voice pleading, 'Stop, Imush, I'm frightened, stop, Imush, enough.' I shook myself and took him down from the swing and saw that his face was greenish and he said he didn't feel well, and a stream of vomit suddenly spewed out onto his shoes.

I cleaned his face and clothes and gave him a drink of water and asked if he felt better, and he raised a pale face to mine. In the strong sunlight the honey-coloured flecks in his eyes shone and he twisted his mouth, and as if afraid to be a cause for worry, he whispered, 'Yes, better.' 'So what shall we do next?' I asked him and he suggested, 'Let's slide on the Monster?' and we drove to Kiryat Yovel.

A red, white and black monster lay on its belly as if brooding on an egg and looked at us with its squinty eyes, playfully pulling forked serpents' tongues at us. Laughing children climbed up and slid down the long tongues, and Yoavi announced, 'By myself,' broke away from me and disappeared behind the monster. I ran after him, but he'd already vanished into its dark womb. I walked around it and stood at its feet, waiting for Yoavi to exit its curled lips and slide down on his bottom right into my arms. But Yoavi didn't appear. And then it all came back to me. The terror. Cold fingers twined around my throat and my heart pounded as if it was going to burst. I knew that my child would never come back, he'd been swallowed up into the depths of the monster, into the belly of Moloch. In panic I called his name and he didn't answer. My legs barely holding me up, I ran behind the monster, to the steps leading into its belly, and I climbed up and panting reached its wide forehead and saw children playing in the small space on the top of its head, and I called Yoavi's name again and again he didn't answer. It was dark and stifling in there and I wanted to run away, and I sat my behind on one of the tongues and it drew me inside, and far too quickly my bottom thumped onto the damp sand. Yoavi wasn't waiting down below. Again and again I called his name, and my voice was swallowed up in the children's laughter and the roar of passing cars. I sat on the wet sand and wept. With my own hands I had sacrificed my son to Moloch and he had swallowed him. And then I heard a shout, and Yoavi's tiny, blond head was peeping from the monster's lips, and I shouted to him to be careful, not to hurry, Ima's coming, but again he uttered a terrible shout, whether of pleasure or fear I don't know, and then he was sliding down head first on his belly. I got up heavily, ran towards him to hold him lest he fall, but he had already fallen from the end of the slide and was crying, and I saw his scratched and bleeding chin, and I was laughing and sobbing, 'It's nothing,' and I sat him on my knee and licked his grazed chin. A smell of cat piss came from him, wet sand crunched between my teeth, and the sourish taste of my son's blood, and I didn't care, and I said, it'll pass, and licked and licked until his crying turned into a giggle and he said, 'Stop it, Imush, it tickles.' And I remembered how Nachum had once seen me do the same thing to his grazed elbow and shouted that I was behaving like a wild animal, because licking a child's wound wasn't hygienic, and Yoavi told him, 'Imush isn't like an animal, she's like a cat licking her kittens.'

We lay exhausted on the damp sand at the foot of the monster, whose face had softened and become friendly like that of a fat lady returning from the market loaded down with shopping baskets. I thought of sculptress Nikki de Saint Phalleand, of how one small woman could have sculpted such a huge, monstrous work and why she dedicated this frightening sculpture to the children of Jerusalem, of all people.

I looked at the weak afternoon sun, and my eyes filled with tears when I told Yoavi that soon Abba wouldn't be living with us at home. I rubbed my eyes so he wouldn't detect my tears, and my eyeballs burned and I thought that my tears had dried in the sun and formed tiny salt crystals. Yoavi's head suddenly shaded me and his eyes looked into mine: 'So it's like Abba going to the army?' he asked, and I said, 'Yes, my clever boy.'

'But he always comes home from the army,' he persisted. 'It

will be like him going into the army for a long, long time,' I said, trying to soothe him, and Yoavi kissed my lips and said, 'Yuck, you're salty.'

As the day became covered with a darkening curtain, the chilly wind drove us from the playground and we went home. I saw Nachum's car in the parking lot. He greeted us gaily and Yoavi waved his doll and said, 'Look at what Imush bought me today,' and Nachum curled his lip and blurted, 'Lovely,' and told me that the answering machine was loaded with messages from Nechama and asked if we wanted him to fix supper for us. Yoavi shouted joyfully and forgot everything I'd told him and asked to sit on the counter by Abba who was slicing vegetables for a salad. Nachum asked what Yoavi had on his chin, and I said, a graze, and Yoavi eagerly volunteered, 'Imush swung me on the swing and I threw up and then I fell off the monster slide.' Nachum's hands rose and fell angrily on the cutting board, making a cucumber's life a misery, and he looked at me accusingly and asked if I'd disinfected it. I told him I'd kept that pleasure for him. From the bathroom came Yoavi's pleading voice, 'Stop it, Abba, it burns,' and Nachum's scolding voice, 'We've got to clean the cut otherwise it'll fill with pus.'

Before he went to bed I heard him moving around the apartment as usual, going from room to room, switching off lights, locking doors and in his undeviating order lowering the shutters, protecting us from the darkness, and the light, and who knows what else.

'Juliet, are you asleep?' he asked, jolting me with the nickname he'd once used for me, when he had courted me and I had called him Romeo.

I turned my back and said I couldn't talk to him right now.

'We've got to talk,' he said. 'We've got to talk about dividing the property and what's going to happen to you. The apartment's in my name. We've got to find you a new place. What do you think about renting in Gilo? It'll be a lot easier for you.'

I sat up in bed and screamed, 'Is that all you're worrying about right now? Your fucking property? What about your son? Or have you forgotten we've got a son? Right now all I'm concerned about is Yoavi,' and I turned my back on him again.

'Don't shout,' he pleaded, 'Yoavi'll wake up.'

'All of a sudden you're worried about your son?' I asked bitterly.

He was almost weeping when he said that Yoavi was dear to his heart and he would never deny his paternal obligations. He suggested that we remain together until after the divorce, and if by then we hadn't found a suitable apartment, he would look for a suitable place with me, and said that I shouldn't worry about maintenance. He couldn't hold himself back and got out of bed and came back with a sheet of paper and asked me to look at it, pleading, 'Julie, you can't ignore it. We're getting divorced. We've got to talk about brass tacks.' I snatched the paper from him, which was divided into two columns by a heavy line, each one with its own header: 'Nachum's Property' and 'Yael's Property.' Beneath our respective names the assets crawled, one after another, in a straight line. I threw it onto the floor. 'You're a petty, stingy and repulsive man,' I said quietly, but he cleared his throat and read from the sheet as if reciting a grocery list, and I shut my ears and asked him to sleep on the couch in the study. But he mumbled something to the effect that until the divorce the bed was his, too, and he lay down, far away from me.

I awoke in the morning with his arms round me from behind in a rare moment of closeness. When I got up I saw in the bathroom that he'd put toothpaste onto my brush, as he'd done in the early days of our love. In the kitchen, steaming coffee and toast awaited me.

Afterwards I drove to the university and thought about how I'd break the news to my colleagues.

Louisa forestalled me and came into the office without discerning my mournful face as with a smile she gave me a splendid sealed envelope. Her smile infected me. 'What's this?' I asked as if I didn't know, and she urged me, 'Go on, open it.' Cursive gold script in Hebrew and French announced that parents of the bride and groom had the pleasure of inviting me to the marriage of their dear children. I kissed her on the cheek and said, '*Mazal Tov*' and 'You've wasted no time,' and she said, '*Ma chérie*, it's all down to you, you were the matchmaker.' I couldn't restrain myself. 'Great. One of us is getting married and the other's getting a divorce.' Her expression became serious and she sat down on my desk and asked me what I meant. And I said, 'Stop playing the innocent, you've probably heard from Yoram that he's got a lover.' Louisa's eyes rounded, 'I swear I didn't know,' and I fired at her, 'Don't tell me you didn't know. The whole world except for his wife knew he has a lover.' 'Who is she?' she shouted, I'll claw her eyes out,' and I replied, 'His hideous Hagit.' Angrily she said, 'Then how didn't Yoram know, they work together, next door to one another,' and I replied, 'I thought that everyone at the clinic knew. Maybe Yoram didn't tell you because you're my friend.' She slid from the table and hugged me and her bangles thundered in my ears as she said, 'You're staying my best friend. No matter what happens with those men.'

'And the wedding?' I asked hesitantly.

She replied with a question, 'What about the wedding?'

I stated a fact. 'Nachum's surely invited and will probably come with his whore and I don't want to see them.' And she said, 'But Nachum's Yoram's partner and we can't not invite him.' 'Well,' I declared, 'I'm not coming,' and she yelled, 'Are you crazy? You're the guest of honour. This wedding would never have happened if it hadn't been for you.' I dug in my heels, saying, 'I'll come as long as Nachum doesn't,' but Louisa stuck to her guns, 'You can't do this to me. You can't ruin my big day.' But I didn't budge an inch. 'It's your decision, it's either him or me,' and she announced that she'd have to talk to Yoram, and you should know that you're making life very difficult for me and it's impossible to leave Nachum off the guest list. Corrosive acid was already bubbling in my stomach when I said with equanimity, 'Then I won't be there so the best of luck to you both.'

Nachum called in the afternoon and asked what I thought about collecting Yoavi together and going to the mall and finally buying him a proper bed, and then we'd all go to a restaurant. Bitterly I asked what exactly we were celebrating, and he hesitated for a moment and then replied that he wanted to be with us as much as possible, and reported that he'd already contacted the president of the Jerusalem rabbinical court, who purely by chance was a patient of his, and the divorce, so the rabbi had assured him, would go through in a jiffy, less than a month. 'There's no point in dragging it out,' he said, trying to reason with me, 'It's what we both want, right?' And I wanted to yell, 'In a jiffy? Is that how you want to end nine years?' but I held myself in check so he wouldn't think I was hurt.

· Dozens of couches and beds stood side by side in the showroom, like one vast, colourful and soft bed. Yoavi climbed onto one whose headboard was curlicues of latticework, hugged Bobo in his arms and pretended to be asleep. He got down and announced that this was the bed he wanted, but Nachum refused and said it was a girl's bed, and chose the one next to it, a bed of dark blue whose price was much lower, and immediately pulled out his wallet and paid cash, so that the bed would be delivered in the morning. Yoavi gazed longingly at the bed he'd wanted, and I consoled him saying that Abba was right, and the bed he'd get tomorrow morning was a big boy's bed.

Then we went to a restaurant. I chose the most expensive dish on the menu – steak in a mushroom and cognac sauce – and Nachum asked if I was sure I'd manage to finish such a big meal, and I answered that I was hungry and he should mind his own business. When I asked which wine we should choose he said he was tired and had to drive home and that wine would make him drowsy, and apart from that the price of wines in this restaurant was exorbitant, and he ordered a Caesar salad and a glass of water for himself, and a hamburger and chips for Yoavi. Terribly polite, we sat at the table and restricted our conversation to 'Very tasty' or 'Please pass the salt,' and smothered Yoavi and Bobo, who was sitting beside him, with exaggerated and clumsy attention, encouraging him over and over to eat, carefully cleaning his grazed chin, running our fingers over his cropped head, repeatedly mentioning that he was a good boy and he was eating so nicely, just like a big boy. The child sat there between us, miserable and embarrassed, now looking at me and then at Nachum, as if following the ball at a tennis match, and I knew that he knew that we were putting on this oppressive act, this lie, just for him.

After Nachum had put Yoavi to bed, we sat in the kitchen and he suddenly asked, 'Would you like a glass of wine?' 'Aren't you too tired for wine?' I asked spitefully, but he had already got out from somewhere a bottle of Chardonnay I didn't know existed. With a great deal of effort he pulled the cork and sniffed it like a connoisseur, poured the wine into two glasses, and began recalling memories and forgotten stories from the past. He spoke yearningly of our early days, how we'd first met at the students' dental clinic, and how alluring I'd seemed to him, and how he'd wanted me even then. Then he displayed his big-heartedness and announced that immediately after the divorce he'd leave the apartment, despite it being in his name, because he had somewhere to live. 'Chez Hagit,' I said bitterly, and hated myself. 'Yes, at Hagit's,' he confirmed, 'although it won't be that comfortable for Yoavi there.' And he added that in the meantime I could go on living in the apartment until I found one I could rent in a nice neighbourhood. He didn't care how long it took, he said, the main thing was that I shouldn't compromise and should find the most suitable apartment available.

In my morning phone chat with Nechama I told her about Nachum's agreeable behaviour and unexpected generosity, and I heard her exhaling smoke together with a little chuckle, and then she told me in her hoarse voice that Nachum was behaving like a classic cheating husband, and that in all probability I'd experience many pleasurable moments with him. 'It's a pleasure created by the temporary emotional openness you're experiencing at present,' she explained, and added that this stage was vital for reducing the anxiety: 'Nachum, and maybe you, too, are adopting courting behaviour to restore the love and attraction of your partner, even if it ceased to exist a long time ago.'

As Nachum undressed the night before the divorce came through, I looked at his body for the last time, and as if seeing his nakedness for the first time I thought how vulnerable he looked without clothes. His feet were flat and wide like pink rubber fins, the legs long, thin and straight, completely smooth from ankle to halfway up the shin, and from there upwards reasonably hairy. Above the junction of the legs with the pubis there was a shadow of a small paunch, and a cascade of abundant, shiny black hair fell towards it from the heights of the chest. I can't recall his member and its appurtenances, so it would be better if I skipped the descriptions and noted that slightly above the pubis, surrounded by stalks of dark hair, stood a round and protruding navel, far different from my own sunken one. Above that, standing out against the pale skin, were two wide pink nipples surrounded by aureoles of tiny bumps and curly hairs. As he came out the bathroom with his back to me, he bent over slightly to put on his underpants, a broad backside covered with downy hair and red pimples with white heads flashed a vertical smile at me from below the back covered with sun spots and birthmarks I'd never seen. As he moved towards the bed I looked at his face, trying to etch it on my memory. An average man, neither handsome nor ugly, with an ordinary face with nothing worthy of note: a straight nose and wide nostrils, a narrow mouth, a dimpled, slightly upturned chin, pale, unfocused eyes, like those of the short-sighted. Across the too-wide forehead two deep furrows stretched from temple to temple, endowing the face with a degree of maturity and seriousness, and above the hairline, in the thinning, greying forelock, two small bays were in the process of excavation. I thought to myself that if there was any truth in the belief that over the years couples begin resembling one another, the process would be interrupted when we separated, and that it was for the best. I didn't want any part of Nachum's features imprinted on mine.

Thus I lay beside him on that last night, listening to his heavy breathing and annoying snores. Again I tortured myself in an attempt to understand why I'd married him of all people, this man whose wife I would no longer be tomorrow. Who knows, maybe I didn't deserve anything better, perhaps I wasn't entitled to experience a love like that of my parents. I prayed for morning to come and deliver me from my painful thoughts. Over and over I felt a nervous twitch in my bladder and got up to go to the bathroom, until Nachum grumbled that I should let him get some rest, and the next time I went to the bathroom I shouldn't flush, because the noise was driving him crazy. I fell asleep just before dawn.

The movement of his body awakened me.

'Are you awake?' he asked.

'I haven't slept a wink,' I complained, and a hand was suddenly cupping my breast, and the other was in the waistband of my panties and pulling them down and sliding over my belly, feeling its way to my pudenda. Then I felt his weight on top of me, and I automatically spread my legs and helped him hide inside me. Like an asthmatic climbing a mountain he panted into my breasts, and it was all over before it had begun. As his body rolled off me he said he was sorry. I lay frozen on my back, and his semen, warm and sticky and disgusting, slid down the slopes of my thighs.

'The divorce papers aren't ready, go away and come back later,' said one of the black-clad gentlemen, the clip of whose yarmulke barely held on to the sparse hair that was meticulously smoothed down over his scalp. 'It will take another hour,' he promised, as if he was talking to us about a very complicated dish we'd ordered in a fancy restaurant.

'Coffee?' Nachum suggested innocently, and without waiting for an answer he was halfway down the stairs with me in his wake. We went to Café Hillel on Jaffa Road. When I took off my coat Nachum saw the dress I was wearing and asked mockingly, 'In whose honour are you all dolled up? Mine or his? And a long white dress too? Did you forget that we're here to get divorced, not get married?' he asked, trying to make a joke of it. I kept quiet. When the waiter arrived Nachum ordered a fried egg, and I said, 'But you always have scrambled eggs,' and he smiled happily: 'A man can change his habits sometimes, can't he?' and he ate with gusto, wiping his plate with a slice of bread. Some of the viscous yolk dripped onto his chin, but I didn't say a word.

I couldn't understand how he could have such an appetite while my stomach was turning over.

I had herbal tea and looked suspiciously at everyone coming inside and opening their bags for inspection at the entrance, and thought that if one of them decided to blow himself upright now, I'd die and Nachum would be a widower, and Hagit would raise my child. I exhorted him to finish his meal. As we came into the sun, spatters of congealed egg yolk glistened on his chin like sickening acne, and I loved it. Nachum asked, 'What have I got on my chin that you're looking at all the time?' and he rubbed the yellow spots, and dry scales dropped from his face onto the blue jacket he was wearing.

Then he confessed with a smile, 'You know, when I first started courting you, I was scared of eating with you. I thought that as an anthropologist you'd probably draw conclusions from the way I ate.' In a burst of compassion I brushed the crumbs from his jacket, and thought who'd do that for him after I'd gone, and Hagit and her neckline stuck themselves into my face.

We went back to the rabbinate. In the divorce court, three heavily bearded, black-clad men looked down on us and spoke, and enquired, and preached, and explained, and asked me to remove all my rings. The wedding ring that Nachum had slipped onto my finger so long ago had dug itself in so deeply it had become flesh of flesh. Foreign eyes followed me, hurrying me with their look. I tried ripping it off by force until Nachum lost his patience and whispered angrily, 'Why didn't you take care of that at home?' They sent me to the toilet, perhaps soap and water would help. I managed to get it off there, but I didn't want to go back. Let them wait, I don't care, I'm not rushing anywhere. I turned my hand over. A white band showed where the rebellious ring had been, highlighting my tanned skin. I'd only taken it off once in the past, when I was pregnant with Yoavi, when my whole body had swelled up and my fingers became sausages. I buried it in the small pocket in my purse, and wondered what I'd do with it now.

Bleak faces greeted me on my return, and Nachum, whose patience had evaporated, grumbled, 'You were in there for half an hour,' and I replied in a stage whisper, 'I'm constipated.'

A scroll of paper landed in my lap and I was asked to hold it in both hands, take it outside to the balcony, turn to the wall and then turn round and stand. I did as I was told like an automaton, and walked outside and came back, and in the third person they declared, as if I weren't in the room, that I was forbidden to my husband and sexual partner. 'But there's been a mistake,' I wanted to shout, 'I've got no sexual partner. Nachum has. He's partnering another woman. She should be forbidden to him!' but then the words hit me, cruel and solemn: 'You are hereby divorced. You are hereby cast out. You are hereby permitted to any man,' just like an auctioneer offering a piece with no bidders. I wanted to shout that I had been permitted only to Nachum and I'd never known another man, and that I was scared, so scared of not belonging. For now I had no owner, I was an abandoned child left to my own devices.

I thought about the man still standing beside me and how they'd expropriated him from my life in a single moment. I suddenly didn't want him to go. Because out there, without him, I would be permitted to any man. Come one, come all, look, feel, touch, penetrate and throw away. All, that is, except for a man of the priestly sect.

We went out into the corridor together, forbidden to one another by a scrap of paper, and I could hardly control my arm that threatened to link his. I glanced at him and thought I saw a glistening in his eye and I wanted to ask him, 'So what's going to happen?' and then we saw him: a beanpole of a man in threadbare black clothes, his grey beard flying, his eyes red and staring, and his mouth, that revealed nicotine-stained teeth, gaping in a shout, 'Where is she? Where's my little doll? I love you, my heart. You won't get a divorce from me. Never. Ever.' A long moment passed until we realised that the policeman at his side was handcuffed to him and that the lawbreaker's arm was manacled to that of the guardian of the law, body touching body. Roughly, the policeman shoved him into the room we had just left with the words 'permitted to any man' still echoing between its walls, and the prisoner turned and tried to escape towards the stairs, dragging the policeman with him, as the latter cursed his despicable twin.

'You're lucky I didn't refuse to grant you a divorce,' my ex-husband said. The blinding winter sunlight attacked us outside and dazzled my eyes that had become accustomed to the dark. I shaded them. I wanted to stay with him a little longer. I asked him to accompany me to the parking lot. At the gate he shook my hand and asked, 'Can we stay friends?' but didn't wait for a reply and hurried to his clinic because that whore Hagit was probably waiting for him with a cake and champagne.

And before the brain managed to process what the eyes had seen, the adrenalin was already flooding my arteries and my skin bristled as if sensing danger: I saw her. She was walking in front of me with a bunch of keys jangling in her hand. I was sure it was her. The same red coat and the same blonde hair capping her head like a helmet. My eyes were riveted on her back and my feet followed her. I had to talk to her, ask her, and didn't know what I'd say if she suddenly turned round. I lengthened my stride, panting behind her, and caught up with her. It was her. Not a shadow of a doubt. I was sure. My heart screamed in my chest, seeking to leap out and flee. A passing cloud covered the sun and my voice was hoarse and shaking: 'Do you remember me?' She looked through me. Her eyes were foreign and cold and two anger lines ran from her forehead to the bridge of her nose. Her mouth curled as she answered with a question, 'Why do you think I should remember you?' and she immediately lengthened her stride, jangling her keys with much devotion, and me at her side, running. 'We met once,' I panted, and she glanced aside at me and again looked through me. 'I don't remember you. Excuse me, I'm in a hurry.' Again she increased her pace, trying to escape, and I blocked her way. 'I won't let you budge from here until we've talked!' She said, 'I don't know you and we've nothing to talk about.' 'Have you really forgotten?' I shouted, 'Have you forgotten the curse?' I asked, almost bursting into tears, 'The curse you put on my son before he was born?' And I could hear the fermenting sounds inside me, the bile would shortly climb into my mouth and my body would fall apart.

'I'm not in the habit of cursing people,' the woman said in disgust.

'But you cursed my son, when he was still a foetus in my belly. At the "Women in Black" demonstration,' I said in a feeble attempt to refresh her memory.

In the silence I heard the twittering of birds cracking the sky.

'You've ruined my life,' I accused her of the great calamity of my life.

'You're mad.' An evil stare pierced my entrails. She tried to evade me and I begged, 'Let's talk about it, we're both women, we're both mothers, we've got to understand each other.'

'I don't have children,' she interrupted.

'What about your son? You said you had a son, that's what you said, and he was killed by terrorists,' I stammered.

'I don't have any children and I never have had,' the woman insisted, 'and now maybe you'll let me pass, I'm in a hurry.' Roughly, she pushed me out of the way, and my feet caught in the hem of the long white dress I'd worn for the divorce. I lost my balance and fell onto the gravel. Her bare neck moved away from me and her hurrying heels angrily drummed on the gravel, crunch-crunch, crunch-crunch, ticking like the timer of a bomb.

I looked after her disappearing figure for a long time until it became a distant red dot. I could have sworn it was her.

I made my way stumblingly to my car. I cried all the way to Yoavi's kindergarten. In the parking lot I put on some make-up, camouflaging the deep boat-like shadows that had dropped anchor beneath my eyes, combed my hair, put on a big smile and willingly opened my bag for Nikolai the guard.

On the way home I told Yoavi that Abba wouldn't be sleeping at home any more, but Yoavi could sleep at Abba's whenever he wanted. 'Where does Abba sleep at night?' he asked anxiously. 'Abba's sleeping at another apartment,' I replied. 'Where?' he demanded, and I didn't know what to tell him. Where the hell did that whore of Nachum's live? I tried to explain that soon we too would be leaving our old apartment and move into a new one and, after we'd left, Abba would move back into the old apartment, and I knew what I was saying was incomprehensible even to myself,

207

and I tried to get myself out of the mess and said that in the meantime we were staying in the old apartment, and Yoavi's new bed would be staying there. 'When we move to our new apartment I'll buy you another bed,' I promised. 'And will we have a cat too?' he wanted to know, and I said, 'Sure.' Yoavi rubbed his grazed chin that refused to heal, and as if remembering he asked if I'd buy him that bed he'd wanted in the shop and Abba hadn't wanted to buy, and again I said, 'Sure.'

When we got home he became serious and asked the obvious question: 'Doesn't Abba love us any more?' I wanted to die but confidently declared, 'Abba loves you more than anything in the world. He loves you to bits.'

'But Imush, doesn't he love Imush any more?' half asking, half stating a fact, and he brought his face to mine and looked long into my eyes and declared, 'But I love Imush and if Abba doesn't love Imush any more then I'll marry her.' When he kissed my lips with his cherry ones, I admitted to myself that perhaps Nachum's genes weren't so bad after all if we'd had a son like this.

That night I pushed the heap of dolls from his bed and lay down at his side, my backside to the wall and my arms round him. I looked at the moon and the phosphorescent stars I'd stuck onto the ceiling and sang, 'And what do the stars do?' and Yoavi was quiet and I responded for him, 'They fall down on us from above. Fall, fall, fall, to where?' And he piped the answer, 'Nowhere.' Then he suddenly asked: 'What's dying?' and wanted to know when I'd die, and if the terrorists would kill me and what would happen to him and where would he live. Frightened, I told him we'd talk in the morning, but he persisted and I replied, without thinking, that dying was like being a butterfly. 'How?' he asked. I reminded him of the silkworms that Shoshana had brought to the kindergarten, and he nodded eagerly, and together we counted off the stages: egg, larva, pupa and butterfly. And I told him that after the pupa the butterfly remains, and that's what dying is like. Then I crushed him in a hug until he complained that I was hurting him, and I promised that even if Abba wasn't sleeping at home, no terrorist would harm us. He turned his face to me, asked me to buy him a rifle and fell asleep right away, his legs entangled in mine and the ends of my hair caught between his chubby fingers. I hugged him to me. That night I didn't hear our fourth-floor neighbours moving the furniture across my ceiling or Levana shouting in lovemaking.

I woke up early, my white dress damp and sticky on my body, the TV set chirping in the background with the morning kids' programme, and Yoavi smiled into my face: 'Now we're both butterflies.'

Later I called Avshalom. 'I am permitted to any man,' I wanted to tell him, but there was no reply. All day I tried calling, in the evening too, after I'd put Yoavi to bed, but the ringing tone went on and on with no reply. I continued to call him day after day, several times a day, until one morning I was answered by a soft, feminine 'Hello? Who's calling?' and the receiver froze in my hand. 'Hello? Who's calling?' the woman repeated, and I wanted to tell her that was me, Yael, and ask her what she was doing first thing in the morning in the apartment of the man I loved, but I didn't manage to say a word. I tried again next day, and again the woman's voice asked its questions, and my heart dropped together with the receiver. In the evening a man intervened in the uncompleted call, and I heard his deep bass voice telling her, 'Let me answer.' It wasn't the voice I'd expected to hear, and I suddenly found my voice and asked about Avshalom. The bass voice replied: 'He's left, moved.' 'Do you have his new address by any chance?' I asked hopefully. I was answered with a bitter laugh: 'I'm looking for him too. He left an unpaid electricity bill.'

What Do the Children Do? Nothing

Afterwards, silence descended on the house. Avshalom's footprints had vanished, while Nachum's had been erased as if they had never existed. His side of the wardrobe yawned with an empty, dark mouth, and a few wire hangers, the ones you get with your dry-cleaning, hung naked and skeletal on the rail, rocking with the opening of the door as if yearning for his clothes. His comb had vanished, his shaving brush had gone, the shuffling of his slippers had been silenced like the buzzing of his electric toothbrush, the rattle of his keys as they were dropped into the copper bowl was no longer heard. The smell of sweat had dissipated, and the scent of the oils and aftershave, and the clinic smells that sometimes clung to his shirt-tails. Only the apron I'd bought him in London, the one with the plastic breasts, remained behind as a memento of the hours and days he'd spent in it at the sink.

The running of the house changed after he left. Suppers that had been served on time, the dishwashing after every meal, changing the bed linen once a week, entertaining friends on Friday evenings, going to the cinema on Saturday evenings, had all collapsed like a house of cards. Times were changed, habits had disappeared, disorder and breakdown reigned supreme, and my home resembled my mother's. The beds remained unmade all day, filthy dishes accumulated in the sink, leftovers mouldered in the fridge, a tap dripped, light bulbs expired one after the other, clothes taken off were thrown onto the floor, and the TV set was on in the background all day long without anybody watching it.

On Mondays and Thursdays, orderly, methodical Nachum collected Yoavi from the kindergarten and brought him home at seven on the dot, as the divorce agreement stipulated. When he couldn't make it on time, I'd find Hagiti and Yoavi hand in hand on the doorstep. Then the scar on my belly would open and my empty womb would contract as if in labour, and I'd want to yell, 'Lay not a hand upon the lad,' he's mine, I conceived him and bore him and it's my belly that was cut open to bring him out, and it's my blood that flowed, but I'd find myself smiling at her and asking what he'd had to eat and where they'd been, and Yoavi would always announce, 'Imush, look at what Hagiti bought me,' and show me a cheap plastic toy.

One day, about a month after the divorce, I didn't go into work and in the morning I called Nechama and told her to come quickly and dress Yoavi and take him to the kindergarten, because I didn't have the strength any more. She used the key I'd given her and burst into my bedroom and tut-tutted at the sight of the dirt and neglect everywhere. 'You've got to get a grip of yourself,' she grumbled and went into Yoavi's room, and then I heard her preaching at him from the toilet that now Ima was a bit sick he must learn to wipe his own bottom. Yoavi asked, 'What's Imush got?' he asked, and wanted to know if you died from my illness, and Nechama soothed him, saying, 'Ima's a little weak and tired, and she'll probably feel much better tomorrow.' Shining bright and clean, his still-damp curls stuck to his head, Yoavi came to my bed and gave me a solemn kiss, the way you do with sick people, and said officially, 'Get well, Imush,' and off he went with Nechama and I disconnected the phone and sank into a sleep filled with nightmares and woke up with a dry mouth and drank some water straight from the tap in the bathroom and went back to bed.

'So we're going to carry on living?' Nechama asked me reprovingly when she suddenly appeared at my bedside. 'What's the time?' I asked, and she groused, 'Time to live,' and raised the shutters. The pink light of the setting sun stole in through the window and Nechama sat down on the end of my bed: 'So in spite of everything we'll go on living, we'll get up in the morning, brush our teeth, make Yoavi's breakfast, take him to the kindergarten, go to work, do some cooking, go out a bit, have some fun, go to sleep at night and get up in the morning,' she said gently, then suddenly raised her voice, '*Yalla*, get your arse in gear, stop feeling sorry for yourself and go take care of your son, he needs his mother.' Obediently and submissively I got out of bed and went to the bathroom and brushed my teeth and washed my face and asked Nechama to bring Yoavi home. Five minutes later Levana was at the door holding a pot of chicken soup and on it a plate of chocolate cookies, and said she'd heard I hadn't been too well, and that I shouldn't hesitate to ask her for help, and meanwhile I should eat the soup and the cookies and get my strength back and she'd take care of the rest.

I sat down in the kitchen in my filthy robe, gnawed on a drumstick and sipped the soup straight from the pot, and the fatty liquid wet my unkempt hair. Levana went out onto the utility balcony and loaded the washing machine, and then went from room to room, collected Yoavi's toys, changed the bedclothes, dusted, washed the dishes, and cleared the fridge of mouldy food. And I trailed after her, 'Enough, Levana, I'll do it,' but she went right on: 'What are friends for?'

Next day I called an estate agent and announced that I wanted to rent an apartment in central Jerusalem.

Afterwards the puddles dried up, municipal workers cleaned up the branches that had broken in the gales and snapped under the weight of the snow, and Louisa got married in the spring, without me. In the spring the green velvet of grass sprouted over the hills, and bluish foliage on the trees' skeletons in Gazelle Valley, and a brown scab on Yoavi's grazed chin. And by the time the scab dropped off, the buttons of buds had opened on the branches, and the trees were resplendent in their bridal gowns, adorned with masses of pink and white stars. And the blossom fell and fruit hung green from the branches and would soon have a blush on its cheeks.

In the spring we moved into our new apartment on the third floor of a building in the German Colony, in a quiet lane with no vehicle access. The walls of our new home shone in their whiteness, we had a small balcony overlooking the garden around the house, and children of Yoavi's age played there unsupervised. I covered the bare walls with artwork posters I bought at the Israel Museum, painted the walls of Yoavi's room in 'the colour of oranges' and the ceiling in 'the blue of the sky,' bought him the bed with the latticework headboard, and pampered myself with a new double bed with a sprung mattress, so that Yoavi could jump on it like a trampoline and nobody would shout at him.

In those first days of spring I walked the neighbourhood lanes, enjoying the fragrance of jasmine and honeysuckle that climbed the walls protecting the well-tended gardens, peeping through the fences and inspecting the old stone Templar houses that had been built with European charm. Every morning I made the beds before we left, washed the dishes right after we'd eaten, and took out the garbage every evening at the set time. By the garbage cans I'd meet Greta, my elderly neighbour on the second floor, doing her best to take her sick dog, whose wasted belly hung down to the ground, for a walk. She'd greet me with a 'Gut efening,' enquire about 'Your darlink leetle boy,' and drag her Mutzi behind her as he staggered along on his arthritic legs. I'd look at them and think about surprising Yoavi with a pet of his own, and I also promised myself that I'd register for a yoga course and maybe bridge, too, and go to the folk dancing at the cultural centre, five minutes' walk away from our new apartment.

Soon the hot, dry summer winds would be knocking at the door, huffing and puffing with their burning breath. And from Yoavi's room came the sound of his favourite song, and he was singing along: 'What do the trees do? Grow. And what do the houses do? Stand. And the clouds? Fly, fly. And the thorns? They make fires.'

By early summer I'd forgotten the expression in his eyes, I couldn't remember the colour of his skin, and the sound of his voice had disappeared. I could only see his hands, peeping from the sleeves of his black jacket, and I knew I'd be able to recognise them even if a thousand pairs of hands were thrust towards me.

I'd walk the streets of the ultra-Orthodox neighbourhoods, hoping to bump into him, asking religious college students I met in the course of my research on evening computer courses, and ultra-Orthodox housewives, and yeshiva students, about him but nobody knew or had heard a thing. The contents of my interview file grew, and I informed Prof. Har-Noy that I was ready to begin writing my thesis. He raised his hairy eyebrows: 'What's the hurry? We've waited a long time. We started a subject. We abandoned a subject. Wait. Maybe you'll change your mind, and maybe you'll decide to go to New Zealand and study the tattoo motifs on the faces of the Maoris.' I smiled at him, and he patted my shoulder in a fatherly way and told me how proud of me he was, that in spite of everything I'd been through we were carrying on, we weren't giving up.

*

Twice a week, as always, on Sunday and Wednesday afternoons, Nechama and Yoeli would come over, and the two tots, who had been dubbed 'Max und Moritz' after the two fictional mischief-makers, would shut themselves up in Yoavi's room and leave us to talk.

At the time it seemed that Yoavi had grown up before his time. He'd consider my needs just like a considerate husband, didn't take advantage of my weaknesses and enlisted all his comic talents to make me laugh and bring happiness into my life. In his eagerness to fill my needs he'd neglect his own desires, and I thought how hard it was for us adults to endure the touch of this world, and here was this toddler shouldering both our burdens.

In his last week at kindergarten before the summer vacation, I remembered that I'd never been asked to bring a cake to the Shabbat Eve ceremony like the other mothers. I asked Shoshana the teacher about it, and she smiled and told me that every time she'd asked Yoavi to tell me that it was my turn next week, he would declare importantly that his mother was a busy woman and she worked at the university and she didn't have time for baking cakes.

Just as my Yoavi was kind and considerate, Nechama's Yoeli was wild and unruly. When she wouldn't give in to his demands he'd scream, throw himself to the floor, and yell at her, 'You're not my mother,' and make fun of her fatness. During these attacks of anger Yoavi would curl himself up on my knee and watch the scene bewildered, and I'd fight my desire to get up and smack Yoeli's bottom. Nechama would sit there, indifferent and apathetic, waiting for the child to calm down. Only when Yoeli insisted on screaming for a very long time would she get up with irritating slowness, press the child's back to her ample body, hold him in her arms, kiss him on the head and loudly declare that she loved him. And wonder of wonders, the child would relax, and within a few moments he'd calm down and ask forgiveness, and she'd let him go without giving him a sermon. Then she'd triumphantly look at me as if to say, 'See? My son knows how to express his anger and frustrations. That's how normal children behave.' And I'd look at my Yoavi, my Angel Gabriel, and think about when the genie would finally burst out of the lamp. It was lying in wait for me, looking for the right time to come in through the front door. Like an uninvited guest claiming his place by force, it would push its way in, take over the rooms, lie on the new beds and couches with its filthy shoes, seeking to push us out, bring in its demon friends who together sought to drive thick wedges into the fortified wall of my friendship with Nechama.

That day, in the afternoon, as I sat in the living room with Nechama, we heard voices mimicking shots and explosions coming from Yoavi's room. We stole in, and through the half-open door saw the deadly serious faces of Max und Moritz, as if they were holding some kind of ritual. They stood there shooting at each other with imaginary rifles, and Yoavi fell to the rug with his eyes closed, arms and legs fluttering, saying, 'I'm dead,' while Yoeli went on making explosion noises and shouting, 'I'm a suicide bomber, I'm a *shaheed*, I've come to kill Jews,' and holding his stomach fell onto the naked corpse of Bobo, who had been divested of his diaper. For a long time the two children lay in their death throes on the rug. Nechama and I slipped back to the living room, and Nechama said that there was nothing we could do, even if we protected them and kept them in isolation, children pick up on everything that's happening here and that's the sad reality of our lives and theirs, and it's a healthy way of dealing with the anxieties and thorny questions that we grown-ups are incapable of dealing with. 'You saw what was happening in there,' I said, 'it wasn't just kids playing war.' And she replied that these games released their tension, that playing was a releasing activity that helped children to reinforce the power of their ego, a creative act that bridged between inner and external reality. 'Cut the crap,' I said, 'they're not playing that kind of game in my house,' and added that we'd apparently failed in their upbringing. We hadn't given them guns and they'd made themselves imaginary ones. And she said, 'We mustn't take them away from them, because in the present situation it's impossible to prevent children playing war games.'

I disagreed and argued that we had to try and get them interested in positive, non-destructive games. 'That game's copying the loathsome actions of murderers,' I asserted, and Nechama lost her patience and yelled, 'So what do you want? Those murderers are suffering in their camps, with the closures and encirclements and the curfew, call it what you will. In a pitiless and oppressive state like yours, the conquered shouldn't rebel? If I were a Palestinian, I'd become a *shaheed* myself!'

And as if I'd been kicked in the belly, I doubled over and panted and hissed that I couldn't believe my ears, and how could she talk like that about those animals, those cowardly, conscienceless creatures who were systematically murdering innocent people, women and children and the aged, and the people who despatched them had promised that they'd be able to fuck any number of virgins in the next world. She raised her voice to a shout, 'But you don't understand, we've all become their enemies, you, me, and our children. And until we withdraw from all the Occupied Territories they'll blow themselves up everywhere and try and kill as many of us as they can.'

'I was there when that bus blew up,' I reminded her, 'you just read about these atrocities in the paper,' and she fired back, 'We made them the way they are. They're the refugees, they're the dispossessed, and by fighting the occupation I'm fighting against the bombings. And until we return everything, eve-ry-thing, life in this country will be bad.' And I tried to shout her down, and yelled that she was suffering from self-hatred, and she asked derisively, 'Since when have you been a psychologist?' and I ignored the question and told her she was naive, and that even if we did give everything back, eve-ry-thing, they'd demand the right of return and then shut us up in a cramped ghetto, and I could hear my father speaking from my mouth and shouting with me. She looked at me in horror and said that since that trauma I'd gone off the rails completely. On hearing our shouts Yoavi and Yoeli came in and looked at us with concern, and I picked up my son and Nechama picked up hers, and she said sweetly that even grown-ups were sometimes allowed to argue and shout. Yoavi's warm, heavy body cuddling into mine calmed me down and I showered his head with kisses and guided the conversation to Shoshana and the kindergarten end-of-year party, and we said goodbye as usual with a kiss on the cheek and a promise to meet again on Sunday afternoon.

A few days later I opened the front door and bits of wool, pieces of straw and flakes of sponge danced on the floor in front of me and covered the couches and rugs with a thin, soft layer. Soft pools of coloured rags stood in small piles and led towards the kitchen. Orli the babysitter was dozing in front of the TV set, and Max und Moritz, who hadn't heard me come in, were busily engaged in a rampage of systematic destruction: the first to greet me was Bobo's head, whose body had vanished, and at its side were heaped massacred soft toys and limbless dolls. Appalled, I saw Yoeli wielding a pair of toy scissors, completely focused on ripping out the belly of Yoavi's beloved Teddy Bear. When he finally managed to tear into it, the two plunged their hungry fingers into its entrails and ripped out bits of wool and straw. Ice water flowed through my veins until Yoavi, who suddenly sensed my presence, gave me a honeyed look filled with innocence.

And the song played in my head: 'What do the children do? Nothing.'

'What are you doing?' I asked, unable to control the tremor in my voice, and Orli awoke in fright.

'Don't you see that we're doing a bombing?' said Yoeli, stating the obvious and looking at me with his star-filled eyes. 'We're *shaheeds* and they're dead Jews,' echoed Yoavi, completing the sentence and pointing at the pile of victims.

I choked back the nausea that rose in my throat and rushed into the kitchen. I drank water straight from the tap, washed my face and leant helplessly against the draining board. Orli quickly came in and tried to make excuses but I refused to listen. I waved my hand to shut her up and pulled a few notes from my purse. She repeated that she was sorry, but I didn't reply. I didn't want to make it any easier for her.

I angrily ripped off a black plastic garbage bag from the roll, shook it open, and with my last remaining strength went back into the living room.

In icy tones I said, 'Now collect all the animals and dolls you've torn up and put them into the bag,' and fled to the bedroom and lay down in my clothes and shoes on the counterpane. Yoavi ran after me and stuck his head into the doorway and asked, 'Is Imush angry?' 'Very, very angry,' I replied, and he wailed contritely, 'But Abba said I wasn't a girl, and all my games were girls' games, and we had to throw all my old dolls and animals into the bin, and he promised to buy me new toys.' Without turning my head to him I ordered him back to the living room and with Yoeli to put everything into the bag, and then we'd talk. When Nechama arrived to collect Yoeli, the damning evidence was waiting for her at the door, a bloated black plastic bag, filled to the top.

'See? This is your healthy way of coping with anxieties,' I said icily, opening the bag and shaking its contents onto the floor: headless dolls, severed limbs, maimed soft toys whose bellies had been ripped open and were now empty, all fell onto the floor in a disgusting pile.

'Just look at this pogrom. So much for the education you give your son, so he can come along and destroy other kids' toys, so he can play *shaheeds* and Jews. You can take your little *shaheed* home now, and tell him that the *shaheeds* are just poor unfortunates who want their lost country back. And maybe in your own apartment you can destroy a few toys together, or is that only allowed in other people's homes?'

Nechama paled and quickly took Yoeli's hand and they ran downstairs together. I followed her out and called after her in the darkened stairwell: 'That's it, run away, ignore it, carry on corrupting pure young souls!' I slammed the door and leant against it, panting heavily. Yoavi was sitting on the floor, sobbing quietly as he made a pitiful effort to erase the signs of the massacre, shoving the remnants of the mutilated cadavers back into the bag, and picking up bits of wool and toy stuffing that had stuck to the rug and couches. I hugged him, hurting, and he sobbed against my chest and asked if he wouldn't be seeing Yoeli again because I was angry with Yoeli and his Ima. And I replied, 'Of course you'll see him again at kindergarten,' but he reminded me that next year he'd be at a new kindergarten without Yoeli, and begged, 'I want to play with him in our house,' and urged me to call Nechama and beg her pardon because I'd offended them. I said that first I had to calm down, and then I'd think about what he wanted.

When I got home the following afternoon, the black bag was standing by the door, and there was a stammering apology on the answering machine. Nechama invited me for a meal at Café Caffit so we could talk things over.

I throttled the bag and swung it in the air.

'What are we going to do with this bag?' I asked Yoavi.

'We've got to bury them,' he declared. 'they're all dead. And the dead are buried in the ground.'

When I took him to the kindergarten next day, he didn't ask about the black bag, and when Hagit brought him home in the afternoon he was carrying a small, pink plastic rifle. 'Look what Hagit bought me,' he boasted. I gave her look of hatred and hissed in English that I didn't like her buying him weapons, and she asked, 'What? What?' and I repeated what I'd said in Hebrew, and she shrugged and said innocently, 'But he asked. You know how hard it is to refuse when he asks, he's so sweet. And apart from that,

Nachum said it was all right,' she summed up lightly, kissed him on the cheek and said, 'See you on Thursday,' and I quickly slammed the door behind her and leant against it as if fearing that she'd come back and ask to come in.

On Thursday Nachum brought Yoavi home early and sent him to his room, because he had to talk to Ima. In the doorway he informed me that he'd been invited to a year's internship in gum surgery at a New York dentistry hospital. I remained silent, and he tried softening the blow and said that I could send Yoavi to him at vacation time. I gulped air: 'When exactly are you planning to go?' and he replied, 'This month.'

'And Hagit's going with you,' I said, stating a fact, and again that bitter bolus threatened to choke me. 'Tell me the truth, when did you get this invitation?' I scratched at the scabs of my wounds, 'Just tell me if it was before or after the bus blew up.' 'Before,' he confessed in a whisper, and my anger boiled over, 'You son-of-a-bitch, how could you not have told me,' and I armed myself with Yoavi and told him that now he'd decided to divorce his son as well, and all these troubles were hitting this poor child almost all at once, first the bombing and then the divorce and now this. And Nachum announced solemnly, as if he'd been waiting for just this moment, 'If it's difficult for you to take care of the child, I'm willing to take him.' 'Over my dead body,' I shot back, and he said irrelevantly, 'Don't worry, you'd still get the maintenance every month.' And I heard myself screaming hoarsely, 'Is that what you think concerns me, your lousy maintenance?' and he replied, 'I didn't come here to fight with you, and keep your voice down, the child can hear.' 'Have you told Yoavi?' I asked, and he said, 'Not yet, I thought you'd do it better.' I told him he was a bastard, because he was the one who was leaving and not me, and before he could reply I called to Yoavi, and he came with his head lowered, and I told him that Abba had something important to tell him, and a flicker of hope lit up his golden eyes, and Nachum glared at me sourly and knelt down and trapped the child between his knees and said, 'Abba's going abroad, to America, and he'll come back very soon, with lots of presents.' 'That's all?' Yoavi shrugged, and Nachum told him, 'That's all,' and Yoavi said, 'Well I'm going back to my room, because I'm in the middle of a game.' Nachum looked at me as if to say, 'You see, he doesn't care at all,' and I said, 'Now go, I don't feel well.'

When I put Yoavi to bed, I said that Abba would come to visit him from America, and if I had enough money we'd go to America and have a great time, and maybe we'd even go to Disneyland. And he said, 'Good,' and looked at me as if in understanding. Afterwards I called Nechama and arranged to meet her for lunch at Caffit.

In the morning I rushed into Yoavi's room and my fingers groping under his body found a warm, dry sheet.

Time Passes and the Earth Rests

'And now he's taking off to America and leaving his child here,' I complained to Nechama at our conciliation meeting at Caffit. She gave me a long look and smiled, 'Be truthful, you're going to miss your two free afternoons when he takes Yoavi.' I ignored the barb. 'Just imagine, that shit planned this trip long before we talked about getting divorced, *and* he meant to take his whore with him.' 'Stop calling them names,' she rebuked me, and added that it was sometimes preferable to raise a child on your own rather than with a distant partner.

A sudden motorbike backfire sent me leaping out of my seat.

'Just take a look at yourself,' Nechama said, 'you're a nervous wreck, jumping at the smallest sound,' and immediately volunteered a diagnosis: 'You're still suffering from post-traumatic stress disorder. Your body can't forget, and you'll carry on experiencing the trauma over and over,' she added, and said that in her opinion I should have psychological therapy as soon as possible, because if I didn't I'd find myself shutting myself up at home and falling into depression.

Although I knew she'd laugh at me I told her that I still missed him. Avshalom. 'He suddenly disappeared from my life,' I said sadly, 'and that's the only reason I'm so jumpy, nothing else.'

But Nechama had already decided for me. 'You're going to call her today and make an appointment,' she said, throwing onto the table an impressive-looking visiting card bearing the legend 'Dr Shaula Wachtel, Clinical Psychologist' in cursive lettering. I told her I didn't trust people whose visiting cards were so ostentatious, but she wouldn't listen and stated a fact: 'You're going to speak to

221

her right now,' as she dialled the number on her cellphone and I heard her say sweetly, 'Hi, Shaula, remember me telling you about my friend who suffered a trauma? Well she's right here and wants to make an appointment to see you,' and she flashed me a wicked smile as she handed me the phone. Gloomily I said hello, and Shaula Wachtel told me in a deep and authoritative voice that her diary was full until after the High Holy Days. I heaved a sigh of relief and said, 'That's OK by me, I'm busy too, so we'll meet after the holidays,' but she suddenly said firmly, 'Just a minute, Nechama said that your case can't be put off. I can see you tomorrow at six in the evening. At six precisely. Sixty-two Emek Refa'im Street.' 'Ah, we're almost neighbours,' I said with dumb gaiety, 'I'll just check my diary.' But Nechama transfixed me with a glare, snatched the phone and said, 'That's fine, she'll be there at six.' She said goodbye with a few polite words, stared at me angrily and mashed her cigarette in the Thousand Island dressing of her almost-untouched salad. The cigarette hissed and its orange filter fell off, and golden curls spread over the plate like the spores of an epidemic. 'Don't you dare cry off. She's the most prestigious psychologist in Jerusalem, and you're playing hard to get with her? I'll take Yoavi home and he'll have supper with us.' I thanked her inaudibly and toyed with the pile of lettuce on my plate. I'd lost my appetite.

I tossed and turned all night. I didn't know what I was supposed to do at the psychologist's and what to tell her. In the morning I met Nechama at Shoshana's kindergarten and she told me, 'Talk to her about anything you like, about everything that's troubling you. Your fantasies, your childhood, your relationship with your mother, about Nachum, about Avshalom, in short, about anything that comes to mind. You can talk freely, nothing leaves her room.' I asked how much it would cost me, and she patted me on the shoulder and said that the first visit was on her, she'd already taken care of it: 'It's my present for your next birthday,' she said, waiting to hear my words of gratitude, and when they didn't come she added that each visit would cost four hundred shekels. 'Four hundred shekels?' I yelled. 'Four hundred shekels a visit is two thousand a month, where am I going to find that kind of money?' Nechama lit a cigarette, exhaled smoke and said it was worth every penny. Afterwards she walked me to my car and predicted that I'd very rapidly find myself waiting impatiently for my visits to

Shaula, because psychological therapy was an unparalleled luxury for the psyche. Sometimes it was even preferable to starve than miss out on it, and one day, once my eyes had been opened, I'd thank her for it.

Five forty-five. Pinkish woolly clouds dozed standing in the blue sky and soon darkness would descend on my city. Soft lights came through the café windows into the street and my car was describing circles through the narrow alleys of the German Colony. I was looking for a parking space, retracing my movements to the main road, Emek Refa'im Street, and thinking about the awful name it had been given, Valley of the Dead. I finally found a narrow space on the pavement on one of the adjacent streets, and the car climbed up onto it with great effort, banging its oil sump and sending a shock right through me. Hoping that a traffic warden wouldn't drop on me at that hour, I walked along the street, looking for Dr Wachtel's house. At five minutes to six I came to a grey, two-storey villa with a sign in the entrance announcing that this building had served as a Templar committee house. I pushed the gate, which opened with difficulty and a grating squeak. A whispering canopy of ancient pines hung over me shedding prickly needles that stuck in my hair, and drizzling droplets of water onto my blouse that shone in the glow of the street lighting. I glanced upwards to the treetops, between which delicate webs marking the procession swayed in the wind. I crossed the garden at a run, frightened of those furry worms whose touch was evil and burnt the skin. I thought that perhaps I'd talk to Shaula about my fear of worms, but by the time I reached the vestibule, panting, the whole thing had been forgotten.

On the door was an Armenian ceramic lion decorated with arabesques and bearing the cursive legend: Welcome to the Home of Dr Shaula Wachtel. Next to the doorbell was a yellowing slip of paper containing two lines of flamboyant handwriting: Please Do Not Ring. Please Open the Door and Wait on the Bench. I did as I'd been told and sat down on the wooden bench whose back bore carved hunting scenes of African warriors. A wide wicker basket, overflowing with the *National Geographic* and its Hebrew counterpart, which indicated the lady of the house's good taste and broad horizons, stood next to the bench, while all I wanted was to reduce my tension with *Woman's Weekly*. At five minutes past six a side door, which I hadn't noticed, opened and a blonde head popped out through the doorway and its lips curled upwards with a slightly wicked twist: 'Yael Maggid?' asked Dr Wachtel, as if she didn't know it was me, and didn't even apologise for being a bit late. I nodded and she ordered, 'Come into here.' I followed her in and didn't know where to sit, and she moved a comfortable-looking armchair towards me that was full of cushions covered with variegated, shiny Thai silk, as if to say, 'Sit there,' and relaxed facing me on an identical chair. Although the chairs appeared to be identical, hers was slightly higher, and I had to look up at her. She returned my look unblinkingly. I felt naked and exposed. I broke eye contact and let my eyes wander over the room. Persian prayer mats painted gay blotches of colour on the brown wooden floor that glowed with much polishing, and oils and pastels by famous Israeli artists covered the shining white walls. A small corner bookcase, filled with thick, leather-bound tomes with gold letters glinting on their spines, stood where two of the walls met, and on either side of it were hammered copper bowls holding well-tended houseplants. A carved antique mahogany desk with lions' paws crouched behind the doctor's armchair, and on its shining top there was a copper lamp-stand whose shade was made of illustrated parchment, and at its side a box of tissues.

Dr Wachtel followed my roaming eyes in silence and moved the box closer to me as if to say, You'll probably need them to dry your tears and blow your nose. Despite the noise of the traffic on Emek Refa'im Street an oppressive silence filled the room, and only a muted roar that smashed itself against the double-glazed window hinted that outside the world was carrying on according to its own rules. The room was pleasantly warm and I felt my body relaxing, and I prayed for the moment that she'd ask, 'Tea or coffee?' but Dr Wachtel's lips remained sealed and the cracks of her green eyes inspected me without a blink of compassion. I thought that her clothes suited this room of hers, and I was ashamed of the smart black gabardine trousers, their weave shining with age, that I was wearing for the occasion. She was wearing a white linen trouser suit, a blood-red Pashmina shawl softly covered her shoulders, and her feet were swallowed up in a pair of flam-boyant high-heeled, pointy-toed cowboy boots, studded with glittering turquoises and strips of crocodile skin. I thought that the boots didn't blend in with the decorous ambience of the room that was both restrained and imposing, but immediately told myself that everybody, even Jerusalem's most noted psychologist, has a right to their own private obsession. I wanted to compliment her on her boots and ask where she'd bought them, but then I thought it was too personal a question. I took my eyes from her boots and focused on her fascinating features. A severe parting split her hair in a ruler-straight line and on both sides, from under the blonde, cheeky white and dark-grey roots peeped, making me happy, as if I'd found a hidden treasure. She turned her profile towards me, as if asking me to admire her face from every possible angle. A small, tight bun lay balled on her nape.

I knew she was following my admiring glances, and it seemed that she was used to this kind of response, because the corners of her mouth turned slightly upwards in a satisfied smile, and I asked: 'Should I talk?' She nodded and stretched out her legs as if to underscore the beauty of her shiny boots beside my old shoes. Embarrassed, I tucked my feet under my chair and asked again, 'Should I talk?' and again she nodded and a bored expression spread over her face that said, 'I've seen and heard it all before, and nothing you say can possibly shock me.' I shifted my look from her boots and focused on a spot at the middle of her throat and asked, 'Where should I begin?' and she replied, 'With what's important to you.' Once more I saw the bus going up in flames and I wanted to justify my visit and told her that my life was in ruins and I had a terrible feeling of emptiness and loneliness, and she said, 'Elaborate.'

I didn't know how to begin and what to say in the fifty minutes she'd allocated me, and finally I came out with everything I thought I needed to say. I dumped my distress on her, my concern for Yoavi, my father's death, my divorce, I also told her about Hagit and Louisa, but didn't tell her about the woman in red and the bus blowing up, and I didn't mention Davidl, and didn't bring Avshalom's name to my lips, as if protecting them in my own secret corner, refusing to give her my approval for nosing around in my life.

I peeped at her. She extended her arms, inspected her reddened nails for a long time, and then suddenly interrupted me by elegantly announcing, 'Our time's up,' and without even consulting me said, 'Same day next week, six o'clock precisely.' As I rummaged in my purse she informed me, without mentioning

Nechama's name, that I was exempt from payment for the first session. I said thank you without really knowing what I was thanking her for, and she courteously opened the door for me and closed it behind me.

I heard the phone ringing from the hall. I ran up the stairs and opened the door panting and left it open and then I heard Nechama's voice in my ear: 'So how was it?' and she didn't wait for a reply and decided, 'You're probably feeling relief already,' and added, 'Isn't she wonderful?' I cut her off in full flow and told her I was a bit confused. 'I talked and talked and she listened and didn't open her mouth,' I complained. 'Of course,' Nechama said with some satisfaction, 'that's how it should be. You're supposed to examine yourself as you talk about yourself.'

The following Thursday at five-fifty I was waiting for her on the wooden bench and leafing through a *National Geographic*. The minutes ticked by slowly before she opened the door. I obediently followed Dr Wachtel into the room, leant back in the chair and inspected her elegant black dress and the high-heeled patent leather shoes that were fastened to her feet with a gold buckle bearing the logo of a designer I hadn't heard of. I noticed that the roots of her hair had been coloured and the grey had been covered without trace. Again I asked, 'Should I talk?' and she nodded. This time I chose to adopt Nechama's professional terminology, and said I'd tell her about a severe trauma I'd undergone on a winter morning last year, and claimed that since that day time had split for me, and my life was divided into the life I'd had up till then, and the one I'd had since. 'Just like BCE and CE,' I said, trying to illustrate it, and with great difficulty I described what had happened with the bus, and I described the little boy I'd thought was a girl, but didn't say a word about Avshalom. I suddenly came apart and, blinded by tears, felt for the box of tissues, and she put it into my lap and I thanked her and thought how pitiful my weeping was in this splendid room of hers.

Now I longed to hear some words of support from her, I wanted her to love me, to take me in her arms, but she was looking interestedly at how I was blowing my nose and balling a wad of tear-stained tissues, and her unchanging expression again announced that she'd seen and heard it all before, and nothing could shock me. I hadn't felt the time passing until she glanced at her watch, and I was angry with her for calculating how much time

I had left until I took myself off, so that she could rake in her fee and get ready for the next poor sod. In the end she stopped my flow of words with her outspread hand, said 'Our time's up,' and stood up. I looked at my watch and saw that we still had another three minutes exactly, but I didn't say anything and she stretched out her hands, inspected the glittering rings that adorned her fingers up to the knuckles, and announced with bored indifference, as if my terrible story had already been erased from her memory, 'Four hundred shekels.'

'I'm not feeling any relief, this time too only I talked and she listened,' I told Nechama, and she proudly gave me a cup of foaming cappuccino she'd made with the new espresso machine she'd bought herself for her birthday. I carried on complaining as I sipped the coffee. 'I told her exactly what I've told you, and Louisa in a slightly censored version, but unlike you she demanded money from me, a lot of money, and she didn't even bother to offer me coffee and cake.' Nechama said that I had to be patient and take into account that the therapy might continue for a few months. Then as if remembering something she asked, 'Want some cake? I've got a great carrot cake,' and served me a thick slice with white icing and a dwarf carrot adorning it. I pulled the marzipan carrot from its sugary bed, sucked its orange sweetness and thought how good it was that I had a friend like her, and asked where she'd bought the great cake, and just then Max und Moritz burst into the kitchen. 'Want some cake?' Nechama asked them, and in unison they asked, 'What kind?' and she piped, 'Carrot cake.' She showed her upper teeth, made a rabbit face, put her hands at both sides of her head, and waved them like ears. They both laughed as if she'd told them a good joke, made noises of disgust, and sang, 'Yuck, carrot cake.'

The following Thursday, despite my request, Prof. Har-Noy refused to bring forward the academic committee meeting that had been arranged for four thirty on the dot, and said that the traditional time must not be changed and it was out of the question to change the time or date because of one committee member. The meeting finished at five forty-five, and I got to the doctor's out of breath at seven minutes past six.

Shaula was waiting for me in her armchair, her legs crossed in their nylon stockings making an irritating rustling sound.

She gave me a severe look and said that because of my late

arrival she would have to cut the session short, as it wasn't fair to keep her next patient waiting because of my tardiness. I sat facing her, angrily and silent, and she kept silent with me. We sat that way for a while until I finally broke my silence and asked, 'Should I talk?' and she replied indifferently, 'Whatever you want.' 'What about?' I asked and she volunteered a suggestion: 'Perhaps begin with your childhood.'

Childhood memories began crowding in on me, vying with each other to be first in line to bring back things past. I stood helpless before them. I wanted only the good, friendly ones, the ones I loved. I didn't know which to choose and said embarrassedly, 'But what has my childhood to do with the bus and the trauma I suffered?' and she said, 'Everything's connected. Perhaps begin with your relationship with your father?' And memories of my father stepped proudly forward, sticking out their tongues at those that hadn't been asked, and I wanted to push them out of the way and said, 'But I want to talk about what's happening to me now. About the state I'm in today,' and she persisted, 'Why aren't you interested in talking about your childhood, about your father?'

I opened a little gate to memories I wanted to remember and said that Father had come from 'There,' and had he told me about everything he'd gone through, I would have been able to fill entire volumes. But she cut me short and asked, 'What kind of a father was he?' I told her that he'd read me books in Hebrew, but that he'd woven his dreams in Ladino. 'What did you feel towards him?' she asked impatiently, and I told her how he'd sit at my bedside, hold my hand during bad nights and rub me with arak when I was sick. 'When he did that, did he touch you in forbidden places?' she suddenly interrogated me with interest, and I said only that 'my father was afraid for me,' and started to recite a list of fears – father was afraid of the Arabs, our neighbours, and he was afraid of road accidents and fires and snakes and scorpions, and he was afraid I'd go out with boys who'd touch me, and afraid that I'd sit on a contaminated seat in a public toilet. And she nodded and remained silent, and I kneaded my pain and told her, completely unintentionally, about his final days when his condition had deteriorated, and how he'd sat next to me in Minimush when I'd taken him to the doctor and he'd suddenly called me a whore, a whore-daughter of a whore, and I'd looked at him sideways and saw the pallor flooding his face, his lips sucked in and the narrow

228

slit that replaced them like an open wound curling towards me in mocking evil. 'Whore-daughter of a whore,' he said, spraying the words together with drops of saliva, like a wicked boy saying rude words. Spittle gathered at the corners of his mouth, and I didn't understand why he hated me so much, and from where he was drawing the strength for this great hatred. I huddled in my seat and gripped the wheel, afraid I'd lose my grip on it, my knuckles white with effort as I tried to concentrate on the traffic. But he wouldn't desist: 'Whore-daughter of a whore,' he hummed, his skeletal body swaying back and forth and his long fingers, twisted with arthritis, holding on to an imaginary side-lock, twisting it around one of fingers and curling, curling it, and his other hand stroked the beard he didn't have. His body again swayed backwards and forwards with the words. Whore-daughter of a whore. And I wept, wiping the tears with my blouse sleeve and begging him, 'Stop it, Abba, enough.' But to no avail. Enthused, he repeated the words and they came from his lips in a bitter hicup, and his breath stank. I put my hand on his knee, trying to soothe him, and he turned his empty eyes to me and spat at me. His spittle, sticky and foamy, slid down his chin onto his best jacket, and a small blob of mucus dripped onto his trousers, soaking into the heavy weave and leaving a dark stain. I was scared of him. I knew that I didn't know this stranger, he wasn't the father I'd had, my beloved father, who'd taught me to ride a bike and who'd sat at my bedside for entire nights, making sure I was breathing.

A light was kindled in Shaula's eyes and she suddenly interrupted me and asked if when I was a child I'd been sexually abused by my father. Stunned and stammering, I asked what made her think that, but she looked at her watch and announced, 'Our time's up.'

I left her room sobbing and saw my father sitting in the waiting room and swaying back and forth like a yeshiva student, and staring mindlessly at me. Fucking bitch.

I wept on the way to the car, a pitiful weeping, overflowing with self-pity, weeping for the father who had once been mine. I ignored the compassionate glances of the people passing and didn't bother to wipe away the tears. Then I sat behind the wheel and, relieved he wasn't sitting next to me, started the car. I drove slowly, as if in a funeral car, ignoring the cars honking impatiently behind me, the ones that overtook me wildly, and the angry glances that were shot at me. Indifferent to the tumult all around, my car progressed slowly, because only on a slow drive like that was I able to reconstruct it all. I stopped at a red light and saw him again, shrivelled, bent and ashamed, walking between two tall male nurses in white, greeting the passing people with his arm raised in the Nazi salute. I followed his back retreating down the corridor until he was swallowed up into the elevator, and I knew that it had been my father's death march. They took him to another place, from where he would not return. I didn't notice the red light change to green and didn't hear the impatient honking, and I wept, my head on the wheel. I was to blame. I had led him to that final place.

A man's face looked at me through the window and I heard a concerned voice saying, 'Are you all right, do you need help?' I shook my head, burst into the junction and heard the screech of brakes, and the horns, and the cries of 'Madwoman' that accompanied me on my way, all testimony to the fact that I'd run a red light.

Over a cup of cappuccino I again told Nechama that there was no change. I didn't feel any relief. And how the hell was I supposed to feel relief when Shaula dared presume that I'd been sexually abused as a child. And Nechama again soothed me, give her another chance, it's still too soon, I believe you'll feel a change shortly.

So I gave Dr Shaula Wachtel another chance and another and another, and at the next sessions, as I talked and she kept silent, I etched on my memory the bored expression on her face until with eyes closed I could draw every line that appeared at the corner of her mouth and on her forehead, and I tried to guess what was passing through her mind and what she was feeling towards me: Was she bored to death and counting the minutes to the end of the session? And maybe she was counting the number of people who'd visited her today and calculating how much she'd made? And in my mind I was making my own calculations and multiplying, and adding and counting fabulous sums: An average of six people per days times four hundred shekels per patient, times five days a week and four weeks a month. Envy choked me and I hated her, this woman glorying in such an expensive house that had been bought with our heartache and damaged psyches. But then she looked at me glassily as if I were transparent, and I thought that maybe she was reconstructing the fuck she'd had last night and perhaps fantasising about the next one? I banished those troublesome thoughts and with all my might tried to make me like her, and her me. I assumed that Dr Wachtel was a married woman, and that the glassy look in her eyes was only the look of a woman thinking about what to cook for her husband when he got home from work. And I made a mental note to question Nechama about Shaula's marital status, for it was unthinkable that this woman should know almost everything about me and I didn't know a thing about her.

I couldn't restrain myself and asked her if my stories were boring her, and she replied with a question, 'Why do you ask?' I said I had the feeling I was wasting her time, and didn't dare, Heaven forbid, mention my own time or money. She remained silent for a long time until she again replied with a question, 'And what makes you think that?' I stammered that I was a bit frustrated, and that it was hard for me to go on talking when she never reacts, but she didn't allow me to finish, stood up and said gravely, 'Our time's up.'

'At the next session I'll make her talk, and if she doesn't I'll tell her straight out that I'm not interested in seeing her again,' I told Nechama when I went to collect Yoavi.

And she yelled and preached and said something like the psychologist's advantage of listening, and I said that this Shaula was taking a lot of money from me for this listening and that it wasn't particularly difficult to look attentive when you're being paid, and apart from that she knew almost everything about me and I didn't know anything about her and there was an imbalance here. Nechama remained silent and I added that Shaula Wachtel was a cold woman who lacked compassion. Nechama was shocked, 'Every therapist must be blessed with the qualities of compassion, kindness, human warmth and honesty.' And she added that with this remark I had proved that the therapy was working. It was a clear act of transference, and she emphasised the English word 'transference,' and that these were feelings that I, the patient, was transferring from an important and earlier figure in my life to Shaula the therapist's figure, who in fact had no contact with the origins of these feelings. 'You're on the right road,' she summed up, 'I believe that Shaula reminds you of your mother.'

The following Thursday, at four thirty in the afternoon, Louisa chaired the academic committee meeting and assured me that this time the meeting would be particularly short. That was so I could get to Dr Shaula Wachtel's on time and inform her that this would be our last session, and so that she and Yoram could go to her gynaecologist for an examination.

That day over morning coffee, we exchanged confidences about our frustrations and decided to go and see Prof. Har-Noy and ask for a change. Smiling, so he would understand that we were not overly serious, Louisa suggested a subject for an enthralling and innovative study, dedicatedly rattling her bangles, and Prof. Har-Noy's eyes were trapped by her bracelets, and he dramatically announced that he could smell a plot being hatched against him in this room. I gravely stated that we were both interested in conducting a new experiment: 'The Manner in Which Academic Meetings Are Conducted As a Correlation of Gender Needs.' The professor angrily arched his brows: 'Which gender are you talking about, dammit?' Without batting an eyelid I replied, 'The gender that runs the meetings.' Har-Noy shifted his eyes to Louisa and then back to me, and then he clutched his head with both hands and his long white curls covered his fingers with small patches of snow, and he declared despairingly, 'I don't understand what these women want of my life.' And Louisa said compassionately, as if talking to a child hard of understanding, that we'd both reached the conclusion that there was a difference in the way our department's meetings were run, and that the difference was in a single fact, the gender that ran the meetings, and that if we were given the chance of running one of the upcoming meetings, he would certainly come to the conclusion that women are far more decisive than men. They have far too much to do to sit in meetings and waste their time on talk. Prof. Har-Noy looked at her with false gravity and declared, 'All right, I give in, you run today's meeting, and Yael will run the following one,' and winked so I'd know that this whole game was very amusing and that he wasn't at all hurt. I replied, 'For a change, you take the minutes.' And he chuckled and waved us away as if to say, 'Get out, can't you see I'm busy?' and shooed us out of his office.

'The department will be hosting a guest lecturer next week,' Louisa announced at the opening of the meeting, maintaining the tension, and added, 'From Oxford.' She waited for a reaction, and when it didn't come she solemnly declared, 'Professor Charles

Bailey,' and again she waited, as if expecting applause. 'Professor Bailey will deliver a lecture at the Van Leer auditorium on ... ' she began again, and fell into an embarrassed silence and looked at the papers in front of her, irritably leafed through them and looked at Prof. Har-Noy who was sitting beside her with a yellow legal pad in front of him. But he ignored her and pretended to be occupied. Louisa's voice sharpened slightly, and she repeated, 'He will deliver a lecture at the Van Leer auditorium on ... ' and then she sweetened her tone and said, 'Please Professor Har-Noy, would you be so good as to inform those present of the date of Professor Bailey's lecture?' Prof. Har-Noy put down his pen, waited a moment, looked at the gathering, and triumphantly announced in a voice that sounded remarkably like a trumpet blast: 'Professor Bailey will deliver his lecture next Thursday, the four-teenth of the month, at seven pm, at the Van Leer auditorium.' And he couldn't resist saying to Louisa, 'My dear lady, whoever chairs a meeting must have the details at his or her fingertips, even if they are considered negligible,' and said he was going to add a note in this regard to the minutes. Louisa blushed and read Prof. Bailey's itinerary from a sheet of paper, but Prof. Har-Noy didn't let her off the hook, and with an innocent expression asked on what subject the esteemed guest from Oxford would be lecturing. Louisa jangled her bangles in embarrassment and he looked at them mesmerised, and quickly answered his own question, and again made a note in the minutes.

On the way to Dr Wachtel I gave Louisa a lift to her home in the Greek Colony. 'See how that chauvinist had a go at us for no reason?' she asked bitterly. 'If he'd really wanted me to be famil-iar with all the details, he would have given me access to all the documentation.' And she immediately reminded me that I would be running the next meeting, 'And I warn you, do your homework so he won't have any ammunition.' I said goodbye with a kiss on the cheek, and she asked me to kiss that hunk Yoavi for her and tell him that the kiss was from Louisa.

The moment I sat down in my armchair in Shaula's room, I told her that I had something important to tell her, 'And I'm not sure you'll like what I've got to say,' I added. She stretched her neck and raised her chin, listening attentively, and I toyed with the expression, 'All ears' and I wanted to laugh, but immediately turned serious, because I wanted to endow my words with a measure of drama. I said I'd thought a lot about our sessions, and in the end I'd decided to discontinue the therapy because I'd come to the conclusion that I was wasting her time and mine. I wanted to add, 'And my money too,' but decided to ignore the financial aspect so she wouldn't think I was a miser. 'Why do you think that?' she asked, and I was happy she'd reacted and I said petulantly, 'I'm not getting any feedback from you. I sometimes think it'd be better for me to sit in a café with a good friend and talk to her about my problems, it would be nicer, and would cost me a great deal less than four hundred shekels,' I said, unable to restrain myself. Shaula's face darkened and her self-satisfied expression was wiped off her face. She sank into deep thought, or so it seemed, and I began to egg her on: 'Come on, say something, ask a question, react, look, you know me, you've heard all my stories, what have you got to say to me, or about me?' And she cleared her throat and asked gravely, 'Did you at any time during your childhood suffer from penis envy?'

'And that's all she had to ask me,' I said, trumpeting the story to Nechama, contentedly sipping a cup of cappuccino and nibbling a piece of cake. 'And that was after me sitting there in her room for hours on end and pouring my life out for her.'

But then, when she said what she said, I pulled my chequebook from my purse, and quietly, but with shaking hands, I wrote her a cheque and told her not to bother writing a receipt, and said I was paying for a full hour although I'd only been there a few minutes. Then I got up and stretched, and she said, 'So why are you going? We haven't finished. We've still got thirty minutes,' but I was already putting on my coat and I left Shaula Wachtel's house, never to return.

I was flooded by a wonderful feeling of release and thought that Shaula had perhaps inadvertently helped me. I pressed the button for the army radio station and bounced on my seat to the strains of the music until I reached Nechama's home, where not only Yoavi awaited me, but also love and compassion and a cup of cappuccino and a bought carrot cake.

And He Caused the Woman to Drink the Bitter Water That Causes the Curse

(Numbers 5, 24)

Stones were cast at me in my sleep. Veiled women wrapped in long black fur mantles pinned me with their evil eyes, and bony, long-nailed fingers pointed at me. Hidden lips mouthed accusations at me, and the word '*sotah*,' 'pervert,' dripped onto me like slim venomous snakes from the gaps in the garment.

And I pleaded for my life.

'I didn't do it, I haven't done anything!' but they turned a deaf ear and as one they bent until their nails reached the ground, tearing stones and clods of earth from it. I wanted to tell them that I had been declared permitted to any man, and I hadn't been defiled, I hadn't committed adultery and had only loved, and that for love I shouldn't be stoned. But my belly, a cask that had been filled with water bitter from the ashes of the Temple, dragged my body down, and my feet caught in the long white dress I was wearing. I fell and covered my head against the shower of stones flying all around me. Covered with dust and stones I lay on the ground, and they moved ever closer to me. Among the fur mantles I suddenly saw a red coat and that woman's hate-twisted face. She came up behind me, put her hands under my arms, gripped my shoulders and clasped me to her body, like Nechama does with her Yoeli when he runs wild. Two of the others knelt in front of me, trapped my flailing legs, grasped them tightly and spread them as if in a steel vice. And now Louisa was coming towards me and her bangles were ringing a warning. I was glad to see her and begged her to save me, but she just contorted her face into a smile and

235

whispered, as if telling me a secret: '*Ma chérie*, I'm doing this for your own good, only for your own good. You won't suffer any longer now.' I saw the razor gleaming in her hand and she plunged it between my legs, and a sharp pain pierced me, and I screamed and heard her laugh rolling towards me: 'For your own good, for your own good, for your own good.' The women crowded around me, pushing and shoving to see what was being done to me. And as I screamed with pain their fingers strummed their lips in ululations of joy.

Then lamps were lit and the pyre burned and Moloch sat facing me, his hollow belly filled with hissing coals. And a procession of women in black approached him led by the woman in red, bearing above their heads the prayer shawl-shrouded sacrifice. I shook off the stones and soil from my broken body, wiped away my tears so I could see, and hurt and bleeding I crawled to them. I pulled myself along the ground after them, holding onto the hems of their garments, begging them to remove the prayer shawl so I could see the child's face, and they ignored me. With difficulty I lifted myself up, stood on tiptoe and raised the prayer shawl. Dark holes stared at me, a smile revealing tiny milk teeth flashed at me, mocking and evil, and fat white maggots wriggled over the whitening bones, entering and exiting the holes in the skull. And I screamed: 'Whose child is this? Whose is he?' and they answered me with a hyena laugh and pointed at me: 'Yours, yours, yours.' And a child's weeping was heard, and my heart beat wildly. My whole body in a sweat I ran into his room, and he said he had pipi and it had almost leaked out. I carried him to the toilet and afterwards we went back into his room and I put him to bed and covered his body with a sheet. I sat beside him for a long time, counting his breaths one after the other and guarding his life from the woman in red and the women in black.

'If we knew about ourselves during wakefulness what we know when dreaming, we'd never go to sleep. And if we'd forget when dreaming what we repress during wakefulness, we wouldn't be willing to wake up,' Nechama said next morning when I told her about the dream.

On the Wednesday of that week I met Prof. Charles Bailey, the social anthropologist from Oxford. Louisa, who was hosting him on the department's behalf, begged me to entertain him. She and her Yoram were busy getting pregnant, she didn't have the time for guests, and she'd never forget this favour as long as she lived. That apart, she assured me that I'd enjoy every minute because he was young and cute, gave me an open cheque so I'd be able to take him to a restaurant, and winked as she said that I shouldn't spare any expense, and that it would do me no harm to have a bottle of wine, even champagne, because the department was footing the bill.

I waited for him in the lobby of the modest YMCA Hotel. A tall, handsome young man was suddenly standing before me, he looked at me and asked in a pleasant voice, but with the wrong Hebrew inflection, 'Ya-el?' I nodded and couldn't understand why I hadn't noticed him earlier. He gave me a particularly broad smile, and I was glad to see that he had even, healthy teeth. We were silent for a long, embarrassed moment until I asked, 'French, eastern or ethnic?' and he ran his fingers through his tight blond curls and said gently, 'I suggest we cross the road and eat at the King David. I've always wanted to eat there.' I nodded happily. Perhaps he, too, was afraid of walking through the centre of town.

A doorman in a red uniform with gold stripes greeted us and opened the door. In the magnificent lobby, empty of tourists, Charles looked up at the decorated ceiling, sighed with satisfaction and said that the hotel had been superbly refurbished. 'At least your underground warned the British in good time before they blew it up,' he remarked. I praised his knowledge of local history and he said, self-effacingly, 'My uncle, my mother's brother, served here as the head telephone operator, and it was he who received the warning about the bomb and reported it to headquarters. But he was only one of the few who believed the warning, so he left the building on the pretext of having a headache, and that's how he escaped injury or worse,' he said apologetically. I walked at his side on the soft purple carpet into the restaurant with its glass walls, and a half-asleep waiter led us to a window table. The illuminated walls of the Old City provided a beautiful backdrop. I looked around the empty restaurant and asked him if he was bothered by us being the only diners, and he smiled: 'But that was precisely my intention. I booked the whole restaurant for us, especially for this evening,' and he pulled out my chair, waited until I was seated, and only then sat down and glared at a couple of American tourists who had come in and were loudly admiring the view.

237

Then he studied the wine list and asked for my help. I confessed that I wasn't a great connoisseur of wines, and he shrugged embarrassedly and said that he, too, wasn't au fait with Israeli wines, 'So in that case we must select the most expensive wine,' he said, and went into consultation with the waiter. Diapered like a baby in a white cloth, a bottle was reverently brought to the table and a little wine was decanted into a glass for tasting. Like an experienced sommelier Charles examined the wine's translucency against the flickering flame of the candle on the table, praised its deep purple hue, rolled it around in the glass, sipped, kept the wine in his mouth and then nodded to the anxious waiter. Our meal arrived with the second glass, and as he poured the third he told me about the lecture he was to deliver at the Van Leer Institute: The Role of the Maternal Grandmother in the Life of the Child. 'Here's to the grandma,' he said, raising his fourth glass, his blue eyes sparkling in the candlelight, and his long, silky, almost feminine lashes fluttered heavily. I asked him to tell me a bit about his subject, and he, delighted, asked if we were familiar with the teachings of Charles William Merton Hart, who in 1920 had studied the hunter-gatherer Tiwi tribes of Australia. I was afraid he'd suspect me of the most awful ignorance and immediately put on a grave expression and said I remembered. 'And do you recall what he said about grandmothers?' he asked and without waiting for my reply, said, 'They are a terrible nuisance and physically quite revolting.' This wretched researcher didn't understand that it is the grandmother who preserves the familial memory, and she is the key to the understanding of human prehistory.' Then he declared dramatically that in a study he'd conducted he'd discovered in some societies the key to the survival of male grandchildren was to be found, strangely enough, in the maternal grandmother. I thought about my mother and her contribution to Yoavi's development, and immediately banished her image from my mind. 'A baby born in Gambia, one of the poorest African countries,' he said, summing up his study there, 'even if it's breastfed for a relatively long time and its immune system relatively strong, the presence of its grandmother, its mother's mother, increases its chances of survival by fifty per cent compared with a baby raised in identical conditions, but which doesn't have a grandmother.' I nodded politely over my still full plate, and Charles finished off his fourth glass and said, 'Louisa told me you have a son. Does he have a grandmother, that is, is your mother still alive?' he asked as if apologising for this intrusion into my private life, and I suspected he'd already obtained some comprehensive research on me from Louisa, and that chatterbox had surely volunteered a mountain of information.

Again I nodded and glanced at Charles's still full plate.

'Does she live near you?' he asked, turning me into one of his research subjects.

'No.'

'Does she see her grandson often?' he asked.

I replied that she lives in another city, in Jaffa, and so she only sees the child once a month or on Jewish festivals. Charles nodded and said, 'That's a shame,' and emphasised that in Gambia, the grandmother's status in the grandchild's life was more important than the father's. 'It surprised me, too,' he confessed when he saw my eyebrows raised in surprise. 'The father doesn't increase the child's chances of survival. His death or absence make no difference to the child mortality statistics, only the grandmother, but on one condition, that she is the matriarchal, not the patriarchal grandmother.'

I can't remember what I ate that evening. Only the taste of the strong coffee we drank at the end of the meal is still with me, and the sight of Charles's extended little finger as he held his cup. I thought about how people who extended their little fingers when drinking repelled me; and he, as if reading my mind, hurried to correct the impression, took his cup in the palm of his hand, sniffed the aroma of the dark liquid with evident pleasure and then sipped slowly, savouring the taste, as if there was no rush and it wasn't late. At that moment I wondered if that was how he made love.

I asked for the bill and Charles insisted on paying it, despite my explanations that the money wasn't coming from my own pocket, and when I didn't succeed in convincing him I waved Louisa's open cheque that bore two signatures. But his insistence prevailed when he said that as an English gentleman he couldn't countenance a lady paying for his meal. While we were arguing the waiter was standing shamefaced at the table, and in the end I gave in to Charles's importuning and he slid his hand over my shoulder in a gesture of thanks, and his fingers almost absently fluttered over the nape of my neck. My flesh crawled. 'If you're free tomorrow, we can use your cheque after my lecture,' he said.

As we left and I said goodbye, he asked me to his hotel room. I was amazed at the hackneyed pretext, 'From there you can see the most enchanting view of the Old City and David's Tower.' I knew full well why I followed him into the lobby and with him stole into the narrow elevator, and I was afraid he'd sense that I hadn't slept with a man for a long time.

In the elevator we kissed for the first time. As we entered his room he embraced me from behind, cupped my breasts as if they had always been his, and only freed them to get a drink from the minibar, as he asked me to sit down on the bed. I sat on the end of the bed, taking care not to wrinkle the tightly stretched counterpane, and saw my reflection in the mirror facing me. From my pale face stared two eyes encircled by dark rings of tiredness and black, smeared mascara; my greasy red lipstick, which was supposed to be non-smear even after a hearty meal or torrid kissing, had vanished completely. I knew that I'd vanish from there, too, like the ghosts of the previous occupants of the room who had also looked at their reflections in that very mirror. I thought about the bodies that had made love on the softness of the mattress I was sitting on: scores? Hundreds? And about the sweat, and the saliva, and the semen, and the tears and all the rest of the bodily fluids that had been spilled onto it.

'Have you been circumcised?' I asked suddenly and fearfully, as he turned his back and bent to get a drink from the minibar.

He straightened up and turned to me, and with an apologetic smile replied that he hadn't. In the light of the halogen lamp standing in the corner of the room I discerned his rubicund nose and the tiny capillaries etched on his cheeks, intertwining as in a piece of reddish lace, the results of overindulgence in liquor.

'Since the British National Health Service stopped paying for infant circumcision, it isn't the accepted thing in England. They managed to do Prince Charles, but I escaped the scalpel. Why do you ask?'

I lowered my eyes to the toes of my shoes and regretted my question.

'I thought that only Louisa was interested in that subject. Is it a women's pastime in this country?' he asked, in an unsuccessful attempt at humour.

'I want to see what it looks like,' I demanded, as if wanting to test the merchandise before I bought it.

Amused, Charles stood before me. Unembarrassed, he took off his shoes, trousers and underpants, and lifted his long shirt-tail; I saw how he sucked in his belly as he did so. I looked at the man standing before me in his brown socks, the lower half of his body naked. As if randomly sprayed onto his belly I saw dull, sparse hair that oozed downwards. The tip of his reddened member, quivering with excitement, burst forth from the folds of skin that encased it, like an aged turtle peeping curiously from its armoured home.

Charles looked into my eyes as I looked at him.

'It's different,' I noted after meticulous scrutiny.

His member suddenly shrank and retreated, its head hidden under a thin, pink covering of skin.

'Does it disgust you?' he asked fearfully.

Like a woman well versed in love I raised my arms, embraced him round the waist and pulled him onto the bed. We sat side by side. He undressed me with patient slowness, as if in no hurry to make love, his mouth on mine and his fingers fluttering over my breasts, undoing the buttons of my blouse one at a time and feeling for the hooks of my bra. He took it off with one hand. My breasts fell heavy and tiredly and the nipples stuck to my belly; I straightened my back to lift them, and his hands cupped them for a moment and then felt for the zipper of my trousers and slid them off together with my panties. Foreign fingers slid over my body, investigating, feeling, probing, and then suddenly froze as they encountered the prominent scar on my belly. I shrank in shame, tried to move his fingers away, and he asked, 'A Caesarean?' I nodded and tried to turn off the light but he imprisoned my hands in his and said hoarsely, 'I want to see it,' and he laid me on the bed and looked at me for a long time. I wanted to tell him that the light bothered me, dazzled me, and I closed my eyes, but the light refused to go away, it penetrated my eyelids and flickered in black rings in the dark. His soft tongue was already feeling for the scar, kissing and licking it from end to end, seeking to erase its protrusions and ease the pain. And his tongue whispered from my belly, 'Let me taste you,' and without waiting for an answer it was spreading my lower lips, and dark and insistent it fluttered around me like a moth sucking my juices. I heard sounds and couldn't believe they were coming from me, and he gasped, 'Now?' and I answered in a choked voice, and his tongue stopped, and again his face was suspended over mine, his mouth dripping with my juices, and I licked them, and he came into me slowly and gently, kissing my eyes and lips, saying over and over, 'You're so beautiful.' And I, touching on despair and so proud, moved my hips in an unfamiliar rhythm, slowly, slowly, slowly. Together with him I was feeling for my longing for Avshalom, his warmth, his hands, his lips, his love that I had never known. I wrapped my legs around him and rocked with him, demanding, with organs filled with honey, the pleasure I deserved. 'More? Do you want more?' he asked, and I shouted, 'Yes, yes, yes,' and he filled the quota of his obligations and my pleasures, filling the void, the bottomless pit that yawned again and again begged to be filled. Afterwards, as I lay under him exhausted and sated, he asked, 'May I?' and after receiving my permission began moving inside me, slowly at first and then faster, increasing the rhythm, controlling his movements, beating his member against the walls of my crevice, his eyes wide open, their blue gradually blackening, his mouth panting into mine, until he climaxed inside me with a great sigh and spurted his warm, sticky seed deep into me, and yelled 'Ya-el!' For a long time afterwards he held me and caressed my body and whispered in my ear that he'd wanted me the moment he'd met me, and asked me to stay and sleep with him. He wouldn't hear any excuses, Louisa had told him that my son was sleeping over at my friend Nechama's. 'And what else did she tell you about me?' I asked, and he laughed and said, 'Everything a man needs to know about a woman.' I wanted to ask if she'd told him that Nachum had been the only man in my life but didn't, and said only that she'd be hearing from me in the morning, and covered myself with the blanket, and he pulled it down to my breasts and looked at them, and then slapped his forehead as if suddenly remembering something: 'D'you know we haven't talked about your research? I've talked and talked, so tell me about what you're doing.' Too tired to answer I asked if he snored because, if he did, I wouldn't manage to fall asleep, and he smiled and whispered, 'For you I'll stay awake all night.' I turned to him and fell asleep in his warmth, and nothing troubled my sleep that night, neither bad dreams nor pangs of conscience. I awoke to pinkish sunbeams coming through the slats of the window shutters and walking over my face. He was already awake, lying at my side, his head on his hand, looking at me. Nachum had never looked at me that way.

'Good morning, what's up?' he said in Hebrew and embraced me from behind so gently and carefully it warmed my heart. I felt his erection, hard and demanding, against my back. I extricated myself from his arms and said I had to get moving, they were expecting me at the office, and he pulled me to my feet, held me from behind, and with his pride and joy tickling the cleft of my buttocks led me to the window and opened the shutter wide so together we could see the sun coming up over the Old City's walls. 'So beautiful,' he sighed, with a hint of sorrow. Our clothes lay strewn on the floor like fly-by-nights that had awoken in someone else's house, and again I said that I had to go. But he turned to me and with a dry mouth that smelt of teeth in need of brushing, kissed me deeply. I repelled his tongue with mine, but it refused to submit and fought against my clenched teeth, then it gave up and moved downward, describing circles on my breasts and licking them. I broke away and escaped to the bathroom to wash away his saliva and congealed semen and our dried perspiration. Like an uninvited guest he followed me inside, closed the toilet lid and sat down, legs apart, and his uncircumcised prick lay on the plastic lid in a pink pool of thin skin, like the sloughed-off skin of a snake whose body is already somewhere else.

Into the bath I emptied a small plastic vial that assured me it would bubble and opened a strong flow of water onto its oily pool, but it disappointingly refused to foam and bubble. I lay in the warm, still, shallow water and he asked to wash my back. I looked at this stranger about whom I'd known almost nothing until last evening, ashamed of this suddenly enforced intimacy, and I refused. He looked at me with his researcher's eyes as I soaped my armpits and breasts and he asked if he could join me in the bath, but I asked him to leave and wait for me in the room. He obediently lowered his head and left, and from the back he looked so vulnerable, and his footsteps revealed the latent shyness of a man who'd been refused. I caught a flash of a broad back and the white segments of smooth, solid buttocks with two deep dimples adorning them on both sides, like an athlete's backside. I heard him impatiently pacing the room back and forth on the carpet that didn't muffle his steps, again and again and again and again.

My bladder was bursting. I was afraid of peeing in the toilet bowl lest he hear the sounds, so I did it in the bath. Afterwards I washed my body off under the shower, and as I turned off the tap he came back into the bathroom; like a matador he held open a bath towel, inviting me into its softness. I relented, and the towel tightened around my body and encased me in its soft warmth, and he gently massaged and rubbed my shrouded flesh and whispered in my ear, either asking or stating: 'Will I see you after the lecture tonight?' and I said no, not tonight, Yoavi will be at home, and I didn't want to add that it was doubtful we'd meet the next day either. I thought that what I'd got from him last night would keep me going for a year, maybe two, until I met Avshalom again. For we'd be together in the end, me and Avshalom. Fate had decreed it. And apart from that, in a few days' time Charles would be flying back to his fortified Oxford, and I'd remain with the memories: incidents like this should be killed off at birth.

Exposed and vulnerable, like a naked man in the presence of a dressed woman, Charles sat on the unmade bed and watched me dressing. Panties and trousers already on, and embarrassed and confused by his looks, I packed my breasts into the bra cups, slipped the straps over my shoulders and reached behind me to close the hooks. I'd always put on my bra the wrong way round, first putting it around my waist and closing the hooks, then bringing the cups to the front, and only then bringing them up to my breasts. But Hollywood movies and my mother and Louisa had ganged up on me and demonstrated how to put on a bra with feminine gracefulness, which was what I was unsuccessfully trying to do right now, my untrained hands fumbling and slipping on my back. He came over and asked which row of hooks I wanted, and I replied, 'It doesn't matter,' and was happy that for this assignation I'd worn my good bra, the lacy one that gave a lovely uplift to my breasts, and he fastened it for me, brushing my damp hair away from my nape and kissing it, and a shudder ploughed through my flesh. And I thought how could it be possible that we'd reached such a point after only one night, a point I'd never had with Nachum, and I'd believed I'd liked him when he told me worriedly that he'd been afraid to fall asleep because he hadn't wanted his snoring to disturb my sleep. He gently remarked that I'd probably been very tired because I'd ground my teeth all night, and perhaps it had been the wine that had caused it. I didn't know whether Louisa had told him about 'that day,' and agreed that I was probably very tired. I declined his offer of breakfast, and lied that I never had breakfast, and that I'd have a cup of coffee in the office.

He embraced me at the door, still naked, and said that he didn't want to wash because he wanted to smell me all day. I giggled in embarrassment, and he said almost apologetically, 'It was so sudden for me,' and I thought for me too, and he kissed me again and begged, 'Perhaps you'll still be able to come to the lecture?' but I didn't reply, and with wet hair got into my car and drove to the university.

At noon Louisa came into the office with a mischievous look in her eye. 'So how was it?' she enquired, and didn't wait for a reply and looked me straight in the eye and noted, as if to herself, 'So the wine helped, eh?' and tried to prise details of my night's experiences out of me. I remained silent, and she asked with surprising rudeness if Charles was circumcised, and I was shocked and said, 'Enough, Louisa, stop right there.' But she persisted and immediately expanded on her favourite subject, and again remarked, for the umpteenth time, that sex with an uncircumcised man is more pleasurable than with a circumcised one. I knew that she was speaking from experience, but didn't ask her to expand further, although I knew she'd have been happy to. I pretended I was hard at it and pleaded with her, 'Please, Louisa, not now, can't you see I'm busy?'

'So will we see you at the lecture at five?' she asked in the plural, as if she were Charles's co-conspirator.

I lowered my head to the students' papers covering my desk and said, 'I heard his lecture last night and I've been given an exemption, but apart from that we've got to talk. How come you're talking about me behind my back? He knew everything about me.' Louisa pursed her lips as if hurt, and before acceding to my request to shut the door behind her turned and said, 'There are times when I can't understand you at all. I thought that after everything you've been through it wouldn't do you any harm to spend a night with a nice guy. I did it for you, don't you see?'

When she'd left I called my mother.

'Yoavi needs his grandmother,' I informed her, inspired by Charles, and she quickly promised she'd come for the weekend. 'And I hope you don't have a problem with Yoskeh coming with me,' she added. I told her I had no problem at all with Yoskeh, and she quickly decided on the sleeping arrangements: 'Then we'll sleep in your bedroom, and you'll move in with Yoavi.'

As I replaced the receiver I wanted to see Charles so much. In the afternoon I left Yoavi with Nechama and went to the Van Leer auditorium. At the entrance to the hall I saw a small crowd, and Charles's blond head shining above them all; he was speaking and they were listening, and I saw Louisa among them, leaning her head backwards, running her fingers through her auburn curls and laughing aloud. I bypassed the crowd and stole into the auditorium, but Charles grasped my arm and said, 'Ya-el, I'm so glad you could make it.' I saw the corners of Louisa's mouth curling upwards in a smile, and red faced I sat down on the end chair of the last row, and thought that now everybody knew I'd slept with him last night, and that those who didn't would get the news from Louisa.

The hall was quickly filled to capacity, and Louisa, in a short skirt that set off her curvaceous legs, solemnly led Charles down to the first row that was reserved for guests. Then she got up onto the stage and in English caressed with her lovely French accent introduced Charles as one of Oxford University's rising stars, detailed his academic achievements, and with an elegant gesture invited him to deliver his lecture. Charles ignored the three wooden steps up to the stage and jumped easily onto it, stood behind the lectern and pushed away the microphone. In his beautifully tailored suit he seemed to have shed his vulnerability and taken on a new appearance of a serene and self-assured man, who carried his body as a matter of course.

'This evening is dedicated, as always, to my favourite woman, my grandmother, my mother's mother,' he began. 'The grandmother is a central figure in the life of the grandchild. If you ask the Nobel Literature laureate, Gabriel García Márques, what are the required conditions for a person to become an author, he will probably tell you that the first is a grandmother who told stories.'

I wondered if his fingers still bore the smell of my depths, and whether Louisa with her sharp senses had detected it, and which of this evening's dignitaries had shaken his hand still permeated with my smell. I thought about his backside and realised why I'd so much wanted to sleep with him last night, and why I'd come to the lecture despite thinking that I wouldn't.

Charles spoke about the universal grandmother, her importance in the lives of her grandchildren, he cited studies, presented the Gambia statistics, backed them up with similar data gathered by various researchers in northern India and pre-modern Japan, and summed up with studies conducted in Europe. For a moment Avshalom was forgotten, and I wanted to get up onto the stage, encircle him with my arms, kiss his lips and show everybody that he was mine; but instead I raised my hand and asked how the researchers explained the fact that it was the matriarchal, not the patriarchal grandmother who increased her grandchild's chances of survival. Charles smiled and said intimately, as if we were alone in the hall, 'That's an excellent question, Ya-el, and I'm pleased you asked it.' Looks were directed at me and I thought I could see Louisa's head turning towards me from the first row. 'I have to admit that I don't have a clear-cut answer. The simplistic and obvious answer is, of course, the ancient assumption that the mother is a matter of fact, and the father a matter of belief. The matriarchal grandmother can be one hundred per cent sure that the grandchild born to her is her direct descendant, a certainty not enjoyed by the patriarchal grandmother, whose relationship with her daughter-in-law is more doubtful, even on the subconscious level ... ' I heard sounds of laughter from the audience and Charles continued, but I was no longer listening and left the auditorium and drove to Nechama's.

'Tell it to your grandma,' said Nechama ironically when I told her about the lecture, but afterwards she was willing to admit that it sounded interesting. 'On second thoughts,' she said, 'this study proves itself in my case too: My mother helps me and nurtures Yoeli, and his mother ignores the fact that a grandchild was born to her,' and laughed at her own joke and said that if it were true, it was time to ask my mother to reach out and form a quality relationship with her grandson. I told her that I'd already invited her, but she was coming with her Yoskeh, and that I found it hard to believe that she'd find the time for her classic grandmotherly role. As I was about to leave, she addressed Yoavi who was in my arms: 'Yoavi, honey, tell your grandma to watch out for the wolf.' And in the stairwell Yoavi asked me who this wolf was that Grandma had to watch out for, and whether he was more dangerous than the terrorists. I told him it was an old fairytale and promised to tell it to him that evening, when he was in bed.

'Grandma, what big eyes you have,' Yoavi said to my mother as she stood in the doorway with Yoskeh, even before she'd managed to put her pot of soup down on the kitchen counter.

And she, playing the game, opened her eyes wide and answered in a gruff voice, 'All the better to see you with, my boy.'

'And Grandma, what big ears you have,' the child giggled, happy with her cooperation.

And she growled, 'All the better to hear you with, my boy.'

'And Grandma, what big teeth you have.'

'All the better to eat you up with,' she roared and went into the kitchen with Yoskeh, loaded down, tagging along behind her, and she put the pot down on the counter, took out her dentures and snapped them like castanets, and Yoavi screamed in fake fright and ran into his room with her after him, her teeth in her hands, her gums bare, and the growls of a ravening wolf coming from her throat. I heard their screams of joy coming from the room and asked Yoskeh to put their things in my bedroom and what he'd like to drink.

Afterwards, in the kitchen, with me peeling potatoes, she slicing greens for a salad, and Yoavi sitting on the floor playing with the new toys I'd bought him, the phone rang and she picked it up as if she owned the place, and I heard her speaking English and asking with exaggerated politeness, 'Who is calling, please? One moment, please.' She handed me the receiver, covered the mouthpiece with her hand, and said, 'Some Charles wants to speak to you, he sounds awfully nice.' I took the phone that had parsley leaves sticking to it and answered brusquely: 'Yes,' 'No,' and again 'No,' and 'Goodbye,' and disconnected. She just had to know. 'Who was it?' and I said, 'A colleague from Oxford who's here on a visit,' and she asked, 'He wanted to see you, didn't he?' I looked at her over the pot of potatoes and nodded. 'And why did you say no?' she asked, 'it will do you no harm to go out with men after everything you've been through.' I wondered if she'd been talking to Louisa, and then remembered that they didn't know one another, and replied, 'How can I go out with you here?' My mother suddenly raised her voice: 'That's why we're here,' she shouted, 'we'll look after Yoavi and you'll go out and have a good time right after dinner. Right, Yoavi'leh?' she asked the child. 'You want to be with Grandma for while?' And Yoavi, that treacherous collaborator, was overjoyed: 'Yes!' 'You see?' she said, 'so call him back and tell him to pick you up after dinner. Actually, maybe it would be better to ask him here, he sounds so nice.' And I wasn't overeager to have them together, but I longed to see him

248

again, and I called the hotel and asked to be put through to his room. I heard an engaged tone, and put down the phone. 'Well?' she enquired. 'It's engaged,' I replied. 'So try again,' she urged me, and I called again, and this time Charles answered, and I invited him for Sabbath dinner, and heard the disappointment in his voice: 'Just a moment ago Louisa invited me over.' 'Fine, and have a good weekend,' I replied, and was about to disconnect when he stopped me. 'Ya-el, just a minute,' and then asked, 'who answered the phone when I called?' I could see my mother's ears pricking up. 'My mother,' I replied, and heard the smile from the other end of the line: 'Give me a minute,' he said, 'and I'll get right back to you.' When the phone rang again my mother looked at me with an 'I told you so' expression on her face, and I nodded, asking her to pick it up. She wiped her hands on the apron with the plastic breasts that Nachum had refused to take with him to his new home, and I heard her trilling and inviting 'Hello?' And as if they'd been pals for years, she told him in the posh English she'd learnt from her British suitors during the Mandate: 'Charles, my dear, I'm so delighted you're coming and I'll set another place right away. We dine at eight. You don't have to bring wine.' And then she giggled like a girl to a suitor, and asked him where he was coming from, and dictated our address, and added that he should tell the taxi driver to switch the meter on, and that he should get a taxi from a Jewish company.

As she replaced the receiver she ordered me out of the kitchen because she'd take care of the rest, and sent me to take a shower and get dressed, 'And put on some perfume and lipstick and blush, you look pale.'

A festive bouquet of red roses appeared in the doorway followed by Charles's face, and I wondered if he'd bought it for Louisa. My mother was overjoyed at the sight of the bouquet and kissed his cheek in thanks, and shook Yoskeh who was sprawled out watching *This Week* and told him with ill-concealed reproof, 'Look at the lovely flowers he's brought me.' Then she relieved me of all my duties as hostess, sat Charles at her side at the table, piling his plate with food again and again, interrogating, laughing, being girlish, acting silly, and still finding time for Yoavi, coaxing him to eat. And Charles sat beaming at her side, focused on her alone. He devoured her dishes like a starving man, complimented her on the seasoning, the table setting, her devoted care of her grandchild, and shot me brief evasive glances for compensation; on one occasion I even felt his hand squeezing my thigh, and I removed it with a light slap.

After coffee and cake my mother ordered me in Hebrew, 'Now take him back to his hotel, and don't worry, we're here with Yoavi, and come home whenever you like.'

On the way to the hotel Charles didn't stop praising my mother. She's a very special, dynamic and intelligent woman, he said, and she looks far younger than her age, she must have been really beautiful when she was young. He also didn't forget to laud her function as Yoavi's grandmother and express his wonderment at their warm relationship. I listened in silence, and then said venomously that I was surprised how a man like him didn't use his researcher's instincts. 'Your impressions are completely superficial,' I asserted, 'and you can't form an opinion of somebody after knowing them for just one evening.' He glanced at me sideways and said softly, 'I hope you're not jealous, Ya-el. Don't compete with your mother, otherwise you won't be able to allow her to fill her role as a grandmother.' And I answered him derisively, and I couldn't understand how I'd blurted out that terrible sentence: 'You're invited to court her, she's a widow.' He looked at me with sudden hostility and said, 'Ya-el, that was an appalling remark I wouldn't have expected of you, especially after everything that's happened between us.' And he fell silent. We drove the rest of the way in silence, and when I parked outside the YMCA Hotel and switched off the engine, I contritely begged his forgiveness. I expected him to ask me up to his room, but he said goodnight drily, courteously thanked me for the invitation to dinner and pecked my cheek with a cold kiss. Then he got quickly out of the car without bothering to close the door behind him, and all the way home I cursed myself and him and my mother, who had once more stolen my thunder.

I was welcomed by a dark apartment and a huge bunch of red roses waved from a vase on the table that had been cleared of the remains of the meal. I went into the kitchen, hoped to find a pile of dishes waiting to be washed in the sink, but the sink shone in the darkness, empty and gleaming. I opened the fridge and found the leftovers stored in well-sealed plastic containers. Disappointed that my mother had not given me new grounds to be angry with her, I went into Yoavi's room and lay down on the spare bed she

250

had offered me, and he turned to me and said from the depths of sleep, 'What a big mouth you've got.' From my bedroom I heard groaning, and Yoskeh whispering to my mother in his thick voice, 'Shhh, she's home.'

When I awoke in the morning I heard my mother in the kitchen chopping vegetables for the Shabbat salad, and I went in. Yoavi was sitting on the counter by her side, nibbling at a carrot and happily swinging his legs.

'Good morning Sleeping Beauty,' she greeted me warmly, and Yoavi giggled in agreement: 'My Imush is the most beautiful of all.'

'Coffee, where's the coffee,' I croaked, and she hurried to pour the revitalising liquid into a mug bearing the green legend 'Israeli Dental Practitioners' Congress Spring 1995.' I thought that perhaps the time had come to smash it to smithereens.

'You were back early,' she stated, and I nodded and wanted to bury my face in the apron's plastic breasts, and cry and feel sorry for myself, and feel her rough hand ruffling my hair.

'Yoavi darling, go and see what Uncle Yoskeh's up to in the living room,' she urged, helping him slide off the counter and sending him on his way with a light smack on the bottom, and then fixing me with compassionate eyes. 'So what's going to happen?' she asked, and I replied, 'Whatever.' She lowered her eyes to her lined hands and immediately turned them over and inspected their backs, and I saw the liver spots that had spread over them. With thumb and forefinger she absently pinched the skin and let it go: the skin remained pinched in a tiny and ugly fold, and she sighed and said, 'Old age.' And she asked again, 'So what's going to happen?' and I didn't reply, and went to my room and closed the door behind me. I looked at my hands, turned them over, and like her pinched the skin and let it go: my skin, loyal and supple, sprang back into place. Then I stood facing the mirror and looked at my face. I saw skin that had lost its freshness and eyes whose corners had fallen slightly downwards, and I took off my shift and touched the scar that split my belly, and slid my hands over my thighs that had become over-rounded, and found consolation in my breasts. I stuck a pencil under one and the pencil fell and rolled onto the floor, telling me that my breasts were still firm and uptilted. Encouraged, I got dressed and went into the kitchen to help my mother. I found Yoskeh playing with Yoavi, the child

251

calling him 'Grandpa', and he, overjoyed with the appellation, dancing with him on his back, making faces like an out of work clown and rubbing his sunken, bristly cheeks against Yoavi's smooth face, until the child's skin reddened and he pleaded, 'Stop, stop,' with hiccuping laughter. What a pity that Yoavi hadn't known my father, I thought, and a heart-warming picture arose in my memory – the month-old Yoavi cradled in the arms of my father, whose mind had not yet gone, and he was telling the baby stories about himself and his parents and 'There,' and Yoavi was looking at him as if he understood every word, and my father laughed joyfully, and kissed the baby's head over and over, the head with its tonsure of black hair, like that of a Dominican friar, and was telling everybody in the room at the time that this child is something, he's no ordinary baby, he understands everything you say. And I said, 'Abba, don't exaggerate, he's an ordinary baby.' And my father looked at me and said sternly and quietly, 'Don't you ever say that your son is ordinary. You can already see that this baby will grow up and be a human being.' I wanted to reply, 'And what did you think? That he'd grow up and be a monkey?' but the aggressive look in my mother's eyes kept my mouth shut, and I only tore the baby from his arms and said I had to feed him, and I shut myself up with him and thought to myself, 'I only hope that my father doesn't fill his tiny head with rubbish the way he tried to fill mine.'

In the afternoon when they packed their things and we went downstairs to say goodbye to them, I thought I'd like them to stay a little longer, just a short while, and I said to Yoskeh, 'Come more often.' He blushed and buried his head in the car boot and arranged and rearranged their bags, pushing them in and making room, and my mother hugged me and whispered, 'Try and understand me. It was different with Abba. It was crowded in bed with him.' And I asked worriedly, 'Weren't you comfortable in my bed?' and she laughed, 'Not your bed. Our bed in the house in Jaffa. His whole family were in bed with us, his whole family and another six million.' And as the car moved away and she waved to me, I knew why she had told me about it just then.

In the evening I called the hotel and asked to speak to Charles. The ringing went unanswered, and the answering machine announced metallically that the guest in room 517 is unavailable at the moment – please leave a message. I hesitated for a few moments, and then I wanted to disconnect and call later, but I was afraid that the machine had already recorded my heavy breathing, and I cleared my throat and declaimed that I was sorry for everything that had happened. Afterwards, when I replaced the receiver, I thought about my voice that had probably sounded panicky and overeager, and regretted the foolish wording of the message, that could be mistakenly interpreted as if I regretted the night we'd spent together in his room. I called the hotel again, and the operator told me in English with a thick Arabic accent that it was impossible to erase the message but, if I wanted, I could leave another one. I pleaded with her, but she was insistent and repeated her original sentence, this time with exaggerated slowness, masticating the words with a kind of sadistic pleasure, like a kindergarten teacher repeating the rules of a game to a slow child. In my desperation I committed an error and told her, 'As a woman you should identify with me,' but she answered mockingly, 'You should have thought before leaving a message,' and cut me off. I was willing to swear that the witch had immediately listened to the pitiful message I'd left for Charles.

Later that night he still hadn't returned to his room, and I called Louisa's house and heard her answering machine announce with exaggerated gaiety: 'You have reached the home of Louisa and Yoram, we're very happy, and if you leave a message we'll be even more happy to return your call.' I disconnected and tried his room again, and the same operator answered me impatiently that the guest in room 517 had not yet returned. I called again towards midnight after first deciding to disconnect if I heard that evil-minded woman's voice. I was happy to hear a man's voice and he connected me to Charles's room. The phone kept on ringing and was not answered.

Next morning, on the office answering machine, I found an apologetic message from Charles. He'd got back very late last night and so was unable to return my call. He was in Ramallah at the moment, and would try and speak with me when he returned.

By the evening I still hadn't heard from him. Then I decided to switch the phone on to mute, so that he'd suffer a bit if he called and didn't find me. But late at night, when I listened to my messages, I didn't find one from him.

Next morning Louisa told me that Charles had returned to England. He'd brought his flight forward by two days, and had even paid the excess on the return ticket. No, she had no idea why he'd left so hurriedly, she said, giving me a meaningful look, as if I had the answer.

After she left the office I remembered that I'd forgotten to ask him if he was married, but immediately thought that it wasn't really important. He didn't owe me a thing, I mollified myself. He had needed me and I him, and it had been good for both of us. Apart from which he'd returned to his own country, and I probably wouldn't see him again in my life.

And as a talisman against troubling thoughts, I again dredged up Avshalom's hands from the depths of my memory, and for the rest of the day I tried concentrating on them alone.

And What Do I Do? Nothing

A streak of grey lightning leapt onto me in the semi-darkness of the stairwell, snared my trouser cuffs, hung onto them with its hooks, quickly climbed onto my shoulder and settled there, very close to my left ear, and let out a triumphal purr. Stunned, I stood there frozen, and Yoavi pranced around me waving his arms in a kind of Red Indian war dance, and in his excitement he stammered a bit and finally managed to say, 'Imush, it's a cat.'

I shook myself and tried to detach the daring mountaineer, but he stuck his curved claws into my blouse and refused to budge. I sat down helplessly on the bottom step and he, woolly and stubborn, held onto my shoulder and tasted my ear with his rough tongue. Shuddering, I asked the stairwell, 'What am I doing?' and Yoavi, choking with excitement, announced, 'Nothing. We're going home. With him.' I took Yoavi's hand and together we climbed the stairs with the cat on my shoulder looking down at us, and Greta's Mutzi from the second floor suddenly burst into loud bass barks from the other side of the armoured door. Greta opened her door a crack and immediately closed it, and from her apartment I heard her trying to calm the excited Mutzi.

As I opened the door of our apartment the cat leapt down lightly, and as if it knew the apartment inside out went right into the kitchen, sat down facing the fridge and began yowling. At that moment the phone rang, it was Nachum wanting to speak to Yoavi. I handed him the receiver, and after answering, 'Fine', to Nachum's first question, I heard him say, 'But Abba, I can't talk right now 'cos I've got a new cat,' and he passed me the phone and ran to stroke the cat. 'So a new toy stops him talking to his father in America,' Nachum said angrily, and I replied tartly, 'So it seems,' without bothering to explain that it wasn't a toy but a real live cat.

Yoavi's coloured plastic plates were already set out on the floor, filled with all kinds of foodstuffs: one contained halvah, another cocktail nibbles, a third pasta, and beside them a bowlful of breakfast cereal and milk. Confused, the cat ambled from one to another and sniffed them with turned-up whiskers. 'He probably wants to eat cat food,' I suggested, and together we went to the grocery store where we deliberated for a long time on the cans of food with various flavours, until Yoavi chose a chicken-flavoured one and explained that the cat probably didn't like fish and hated liver, and you mustn't force cats to eat things they don't like. When we got home I put the food onto a plate and the cat slowly walked to it and with kingly dignity and exaggerated refinement was gracious enough to sniff the pile of food. Then he stuck out his pink tongue, wiggled his whiskers and fell onto it ravenously, his mouth and tongue making damp smacking noises. By the time the bowl was empty Yoavi declared, 'Pussy's thirsty,' and we put a soup bowl of water in front of him, and his tongue, like a rose petal, cautiously tried the water and then sucked it quickly into his mouth. His belly full, he sat in the centre of a transparent pool of sunlight, and his silky grey coat, adorned with fine silvery streaks, glittered in the light. Aware of the admiration he was being given, he licked one of his paws and with it brushed his ears and face. We watched him mesmerised, and Yoavi asked if he could wash that way too, like a cat, and I said that cats don't really wash, they just wipe themselves with cat spit, and Yoavi laughed, and we both looked at the cat that had finished his ablutions and was slowly stretching. Then he sat on his backside with his ears pricked, as if listening to sounds beyond the range of human ears, and his greenish eyes, gleaming eyes, were fixed on sights hidden from human vision.

In the evening he dug himself a hole in the sandbox we put out on the balcony, sat in it and for a long time afterwards he obscured and covered any traces. 'How does he know to cover his kaki with sand like that?' Yoavi asked, and I replied, 'His mother must have taught him.' Yoavi picked him up and sniffed his belly the way I used to do with him when he was a baby, and the cat quickly escaped and curled up on the best armchair in the living room, the one that had been Nachum's, with Yoavi's Tutti as a sheet.

The cat's tiny personality rapidly took over the household, and we became lodgers, at his beck and call. He'd rub his striped coat against our legs, sharpen his claws on the new furniture I'd bought, awaken us with his yowling in the morning. And we, a pair of soft-hearted giants, were at his service, eager to please and fulfil his every whim. I thought to myself about how a small ball of fur could dominate us this way, and how was it possible that such contradictory attributes could exist side by side in this creature; for he'd be loving one moment and then indifferent, cunning and then innocent, frisky and then lazy, gentle and cruel, and his nine lives appeared before us all together. New rules, that we didn't dare break, were enacted in the apartment, and odd sleeping arrangements were imposed upon us. He'd start the night in Yoavi's arms, and from there he'd come to me, warm and fragrant, carrying the scent of my sleeping child. Then he'd curl up on my tummy, purring loudly and awakening me from sleep that in any case was light. Then he'd go back to Yoavi, and then remember me at dawn and jump onto my bed with a loud noise, and demandingly miaow in my ear and turn me into a butterfly against my will, for I'd trudge after him red-eyed to the fridge and feed him. At night, as I sat at the computer typing up the interviews I'd conducted with ultra-Orthodox women, yeshiva and religious college students, he'd jump into my lap and from there to the desk, sit in front of the screen blocking my view, and with his velvety paws with their withdrawn claws try and catch the letters flickering in front of him. Then I'd sit him on my knee, listen to his contented purring and watch his paws opening and closing in the suckling movements of a kitten. I'd work that way until my back ached and my eyes clouded, and after I'd switched off the computer I'd stand for a long time watching the cat as he tried to catch the screen saver's fish.

One morning, as I sniffed the fragrance of rain that was yet to fall, I knew that summer was almost over and chilly, lovelier days were on their way. The leaves would soon be painted orange and fall from the trees, and yellow would cover the city's pavements and infiltrate between the gusts of wind and the sky would wrap itself up in the cloudy scarves of the first rain. And we celebrated Rosh Hashana with my mother and Yoskeh, and the rest of the High Holy Days made their pilgrimage to us, and the autumn crocuses and the squills bloomed, and Yoavi spent his first days at the new nursery school, and I did my moral stocktaking of the past year. Cold nights drove me to air the quilts from the smell of moth-balls and sort out the winter clothes. I spent a whole evening on Yoavi's and was amazed to see how much my child had grown since last winter.

Just before the High Holy Days and the long school break, Nechama and Yoeli visited us more frequently, both to see the cat and visit Yoavi who was now at his new nursery school without Yoeli. And as they played with the cat, it seemed that the echoes of the *shaheeds'* explosions were almost forgotten. During those quiet days of stocktaking, Nechama and I patched up our relation-ship and finally agreed that we wouldn't talk about psychology and politics, and more particularly we decided to avoid words like '*shaheed*,' 'occupation,' 'closure' and 'curfew.' And Nechama told me then, as if giving me a compliment, 'Now I really feel that you're coming out of it,' and I replied that she was right, I really was coming out of it. I thought about how life goes on, people sit in cafés, even those that were or would be blown up, and travel by bus, even on the routes that were or would be shattered, and the malls hum with people, and people take trips, and couples get married and children are born, and I remembered our children and said to Nechama that it was suspiciously quiet in Yoavi's room. We peeped in at them through the half-open door and saw them trying to put a doll's shirt on the cat, and he rebelled and extended his claws and tried to evade them. When they came out, their hands scratched, Nechama washed their hands and put antiseptic on them, and said that cats don't need clothes because they've got their own coats. Then she warned Yoeli to not even think about opening the cat's belly with the scissors, because all that would come out would be blood and a lot of intestines.

'Mr Grey,' that's what Yoavi called the cat, and he grew and put on weight, and one fine day he disappeared only to be found later in my wardrobe, lying peacefully on a bed of my blouses and six kittens in a variety of colours stuck to his nipples. That day I had to have a long and draining talk with my son, who was toying with the idea that boys could give birth, and I explained that Mr Grey was a female and that we just hadn't known, because cats are different from people. At the same time we changed his name to 'Mrs Grey,' and Yoavi said he wasn't all that happy that the cat was a girl, because he didn't like girls. Despite the enforced sex change, we carried on talking about and to him in the masculine, and at the Shabbat Eve assembly at his new nursery school, when Yoavi told the children about his male cat that had had kittens, he became the hero of the hour. Since then he came home every day with new friends who wanted to see the kittens.

A month after Mrs Grey's confinement, I received the news in a thick, fancy white envelope that was among the dozens of letters and journals stuffed into my mailbox. On the envelope were a few stamps proudly bearing the pinkish likeness of Elizabeth II in her golden jubilee year. I turned it over and discovered on the flap, instead of the sender's name and address, the splendidly embossed seal of the University of Oxford. Eager to find out what it contained, I tore it open together with the letter's upper edge, which bore my address and the salutation 'Dear Madam.' In solemn officialese the letter informed me that I was invited to serve as a visiting fellow at the university's department of anthropology in the coming academic year. At the end of the letter, in fine print, I was assured of modest but certainly reasonable lodgings, and a bursary that was equivalent to my yearly salary at the university here. As I was about to throw the envelope into the wastepaper basket, a small note fell out with a beautifully embossed letterhead: 'Professor Charles Bailey.' In a few words and in rounded handwriting he begged my forgiveness for not managing to meet me the night before he left, and asked me to consider the proposal in a positive light; he would be very happy to meet me again and help me however he could. With the letter in my hand I ran to my office, and Louisa was already there and flashed me a conspiratorial smile, waved her arms enthusiastically and jingled the bells of her bangles, whose number had increased since her wedding day. 'So you finally got the letter,' she laughed, and raining on my parade somewhat she told me that about a month ago she'd received a similar one but had been forced to decline, because the wedding hadn't been all that long ago, and Yoram's career was no less important than hers, and they were trying to get pregnant and couldn't sever the ties with their doctor in Israel. So as not to send them away empty-handed, so she said, she had recommended that they ask me, and she hadn't been sure that they'd accepted her recommendation and so she hadn't bothered to tell me so I wouldn't be disappointed. I didn't understand why she had to tell me all this,

259

and I feigned indifference and said that I didn't believe I'd go, because it would compel me to postpone my research, and she reproached me and said that had she known I'd turn down such a tempting invitation, she would have recommended another researcher, and now I was putting her in an invidious position. To mollify her I said I'd consider it, but first I had to talk about it with Prof. Har-Noy.

'Go, my child, go, you've had a hard year,' the professor trumpeted, and I knew that Louisa had already made him her co-conspirator. 'Your *dossim* can wait. And apart from that, perhaps you'll find some no less interesting material in the libraries there.' I looked at the withered bags suspended beneath his eyes and his bobbing Adam's apple, covered with red hummocks, and I thanked him. He suddenly reached out and stroked my head, and I knew that he'd always wanted to do that and now he had been given the chance. I evaded him and went back to my office and wrote a long and detailed letter in which I thanked them for choosing me, and so as not to appear overeager I wrote that I was considering the matter, and asked when I had to give them a final answer.

At home I came to the conclusion that I deserved this trip. So far, I told myself, I'd accepted the reality of my life as a decree of fate. I thought about my present that had been lost, my life that had run itself of its own accord almost without being affected by me, and about the time that had passed not of its own accord, dragging me powerless behind it. I wanted to break this vicious circle, and I decided that the time had come to live a quiet life where no buses would threaten to blow up on us. I tore up the mild letter I'd written and replaced it with another, in which I thanked them for the invitation and asked when I could get there.

The letter from Oxford destabilised our daily and nightly routine. I began dreaming about airports, suitcases not reaching their destination, a dark and gloomy apartment that would await us there, books I'd forgotten to return to the university library and the warning letters regarding asset attachment that would follow me to Oxford. Yoavi cried a little and declared that he didn't want to say goodbye to Yoeli who's his best friend, and I promised him that Yoeli and Nechama would certainly come and visit him. He calmed down a bit until he remembered Mrs Grey, and insisted that he'd only go if he came with us. I sat facing him, the cat on my knee and the kittens running round the apartment, and explained that it was very difficult to go abroad with a cat, because when we got there they'd take him away and put him into quarantine, and only release him after a very long time. And Yoavi got frightened and looked at me with his round eyes and asked hesitantly, 'Quarantine?' and the fear was evident in his voice when he asked, 'Like what we do to the Palestinians?' I was at a loss and didn't know where he'd picked up the word, and suspected he'd heard it at Nechama's, and for a long time I tried to explain the difference between the quarantine for cats and the closure of the Palestinians, and he looked at me confusedly and asked, 'So when the Palestinians go to England they put them into quarantine like the cats?' I replied that cats are put into a special quarantine for cats and he shouted in understanding, 'And they put the Palestinians into a special quarantine for Palestinians!' And I knew I was in trouble and was forced to tell him that every time a bomb went off in Israel, 'Of a suicide bomber,' he interjected, completing my sentence, we impose a closure on the Palestinians' towns and villages and don't allow them out so we can catch the people who did it. And he said, 'But that's not what Nechama said.' 'And what did she say?' and I could feel the old anger rising in my throat. 'She said that we're bad and we do them a closure that's like putting them in prison and they can't get out even if they're sick and have got to go to hospital.'

Then I changed my story and said that cat quarantine in England was actually a hospital, where they'd examine Mrs Grey to see if she was healthy, so that she wouldn't infect the English cats with diseases, and then we'd be able to go there and take her.

'What about the kittens?' he asked, about to burst into tears.

'We'll give the kittens as a present to other children who want them.'

'Yoeli too?'

'First Yoeli, but only if his mother says it's OK.'

A week later Yoavi adopted a new custom.

'Imush, I've got a visitor who wants to see the kittens,' I heard him announce from the doorway and found him standing there with a young soldier who flashed me an apologetic smile and said that Yoavi had met him in the street and asked him to come home with him to see the kittens. 'And by chance I like cats,' he added and

261

introduced himself as Yishai. I smiled at him and said, 'You can help yourself to one, because we're going abroad shortly and I've got to find them good homes.' Yishai apologised and said that his base was far away and he'd just got home on leave, and he was afraid that there was nobody to take care of the cat in his absence, but he'd be happy to play with them and Yoavi while he was home, as he lived with his parents in the next-door building. Then they shut themselves up in Yoavi's room and I heard Yoavi asking him about his marital status, and Yishai roar with laughter as he replied, 'I haven't got a wife, I'm not married, but I've got a girlfriend.'

'Are you going to marry her?' came Yoavi's worried voice, and Yishai replied, 'Maybe, if she asks me nicely.' Then I heard them singing, 'What do the trees do? Grow,' and Yoavi insisting that they sing all the verses: 'And what do I do? No-o-o-thing.' Only after they came out of the room and Yishai went on his way, Yoavi told me that Yishai could be a good father for him, because he liked cats too. I choked as I told him that you have only one father.

'But he's in America,' he frowned and persisted, 'If Yishai married you, then he'd be my Abba.' I brushed some soft curls from his forehead and promised him faithfully that Abba would come to London and visit him.

Later, as I put him to bed, I told him he had to be careful, and that he couldn't bring home strangers he met in the street. I added that Yishai was a nice boy, but there were also bad people out in the streets, and not all of them liked children, and I demanded that he promise me that if he brought new friends home, it would only be on condition that I was in, and if he took them into his room, the door had to stay open. And Yoavi smiled and said, 'Of course, Imush, you've got to be at home, because you've got to see them too so you can choose me a new Abba.'

The journey came ever closer and numerous cartons piled up in the apartment, and I ran between them thinking about what to pack and what to leave. I informed the landlord that I was leaving for a year, and that I didn't want to give up the apartment, and we agreed that I'd look for a subtenant. Yoavi was very excited by the upcoming journey, and he, too, packed his books in a carton, and he handed me his Tutti and said he didn't need it any more because he was a big boy, and soon he'd be going to England and he'd learn English there.

262

About a month before we were due to leave we bought Mrs. Grey a plastic pet carrier and took her for an examination and immunisation at Yonit the vet's, who at my request soothed Yoavi and explained that Mrs Grey would be staying at a cat hotel and would meet lots of new friends there. 'And how will he talk to them?' he asked and I could hear the concern in his voice, 'In Cattish,' Yonit replied soothingly, and Yoavi's eyes shone as he told her that he'd be making lots of new friends in England and he'd talk to them in English.

About a week before the journey I again heard Yoavi's excited call from the door way: 'Imush, Imush, I've got a visitor who wants to see the kittens.' And I, surrounded by the cartons in which I'd packed up my life, was standing in a tattered shirt and Nachum's apron with the plastic breasts at the sink washing dishes, and I turned my head slightly and looked at the tall, slim visitor who was wearing new jeans with the bottoms turned up, and I saw smooth blond hair combed into a parting, and said offhandedly, 'Hello, visitor.' The stranger flashed me an apologetic smile and his eyes dwelt on my plastic breasts, and I thought he was a very good looking man, and heard him say, 'I hope it's OK, the boy met me outside and invited me in to see the kittens, and I'm interested in adopting one.' And I replied happily, 'There's only two left, choose whichever one you want.'

I went back to scrubbing dishes and thought that Yoavi had superior taste in men, because every one he'd brought home so far had been extremely good looking, and all of them, without exception, were nice; and I thought further that this man's face was somehow familiar, and that I'd probably seen him in the neighbourhood, at the grocery shop or in a queue at the post office. I took off the apron and decided it was high time I got rid of it, because I certainly had no intention of taking it with me to Oxford, and I stuffed it into the black garbage bag standing by the door, that was filled with the remnants of my previous life that I wanted to forget.

From Yoavi's room came the sounds of the conversation that was carried on in the format he'd recently adopted.

'Have you got a wife?' asked my son, and there was a brief silence, and then I heard the child say in a voice filled with hope: 'If you're not married, then you haven't got any children.' The stranger evidently replied with a shake of the head. Then I heard Yoavi telling him that we'd called our cat Mr Grey because we thought he was a boy, until one day he'd had kittens in Ima's wardrobe, and the stranger's voice roared with laughter that came from the heart, and I heard him telling Yoavi that when he was a child he'd had cats, and that when they're little it's hard to tell if they're boys or girls. Then Yoavi told him that we were going to England because Ima had work there, and asked him which kitten he'd like, and I heard soft mewling and the stranger's voice saying that it was late and he had to go.

A striped kitten was hugged to the man's chest as he came out of Yoavi's room.

At the front door he looked at me and his eyes smiled as he wished us bon voyage, and Yoavi ran to open the door for him, kissed the kitten's head that was cradled in the stranger's big hand, and he asked fearfully: 'Will you come and visit me one more time before I go to England?' and the stranger replied, 'If your mother says it's all right,' and he extended his other hand and warmly stroked my son's head.

I saw the most beautiful hand in the world toying with my son's curls.

'Imush, it's all right isn't it?'

I got up painfully from the armchair and came closer and looked into the clear eyes. The stranger blushed and lowered his eyes a little. The kitten mewed in his hand and I was afraid that he was unintentionally crushing it, and his fingers again played embarrassedly with Yoavi's curls.

Yoavi pulled at my shirt: 'Imush, say it's all right for him to come and visit us and the kittens again tomorrow.'

Two deep blue pools opened at me and I curled up in his look, sinking into the heavenly softness of fluffy clouds. Serenity flooded me, and I wanted to fall into his arms and weep and laugh and question and interrogate and ask. But Yoavi who was standing beside me pulled at my hand and led me back into reality and repeated, 'Say it's all right for him to come and visit us and the kittens again tomorrow.' And wordlessly I nodded and held Yoavi's hand and together we accompanied the man with the grey kitten in his arms to the landing.

I followed his descending footsteps with my finger hovering over the light switch, to light his way lest darkness descend upon him.